'Like Miéville and Gaiman, Sapkowski takes the old and makes it new'   Foundation

'Like a complicated magic spell, a Sapkowski novel is a hodge podge of fantasy, intellectual discourse and dry humour. Recommended'   *Time Magazine*

'An extraordinary tale which highlights Sapkowski's masterful character creation . . . one of the best fantasy sagas of all time'
                                                    Fantasy Book Review

'The Witcher series is something quite special'   SF Book

'An incredibly nuanced, well-articulated novel, imbued with a self-assured command of description and brimming with Eastern European folklore'   *Starburst*

'Character interplay is complex, unsentimental and anchored in brutal shared history'   *SFX*

'There's lots of imagination on show, the writing has a strong voice, and the Witcher is an entertaining character'   Mark Lawrence

'Refreshing and a lot of fun to read'   *Grimdark Magazine*

'Captivating, often nerve-wracking, and truthfully . . . rip-roaring fun'   Fantasy Hive

THE LAST WISH

ANDRZEJ SAPKOWSKI

Translated by Danusia Stok

This paperback first published in Great Britain in 2020 by Gollancz
First published in Great Britain in 2007 by Gollancz
an imprint of The Orion Publishing Group Ltd
Carmelite House, 50 Victoria Embankment
London EC4Y 0DZ

An Hachette UK Company

17

Originally published in Polish as *Ostatnie Zyczenie*
This publication has been funded by the Book Institute
– the © POLAND Translation Program
Published by arrangement with The Patricia Pasqualini Literary Agency

A CIP catalogue record for this book is
available from the British Library.

ISBN (Mass Market Paperback) 978 1 473 23106 1
ISBN (eBook) 978 0 575 09991 3

Typeset by Input Data Services Ltd, Somerset
Printed in Great Britain by Clays Ltd, Elcograf S.p.A.

MIX
Paper from
responsible sources
FSC
www.fsc.org FSC® C104740

www.gollancz.co.uk

THE VOICE OF REASON 1

She came to him towards morning.

She entered very carefully, moving silently, floating through the chamber like a phantom; the only sound was that of her mantle brushing her naked skin. Yet this faint sound was enough to wake the witcher – or maybe it only tore him from the half-slumber in which he rocked monotonously, as though travelling through fathomless depths, suspended between the sea bed and its calm surface amidst gently undulating strands of seaweed.

He did not move, did not stir. The girl flitted closer, threw off her mantle and slowly, hesitantly, rested her knee on the edge of the large bed. He observed her through lowered lashes, still not betraying his wakefulness. The girl carefully climbed onto the bedclothes, and onto him, wrapping her thighs around him. Leaning forward on straining arms, she brushed his face with hair which smelt of chamomile. Determined, and as if impatient, she leant over and touched his eyelids, cheeks, lips with the tips of her breasts. He smiled, very slowly, delicately, grasping her by the shoulders, and she straightened, escaping his fingers. She was radiant, luminous in the misty brilliance of dawn. He moved, but with pressure from both hands, she forbade him to change position and, with a light but decisive movement of her hips, demanded a response.

He responded. She no longer backed away from his hands; she threw her head back, shook her hair. Her skin was cool and surprisingly smooth. Her eyes, glimpsed when her face came close to his, were huge and dark as the eyes of a water nymph.

Rocked, he sank into a sea of chamomile as it grew agitated and seethed.

THE WITCHER

I

Later, it was said the man came from the north, from Ropers Gate. He came on foot, leading his laden horse by the bridle. It was late afternoon and the ropers', saddlers' and tanners' stalls were already closed, the street empty. It was hot but the man had a black coat thrown over his shoulders. He drew attention to himself.

He stopped in front of the Old Narakort Inn, stood there for a moment, listened to the hubbub of voices. As usual, at this hour, it was full of people.

The stranger did not enter the Old Narakort. He pulled his horse further down the street to another tavern, a smaller one, called The Fox. Not enjoying the best of reputations, it was almost empty.

The innkeeper raised his head above a barrel of pickled cucumbers and measured the man with his gaze. The outsider, still in his coat, stood stiffly in front of the counter, motionless and silent.

'What will it be?'

'Beer,' said the stranger. His voice was unpleasant.

The innkeeper wiped his hands on his canvas apron and filled a chipped earthenware tankard.

The stranger was not old but his hair was almost entirely white. Beneath his coat he wore a worn leather jerkin laced up at the neck and shoulders.

As he took off his coat those around him noticed that he carried a sword – not something unusual in itself, nearly every man in Wyzim carried a weapon – but no one carried a sword strapped to his back as if it were a bow or a quiver.

The stranger did not sit at the table with the few other guests. He remained standing at the counter, piercing the innkeeper with his gaze. He drew from the tankard.

'I'm looking for a room for the night.'

'There's none,' grunted the innkeeper, looking at the guest's boots, dusty and dirty. 'Ask at the Old Narakort.'

'I would rather stay here.'

'There is none.' The innkeeper finally recognised the stranger's accent. He was Rivian.

'I'll pay.' The outsider spoke quietly, as if unsure, and the whole nasty affair began. A pockmarked beanpole of a man who, from the moment the outsider had entered had not taken his gloomy eyes from him, got up and approached the counter. Two of his companions rose behind him, no more than two paces away.

'There's no room to be had, you Rivian vagabond,' rasped the pockmarked man, standing right next to the outsider. 'We don't need people like you in Wyzim. This is a decent town!'

The outsider took his tankard and moved away. He glanced at the innkeeper, who avoided his eyes. It did not even occur to him to defend the Rivian. After all, who liked Rivians?

'All Rivians are thieves,' the pockmarked man went on, his breath smelling of beer, garlic and anger. 'Do you hear me, you bastard?'

'He can't hear you. His ears are full of shit,' said one of the men with him, and the second man cackled.

'Pay and leave!' yelled the pocked man.

Only now did the Rivian look at him.

'I'll finish my beer.'

'We'll give you a hand,' the pockmarked man hissed. He knocked the tankard from the stranger's hand and simultaneously grabbing him by the shoulder, dug his fingers into the leather strap which ran diagonally across the outsider's chest. One of the men behind him raised a fist to strike. The outsider curled up on the spot, throwing the pockmarked man off balance. The sword hissed in its sheath and glistened briefly in the dim light. The place seethed. There was a scream, and one of the few remaining

3

customers tumbled towards the exit. A chair fell with a crash and earthenware smacked hollowly against the floor. The innkeeper, his lips trembling, looked at the horribly slashed face of the pocked man, who, clinging with his fingers to the edge of the counter, was slowly sinking from sight. The other two were lying on the floor, one motionless, the other writhing and convulsing in a dark, spreading puddle. A woman's hysterical scream vibrated in the air, piercing the ears as the innkeeper shuddered, caught his breath, and vomited.

The stranger retreated towards the wall, tense and alert. He held the sword in both hands, sweeping the blade through the air. No one moved. Terror, like cold mud, was clear on their faces, paralysing limbs and blocking throats.

Three guards rushed into the tavern with thuds and clangs. They must have been close by. They had truncheons wound with leather straps at the ready, but at the sight of the corpses, drew their swords. The Rivian pressed his back against the wall and, with his left hand, pulled a dagger from his boot.

'Throw that down!' one of the guards yelled with a trembling voice. 'Throw that down, you thug! You're coming with us!'

The second guard kicked aside the table between himself and the Rivian.

'Go get the men, Treska!' he shouted to the third guard, who had stayed closer to the door.

'No need,' said the stranger, lowering his sword. 'I'll come by myself.'

'You'll go, you son of a bitch, on the end of a rope!' yelled the trembling guard. 'Throw that sword down or I'll smash your head in!'

The Rivian straightened. He quickly pinned his blade under his left arm and with his right hand raised towards the guards, swiftly drew a complicated sign in the air. The clout-nails which studded his tunic from his wrists to elbows flashed.

The guards drew back, shielding their faces with their arms. One of the customers sprang up while another darted to the door. The woman screamed again, wild and ear-splitting.

4

'I'll come by myself,' repeated the stranger in his resounding, metallic voice. 'And the three of you will go in front of me. Take me to the castellan. I don't know the way.'

'Yes, sir,' mumbled the guard, dropping his head. He made towards the exit, looking around tentatively. The other two guards followed him out backwards, hastily. The stranger followed in their tracks, sheathing his sword and dagger. As they passed the tables the remaining customers hid their faces from the dangerous stranger.

II

Velerad, castellan of Wyzim, scratched his chin. He was neither superstitious nor faint-hearted but he did not relish the thought of being alone with the white-haired man. At last he made up his mind.

'Leave,' he ordered the guards. 'And you, sit down. No, not there. Further away, if you please.'

The stranger sat down. He no longer carried his sword or black coat.

'I am Velerad, castellan of Wyzim,' said Velerad, toying with a heavy mace lying on the table. 'And I'm listening. What do you have to say to me, you brigand, before you are thrown into the dungeon? Three killed and an attempted spell-casting; not bad, not bad at all. Men are impaled for such things in Wyzim. But I'm a just man, so I will listen to you, before you are executed. Speak.'

The Rivian unbuttoned his jerkin and pulled out a wad of white goat leather.

'You nail this crossways, in taverns,' he said quietly. 'Is what's written here true?'

'Ah.' Velerad grunted, looking at the runes etched into the leather. 'So that's it. And I didn't guess at once. Yes, it's true. It's signed by Foltest, King of Temeria, Pontar and Mahakam, which

5

makes it true. A proclamation is a proclamation, witcher, but law is law – and I take care of law and order in Wyzim. I will not allow people to be murdered! Do you understand?'

The Rivian nodded to show he understood. Velerad snorted with anger.

'You carry the witcher's emblem?' The stranger reached into his jerkin once more and pulled out a round medallion on a silver chain. It pictured the head of a wolf, baring its fangs. 'And do you have a name? Any name will do, it's simply to make conversation easier.'

'My name is Geralt.'

'Geralt, then. Of Rivia I gather, from your accent?'

'Of Rivia.'

'Right. Do you know what, Geralt? This,' Velerad slapped the proclamation, 'let it go. It's a serious matter. Many have tried and failed already. This, my friend, is not the same as roughing up a couple of scoundrels.'

'I know. This is my job, Velerad. And that proclamation offers a three thousand oren reward.'

'Three thousand,' Velerad scowled. 'And the princess as a wife, or so rumour says, although gracious Foltest has not proclaimed that.'

'I'm not interested in the princess,' Geralt said calmly. He was sitting motionless, his hands on his knees. 'Just in the three thousand.'

'What times,' sighed the castellan. 'What foul times! Twenty years ago who would have thought, even in a drunken stupour, that such a profession as a witcher would exist? Itinerant killers of basilisks; travelling slayers of dragons and vodniks! Tell me, Geralt, are you allowed beer in your guild?'

'Certainly.'

Velerad clapped his hands.

'Beer!' he called. 'And sit closer, Geralt. What do I care?'

The beer, when it arrived, was cold and frothy.

'Foul times,' Velerod muttered, drinking deep from his tankard. 'All sorts of filth has sprung up. Mahakam, in the mountains, is teeming with bogeymen. In the past it was just wolves howling in the woods, but now it's kobolds and spriggans wherever you spit, werewolves or some other vermin. Fairies and rusalkas snatch children from villages by the hundreds. We have diseases never heard of before; it makes my hair stand on end. And now, to top it all, this!' He pushed the wad of leather back across the table. 'It's not surprising, Geralt, that you witchers' services are in demand.'

'The king's proclamation, castellan,' Geralt raised his head. 'Do you know the details?'

Velerad leant back in his chair, locked his hands over his stomach.

'The details? Yes, I know them. Not first-hand perhaps, but from a good source.'

'That's what I want.'

'If you insist, then listen.' Velerad drank some beer and lowered his voice. 'During the reign of old Medell, his father, when our gracious king was still a prince, Foltest showed us what he was capable of, and he was capable of a great deal. We hoped he would grow out of it. But shortly after his coronation Foltest surpassed himself, jaw-droppingly: he got his own sister with child. Adda was younger and they were always together, but nobody suspected anything except, perhaps, the queen . . . To get to the point: suddenly there is Adda with a huge belly, and Foltest talking about getting wed to his sister. The situation was made even more tense because Vizimir of Novigrad wanted his daughter, Dalka, to marry Foltest and had already sent out his envoys. We had to restrain Foltest from insulting them, and lucky we did, or Vizimir would have torn our insides out. Then, not without Adda's help – for she influenced her brother – we managed to dissuade the boy from a quick wedding.

'Well, then Adda gave birth. And now listen, because this is where it all starts. Only a few saw what she bore, but one midwife jumped from the tower window to her death and the other lost her senses and remains dazed to this day. So I gather that the royal bastard – a girl – was not comely, and she died immediately.

7

No one was in a hurry to tie the umbilical cord. Nor did Adda, to her good fortune, survive the birth.

'But then Foltest stepped in again. Wisdom dictated that the royal bastard should have been burned or buried in the wilderness. Instead, on the orders of our gracious king, she was laid to rest in a sarcophagus in the vaults beneath the palace.'

'It's too late for your wisdom now.' Geralt raised his head. 'One of the Knowing Ones should have been sent for.'

'You mean those charlatans with stars on their hats? Of course. About ten of them came running later, when it became known what lay in the sarcophagus. And what scrambled out of it at night. Though it didn't start manifesting straight away. Oh, no. For seven years after the funeral there was peace. Then one night – it was a full moon – there were screams in the palace, shouting and commotion! I don't have to tell you, this is your trade and you've read the proclamation. The infant had grown in the coffin – and how! – grown to have incredible teeth! In a word, she became a striga.

'Pity you didn't see the corpses, as I did. Had you, you'd have taken a great detour to avoid Wyzim.'

Geralt was silent.

'Then, as I was saying,' Velerad continued, 'Foltest summoned a whole crowd of sorcerers. They all jabbered at the same time and almost came to blows with those staffs they carry – to beat off the dogs, no doubt, once they've been set loose on them. And I think they regularly are. I'm sorry, Geralt, if you have a different opinion of wizards. No doubt you do, in your profession, but to me they are swindlers and fools. You witchers inspire greater confidence in men. At least you are more straightforward.'

Geralt smiled, but didn't comment.

'But, to the point.' The castellan peered into his tankard and poured more beer for himself and the Rivian. 'Some of the sorcerers' advice didn't seem so stupid. One suggested burning the striga together with the palace and the sarcophagus. Another advised chopping her head off. The rest were keen on driving aspen stakes into her body during the day, when the she-devil was

8

asleep in her coffin, worn out by her night's delights. Unfortunately one, a jester with a pointed hat and a bald pate, a hunch-backed hermit, argued it was magic: the spell could be undone and the striga would turn into Foltest's little daughter, as pretty as a picture. Someone simply had to stay in the crypt throughout the night, and that would be that. After which – can you imagine such a fool? – he went to the palace for the night. Little of him was left in the morning, only, I believe, his hat and stick. But Foltest clung to his idea like a burr to a dog's tail. He forbade any attempt to kill the striga and brought in charlatans from all corners of Wyzim to reverse the spell and turn her into a princess. What colourful company! Twisted women, cripples, dirty and louse-ridden. It was pitiful.

'They went ahead and cast spells – mainly over a bowl and tankard. Of course some were quickly exposed as frauds by Foltest or the council. A few were even hung on the palisades, but not enough of them. I would have hung them all. I don't suppose I have to say that the striga, in the meantime, was getting her teeth into all sorts of people every now and again and paying no attention to the fraudsters and their spells. Or that Foltest was no longer living in the palace. No one lived there anymore.'

Velerad paused, drank some beer, and the witcher waited in silence.

'And so it's been for seven years, Geralt, because she was born around fourteen years ago. We've had a few other worries, like war with Vizimir of Novigrad – fought for real, understandable reasons – over the border posts, not for some princess or marriage alliance. Foltest sporadically hints at marriage and looks over portraits from neighbouring courts, which he then throws down the privy. And every now and then this mania seizes hold of him again, and he sends horsemen out to look for new sorcerers. His promised reward, the three thousand, has attracted any number of cranks, stray knights, even a shepherd known throughout the whole region as a cretin, may he rest in peace. But the striga is still doing well. Every now and again she gets her teeth into someone. You get used to it. And at least those heroes trying to reverse the spell have a use – the beast stuffs herself on the spot and doesn't roam beyond her palace. Foltest has a new palace, of course, quite a fine one.'

'In seven years,' Geralt raised his head, 'in seven years, no one has settled the matter?'

'Well, no.' Velerad's gaze penetrated the witcher. 'Because the matter can't be settled. We have to come to terms with it, especially Foltest, our gracious and beloved ruler, who will keep nailing these proclamations up at crossroads. Although there are fewer volunteers now. There was one recently, but he insisted on the three thousand in advance. So we put him in a sack and threw him in the lake.'

'There is still no shortage of fraudsters then.'

'No, far from it,' the castellan agreed without taking his eyes off the witcher. 'That's why you mustn't demand gold in advance when you go to the palace. If you go.'

'I'll go.'

'It's up to you. But remember my advice. As we're talking of the reward, there has been word recently about the second part of it. I mentioned it to you: the princess for a wife. I don't know who made it up, but if the striga looks the way they say then it's an exceptionally grim joke. Nevertheless there's been no lack of fools racing to the palace for the chance of joining the royal family. Two apprentice shoemakers, to be precise. Why are shoemakers so foolish, Geralt?'

'I don't know. And witchers, castellan? Have they tried?'

'There were a few. But when they heard the spell was to be lifted and the striga wasn't to be killed they mostly shrugged and left. That's one of the reasons why my esteem for witchers has grown, Geralt. And one came along, younger than you – I forget his name, if he gave it at all. He tried.'

'And?'

'The fanged princess spread his entrails over a considerable distance.'

Geralt nodded. 'That was all of them?'

'There was one other.'

Velerad remained silent for a while, and the witcher didn't urge him on.

'Yes,' the castellan said finally. 'There was one more. At first, when Foltest threatened him with the noose if he killed or harmed the striga, he laughed and started packing his belongings. But then—' Velerad leaned across the table, lowered his voice to almost a whisper. '—then he undertook the task. You see, Geralt, there are some wise men in Wyzim, in high positions, who've had enough of this whole affair. Rumour has it these men persuaded the witcher, in secret, not to fuss around with spells but to batter the striga to death and tell the king the spell had failed, that his dear daughter had been killed in self-defence – an accident at work. The king, of course, would be furious and refuse to pay an oren in reward. But that would be an end to it. The witty witcher replied we could chase strigas ourselves for nothing. Well, what could we do? We collected money, bargained . . . but nothing came of it.'

Geralt raised his eyebrows.

'Nothing,' repeated Velerad. 'The witcher didn't want to try that first night. He trudged around, lay in wait, wandered about the neighbourhood. Finally, they say, he saw the striga in action, as she does not clamber from her crypt just to stretch her legs. He saw her and scarpered that night. Without a word.'

Geralt's expression changed a little, in what was probably supposed to be a smile.

'Those wise men,' he said, 'they still have the money, no doubt? Witchers don't take payment in advance.'

'No doubt they still do,' said Velerad.

'Does the rumour say how much they offer?'

Velerad bared his teeth in a smile. 'Some say eight hundred—'

Geralt shook his head.

'Others,' murmured the castellan, 'talk of a thousand.'

'Not much when you bear in mind that rumour likes to exaggerate. And the king is offering three thousand.'

'Don't forget about the betrothal,' Velerad mocked. 'What are you talking about? It's obvious you won't get the three thousand.'

'How's it obvious?'

Velerad thumped the table. 'Geralt, do not spoil my impression of witchers! This has been going on for more than seven years! The striga is finishing off up to fifty people a year, fewer now people are avoiding the palace. Oh no, my friend, I believe in magic. I've seen a great deal and I believe, to a certain extent, in the abilities of wizards and witchers. But all this nonsense about lifting the spell was made up by a hunch-backed, snotty old man who'd lost his mind on his hermit's diet. It's nonsense which no one but Foltest believes. Adda gave birth to a striga because she slept with her brother. That is the truth, and no spell will help. Now the striga devours people – as strigas do – she has to be killed, and that is that. Listen: two years ago peasants from some God-forsaken hole near Mahakam were plagued by a dragon devouring their sheep. They set out together, battered the dragon to death with stanchions, and did not even think it worth boasting about. But we in Wyzim are waiting for a miracle and bolting our doors every full moon, or tying our criminals to a stake in front of the palace, praying the beast stuffs herself and returns to her sarcophagus.'

'Not a bad method,' the witcher smiled. 'Are there fewer criminals?'

'Not a bit of it.'

'Which way to the palace, the new one?'

'I will take you myself. And what about the wise men's suggestion?'

'Castellan,' said Geralt, 'why act in haste? After all, I really could have an accident at work, irrespective of my intentions. Just in case, the wise men should be thinking about how to save me from the king's anger and get those fifteen hundred orens, of which rumour speaks, ready.'

'It was to be a thousand.'

'No, Lord Velerad,' the witcher said categorically. 'The witcher who was offered a thousand ran at the mere sight of the striga, without bargaining. So the risk is greater than a thousand. Whether it is greater than one and a half remains to be seen. Of course, I will say goodbye beforehand.'

'Geralt?' Velerad scratched his head. 'One thousand two hundred?'

'No. This isn't an easy task. The king is offering three, and sometimes it's easier to lift a spell than to kill. But one of my predecessors would have done so, or killed the striga, if this were simple. You think they let themselves be devoured out of fear of the king?'

'Then, witcher,' Velerad nodded wistfully, 'our agreement stands. But a word of advice – say nothing to the king about the danger of an accident at work.'

III

Foltest was slim and had a pretty – too pretty – face. He was under forty, the witcher thought. The king was sitting on a dwarf-armchair carved from black wood, his legs stretched out toward the hearth, where two dogs were warming themselves. Next to him on a chest sat an older, powerfully-built man with a beard. Behind the king stood another man, richly dressed and with a proud look on his face. A magnate.

'A witcher from Rivia,' said the king after the moment's silence which fell after Velerad's introduction.

'Yes, your Majesty.' Geralt lowered his head.

'What made your hair so grey? Magic? I can see that you are not old. That was a joke. Say nothing. You've had a fair amount of experience, I dare presume?'

'Yes, your Majesty.'

'I would love to hear about it.'

Geralt bowed even lower. 'Your Majesty, you know our code of practice forbids us to speak of our work.'

'A convenient code, witcher, very convenient. But tell me, have you had anything to do with spriggans?'

'Yes.'

'Vampires, leshys?'

'Those too.'

Foltest hesitated. 'Strigas?'

Geralt raised his head, looking the king in the eyes. 'Yes.'

Foltest turned his eyes away. 'Velerad!'

'Yes, Gracious Majesty?'

'Have you given him the details?'

'Yes, your Gracious Majesty. He says the spell cast on the princess can be reversed.'

'I have known that for a long time. How, witcher? Oh, of course, I forgot. Your code of practice. All right. I will make one small comment. Several witchers have been here already. Velerad, you have told him? Good. So I know that your speciality is to kill, rather than to reverse spells. This isn't an option. If one hair falls from my daughter's head, your head will be on the block. That is all. Ostrit, Lord Segelen, stay and give him all the information he requires. Witchers always ask a lot of questions. Feed him and let him stay in the palace. He is not to drift from tavern to tavern.'

The king rose, whistled to his dogs and made his way to the door, scattering the straw covering the chamber floor. At the door he paused.

'If you succeed, witcher, the reward is yours. Maybe I will add something if you do well. Of course, the nonsense spread by common folk about marrying the princess carries not a word of truth. I'm sure you don't believe I would give my daughter's hand to a stranger?'

'No, your Majesty. I don't.'

'Good. That shows you have some wisdom.'

Foltest left, closing the door behind him. Velerad and the magnate, who had been standing all the while, immediately sat at the table. The castellan finished the king's half-full cup, peered into the jug and cursed. Ostrit, who took Foltest's chair, scowled at the witcher while he stroked the carved armrests. Segelin, the bearded man, nodded at Geralt.

'Do sit, witcher, do sit. Supper will soon be served. What would you like to know? Castellan Velerad has probably already told you

14

everything. I know him, he has sooner told you too much than too little.'

'Only a few questions.'

'Ask.'

'The castellan said that, after the striga's appearance, the king called up many Knowing Ones.'

'That's right. But don't say striga, say princess. It makes it easier to avoid making a mistake in the king's presence – and any consequent unpleasantness.'

'Was there anyone well-known among the Knowing Ones? Anyone famous?'

'There were such, then and later. I don't remember the names. Do you, Lord Ostrit?'

'I don't recall,' said the magnate. 'But I know some of them enjoyed fame and recognition. There was much talk of it.'

'Were they in agreement that the spell can be lifted?'

'They were far from any agreement,' smiled Segelin, 'on any subject. But such an opinion was expressed. It was supposed to be simple, not even requiring magical abilities. As I understand it, it would suffice for someone to spend the night – from sunset to the third crowing of the cock – by the sarcophagus.'

'Simple indeed,' snorted Velerad.

'I would like to hear a description of the . . . the princess.'

Velerad leapt up from his chair. 'The princess looks like a striga!' he yelled. 'Like the most strigish striga I have heard of! Her Royal Highness, the cursed royal bastard, is four cubits high, shaped like a barrel of beer, has a maw which stretches from ear to ear and is full of dagger-like teeth, has red eyes and a red mop of hair! Her paws, with claws like a wild cat's, hang down to the ground! I'm surprised we've yet to send her likeness to friendly courts! The princess, plague choke her, is already fourteen. Time to think of giving her hand to a prince in marriage!'

'Hold on, Velerad,' frowned Ostrit, glancing at the door. Segelin smiled faintly.

'The description, although vivid, is reasonably accurate, and that's what you wanted, isn't it, witcher? Velerad didn't mention

15

that the princess moves with incredible speed and is far stronger for her height and build than one would expect. And she is fourteen years old, if that is of any importance.'

'It is,' said the witcher. 'Do the attacks on people only occur during the full moon?'

'Yes,' replied Segelin, 'if she attacks beyond the old palace. Within the palace walls people always die, irrespective of the moon's phase. But she only ventures out during the full moon, and not always then.'

'Has there been even one attack during the day?'

'No.'

'Does she always devour her victims?'

Velerad spat vehemently on the straw.

'Come on, Geralt, it'll be supper soon. Pish! Devours, takes a bite, leaves aside, it varies – according to her mood, no doubt. She only bit the head from one, gutted a couple, and a few more she picked clean to the bone, sucked them dry, you could say. Damned mother's—!'

'Careful, Velerad,' snarled Ostrit. 'Say what you want about the striga but do not insult Adda in front of me, as you would not dare in the king's presence!'.

'Has anyone she's attacked survived?' The witcher asked, apparently paying no special attention to the magnate's outburst.

Segelin and Ostrit looked at each other.

'Yes,' said the bearded man. 'At the very beginning, seven years ago, she threw herself at two soldiers standing guard over the crypt. One escaped—'

'And then,' interrupted Velerad, 'there was another, the miller she attacked near the town. You remember . . . ?'

IV

The following day, late in the evening, the miller was brought to the small chamber above the guardhouse allocated to the witcher. He was led in by a soldier in a hooded coat.

16

The conversation did not yield any significant results. The miller was terrified; he mumbled and stammered, and his scars told the witcher more than he did. The striga could open her jaws impressively wide and had extremely sharp teeth, including very long upper fangs – four of them, two on each side. Her claws were sharper than a wildcat's, but less curved. And it was only because of that the miller had managed to tear himself away.

Having finished his examination Geralt nodded to the miller and soldier, dismissing them. The soldier pushed the peasant through the door and lowered his hood. It was Foltest himself.

'Sit, do not get up,' said the king. 'This visit is unofficial. Are you happy with the interview? I heard you were at the palace this morning.'

'Yes, your Majesty.'

'When will you set about your task?'

'It is four days until the full moon. After that.'

'You prefer to have a look at her yourself beforehand?'

'There is no need. But having had her fill the— the princess will be less active.'

'Striga, master witcher, striga. Let us not play at diplomacy. She will be a princess afterwards. And that is what I have come to talk about. Answer me unofficially, briefly and clearly: will it work or not? Don't hide behind your code.'

Geralt rubbed his brow.

'I confirm, your Majesty, that the spell might be reversed. And, unless I am mistaken, it can be done by spending the night at the palace. The third crowing of the cock, as long as it catches the striga outside her sarcophagus, will end the spell. That is what is usually done with strigas.'

'So simple?'

'It is not simple. First you have to survive the night. Then there are exceptions to the rule, for example, not one night but three. Consecutively. There are also cases which are . . . well . . . hopeless.'

'Yes,' Foltest bristled. 'I keep hearing that from some people. Kill the monster because it's an incurable case. Master witcher, I

17

am sure they have already spoken to you. Am I right? Hack the man-eater to death without any more fuss, at the beginning, and tell the king nothing else could be done. I won't pay, but they will. Very convenient. And cheap. Because the king will order the witcher beheaded or hanged and the gold will remain in their pockets.'

'The king unconditionally orders the witcher to be beheaded?' Geralt grimaced.

Foltest looked the Rivian in the eyes for a long while.

'The king does not know,' he finally said. 'But the witcher should bear such an eventuality in mind.'

Geralt was silent for a moment. 'I intend to do what is in my power,' he said. 'But if it goes badly I will defend my life. Your Majesty, you must also be prepared for such an eventuality.'

Foltest got up. 'You do not understand me. It's obvious you'll kill her if it becomes necessary, whether I like it or not. Because otherwise she'll kill you, surely and inevitably. I won't punish anyone who kills her in self-defence. But I will not allow her to be killed without trying to save her. There have already been attempts to set fire to the old palace. They shot at her with arrows, dug pits and set traps and snares, until I hung a few of her attackers. But that is not the point. Witcher, listen!'

'I'm listening.'

'After the third crowing of the cock, there will be no striga, if I understand correctly. What will there be?'

'If all goes well, a fourteen-year-old girl.'

'With red eyes? Crocodile's teeth?'

'A normal fourteen-year-old. Except that . . .'

'Well?'

'Physically.'

'I see. And mentally? Every day, a bucket of blood for breakfast? A little girl's thigh?'

'No. Mentally . . . There is no telling. On the level, I think, of a three- or four-year-old child. She'll require loving care for a long while.'

'That's obvious. Witcher?'

18

'I'm listening.'

'Can it happen to her again? Later on?'

Geralt was silent.

'Aha,' said the king. 'It can. And what then?'

'Should she die after a long swoon lasting several days, her body will have to be burned. Quickly.'

Foltest grew gloomy.

'I do not think it will come to that,' added Geralt. 'Just to be sure, I will give you some instructions, your Majesty, to lessen the danger.'

'Right now? Is it not too soon, master witcher? And if—'

'Right now,' interrupted the Rivian. 'Many things may happen, your Majesty. It could be that you'll find a princess in the morning, the spell already broken, and my corpse.'

'Even so? Despite my permission to defend yourself? Which, it seems, wasn't that important to you.'

'This is a serious matter, your Majesty. The risk is great. That is why you must listen: the princess should always wear a sapphire around her neck, or better, an inclusion, on a silver chain. Day and night.'

'What is an inclusion?'

'A sapphire with a pocket of air trapped within the stone. Aside from that, every now and then you should burn juniper, broom and aspen in the fireplace of her chamber.'

Foltest grew pensive. 'I thank you for your advice, witcher. I will pay heed if— And now listen to me carefully. If you find the case is hopeless, kill her. If you undo the spell but the girl is not . . . normal. If you have a shadow of a doubt as to whether you have been entirely successful, kill her. Do not worry, you have nothing to fear from me. I'll shout at you in front of others, banish you from the palace and the town, nothing more. Of course I won't give you the reward, but maybe you'll manage to negotiate something from you know who.'

They were both quiet for a while.

'Geralt.' For the first time Foltest called the witcher by his name.

'Yes.'

'How much truth is there in the rumour that the child is as she is because Adda was my sister?'

'Not much. A spell has to be cast, they don't cast themselves. But I think your congress with your sister was the reason the spell was cast, and this is the result.'

'As I thought. That is what some of the Knowing Ones said, although not all of them. Geralt? Where do such things come from? Spells, magic?'

'I don't know, your Majesty. Knowing Ones study the causes of such phenomena. For us witchers the knowledge that concentrated will can cause such phenomena is enough. That and the knowledge to fight them.'

'And kill them?'

'Usually. Besides, that is what we're usually paid for. Only a few demand the reversal of spells, your Majesty. As a rule, people simply want to defend themselves from danger. If the monster has men on its conscience then revenge can also come into play.'

The king got up, took a few paces across the chamber, and stopped in front of the witcher's sword hanging on the wall.

'With this?' he asked, not looking at Geralt.

'No. That is for men.'

'So I heard. Do you know what, Geralt? I'm going to the crypt with you.'

'Out of the question.'

Foltest turned, his eyes glinted. 'Do you know, sorcerer, that I have not seen her? Neither after she was born, nor later. I was afraid. I may never see her, am I not right? At least I have the right to see my daughter while you're murdering her.'

'I repeat, it's out of the question. It is certain death. For me as well as you. If my attention, my will falters— No, your Majesty.'

Foltest turned away, started towards the door. For a moment Geralt thought he would leave without a word, without a parting gesture, but the king stopped and looked at him.

'You inspire trust,' he said, 'although I know what a rogue you are. I was told what happened at the tavern. I'm sure you killed

20

those thugs solely for word to spread, to shock people, to shock me. It's obvious that you could have dealt with them without killing. I'm afraid I'll never know whether you are going there to save my daughter, or to kill her. But I agree to it. I have to agree. Do you know why?'

Geralt did not reply.

'Because I think,' said the king, 'I think that she is suffering. Am I not right?'

The witcher fixed his penetrating eyes on the king. He didn't confirm it, didn't nod, didn't make the slightest gesture, but Foltest knew. He knew the answer.

V

Geralt looked out of the palace window for the last time. Dusk was falling rapidly. Beyond the lake the distant lights of Wyzim twinkled. There was a wilderness around the old palace – a strip of no-man's land with which, over seven years, the town had cut itself off from this dangerous place, leaving nothing but a few ruins, rotten beams and the remains of a gap-toothed palisade which had obviously not been worth dismantling and moving. As far away as possible – at the opposite end of the settlement – the king had built his new residence. The stout tower of his new palace loomed black in the distance, against the darkening blue of the sky.

In one of the empty, plundered chambers, the witcher returned to the dusty table at which he was preparing, calmly and meticulously. He knew he had plenty of time. The striga would not leave her crypt before midnight.

On the table in front of him he had a small chest with metal fittings. He opened it. Inside, packed tightly in compartments lined with dried grass, stood small vials of dark glass. The witcher removed three.

From the floor, he picked up an oblong packet thickly wrapped in sheep's skins and fastened with a leather strap. He unwrapped it and pulled out a sword with an elaborate hilt, in a black, shiny scabbard covered with rows of runic signs and symbols. He drew the blade, which lit up with a pure shine of mirror-like brightness. It was pure silver.

Geralt whispered an incantation and drank, one after the other, the contents of two vials, placing his left hand on the blade of the sword after each sip. Then, wrapping himself tightly in his black coat, he sat down on the floor. There were no chairs in the chamber, or in the rest of the palace.

He sat motionless, his eyes closed. His breathing, at first even, suddenly quickened, became rasping and tense. And then stopped completely. The mixture which helped the witcher gain full control of his body was chiefly made up of veratrum, stramonium, hawthorn and spurge. The other ingredients had no name in any human language. For anyone who was not, like Geralt, inured to it from childhood, it would have been lethal poison.

The witcher turned his head abruptly. In the silence his hearing, sharpened beyond measure, easily picked out a rustle of footsteps through the courtyard overgrown with stinging nettles. It could not be the striga. The steps were too light. Geralt threw his sword across his back, hid his bundle in the hearth of the ruined chimney-place and, silent as a bat, ran downstairs.

It was still light enough in the courtyard for the approaching man to see the witcher's face. The man, Ostrit, backed away abruptly; an involuntary grimace of terror and repulsion contorted his lips. The witcher smiled wryly – he knew what he looked like. After drinking a mixture of banewart, monk's hood and eyebright the face takes on the colour of chalk, and the pupils fill the entire iris. But the mixture enables one to see in the deepest darkness, and this is what Geralt wanted.

Ostrit quickly regained control.

'You look as if you were already a corpse, witcher,' he said. 'From fear, no doubt. Don't be afraid. I bring you reprieve.'

The witcher did not reply.

'Don't you hear what I say, you Rivian charlatan? You're saved.

And rich.' Ostrit hefted a sizeable purse in his hand and threw it at Geralt's feet. 'A thousand orens. Take it, get on your horse and get out of here!'

The Rivian still said nothing.

'Don't gawp at me!' Ostrit raised his voice. 'And don't waste my time. I have no intention of standing here until midnight. Don't you understand? I do not wish you to undo the spell. No, you haven't guessed. I am not in league with Velerad and Segelin. I don't want you to kill her. You are simply to leave. Everything is to stay as it is.'

The witcher did not move. He did not want the magnate to realise how fast his movements and reactions now were. It was quickly growing dark. A relief, as even the semi-darkness of dusk was too bright for his dilated pupils.

'And why, sir, is everything to remain as it is?' he asked, trying to enunciate each word slowly.

'Now, that,' Ostrit raised his head proudly, 'should really be of damn little concern to you.'

'And what if I already know?'

'Go on.'

'It will be easier to remove Foltest from the throne if the striga frightens the people even more? If the royal madness completely disgusts both magnates and common folk, am I right? I came here by way of Redania and Novigrad. There is much talk there that there are those in Wyzim who look to King Vizimir as their saviour and true monarch. But I, Lord Ostrit, do not care about politics, or the successions to thrones, or revolutions in palaces. I am here to accomplish my task. Have you never heard of a sense of responsibility and plain honesty? About professional ethics?'

'Careful to whom you speak, you vagabond!' Ostrit yelled furiously, placing his hand on the hilt of his sword. 'I have had enough of this. I am not accustomed to hold such discussions! Look at you – ethics, codes of practice, morality?! Who are you to talk? A brigand who's barely arrived before he starts murdering men? Who bends double to Foltest and behind his back bargains with Velerad like a hired thug? And you dare to turn your nose up at me, you serf? Play at being a Knowing One? A Magician? You scheming witcher! Be gone before I run the flat of my sword across your gob!'

The witcher did not stir. He stood calmly.

'You'd better leave, Lord Ostrit,' he said. 'It's growing dark.'

Ostrit took a step back, drew his sword in a flash.

'You asked for this, you sorcerer. I'll kill you. Your tricks won't help you. I carry a turtle-stone.'

Geralt smiled. The reputation of turtle-stone was as mistaken as it was popular. But the witcher was not going to lose his strength on spells, much less expose his silver sword to contact with Ostrit's blade. He dived under the whirling blade and, with the heel of his hand and his silver-studded cuff, hit him in the temple.

VI

Ostrit quickly regained consciousness and looked around in the total darkness. He noticed that he was tied up. He did not see Geralt standing right beside him. But he realised where he was and let out a prolonged, terrifying howl.

'Keep quiet,' said the witcher. 'Otherwise you'll lure her out before her time.'

'You damned murderer! Where are you? Untie me immediately, you louse! You'll hang for this, you son-of-a-bitch!'

'Quiet.'

Ostrit panted heavily.

'You're leaving me here to be devoured by her! Tied up?' he asked, quieter now, whispering a vile invective.

'No,' said the witcher. 'I'll let you go. But not now.'

'You scoundrel,' hissed Ostrit. 'To distract the striga?'

'Yes.'

Ostrit didn't say anything. He stopped wriggling and lay quietly.

'Witcher?'

'Yes.'

24

'It's true that I wanted to overthrow Foltest. I'm not the only one. But I am the only one who wanted him dead. I wanted him to die in agony, to go mad, to rot alive. Do you know why?'

Geralt remained silent.

'I loved Adda. The king's sister. The king's mistress. The king's trollop. I loved her— Witcher, are you there?'

'I am.'

'I know what you're thinking. But it wasn't like that. Believe me, I didn't cast any spells. I don't know anything about magic. Only once in anger did I say . . . Only once. Witcher? Are you listening?'

'I am.'

'It's his mother, the old queen. It must be her. She couldn't watch him and Adda— It wasn't me. I only once, you know, tried to persuade them but Adda— Witcher! I was besotted, and said . . . Witcher? Was it me? Me?'

'It doesn't matter anymore.'

'Witcher? Is it nearly midnight?'

'It's close.'

'Let me go. Give me more time.'

'No.'

Ostrit did not hear the scrape of the tomb lid being moved aside, but the witcher did. He leant over and, with his dagger, cut the magnate's bonds. Ostrit did not wait for the word. He jumped up, numb, hobbled clumsily, and ran. His eyes had grown accustomed enough to the darkness for him to see his way from the main hall to the exit.

The slab blocking the entrance to the crypt opened and fell to the floor with a thud. Geralt, prudently behind the staircase balustrade, saw the misshapen figure of the striga speeding swiftly and unerringly in the direction of Ostrit's receding footsteps. Not the slightest sound issued from the striga.

A terrible, quivering, frenzied scream tore the night, shook the old walls, continued rising and falling, vibrating. The witcher couldn't make out exactly how far away it was – his sharpened hearing deceived him – but he knew that the striga had caught up with Ostrit quickly. Too quickly.

He stepped into the middle of the hall, stood right at the entrance to the crypt. He threw down his coat, twitched his shoulders, adjusted the position of his sword, pulled on his gauntlets. He still had some time. He knew that the striga, although well fed after the last full moon, would not readily abandon Ostrit's corpse. The heart and liver were, for her, valuable reserves of nutrition for the long periods spent in lethargic sleep.

The witcher waited. By his count, there were about three hours left until dawn. The cock's crow could only mislead him. Besides, there were probably no cocks in the neighbourhood.

He heard her. She was trudging slowly, shuffling along the floor. And then he saw her.

The description had been accurate. The disproportionately large head set on a short neck was surrounded by a tangled, curly halo of reddish hair. Her eyes shone in the darkness like an animal's. The striga stood motionless, her gaze fixed on Geralt. Suddenly she opened her jaws – as if proud of her rows of pointed white teeth – then snapped them shut with a crack like a chest being closed. And leapt, slashing at the witcher with her bloodied claws.

Geralt jumped to the side, spun a swift pirouette. The striga rubbed against him, also spun around, slicing through the air with her talons. She didn't lose her balance and attacked anew, mid-spin, gnashing her teeth fractions of an inch from Geralt's chest. The Rivian jumped away, changing the direction of his spin with a fluttering pirouette to confuse the striga. As he leapt away he dealt a hard blow to the side of her head with the silver spikes studding the knuckles of his gauntlet.

The striga roared horribly, filling the palace with a booming echo, fell to the ground, froze and started to howl hollowly and furiously.

The witcher smiled maliciously. His first attempt, as he had hoped, had gone well. Silver was fatal to the striga, as it was for most monsters brought into existence through magic. So there was a chance: the beast was like the others, and that boded well for lifting the spell, while the silver sword would, as a last resort, assure his life.

The striga was in no hurry with her next attack. She approached slowly, baring her fangs, dribbling repulsively. Geralt backed away and, carefully placing his feet, traced a semi-circle. By slowing and quickening his movements he distracted the striga, making it difficult for her to leap. As he walked the witcher unwound a long, strong silver chain, weighted at the end.

The moment the striga tensed and leapt the chain whistled through the air and, coiling like a snake, twined itself around the monster's shoulders, neck and head. The striga's jump became a tumble, and she let out an ear-piercing whistle. She thrashed around on the floor, howling horribly with fury or from the burning pain inflicted by the despised metal. Geralt was content – if he wanted he could kill the striga without great difficulty. But the witcher did not draw his sword. Nothing in the striga's behaviour had given him reason to think she might be an incurable case. Geralt moved to a safer distance and, without letting the writhing shape on the floor out of his sight, breathed deeply, focused himself.

The chain snapped. The silver links scattered like rain in all directions, ringing against the stone. The striga, blind with fury, tumbled to the attack, roaring. Geralt waited calmly and, with his raised right hand, traced the Sign of Aard in front of him.

The striga fell back as if hit by a mallet but kept her feet, extended her talons, bared her fangs. Her hair stood on end and fluttered as if she were walking against a fierce wind. With difficulty, one rasping step at a time, she slowly advanced. But she did advance.

Geralt grew uneasy. He did not expect such a simple Sign to paralyse the striga entirely but neither did he expect the beast to overcome it so easily. He could not hold the Sign for long, it was too exhausting, and the striga had no more than ten steps to go. He lowered the Sign suddenly, and sprung aside. The striga, taken by surprise, flew forward, lost her balance, fell, slid along the floor and tumbled down the stairs into the crypt's entrance, yawning in the floor.

Her infernal scream reverberated from below.

To gain time Geralt jumped on to the stairs leading to the

gallery. He had not even climbed halfway up when the striga ran out of the crypt, speeding along like an enormous black spider. The witcher waited until she had run up the stairs after him, then leapt over the balustrade. The striga turned on the stairs, sprang and flew at him in an amazing ten-metre leap. She did not let herself be deceived by his pirouettes this time; twice her talons left their mark on the Rivian's leather tunic. But another desperately hard blow from the silver spiked gauntlet threw the striga aside, shook her. Geralt, feeling fury building inside him, swayed, bent backwards and, with a mighty kick, knocked the beast off her legs.

The roar she gave was louder than all the previous ones. Even the plaster crumbled from the ceiling.

The striga sprang up, shaking with uncontrolled anger and lust for murder. Geralt waited. He drew his sword, traced circles with it in the air, and skirted the striga, taking care that the movement of his sword was not in rhythm with his steps. The striga did not jump. She approached slowly, following the bright streak of the blade with her eyes.

Geralt stopped abruptly, froze with his sword raised. The striga, disconcerted, also stopped. The witcher traced a slow semi-circle with the blade, took a step in the striga's direction. Then another. Then he leapt, feigning a whirling movement with his sword above her head.

The striga curled up, retreated in a zigzag. Geralt was close again, the blade shimmering in his hand. His eyes lit up with an ominous glow, a hoarse roar tore through his clenched teeth. The striga backed away, pushed by the power of concentrated hatred, anger and violence which emanated from the attacking man and struck her in waves, penetrating her mind and body. Terrified and pained by feelings unknown to her she let out a thin, shaking squeak, turned on the spot and ran off in a desperate, crazy escape down the dark tangle of the palace's corridors.

Geralt stood quivering in the middle of the hall. Alone. It had taken a long time, he thought, before this dance on the edge of an abyss, this mad, macabre ballet of a fight, had achieved the desired effect, allowed him to psychically become one with his opponent,

28

to reach the underlayers of concentrated will which permeated the striga. The evil, twisted will from which the striga was born. The witcher shivered at the memory of taking on that evil to redirect it, as if in a mirror, against the monster. Never before had he come across such a concentration of hatred and murderous frenzy, not even from basilisks, who enjoyed a ferocious reputation for it.

All the better, he thought as he walked toward the crypt entrance and the blackness that spread from it like an enormous puddle. All the better, all the stronger, was the blow received by the striga. This would give him a little more time until the beast recovered from the shock. The witcher doubted whether he could repeat such an effort. The elixirs were weakening and it was still a long time until dawn. But the striga could not return to her crypt before first light, or all his trouble would come to nothing.

He went down the stairs. The crypt was not large; there was room for three stone sarcophagi. The slab covering the first was half pushed aside. Geralt pulled the third vial from beneath his tunic, quickly drank its contents, climbed into the tomb and stretched out in it. As he had expected, it was a double tomb — for mother and daughter.

He had only just pulled the cover closed when he heard the striga's roar again. He lay on his back next to Adda's mummified corpse and traced the Sign of Yrden on the inside of the slab. He laid his sword on his chest, stood a tiny hourglass filled with phosphorescent sand next to it and crossed his arms. He no longer heard the striga's screams as she searched the palace. He had gradually stopped hearing anything as the true-love and celandine began to work.

VII

When Geralt opened his eyes the sand had passed through the hourglass, which meant his sleep had been even longer than he had intended. He pricked up his ears, and heard nothing. His senses were now functioning normally.

He took hold of his sword and, murmuring an incantation, ran his hand across the lid of the sarcophagus. He then moved the slab slightly, a couple of inches.

Silence.

He pushed the lid further, sat, holding his weapon at the ready, and lifted his head above the tomb. The crypt was dark but the witcher knew that outside dawn was breaking. He struck a light, lit a miniature lamp and lifted it, throwing strange shadows across the walls of the crypt.

It was empty.

He scrambled from the sarcophagus, aching, numb, cold. And then he saw her. She was lying on her back next to the tomb, naked and unconscious.

She was rather ugly. Slim with small pointed breasts, and dirty. Her hair – flaxen-red – reached almost to her waist. Standing the lamp on the slab he knelt beside her and leant over. Her lips were pale and her face was bloody where he had hit her cheekbone. Geralt removed his gloves, put his sword aside and, without any fuss, drew up her top lip with his finger. Her teeth were normal. He reached for her hand which was buried in her tangled hair. Before he took it he saw her open eyes. Too late.

She swiped him across the neck with her talons, cutting him deeply. Blood splashed on to her face. She howled, striking him in the eyes with her other hand. He fell on her, grabbing her by the wrists, nailing her to the floor. She gnashed her teeth – which were now too short – in front of his face. He butted her in the face with his forehead and pinned her down harder. She had lost her former strength; she could only writhe beneath him, howling, spitting out blood – his blood – which was pouring over her mouth. His blood was draining away quickly. There was no time. The witcher cursed and bit her hard on the neck, just below the ear. He dug his teeth in and clenched them until her inhuman howling became a thin, despairing scream and then a choking sob – the cry of a hurt fourteen-year-old girl.

He let her go when she stopped moving, got to his knees, tore a piece of canvas from his sleeve pocket and pressed it to his neck. He felt for his sword, held the blade to the unconscious girl's throat, and leant over her hand. The nails were dirty, broken, bloodied but . . . normal. Completely normal.

The witcher got up with difficulty. The sticky-wet greyness of early morning was flooding in through the crypt's entrance. He made a move towards the stairs but staggered and sat down heavily on the floor. Blood was pouring through the drenched canvas onto his hands, running down his sleeve. He unfastened his tunic, slit his shirt, tore and ripped rags from it and tied them around his neck, knowing that he didn't have much time, that he would soon faint . . .

He succeeded. And fainted.

In Wyzim, beyond the lake, a cock, ruffling his feathers in the cold damp, crowed hoarsely for the third time.

VIII

He saw the whitened walls and beamed ceiling of the small chamber above the guardroom. He moved his head, grimacing with pain, and moaned. His neck was bandaged, thickly, thoroughly, professionally.

'Lie still, witcher,' said Velerad. 'Lie, do not move.'

'My . . . sword . . .'

'Yes, yes. Of course, what is most important is your witcher's silver sword. It's here, don't worry. Both the sword and your little trunk. And the three thousand orens. Yes, yes, don't utter a word. It is I who am an old fool and you the wise witcher. Foltest has been repeating it over and over for the last two days.'

'Two—'

'Oh yes, two. She slit your neck open quite thoroughly. One could see everything you have inside there. You lost a great deal of blood. Fortunately we hurried to the palace straight after the third crowing of the cock. Nobody slept in Wyzim that night. It was impossible, you made a terrible noise. Does my talking tire you?'

'The prin . . . cess?'

'The princess is like a princess. Thin. And somewhat dull-witted. She weeps incessantly and wets her bed. But Foltest says this will change. I don't think it'll change for the worse, do you, Geralt?'

The witcher closed his eyes.

'Good. I take my leave now. Rest.' Velerad got up. 'Geralt? Before I go, tell me: why did you try to bite her to death? Eh? Geralt?'

The witcher was asleep.

THE VOICE OF REASON 2

I

'Geralt.'

He raised his head, torn from sleep. The sun was already high and forced blinding golden rays through the shutters, penetrating the chamber with tentacles of light. The witcher shaded his eyes with his hand in an unnecessary, instinctive reflex which he had never managed to shake off – all he needed to do, after all, was narrow his pupils into vertical slits.

'It's late,' said Nenneke, opening the shutters. 'You've slept in. Off with you, Iola.'

The girl sat up suddenly and leant out of bed to take her mantle from the floor. Geralt felt a trickle of cool saliva on his shoulder, where her lips had been a moment ago.

'Wait . . .' he said hesitantly. She looked at him, quickly turned away.

She had changed. There was nothing of the water nymph in her any more, nothing of the luminous, chamomile-scented apparition she had been at dawn. Her eyes were blue, not black. And she had freckles – on her nose, her neckline, her shoulders. They weren't unattractive, they suited her complexion and reddish hair. But he hadn't seen them at dawn, when she had been his dream. With shame he realised he felt resentment towards her, resentment that she hadn't remained a dream, and that he would never forgive himself for it.

'Wait,' he repeated. 'Iola . . . I wanted—'

'Don't speak to her, Geralt,' said Nenneke. 'She won't answer you anyway. Off with you, Iola.'

Wrapped in her mantle the girl pattered towards the door, her bare feet slapping the floor – troubled, flushed, awkward. No longer reminding him, in any way, of—

Yennefer.

'Nenneke,' he said, reaching for his shirt. 'I hope you're not annoyed that— You won't punish her, will you?'

'Fool,' the priestess snorted. 'You've forgotten where you are. This is neither a hermitage nor a convent. It's Melitele's temple. Our goddess doesn't forbid our priestesses anything. Almost.'

'You forbade me to talk to her.'

'I didn't forbid you. But I know it's pointless. Iola doesn't speak.'

'What?'

'She doesn't speak. She's taken a vow. It's a sort of sacrifice through which . . . Oh, what's the point of explaining, you wouldn't understand anyway. You wouldn't even try to understand, I know your views on religion. No, don't get dressed yet. I want to check your neck.'

She sat on the edge of the bed and skilfully unwound the linen bandages wrapped thickly around the witcher's neck. He grimaced in pain.

As soon as he had arrived in Ellander, Nenneke had removed the painfully thick stitches of shoemaker's twine with which they had stitched him in Wyzim, opened the wound and dressed it again. The results were clear: he had arrived at the temple almost cured, if perhaps a little stiff. Now he was sick again, and in pain. But he didn't protest. He'd known the priestess for years and knew how great was her knowledge of healing, how rich and comprehensive her pharmacy was. A course of treatment at Melitele's temple could do nothing but good.

Nenneke felt the wound, washed it and began to curse. He already knew this routine by heart. She had started on the very first day, and had never failed to moan when she saw the marks left by the princess of Wyzim's talons.

'It's terrible! To let yourself be slashed like this by an ordinary striga. Muscles, tendons – she only just missed your carotid artery! Great Melitele! Geralt, what's happening to you? How did she get so close to you? What did you want with her? To mount her?'

He didn't answer, and smiled faintly.

'Don't grin like an idiot.' The priestess rose and took a bag of dressings from the chest of drawers. Despite her weight and low stature she moved swiftly and gracefully. 'There's nothing funny about it. You're losing your reflexes, Geralt.'

'You're exaggerating.'

'I'm not exaggerating at all.' Nenneke spread a greenish mush smelling sharply of eucalyptus over the wound. 'You shouldn't have allowed yourself to get wounded, but you did, and very seriously at that. Fatally even. And even with your exceptional powers of regeneration it'll be months before your neck is fully mobile again. I warn you, don't test your strength by fighting an agile opponent during that time.'

'Thank you for the warning. Perhaps you could give me some advice, too: how am I supposed to live in the meantime? Rally a few girls, buy a cart and organize a travelling house of ill-repute?'

Nenneke shrugged, bandaging his neck with quick, deft movements. 'Am I supposed to give you advice and teach you how to live? Am I your mother or something? Right, that's done. You can get dressed. Breakfast's waiting for you in the refectory. Hurry up or you'll have to make it yourself. I don't intend to keep the girls in the kitchen to midday.'

'Where will I find you later? In the sanctuary?'

'No.' Nenneke got up. 'Not in the sanctuary. You're a welcome guest here, witcher, but don't hang around in the sanctuary. Go for a walk, and I'll find you myself.'

'Fine.'

II

Geralt strolled – for the fourth time – along the poplar alley which led from the gate to the dwellings by the sanctuary and main temple block, which merged into the sheer rock. After brief consideration he decided against returning to shelter, and turned towards the gardens and outbuildings. Umpteen priestesses, clad in grey working garments, were toiling away, weeding the beds and feeding the birds in the henhouses. The majority of them were young or very young, virtually children. Some greeted him with a nod or a smile in passing. He answered their greetings but didn't recognise any of them. Although he often visited the temple – once or even twice a year – he never saw more than three or four faces he knew. The girls came and went – becoming oracles in other temples, midwives and healers specialising in women's and children's diseases, wandering druids, teachers or governesses. But there was never a shortage of priestesses, arriving from all over, even the remotest regions. Melitele's temple in Ellander was well-known and enjoyed well-earned fame.

The cult of Melitele was one of the oldest and, in its day, one of the most widespread cults from time immemorial. Practically every pre-human race and every primordial nomadic human tribe honoured a goddess of harvest and fertility, a guardian of farmers and gardeners, a patroness of love and marriage. Many of these religions merged into the cult of Melitele.

Time, which was quite pitiless towards other religions and cults, effectively isolating them in forgotten, rarely visited little temples and oratories buried amongst urban buildings, had proved merciful to Melitele. She did not lack either followers or sponsors. In explaining the popularity of the goddess, learned men who studied this phenomenon used to hark back to the pre-cults of the Great Mother, Mother Nature, and pointed to the links with nature's cycle, with the rebirth of life and other grandiloquently named phenomena. Geralt's friend, the troubadour Dandilion, who enjoyed a reputation as a specialist in every possible field, looked for simpler explanations. Melitele's cult, he deduced, was a typical woman's cult. Melitele was, after all, the patroness of fertility and birth; she was the guardian of midwives. And a woman in labour has to scream. Apart from the usual cries – usually promising never to give herself to any bloody man ever again in her life – a woman in labour has to call upon some godhead for help, and

36

Melitele was perfect. And since women gave birth, give birth and will continue to give birth, the goddess Melitele, the poet proved, did not have to fear for her popularity.

'Geralt.'

'Nenneke. I was looking for you.'

'Me?' The priestess looked at him mockingly. 'Not Iola?'

'Iola, too,' he admitted. 'Does that bother you?'

'Right now, yes. I don't want you to get in her way and distract her. She's got to get herself ready and pray if something's to come of this trance.'

'I've already told you,' he said coldly, 'I don't want any trance. I don't think a trance will help me in any way.'

'While I,' Nenneke winced, 'don't think a trance will harm you in any way.'

'I can't be hypnotised, I have immunity. I'm afraid for Iola. It might be too great an effort for a medium.'

'Iola isn't a medium or a mentally ill soothsayer. That child enjoys the goddess's favour. Don't pull silly faces, if you please. As I said, your view on religion is known to me, it's never particularly bothered me and, no doubt, it won't bother me in the future. I'm not a fanatic. You've a right to believe that we're governed by Nature and the Force hidden within her. You can think that the gods, including my Melitele, are merely a personification of this power invented for simpletons so they can understand it better, accept its existence. According to you, that power is blind. But for me, Geralt, faith allows you to expect what my goddess personifies from nature: order, law, goodness. And hope.'

'I know.'

'If you know that then why your reservations about the trance? What are you afraid of? That I'll make you bow your head to a statue and sing canticles? Geralt, we'll simply sit together for a while – you, me and Iola – and see if the girl's talents will let her see into the vortex of power surrounding you. Maybe we'll discover something worth knowing. And maybe we won't discover anything. Maybe the power and fate surrounding you won't choose to reveal themselves to us, will remain hidden and incomprehensible. I don't know. But why shouldn't we try?'

'Because there's no point. I'm not surrounded by any vortex or fate. And if I were, why the hell would I delve into it?'

'Geralt, you're sick.'

'Injured, you mean.'

'I know what I mean. There's something not quite right with you. I can sense that. After all, I have known you ever since you were a youngster. When I met you, you came up to my waist. And now I feel that you're spinning around in some damned whirlpool, tangled up in a slowly tightening noose. I want to know what's happening. But I can't do it myself, I have to count on Iola's gifts.'

'You want to delve too deeply. Why the metaphysics? I'll confide in you, if you like. I'll fill your evenings with tales of ever more astounding events from the past few years. Get a keg of beer so my throat doesn't dry up and we can start today. But I fear I'll bore you because you won't find any nooses or vortexes there. Just a witcher's ordinary tales.'

'I'll willingly listen to them. But a trance, I repeat, would do no harm.'

'Don't you think,' he smiled, 'that my lack of faith makes such a trance pointless?'

'No, I don't. And do you know why?'

'No.'

Nenneke leant over and looked him in the eyes with a strange smile on her pale lips.

'Because it would be the first proof I've ever heard of that a lack of faith has any kind of power at all.'

A GRAIN OF TRUTH

I

A number of black points moving against a bright sky streaked with mist drew the witcher's attention. Birds. They wheeled in slow, peaceful circles, then suddenly swooped and soared up again, flapping their wings.

The witcher observed the birds for a long time then – bearing in mind the shape of the land, density of the wood, depth and course of the ravine which he suspected lay in his path – calculated the distance to them, and how long he would take to cover it. Finally he threw aside his coat and tightened the belt across his chest by two holes. The pommel and hilt of the sword strapped across his back peeked over his shoulder.

'We'll go a little out of our way, Roach,' he said. 'We'll take a detour from the highway. I don't think the birds are circling there for nothing.'

The mare walked on, obedient to Geralt's voice.

'Maybe it's just a dead elk,' said Geralt. 'But maybe it's not. Who knows?'

There was a ravine, as he had suspected; the witcher scanned the crowns of the trees tightly filling the rift. But the sides of the gully were gentle, the riverbed dry and clear of blackthorns and rotting tree trunks. He crossed it easily. On the other side was a copse of birches, and behind it a large glade, heath and undergrowth, which threw tentacles of tangled branches and roots upwards.

The birds, scared away by the appearance of a rider, soared higher, croaking sharply in their hoarse voices.

Geralt saw the first corpse immediately – the white of the

sheepskin jacket and matt-blue of the dress stood out clearly against a yellowing clump of sedge. He didn't see the second corpse but its location was betrayed by three wolves sitting calmly on their haunches watching the witcher. His mare snorted and the wolves, as if at a command, unhurriedly, trotted into the woods, every now and again turning their triangular heads to watch the newcomer. Geralt jumped off his horse.

The woman in the sheepskin and blue dress had no face or throat, and most of her left thigh had gone. The witcher, not leaning over, walked by her.

The man lay with his face to the ground. Geralt didn't turn the body over, seeing that the wolves and birds hadn't been idle. And there was no need to examine the corpse in detail – the shoulders and back of the woollen doublet were covered with thick black rivulets of dried blood. It was clear the man had died from a blow to the neck, and the wolves had only found the body afterwards.

On a wide belt next to a short cutlass in a wooden sheath the man wore a leather purse. The witcher tore it off and, item by item, threw the contents on the grass: a tinder-box, a piece of chalk, sealing-wax, a handful of silver coins, a folding shaving-knife with a bone handle, a rabbit's ear, three keys and a talisman with a phallic symbol. Two letters, written on canvas, were damp with rain and dew, smudged beyond readability. The third, written on parchment, was also ruined by damp, but still legible. It was a credit note made out by the dwarves' bank in Murivel to a merchant called Rulle Asper, or Aspen. It wasn't for a large sum.

Bending over, Geralt lifted the man's right hand. As he had expected, the copper ring digging into the swollen, blue finger carried the sign of the armourers' guild: a stylised helmet with visor, two crossed swords and the rune 'A' engraved beneath them.

The witcher returned to the woman's corpse. As he was turning the body over something pricked him in the finger – a rose, pinned to the dress. The flower had withered but not lost its colour: the petals were dark blue, very dark blue. It was the first time Geralt had seen such a rose. He turned the body over completely, and winced.

On the woman's bare and bloody neck were clear bite marks. And not those of a wolf.

The witcher carefully backed away to his horse. Without taking his eyes from the forest edge, he climbed into the saddle. He circled the glade twice and, leaning over, looked around, examining the ground closely.

'So, Roach,' he said quietly, 'the case is reasonably clear. The armourer and the woman arrived on horseback from the direction of the forest. They were on their way home from Murivel, because nobody carries an uncashed credit note for long. Why they were going this way and not following the highway? I don't know. But they were crossing the heath, side by side. And then – again, I don't know why – they both dismounted, or fell from, their horses. The armourer died instantly. The woman ran, then fell and died, and whatever attacked her – which didn't leave any tracks – dragged her along the ground, with her throat in its teeth. The horses ran off. This happened two or three days ago.'

The mare snorted restlessly, reacting to his tone of voice.

'The thing which killed them,' continued Geralt, watching the forest's edge, 'was neither a werewolf nor a leshy. Neither would have left so much for the scavengers. If there were swamps here I'd say it was a kikimora or a vypper . . . but there aren't any swamps here.'

Leaning over, the witcher pulled back the blanket which covered the horse's side and uncovered another sword strapped to the saddle-bag – one with a shining, ornate guard and black corrugated hilt.

'Well, Roach. We're taking a roundabout route; we'd better check why this armourer and woman were riding through the forest not along the highway. If we pass by ignoring such incidents we won't ever earn enough for your oats, will we?'

The mare obediently moved forward, across the heath, carefully sidestepping hollows.

'Although it's not a werewolf, we won't take any risks,' the witcher continued, taking a bunch of dried monkshead from a saddlebag and hanging it by the bit. The mare snorted. Geralt unlaced his tunic a little and pulled out a medallion engraved with a wolf with bared jaws. The medallion, hanging on a silver chain, bobbed up and down in rhythm to the horse's gait, sparkling in the sun's rays like mercury.

II

He noticed the red tiles of the tower's conical roof from the summit of a hill as he cut across a bend in the faint trail. The slope, covered with hazel, dry branches and a thick carpet of yellow leaves, wasn't safe to descend on horseback. The witcher retreated, carefully rode down the incline and returned to the main path. He rode slowly, stopped the horse every now and again and, hanging from the saddle, looked out for tracks.

The mare tossed her head, neighed wildly, stamped and danced on the path, kicking up a storm of dried leaves. Geralt, wrapping his left arm around the horse's neck, swept his right hand – the fingers arranged in the Sign of Axia – over the mount's head as he whispered an incantation.

'Is it as bad as all that?' he murmured, looking around and not withdrawing the Sign. 'Easy, Roach, easy.'

The charm worked quickly but the mare, prodded with his heel, moved forward reluctantly, losing the natural springy rhythm of her gait. The witcher jumped nimbly to the ground and went on by foot, leading her by the bridle. He saw a wall.

There was no gap between the wall and the forest, no distinct break. The young trees and juniper bushes twined their leaves with the ivy and wild vines clinging to the stonework. Geralt looked up. At that same moment, he felt a prickle along his neck, as if an invisible, soft creature had latched on to his neck, lifting the hairs there.

He was being watched.

He turned around smoothly. Roach snorted; the muscles in her neck twitched, moved under her skin.

A girl was standing on the slope of the hill he had just climbed down, one arm resting on the trunk of an alder tree. Her trailing white dress contrasted with the glossy blackness of her dishevelled hair, falling to her shoulders. She seemed to be smiling, but she was too far away to be sure.

'Greetings,' he said, raising his hand in a friendly gesture. He took a step towards the girl. She turned her head a little, following his movements. Her face was pale, her eyes black and enormous. The smile – if it had been a smile – vanished from her face as though wiped away with a cloth. Geralt took another step, the leaves rustled underfoot, and the girl ran down the slope like a deer, flitting between the hazel bushes. She was no more than a white streak as she disappeared into the depths of the forest. The long dress didn't appear to restrict her ease of movement in the least.

Roach neighed anxiously, tossing her head. Geralt, still watching the forest, instinctively calmed her with the Sign again. Pulling the mare by the bridle he walked slowly along the wall, wading through burdock up to the waist.

He came to a sturdy gate, with iron fittings and rusty hinges, furnished with a great brass knocker. After a moment's hesitation Geralt reached out and touched the tarnished ring. He immediately jumped back as, at that moment, the gate opened, squeaking, clattering, and raking aside clumps of grass, stones and branches. There was no one behind it – the witcher could only see a deserted courtyard, neglected and overgrown with nettles. He entered, leading Roach. The mare, still stunned by the Sign, didn't resist, but she moved stiffly and hesitantly after him.

The courtyard was surrounded on three sides by a wall and the remains of some wooden scaffolding. On the fourth side stood the mansion, its façade mottled by a pox of chipped plaster, dirty damp patches, and festooned with ivy. The shutters, with their peeling paint, were closed, as was the door.

Geralt threw Roach's reins over the pillar by the gate and slowly made his way towards the mansion, following the gravel path past a small fountain full of leaves and rubbish. In the centre of the fountain, on a fanciful plinth, a white stone dolphin arched, turning its chipped tail upwards.

Next to the fountain in what, a very long time ago, used to be a flowerbed, grew a rosebush. Nothing but the colour of the flowers made this bush unique – but the flowers were exceptional: indigo, with a faint shade of purple on the tips of some of the petals. The witcher touched one, brought his face closer and inhaled. The flowers held the typical scent of roses, only a little more intense.

The door and all the shutters of the mansion flew open at the same instant with a bang. Geralt raised his head abruptly. Down the path, scrunching the gravel, a monster was rushing straight at him.

The witcher's right hand rose, as fast as lightning, above his right shoulder while his left jerked the belt across his chest making the sword hilt jump into his palm. The blade, leaping from the scabbard with a hiss, traced a short, luminous semi-circle and froze, the point aiming at the charging beast.

At the sight of the sword the monster stopped short, spraying gravel in all directions. The witcher didn't even flinch.

The creature was humanoid, and dressed in clothes which, though tattered, were of good quality and not lacking in stylish and useless ornamentation. His human form, however, reached no higher than the soiled collar of his tunic, for above it loomed a gigantic, hairy, bear-like head with enormous ears, a pair of wild eyes and terrifying jaws full of crooked fangs in which a red tongue flickered like flame.

'Flee, mortal man!' the monster roared, flapping his paws but not moving from the spot. 'I'll devour you! Tear you to pieces!' The witcher didn't move, didn't lower his sword. 'Are you deaf? Away with you!' The creature screamed, then made a sound somewhere between a pig's squeal and a stag's bellowing roar, making the shutters rattle and clatter and shaking rubble and plaster from the sills. Neither witcher nor monster moved.

'Clear off while you're still in one piece!' roared the creature, less sure of himself. 'Because if you don't, then—'

44

'Then what?' interrupted Geralt.

The monster suddenly gasped and tilted his monstrous head. 'Look at him, isn't he brave?' He spoke calmly, baring his fangs and glowering at Geralt with bloodshot eyes. 'Lower that iron, if you please. Perhaps you've not realised you're in my courtyard? Or maybe it's customary, wherever you come from, to threaten people with swords in their own courtyards?'

'It is customary,' Geralt agreed, 'when faced with people who greet their guests with a roar and the cry that they're going to tear you to pieces.'

'Pox on it!' The monster got himself worked up. 'And he'll insult me on top of it all, this straggler. A guest, is he? Pushes his way into the yard, ruins someone else's flowers, plays the lord and thinks that he'll be brought bread and salt. Bah!'

The creature spat, gasped and shut his jaws. The lower fangs protruded, making him look like a boar.

'So?' The witcher spoke after a moment, lowering his sword. 'Are we going to carry on standing like this?'

'And what do you suggest instead? Lying down?' snorted the monster. 'Put that iron away, I said.'

The witcher nimbly slipped the weapon into its scabbard and, without lowering his arm, stroked the hilt which rose above his shoulder.

'I'd prefer you,' he said, 'not to make any sudden moves. This sword can always be drawn again, faster than you imagine.'

'I noticed,' rasped the monster. 'If it wasn't for that you'd have been out of this gate a long time ago, with my bootprint on your arse. What do you want here? How did you get here?'

'I got lost,' lied the witcher.

'You got lost,' repeated the monster, twisting his jaws in a menacing grin. 'Well, unlose your way. Out of the gate, turn your left ear to the sun and keep walking and you'll soon get back to the highway. Well? What are you waiting for?'

'Is there any water?' asked Geralt calmly. 'The horse is thirsty. And so am I, if that doesn't inconvenience you.'

The monster shifted from one foot to the other and scratched his ear. 'Listen you,' he said. 'Are you really not frightened of me?'

'Should I be?'

The monster looked around, cleared his throat and yanked up his baggy trousers.

'Pox on it, what's the harm of a guest in the house? It's not every day I meet someone who doesn't run away or faint at the sight of me. All right then. If you're a weary but honest wanderer I invite you in. But if you're a brigand or a thief, then I warn you: this house does what I tell it to. Within these walls I rule!'

He lifted his hairy paw. All the shutters clattered against the wall once more and deep in the dolphin's stone gullet something rumbled.

'I invite you in,' he repeated.

Geralt didn't move, scrutinising him.

'Do you live alone?'

'What's that to do with you?' said the monster angrily, opening his jaws, then croaked loudly, 'Oh, I see. No doubt you'd like to know whether I've got forty servants all as beautiful as me. I don't. Well, pox, are you going to make use of my generous invitation? If not, the gate's over there.'

Geralt bowed stiffly. 'I accept your invitation,' he said formally. 'I won't slight the right of hospitality.'

'My house is your house,' the monster said in return, just as formally, although a little offhandedly. 'This way please, dear guest. And leave the horse here, by the well.'

The interior was in need of extensive repair, although it was reasonably clean and tidy. The furniture had been made by skilled craftsmen, if a very long time ago. A pungent smell of dust hung in the dark rooms.

'Light!' growled the monster, and the torch in its iron bracket burst into flames and sooty smoke.

'Not bad,' remarked the witcher.

The monster cackled. 'That's it? I see you won't be amazed by any old trick. I told you this house obeys my commands. This way, please. Careful, the stairs are steep. Light!'

46

On the stairs, the monster turned. 'What's that around your neck, dear guest?'

'Have a look.'

The creature took the medallion in his paw, lifted it up to his eyes, tightening the chain around Geralt's neck a little.

'The animal has an unpleasant expression. What is it?'

'My guild's badge.'

'Ah, you make muzzles, no doubt. This way, please. Light!'

The centre of the large room, completely devoid of windows, was taken up by a huge oak table, empty apart from an enormous brass candlestick, slowly turning green and covered with trickles of hardened wax. At the monster's command the candles lit and flickered, brightening the interior a little.

One wall was hung with weapons, compositions of round shields, crossed partisans, javelins and guisarmes, heavy sabres and axes. Half of the adjacent wall was taken up by an enormous fireplace, above which hung rows of flaking and peeling portraits. The wall facing the entrance was filled with hunting trophies – elks and stag antlers whose branching racks threw long shadows across the grinning mounted heads of wild boar, bear and lynx, over the ruffled and frayed wings of eagles and hawks. The place of honour was filled by a rock dragon's head, tainted brown, damaged and leaking stuffing. Geralt examined it more closely.

'My grandpa killed it,' said the monster, throwing a huge log into the depths of the fireplace. 'It was probably the last one in the vicinity when it got itself killed. Sit, my dear guest. You're hungry?'

'I won't deny it, dear host.'

The monster sat at the table, lowered his head, clasped his hairy paws over his stomach, muttered something while twiddling his enormous thumbs, then suddenly roared, thumping the table with his paw. Dishes and platters rattled like pewter and silver, chalices jingled like crystal. There was a smell of roast meat, garlic, marjoram and nutmeg. Geralt did not show any surprise.

'Yes.' The monster rubbed his hands. 'This is better than servants, isn't it? Help yourself, dear guest. Here is some fowl,

47

here some boar ham, here terrine of . . . I don't know what. Something. Here we have some hazel grouse. Pox, no, it's partridge. I got the spells muddled up. Eat up, eat up. This is proper, real food, don't worry.'

'I'm not worried.' Geralt tore the fowl in two.

'I forgot,' snorted the monster, 'that you're not timid. What shall I call you?'

'Geralt. And your name, dear host?'

'Nivellen. But they call me Degen or Fanger around here. And they use me to frighten children.'

The monster poured the contents of an enormous chalice down his throat, after which he sank his fingers in the terrine, tearing half of it from the bowl in one go.

'Frighten children,' repeated Geralt with his mouth full. 'Without any reason, no doubt?'

'Of course not. Your health, Geralt!'

'And yours, Nivellen.'

'How's the wine? Have you noticed that it's made from grapes and not apples? But if you don't like it I'll conjure up a different one.'

'Thank you, it's not bad. Are your magical powers innate?'

'No. I've had them since growing this. This trap, that is. I don't know how it happened myself, but the house does whatever I wish. Nothing very big; I can conjure up food, drink, clothes, clean linen, hot water, soap. Any woman can do that, and without using magic at that. I can open and close windows and doors. I can light a fire. Nothing very remarkable.'

'It's something. And this . . . trap, as you call it, have you had it long?'

'Twelve years.'

'How did it happen?'

'What's it got to do with you? Pour yourself some more wine.'

'With pleasure. It's got nothing to do with me. I'm just asking out of curiosity.'

'An acceptable reason,' the monster said, and laughed loudly. 'But I don't accept it. It's got nothing to do with you and that's

48

that. But just to satisfy your curiosity a little I'll show you what I used to look like. Look at those portraits. The first from the chimney is my father. The second, pox only knows. And the third is me. Can you see it?'

Beneath the dust and spider-webs a nondescript man with a bloated, sad, spotty face and watery eyes looked down from the painting. Geralt, who was no stranger to the way portrait painters tended to flatter their clients, nodded.

'Can you see it?' repeated Nivellen, baring his fangs.

'I can.'

'Who are you?'

'I don't understand.'

'You don't understand?' The monster raised his head; his eyes shone like a cat's. 'My portrait is hung beyond the candlelight. I can see it, but I'm not human. At least, not at the moment. A human, looking at my portrait, would get up, go closer and, no doubt, have to take the candlestick with him. You didn't do that, so the conclusion is simple. But I'm asking you plainly: are you human?'

Geralt didn't lower his eyes. 'If that's the way you put it,' he answered after a moment's silence, 'then, not quite.'

'Ah. Surely it won't be tactless if I ask, in that case, what you are?'

'A witcher.'

'Ah,' Nivellen repeated after a moment. 'If I remember rightly, witchers earn their living in an interesting way – they kill monsters for money.'

'You remember correctly.'

Silence fell again. Candle flames pulsated, flicked upwards in thin wisps of fire, glimmering in the cut-crystal chalices. Cascades of wax trickled down the candlestick.

Nivellen sat still, lightly twitching his enormous ears. 'Let's assume,' he said finally, 'that you draw your sword before I jump on you. Let's assume you even manage to cut me down. With my weight, that won't stop me; I'll take you down through sheer momentum. And then it's teeth that'll decide. What do you think, witcher, which one of us has a better chance if it comes to biting each other's throats?'

Geralt, steadying the carafe's pewter stopper with his thumb, poured himself some wine, took a sip and leaned back into his chair. He was watching the monster with a smile. An exceptionally ugly one.

'Yeeees,' said Nivellen slowly, digging at the corner of his jaws with his claw. 'One has to admit you can answer questions without using many words. It'll be interesting to see how you manage the next one. Who paid you to deal with me?'

'No one. I'm here by accident.'

'You're not lying, by any chance?'

'I'm not in the habit of lying.'

'And what are you in the habit of doing? I've heard about witchers – they abduct tiny children whom they feed with magic herbs. The ones who survive become witchers themselves, sorcerers with inhuman powers. They're taught to kill, and all human feelings and reactions are trained out of them. They're turned into monsters in order to kill other monsters. I've heard it said it's high time someone started hunting witchers, as there are fewer and fewer monsters and more and more witchers. Do have some partridge before it's completely cold.'

Nivellen took the partridge from the dish, put it between his jaws and crunched it like a piece of toast, bones cracking as they were crushed between his teeth.

'Why don't you say anything?' he asked indistinctly, swallowing. 'How much of the rumours about you witchers is true?'

'Practically nothing.'

'And what's a lie?'

'That there are fewer and fewer monsters.'

'True. There's a fair number of them.' Nivellen bared his fangs. 'One is sitting in front of you wondering if he did the right thing by inviting you in. I didn't like your guild badge right from the start, dear guest.'

'You aren't a monster, Nivellen,' the witcher said dryly.

'Pox, that's something new. So what am I? Cranberry pudding?

50

A flock of wild geese flying south on a sad November morning? No? Maybe I'm the virtue that a miller's buxom daughter lost in spring? Well, Geralt, tell me what I am. Can't you see I'm shaking with curiosity?'

'You're not a monster. Otherwise you wouldn't be able to touch this silver tray. And in no way could you hold my medallion.'

'Ha!' Nivellen roared so powerfully the candle flames fell horizontal for a moment. 'Today, very clearly, is a day for revealing great and terrible secrets! Now I'm going to be told that I grew these ears because I didn't like milky porridge as a child!'

'No, Nivellen,' said Geralt calmly. 'It happened because of a spell. I'm sure you know who cast that spell.'

'And what if I do?'

'In many cases a spell can be uncast.'

'You, as a witcher, can uncast spells in many cases?'

'I can. Do you want me to try?'

'No. I don't.' The monster opened his jaws and poked out his tongue, two span long, and very red. 'Surprised you, hasn't it?'

'That it has,' admitted Geralt.

The monster giggled and lounged in his armchair. 'I knew that would,' he said. 'Pour yourself some more, get comfortable and I'll tell you the whole story. Witcher or not, you've got an honest face and I feel like talking. Pour yourself more.'

'There's none left.'

'Pox on it!' The monster cleared his throat, then thumped the table with his paw again. A large earthenware demijohn in a wicker basket appeared next to the two empty carafes, from nowhere. Nivellen tore the sealing wax off with his teeth.

'As no doubt you've noticed,' he began, pouring the wine, 'this is quite a remote area. It's a long way to the nearest human settlement. It's because, you see, my father, and my grandfather too, in his time, didn't make themselves particularly loved by our neighbours or the merchants using the highway. If anyone went astray here and my father spotted them from the tower, they lost – at best – their fortune. And a couple of the nearer settlements

51

were burnt because Father decided the levies were being paid tardily. Not many people liked my father. Except for me, naturally. I cried awfully when what was left of my father after a blow from a two-handed sword was brought home on a cart one day. Grandpa didn't take part in robbery any more because, ever since he was hit on the head with a morningstar, he had a terrible stutter. He dribbled and rarely made it to the privy on time. As their heir, I had to lead the gang.

'I was young at the time,' Nivellen continued, 'a real milksop, so the lads in the crew wound me around their little fingers in a flash. I was as much in command of them as a fat piglet is of a pack of wolves. We soon began doing things which Father would never have allowed, had he been alive. I'll spare you the details and get straight to the point. One day we took ourselves as far as Gelibol, near Mirt, and robbed a temple. A young priestess was there too.'

'Which temple, Nivellen?'

'Pox only knows, but it must have been a bad one. There were skulls and bones on the altar, I remember, and a green fire was burning. It stank like nobody's business. But to the point. The lads overpowered the priestess and stripped her, then said I had to become a man. Well, I became a man, stupid little snot that I was, and while I was achieving manhood the priestess spat into my face and screamed something.'

'What?'

'That I was a monster in human skin, that I'd be a monster in a monster's skin, something about love, blood . . . I can't remember. She must have had the dagger, a little one, hidden in her hair. She killed herself and then—

'We fled from there, Geralt, I'm telling you – we nearly wore our horses out. It was a bad temple.'

'Go on.'

'Then it was as the priestess had said. A few days later, I woke up and as the servants saw me, they screamed and took to their heels. I went to the mirror . . . You see, Geralt, I panicked, had some sort of an attack, I remember it almost through a haze. To put it briefly, corpses fell. Several. I used whatever came to hand – and I'd suddenly become very strong. And the house helped as best it could: doors slammed, furniture flew in the air, fires broke out. Whoever could get out ran away in a panic: my aunt and cousin, the lads from the crew. What am I saying? Even the dogs howled and cowered. My cat, Glutton, ran away. Even my aunt's parrot kicked the bucket out of fear. I was alone, roaring, howling, going mad, smashing whatever came to hand, mainly mirrors.'

Nivellen paused, sighed and sniffed.

'When the attack was over,' he resumed after a while, 'it was already too late. I was alone. I couldn't explain to anyone that only my appearance had changed, that although in this horrible shape I was just a stupid youngster, sobbing over the servants' bodies in an empty manor. I was afraid they'd come back and kill me before I could explain. But nobody returned.'

The monster grew silent for a moment and wiped his nose on his sleeve. 'I don't want to go back to those first months, Geralt. It still leaves me shaking when I recall them. I'll get to the point. For a long time, a very long time, I sat in the manor, quiet as a mouse, not stirring from the place. If anyone appeared, which rarely happened, I wouldn't go out. I'd tell the house to slam the shutters a couple of times, or I'd roar through the gargoyle, and that was usually enough for the would-be guest to leave in a hurry. So that's how it was, until one day I looked out of the window one pale dawn and – what did I see? Some trespasser stealing a rose from my aunt's bush. And it isn't just any old rosebush: these are blue roses from Nazair. It was Grandfather who brought the seedlings. I flew into a fury and jumped outside.

'The fat trespasser, when he got his voice back – he'd lost it when he saw me – squealed that he only wanted a few flowers for his daughter, that I should spare him, spare his life and his health. I was just ready to kick him out of the main gate when I remembered something. Stories Lenka, my nanny – the old bag – used to tell me. Pox on it, I thought, if pretty girls turn frogs into princes, or the other way round, then maybe . . . Maybe there's a grain of truth in these stories, a chance . . . I leapt four yards, roared so loud wild vine tumbled from the wall, and I yelled "Your daughter or your life!" Nothing better came to mind. The merchant, for he was a merchant, began to weep, then confessed that his daughter was only eight. Are you laughing?'

'No.'

'I didn't know whether to laugh or cry over my shitty fate. I felt sorry for the old trader. I couldn't watch him shake like that. I invited him inside, made him welcome and, when he was leaving I poured gold and precious stones into his bag. There was still a fair fortune in the cellar from Father's day. I hadn't quite known what to do with it, so I could allow myself this gesture. The merchant beamed and thanked me so profusely that he slobbered all over himself. He must have boasted about his adventure somewhere because not two weeks had gone by when another merchant appeared. He had a pretty large bag ready with him. And a daughter. Also pretty large.'

Nivellen extended his legs under the table and stretched until the armchair creaked.

'I came to an understanding with the merchant in no time,' he continued. 'He'd leave her with me for a year. I had to help him load the sack onto his mule; he wouldn't have managed by himself.'

'And the girl?'

'She had fits at the sight of me for a while. She really thought I'd eat her. But after a month we were eating at the same table, chatting and going for long walks. She was kind, and remarkably smart, and I'd get tongue-tied when I talked to her. You see, Geralt, I was always shy with girls, always made a laughing stock of myself, even with wenches from the cowshed with dung up to their knees, girls the lads from the crew turned over this way and that at will. Even they made fun of me. To say nothing of having a maw like this. I couldn't even make myself say anything about why I had paid so dearly for a year of her life. The year dragged like the stench following marauding troops until, at last, the merchant arrived and took her away.

'I locked myself in the house, resigned, and didn't react for

54

several months to any of the guests who turned up with daughters. But after a year spent with company, I realised how hard it was to live without anyone to talk to.' The monster made a noise which was supposed to be a sigh but came out more like a hiccough.

'The next one,' he said after a while, 'was called Fenne. She was small, bright and chirpy, a real goldcrest. She wasn't frightened of me at all. Once, on the anniversary of my first haircut, my coming of age, we'd both drunk too much mead and . . . ha, ha. Straight after, I jumped out of bed and ran to the mirror. I must admit I was disappointed, and despondent. The trap was the same as it ever was, if with a slightly more stupid expression. And they say the wisdom of ages is to be found in fairy tales. It's not worth a shit, wisdom like that, Geralt.

'Well, Fenne quickly tried to make me forget my worries. She was a jolly girl, I tell you. Do you know what she thought up? We'd both frighten unwanted guests. Imagine: a guest like that enters the courtyard, looks around, and then, with a roar, I charge at him on all fours with Fenne, completely naked, sitting on my back and blowing my grandfather's hunting horn!'

Nivellen shook with laughter, the white of his fangs flashing. 'Fenne,' he continued, 'stayed with me for a year, then returned to her family with a huge dowry. She was preparing to marry a tavern owner, a widower.'

'Carry on, Nivellen. This is interesting.'

'You think so?' said the monster, scratching himself between the ears with a rasping sound. 'All right. The next one, Primula, was the daughter of an impoverished knight. The knight, when he got here, had a skinny horse, a rusty cuirass and incredible debts. He was as hideous as cow dung, I tell you, Geralt, and spread a similar smell. Primula, I'd wager my right hand, was conceived while he was at war, as she was quite pretty. I didn't frighten her either, which isn't surprising, really, as compared to her parent I might have appeared quite comely. She had, as it turned out, quite a temperament and I, having gained some self-confidence, seized the moment by the horns. After two weeks Primula and I already

55

had a very close relationship. She liked to pull me by the ears and shout "Bite me to death, you animal!" and "Tear me apart, you beast!" and other equally idiotic things. I ran to the mirror in the breaks, but just imagine, Geralt, I looked at myself with growing anxiety. Less and less did I long to return to my former shape. You see, Geralt, I used to be a weakling and now I'd become a strapping fellow. I'd keep getting ill, I'd cough, my nose would run, but now I don't catch anything. And my teeth? You wouldn't believe how rotten my teeth had been! And now? I can bite through the leg of a chair. Do you want me to bite a chair leg?'

'No, I don't.'

'Maybe that's good.' The monster opened his mouth wide. 'My showing-off used to amuse the girls and there aren't many whole chairs left in the house.' Nivellen yawned, his enormous tongue rolling up into a tube.

'This talking has made me tired, Geralt. Briefly: there were two after Primula, Ilka and Venimira. Everything happened in the same way, to the point of boredom. First, a mixture of fear and reserve, then a thread of sympathy re-enforced by small but precious gifts, then "Bite me, eat me up", Daddy's return, a tender farewell and an increasingly discernible depletion of the treasury. I decided to take longer breaks to be alone. Of course, I'd long ago stopped believing that a virgin's kiss would transform the way I looked. And I'd come to terms with it. And, what's more, I'd come to the conclusion that things were fine as they were and that there wasn't any need for changes.'

'Really? No changes, Nivellen?'

'It's true. I have a horse's health, which came with the way I look, for one. Secondly, my being different works on girls like an aphrodisiac. Don't laugh! I'm certain that as a human I'd have to give a mighty good chase to get at a girl like, for example, Venimira, who was an extremely beautiful maid. I don't suppose she'd have glanced twice at the fellow in the portrait. And thirdly: safety. Father had enemies, and a couple of them had survived. People whom the crew, under my pitiful leadership, had sent to their graves, had relatives. There's gold in the cellar. If it wasn't for the fear inspired by me, somebody would come and get it, if only peasants with pitchforks.'

'You seem quite sure,' Geralt remarked, playing with an empty chalice, 'that you haven't offended anyone in your present shape. No father, no daughter. No relative or daughter's betrothed—'

'Leave off, Geralt.' Nivellen was indignant. 'What are you talking about? The fathers couldn't contain themselves for joy. I told you, I was incredibly generous. And the daughters? You didn't see them when they got here in their dresses of sackcloth, their little hands raw from washing, their shoulders stooped from carrying buckets. Even after two weeks with me Primula still had marks on her back and thighs from the strap her knightly father had beaten her with. They walked around like princesses here, carried nothing but a fan and didn't even know where the kitchen was. I dressed them up and covered them with trinkets. At the click of a finger, I'd conjure up hot water in the tin bath Father had plundered for my mother at Assengard. Can you imagine? A tin bath! There's hardly a regent, what am I saying, hardly a lord who's got a tin bath at home. This was a house from a fairy tale for them, Geralt. And as far as bed is concerned, well . . . Pox on it, virtue is rarer today than a rock dragon. I didn't force any of them, Geralt.'

'But you suspected someone had paid me to kill you. Who would have?'

'A scoundrel who wanted the contents of my cellar but didn't have any more daughters,' Nivellen said emphatically. 'Human greed knows no limits.'

'And nobody else?'

'And nobody else.'

They both remained silent, gazing at the nervous flicker of the candle flames.

'Nivellen,' said the witcher suddenly, 'are you alone now?'

'Witcher,' answered the monster after a moment's hesitation, 'I think that, in principle, I ought to insult you, take you by the neck and throw you down the stairs. Do you know why? Because you treat me like a dimwit. I noticed how you've been cocking

57

your ears and glancing at the door. You know perfectly well that I don't live alone. Am I right?'

'You are. I'm sorry.'

'Pox on your apologies. Have you seen her?'

'Yes. In the forest, by the gate. Is she why merchants and daughters have been leaving here empty-handed for some time?'

'So you know about that too? Yes, she's the reason.'

'Do you mind if I ask whether—'

'Yes, I do mind.'

Silence again.

'Oh well, it's up to you,' the witcher finally said, getting up. 'Thanks for your hospitality, dear host. Time I was on my way.'

'Quite right.' Nivellen also got up. 'For certain reasons I can't offer you a room in the manor for the night, and I don't encourage you to spend the night in these woods. Ever since the area's been deserted it's been bad at night here. You ought to get back to the highway before dusk.'

'I'll bear that in mind, Nivellen. Are you sure you don't need my help?'

The monster looked at him askance. 'You think you *could* help me? You'd be able to lift this from me?'

'I wasn't only thinking about that sort of help.'

'You didn't answer my question. Although . . . you probably did. You wouldn't be able to.'

Geralt looked him straight in the eyes. 'You had some bad luck,' he said. 'Of all the temples in Gelibol and the Nimnar Valley, you picked the Church of Coram Agh Tera, the Lionheaded Spider. In order to lift the curse thrown by the priestess of Coram Agh Tera, you need knowledge and powers which I don't possess.'

'And who does?'

'So you are interested after all? You said things were fine as they are.'

'As they are, yes. But not as they might be. I'm afraid that—'

'What are you afraid of?'

The monster stopped at the door to the room and turned. 'I've had enough of your questions, witcher, which you keep asking instead of answering mine. Obviously, you've got to be asked in the right way. Listen. For some time now I've had hideous dreams. Maybe the word "monstrous" would be more accurate. Am I right to be afraid? Briefly, please.'

'Have you ever had muddy feet after waking from such a dream? Conifer needles in your sheets?'

'No.'

'And have—'

'No. Briefly, please.'

'You're rightly afraid.'

'Can anything be done about it? Briefly, please.'

'No.'

'Finally. Let's go, I'll see you out.'

In the courtyard, as Geralt was adjusting the saddle-bags, Nivellen stroked the mare's nostrils and patted her neck. Roach, pleased with the caress, lowered her head.

'Animals like me,' boasted the monster. 'And I like them, too. My cat, Glutton, ran away at the beginning but she came back later. For a long time, she was the only living creature who kept me company in my misfortune. Vereena, too—' He broke off with a grimace.

Geralt smiled. 'Does she like cats too?'

'Birds.' Nivellen bared his teeth. 'I gave myself away, pox on it. But what's the harm. She isn't another merchant's daughter, Geralt, or another attempt to find a grain of truth in old folk tales. It's serious. We love each other. If you laugh, I'll sock you one.'

Geralt didn't laugh. 'You know your Vereena,' he said, 'is probably a rusalka?'

'I suspected as much. Slim. Dark. She rarely speaks, and in a language I don't know. She doesn't eat human food. She disappears into the forest for days on end, then comes back. Is that typical?'

'More or less.' The witcher tightened Roach's girth-strap. 'No doubt you think she wouldn't return if you were to become human?'

'I'm sure of it. You know how frightened rusalkas are of people.

Hardly anybody's seen a rusalka from up close. But Vereena and I . . . Pox on it! Take care, Geralt.'

'Take care, Nivellen.' The witcher prodded the mare in the side with his heel and made towards the gate. The monster shuffled along at his side.

'Geralt?'

'Yes.'

'I'm not as stupid as you think. You came here following the tracks of one of the merchants who'd been here lately. Has something happened to one of them?'

'Yes.'

'The last was here three days ago. With his daughter, not one of the prettiest, by the way. I commanded the house to close all its doors and shutters and give no sign of life. They wandered around the courtyard and left. The girl picked a rose from my aunt's rosebush and pinned it to her dress. Look for them somewhere else. But be careful, this is a horrible area. I told you that the forest isn't the safest of places at night. Ugly things are heard and seen.'

'Thanks, Nivellen. I'll remember about you. Who knows, maybe I'll find someone who—'

'Maybe yes. And maybe no. It's my problem, Geralt, my life and my punishment. I've learnt to put up with it. I've got used to it. If it gets worse, I'll get used to that too. And if it gets far worse don't look for anybody. Come here yourself and put an end to it. As a witcher. Take care, Geralt.'

Nivellen turned and marched briskly towards the manor. He didn't look round again.

III

The area was deserted, wild and ominously inhospitable. Geralt didn't return to the highway before dusk; he didn't want to take a roundabout route so he took a short-cut through the forest. He spent the night on the bare summit of a high hill, his sword on his knees, beside a tiny campfire into which, every now and then, he threw wisps of monkshood. In the middle of the night he noticed the glow of a fire far away in the valley; he heard mad howling and singing and a sound which could only have been the screaming of a tortured woman. When dawn had barely broken he made his way there to find nothing but a trampled glade and charred bones in still-warm ashes. Something sitting in the crown of an enormous oak shrieked and hissed. It could have been a harpy, or an ordinary wildcat. The witcher didn't stop to check.

IV

About midday, while Roach was drinking at a spring, the mare neighed piercingly and backed away, baring her yellow teeth and chewing her bit. Geralt calmed her with the Sign. Then he noticed a regular ring formed by the caps of reddish mushrooms peering from the moss.

'You're becoming a real hysteric, Roach,' he said. 'This is just an ordinary devil's ring. What's the fuss?'

The mare snorted, turning her head towards him. The witcher rubbed his forehead, frowned and grew thoughtful. Then he leapt into the saddle, turned the horse around and started back, following his own tracks.

'Animals like me,' he muttered. 'Sorry, Roach. It turns out you've got more brains than me!'

V

The mare flattened her ears against her skull and snorted, throwing up earth with her hooves; she didn't want to go. Geralt didn't calm her with the Sign; he jumped from the saddle and threw the reins over the horse's head. He no longer had his old sword in its lizard-skin sheath on his back; its place was filled with a shining, beautiful weapon with a cruciform and slender, well-weighted hilt, ending in a spherical pommel made of white metal.

This time the gate didn't open for him. It was already open, just as he had left it.

He heard singing. He didn't understand the words; he couldn't even identify the language. He didn't need to – the witcher felt and understood the very nature, the essence, of this quiet, piercing song which flowed through the veins in a wave of nauseous, overpowering menace.

The singing broke off abruptly, and then he saw her.

She was clinging to the back of the dolphin in the dried-up fountain, embracing the moss-overgrown stone with her tiny hands, so pale they seemed transparent. Beneath her storm of tangled black hair shone huge, wide-open eyes the colour of anthracite.

Geralt slowly drew closer, his step soft and springy, tracing a semi-circle from the wall and blue rosebush. The creature glued to the dolphin's back followed him with her eyes, turning her petite face with an expression of longing, and full of charm. He could still hear her song, even though her thin, pale lips were held tight and not the slightest sound emerged from them.

The witcher halted at a distance of ten paces. His sword, slowly drawn from its black enamelled sheath, glistened and glowed above his head.

'It's silver,' he said. 'This blade is silver.'

The pale little face did not flinch, the anthracite eyes did not change expression.

'You're so like a rusalka,' the witcher continued calmly, 'that you could deceive anyone. All the more as you're a rare bird, black-haired one. But horses are never mistaken. They recognise creatures like you instinctively and perfectly. What are you? I think you're a moola, or an alpor. An ordinary vampire couldn't come out in the sun.'

The corners of the pale lips quivered and turned up a little.

'Nivellen attracted you with that shape of his, didn't he? You evoked his dreams. I can guess what sort of dreams they were, and I pity him.'

The creature didn't move.

'You like birds,' continued the witcher. 'But that doesn't stop you biting the necks of people of both sexes, does it? You and Nivellen, indeed! A beautiful couple you'd make, a monster and a vampire, rulers of a forest castle. You'd dominate the whole area in a flash. You, eternally thirsty for blood, and he, your guardian, a murderer at your service, a blind tool. But first he had to become a true monster, not a human being in a monster's mask.'

The huge black eyes narrowed.

'Where is he, black-haired one? You were singing, so you've drunk some blood. You've taken the ultimate measure, which means you haven't managed to enslave his mind. Am I right?'

The black-tressed head nodded slightly, almost imperceptibly, and the corners of the mouth turned up even more. The tiny little face took on an eerie expression.

'No doubt you consider yourself the lady of this manor now?'

A nod, this time clearer.

'Are you a moola?'

A slow shake of the head. The hiss which reverberated through his bones could only have come from the pale, ghastly, smiling lips, although the witcher didn't see them move.

'Alpor?'

Denial.

The witcher backed away and clasped the hilt of his sword tighter. 'That means you're ─ '

The corners of the lips started to turn up higher and higher, the lips flew open . . .

'A bruxa!' the witcher shouted, throwing himself towards the fountain.

From behind the pale lips glistened white, spiky fangs. The vampire jumped up, arched her back like a leopard and screamed.

The wave of sound hit the witcher like a battering ram, depriving him of breath, crushing his ribs, piercing his ears and brain with thorns of pain. Flying backwards he just managed to cross his wrists in the Sign of Heliotrop. The spell cushioned some of his impact with the wall but even so the world grew dark and the remainder of his breath burst from his lungs in a groan.

On the dolphin's back, in the stone circle of the dried-up fountain where a dainty girl in a white dress had sat just a moment ago, an enormous black bat flattened its glossy body, opening its long, narrow jaws wide, revealing rows of needle-like white teeth. The membranous wings spread and flapped silently, and the creature charged at the witcher like an arrow fired from a crossbow.

Geralt, with the metallic taste of blood in his mouth, shouted a spell and threw his hand, fingers spread in the Sign of Quen, out in front of him. The bat, hissing, turned abruptly, then chuckled and veered up into the air before diving down vertically, straight at the nape of the witcher's neck. Geralt jumped aside, slashed, and missed. The bat, smoothly, gracefully drew in a wing, circled around him and attacked anew, opening its eyeless, toothed snout wide. Geralt waited, sword held with both hands, always pointed in the creature's direction. At the last moment, he jumped – not to the side but forward, dealing a swinging cut which made the air howl.

He missed. It was so unexpected that he lost his rhythm and dodged a fraction of a second too late. He felt the beast's talons tear his cheek, and a damp velvety wing slapped against his neck. He curled up on the spot, transferred the weight of his body to his right leg and slashed backwards sharply, missing the amazingly agile creature again.

The bat beat its wings, soared up and glided towards the fountain. As the crooked claws scraped against the stone casing the monstrous, slobbering snout was already blurring, morphing, disappearing, although the pale little lips which were taking its place couldn't quite hide the murderous fangs.

The bruxa howled piercingly, modulating her voice into a macabre tune, glared at the witcher with eyes full of hatred, and screamed again.

The soundwave was so powerful it broke through the Sign. Black and red circles spun in Geralt's eyes; his temples and the crown of his head throbbed. Through the pain drilling in his ears, he began to hear voices wailing and moaning, the sound of flute and oboe, the rustle of a gale. The skin on his face grew numb and cold. He fell to one knee and shook his head.

The black bat floated towards him silently, opening its toothy jaws. Geralt, still stunned by the scream, reacted instinctively. He jumped up and, in a flash, matching the tempo of his movements to the speed of the monster's flight, took three steps forward, dodged, turned a semi-circle and then, quick as a thought, delivered a two-handed blow. The blade met with no resistance . . . almost no resistance. He heard a scream, but this time it was a scream of pain, caused by the touch of silver.

The wailing bruxa was morphing on the dolphin's back. On her white dress, slightly above her left breast, a red stain was visible beneath a slash no longer than a little finger. The witcher ground his teeth – the cut, which should have sundered the beast in two, had been nothing but a scratch.

'Shout, vampire,' he growled, wiping the blood from his cheek. 'Scream your guts out. Lose your strength. And then I'll slash your pretty little head off!'

You. You will be the first to grow weak, Sorcerer. I will kill you.

The bruxa's lips didn't move, but the witcher heard the words clearly; they resounded in his mind, echoing and reverberating as if underwater.

'We shall see,' he muttered through his teeth as he walked, bent over, in the direction of the fountain.

I will kill you. I'll kill you. I'll kill you.

'We shall see.'

'Vereena!' Nivellen, his head hanging low and both hands clinging to the doorframe, stumbled from the mansion. He staggered towards the fountain, waving his paws unsteadily. Blood stained the cuff of his tunic.

'Vereena!' he roared again.

The bruxa jerked her head in his direction. Geralt, raising his sword to strike, jumped towards her, but the vampire's reaction was much faster. A sharp scream and another soundwave knocked the witcher from his feet. He tumbled onto his back and scraped against the gravel of the path. The bruxa arched and tensed to jump, her fangs flashing like daggers. Nivellen, spreading his paws like a bear, tried to grab her but she screamed straight into his face, throwing him back against the wooden scaffolding under the wall, which broke with a sharp crash and buried him beneath a stack of timber.

Geralt was already on his feet, running, tracing a semi-circle around the courtyard, trying to draw the bruxa's attention away from Nivellen. The vampire, fluttering her white dress, scurried straight at him, light as a butterfly, barely touching the ground. She was no longer screaming, no longer trying to morph. The witcher knew she was tired, and that she was still lethal. Behind Geralt's back, Nivellen was clattering under the scaffolding, roaring.

Geralt leapt to the left, executing a short moulinet with his sword to confuse the bruxa gliding towards him – white and black, wind-blown, terrible. He'd underestimated her. She screamed. He didn't make the Sign in time, flew backwards until he thumped against the wall. The pain in his spine shot all the way to the tips of his fingers, paralysed his shoulders, cut him down at the legs. He fell to his knees. The bruxa, wailing melodiously, jumped towards him.

'Vereena!' roared Nivellen.

She turned – and Nivellen forced the sharp broken end of a three-metre-long pole between her breasts. She didn't shout. She only sighed.

The witcher shook, hearing this sigh.

They stood there: Nivellen, on wide-spread legs, was wielding the pole in both hands, one end firmly secured under his arm.

The bruxa, like a white butterfly on a pin, hung on the other end of the stake clutching it with both hands. The vampire exhaled excruciatingly and suddenly pressed herself hard against the stake.

Geralt watched a red stain bloom on her back, on the white dress through which the broken tip emerged in a geyser of blood: hideous, almost obscene. Nivellen screamed, took one step back, then another, retreating from her, but he didn't let go of the pole and dragged the bruxa behind him. One more step and he leaned back against the mansion. The end of the pole scraped against the wall.

Slowly, as if a caress, the bruxa moved her tiny hands along the stake, stretched her arms out to their full length, grasped the pole hard and pulled on it again. Over a metre of bloodied wood already protruded from her back. Her eyes were wide open, her head flung back. Her sighs became more frequent and rhythmic, turning into a ruckling wheeze.

Geralt stood but, fascinated by the scene, still couldn't make himself act. He heard words resounding dully within his skull, as if echoing around a cold, damp dungeon.

Mine. Or nobody's. I love you. Love you.

Another terrible, vibrating sigh, choking in blood. The bruxa moved further along the pole and stretched out her arms. Nivellen roared desperately and, without letting go of the stake, tried to push the vampire as far from himself as possible – but in vain. She pulled herself closer and grabbed him by the head. He wailed horrifically and tossed his hairy head. The bruxa moved along the pole again and tilted her head towards Nivellen's throat. The fangs flashed a blinding white.

Geralt jumped. Every move he made, every step, was part of his nature: hard learnt, automatic and lethally sure. Three quick steps, and the third, like a hundred such steps before, finished on the left leg with a strong, firm stamp. A twist of his torso and a sharp, forceful cut. He saw her eyes. Nothing could change now. He heard the voice. Nothing. He yelled, to drown the word which she was repeating. Nothing could change. He cut.

He struck decisively, like hundreds of times before, with the centre of the blade, and immediately, following the rhythm of the movement, took a fourth step and half a turn. The blade, freed by the half-turn, floated after him, shining, drawing a fan of red droplets in its wake. The streaming raven-black hair floated in the air, *floated, floated, floated* . . .

The head fell onto the gravel.

There are fewer and fewer monsters?

And I? What am I?

Who's shouting? The birds?

The woman in a sheepskin jacket and blue dress?

The roses from Nazair?

How quiet!

How empty. What emptiness.

Within me.

Nivellen, curled up in a bundle, sheltering his head in his arms and shaking with twitches and shivers, was lying in the nettles by the manor wall.

'Get up,' said the witcher.

The young, handsome, well-built man with a pale complexion lying by the wall raised his head and looked around. His eyes were vague. He rubbed them with his knuckles. He looked at his hands, felt his face. He moaned quietly and, putting his finger in his mouth, ran it along his gums for a long time. He grasped his face again and moaned as he touched the four bloody, swollen streaks on his cheek. He burst out sobbing, then laughed.

'Geralt! How come? How did this— Geralt!'

'Get up, Nivellen. Get up and come along. I've got some medicine in my saddle-bags. We both need it.'

'I've no longer got . . . I haven't, have I? Geralt? Why?'

The witcher helped him get up, trying not to look at the tiny hands – so pale as to be transparent – clenched around the pole stuck between the small breasts which were now plastered with a wet red fabric.

Nivellen moaned again. 'Vereena—'

'Don't look. Let's go.'

They crossed the courtyard, holding each other up, and passed the blue rosebush.

Nivellen kept touching his face with his free hand. 'Incredible, Geralt. After so many years? How's it possible?'

'There's a grain of truth in every fairy tale,' said the witcher quietly. 'Love and blood. They both possess a mighty power. Wizards and learned men have been racking their brains over this

68

for years, but they haven't arrived at anything except that—'
    'That what, Geralt?'
    'It has to be true love.'

THE VOICE OF REASON 3

'I'm Falwick, Count of Moën. And this knight is Tailles, from Dorndal.'

Geralt bowed cursorily, looking at the knights. Both wore armour and crimson cloaks with the emblem of the White Rose on their left shoulder. He was somewhat surprised as, so far as he knew, there was no Commandery of that Order in the neighbourhood.

Nenneke, to all appearances smiling light-heartedly and at ease, noticed his surprise.

'These nobly born gentlemen,' she said casually, settling herself more comfortably in her throne-like armchair, 'are in the service of Duke Hereward, who governs these lands most mercifully.'

'Prince.' Tailles, the younger of the knights, corrected her emphatically, fixing his hostile pale blue eyes on the priestess. 'Prince Hereward.'

'Let's not waste time with details and titles.' Nenneke smiled mockingly. 'In my day, only those with royal blood were addressed as princes, but now, it seems, titles don't mean so much. Let's get back to our introductions, and why the Knights of the White Rose are visiting my humble temple. You know, Geralt, that the Chapter is requesting investitures for the Order from Hereward, which is why so many Knights of the Rose have entered his service. And a number of locals, like Tailles here, have taken vows and assumed the red cloak which becomes him so well.'

'My honour.' The witcher bowed once more, just as cursorily as before.

'I doubt it,' the priestess remarked coldly. 'They haven't come here to honour you. Quite the opposite. They've arrived demanding that you leave as soon as possible. In short, they're here to

70

chase you out. You consider that an honour? I don't. I consider it an insult.'

'The noble knights have troubled themselves for no reason,' shrugged Geralt. 'I don't intend to settle here. I'm leaving of my own accord without any additional incentives, and soon at that.'

'Immediately,' growled Tailles. 'With not a moment's delay. The prince orders—'

'In this temple, I give the orders,' interrupted Nenneke in a cold, authoritative voice. 'I usually try to ensure my orders don't conflict too much with Hereward's politics, as far as those politics are logical and understandable. In this case they are irrational, so I won't treat them any more seriously than they deserve. Geralt, witcher of Rivia, is my guest. His stay is a pleasure to me. So he will stay in my temple for as long as he wishes.'

'You have the audacity to contradict the prince, woman?' Tailles shouted, then threw his cloak back over his shoulder to reveal his grooved, brass-edged breast-plate in all its splendour. 'You dare to question our ruler's authority?'

'Quiet,' Nenneke snapped and narrowed her eyes. 'Lower your voice. Have a care who you speak to like that.'

'I know who I'm talking to!' The knight advanced a step. Falwick, the older knight, grabbed him firmly by the elbow and squeezed until the armour-plated gauntlet grated. Tailles yanked furiously. 'And my words express the prince's will, the lord of this estate! We have got soldiers in the yard, woman—'

Nenneke reached into the purse at her belt and took out a small porcelain jar. 'I really don't know,' she said calmly, 'what will happen if I smash this container at your feet, Tailles. Maybe your lungs will burst. Maybe you'll grow fur. Or maybe both, who knows? Only merciful Melitele.'

'Don't dare threaten me with your spells, priestess! Our soldiers—'

'If any one of your soldiers touches one of Melitele's priestesses, they will hang, before dusk, from the acacias along the road to town. And they know that very well. As do you, Tailles, so stop acting like a fool. I delivered you, you shitty brat, and I pity your mother, but don't tempt fate. And don't force me to teach you manners!'

'All right, all right,' the witcher butted in, growing bored. 'It looks as though I'm becoming the cause of a serious conflict and I don't see why I should. Sir Falwick, you look more level-headed than your companion who, I see, is beside himself with youthful enthusiasm. Listen, Falwick, I assure you that I will leave in a few days. I also assure you that I have no intention to work here, to undertake any commissions or orders. I'm not here as a witcher, but on personal business.'

Count Falwick met his eyes and Geralt realised his mistake. There was pure, unwavering hatred in the White Rose knight's eyes. The witcher was sure that it was not Duke Hereward who was chasing him out, but Falwick and his like.

The knight turned to Nenneke, bowed with respect and began to speak. He spoke calmly and politely. He spoke logically. But Geralt knew Falwick was lying through his teeth.

'Venerable Nenneke, I ask your forgiveness, but Prince Hereward will not tolerate the presence of this witcher on his lands. It is of no importance if he is hunting monsters or claims to be here on personal business – the prince knows that witchers do not undertake personal business. But they do attract trouble like a magnet filings. The wizards are rebelling and writing petitions, the druids are threatening—'

'I don't see why Geralt should bear the consequences of the unruliness of local wizards and druids,' interrupted the priestess. 'Since when has Hereward been interested in either's opinion?'

'Enough of this discussion.' Falwick stiffened. 'Have I not made myself sufficiently clear, venerable Nenneke? I will make it so clear as can't be clearer: neither the prince nor the Chapter of the Order will tolerate the presence of this witcher, Geralt, the Butcher of Blaviken, in Ellander for one more day.'

'This isn't Ellander!' The priestess sprang from her chair. 'This is the temple of Melitele! And I, Nenneke, the high priestess of Melitele, will not tolerate your presence on temple grounds a minute longer, sirs!'

'Sir Falwick,' the witcher said quietly, 'listen to the voice of reason. I don't want any trouble, nor do I believe that you particularly care for it. I'll leave this neighbourhood within three days. No, Nenneke, don't say anything, please. It's time for me to be on my way. Three days. I don't ask for more.'

'And you're right not to ask.' The priestess spoke before Falwick could react. 'Did you hear, boys? The witcher will remain here for three days because that's his fancy. And I, priestess of Great Melitele, will for those three days be his host, for that is my fancy. Tell that to Hereward. No, not Hereward. Tell that to his wife, the noble Ermellia, adding that if she wants to continue receiving an uninterrupted supply of aphrodisiacs from my pharmacy, she'd better calm her duke down. Let her curb his humours and whims, which look ever more like symptoms of idiocy.'

'Enough!' Tailles shouted so shrilly his voice broke into a falsetto. 'I don't intend to stand by and listen as some charlatan insults my lord and his wife! I will not let such an insult pass unnoticed! It is the Order of the White Rose which will rule here, now; it's the end of your nests of darkness and superstitions. And I, a Knight of the White Rose—'

'Shut up, you brat,' interrupted Geralt, smiling nastily. 'Halt your uncontrolled little tongue. You speak to a lady who deserves respect, especially from a Knight of the White Rose. Admittedly, to become one it's enough, lately, to pay a thousand Novigrad crowns into the Chapter's treasury, so the Order's full of sons of money-lenders and tailors – but surely some manners have survived? But maybe I'm mistaken?'

Tailles grew pale and reached to his side.

'Sir Falwick,' said Geralt, not ceasing to smile. 'If he draws his sword, I'll take it from him and beat the snotty-nosed little brat's arse with the flat of his blade. And then I'll batter the door down with him.'

Tailles, his hands shaking, pulled an iron gauntlet from his belt and, with a crash, threw it to the ground at the witcher's feet.

'I'll wash away the insult to the Order with your blood, mutant!' he yelled. 'On beaten ground! Go into the yard!'

'You've dropped something, son,' Nenneke said calmly. 'So pick it up, we don't leave rubbish here. This is a temple. Falwick, take that fool from here or this will end in grief. You know what you're to tell Hereward. And I'll write a personal letter to him; you don't look like trustworthy messangers to me. Get out of here. You can find your way out, I hope?'

Falwick, restraining the enraged Tailles with an iron grip, bowed, his armour clattering. Then he looked the witcher in the eyes. The witcher didn't smile. Falwick threw his crimson cloak over his shoulders.

'This wasn't our last visit, venerable Nenneke,' he said. 'We'll be back.'

'That's just what I'm afraid of,' replied the priestess coldly. 'The displeasure's mine.'

THE LESSER EVIL

As usual, cats and children noticed him first. A striped tomcat sleeping on a sun-warmed stack of wood, shuddered, raised his round head, pulled back his ears, hissed and bolted off into the nettles. Three-year-old Dragomir, fisherman Trigla's son, who was sitting on the hut's threshold doing his best to make dirtier an already dirty shirt, started to scream as he fixed his tearful eyes on the passing rider.

The witcher rode slowly, without trying to overtake the hay-cart obstructing the road. A laden donkey trotted behind him, stretching its neck, and constantly pulling the cord tied to the witcher's pommel tight. In addition to the usual bags the long-eared animal was lugging a large shape, wrapped in a saddle-cloth, on its back. The grey-white flanks of the ass were covered with black streaks of dried blood.

The cart finally turned down a side-street leading to a granary and harbour from which a sea-breeze blew, carrying the stink of tar and ox's urine. Geralt picked up his pace. He didn't react to the muffled cry of the woman selling vegetables who was staring at the bony, taloned paw sticking out beneath the horse-blanket, bobbing up and down in time with the donkey's trot. He didn't look round at the crowd gathering behind him and rippling with excitement.

There were, as usual, many carts in front of the alderman's house. Geralt jumped from the saddle, adjusted the sword on his back and threw the reins over the wooden barrier. The crowd following him formed a semi-circle around the donkey.

Even outside, the alderman's shouts were audible.

'It's forbidden, I tell you! Forbidden, goddammit! Can't you understand what I say, you scoundrel?'

Geralt entered. In front of the alderman, small, podgy and red with rage, stood a villager holding a struggling goose by the neck.

'What— By all the gods! Is that you, Geralt? Do my eyes deceive me?' And turning to the peasant again: 'Take it away, you boor! Are you deaf?'

'They said,' mumbled the villager, squinting at the goose, 'that a wee something must be given to his lordship, otherways—'

'Who said?' yelled the alderman. 'Who? That I supposedly take bribes? I won't allow it, I say! Away with you! Greetings, Geralt.'

'Greetings, Caldemeyn.'

The alderman squeezed the witcher's hand, slapped him on the shoulder. 'You haven't been here for a good two years, Geralt. Eh? You can never stay in one place for long, can you? Where are you coming from? Ah, dog's arse, what's the difference where? Hey, somebody bring us some beer! Sit down, Geralt, sit down. It's mayhem here because we've the market tomorrow. How are things with you, tell me!'

'Later. Come outside first.'

The crowd outside had grown two-fold but the empty space around the donkey hadn't grown any smaller. Geralt threw the horse-blanket aside. The crowd gasped and pulled back. Caldemeyn's mouth fell open.

'By all the gods, Geralt! What is it?'

'A kikimora. Is there any reward for it?'

Caldemeyn shifted from foot to foot, looking at the spidery shape with its dry black skin, that glassy eye with its vertical pupil, the needle-like fangs in the bloody jaws.

'Where— From where—?'

'On the dyke, not some four miles from town. On the swamps. Caldemeyn, people must have disappeared there. Children.'

'Well, yes, true enough. But nobody— Who could have guessed— Hey, folks, go home, get back to work! This isn't a show! Cover it up, Geralt. Flies are gathering.'

Back inside the alderman grabbed a large jug of beer without a word and drank it to the last drop in one draught. He sighed deeply and sniffed.

'There's no reward,' he said gloomily. 'No one suspected that there was something like that lurking in the salt marshes. It's true that several people have disappeared in those parts, but . . . Hardly anyone loitered on that dyke. And why were you there? Why weren't you taking the main road?'

'It's hard for me to make a living on main roads,Caldemeyn.'

'I forgot.' The alderman suppressed a belch, puffing out his cheeks. 'And this used to be such a peaceful neighbourhood. Even imps only rarely pissed in the women's milk. And here, right next to us, some sort of felispectre. It's only fitting that I thank you. Because as for paying you, I can't. I haven't the funds.'

'That's a shame. I could do with a small sum to get through the winter.' The witcher took a sip from his jug, wiped away the froth. 'I'm making my way to Yspaden, but I don't know if I'll get there before the snows block the way. I might get stuck in one of the little towns on the Lutonski road.'

'Do you plan to stay long in Blaviken?'

'No. I've no time to waste. Winter's coming.'

'Where are you going to stay? With me perhaps? There's an empty room in the attic. Why get fleeced by the innkeepers, those thieves. We'll have a chat and you can tell me what's happening in the big, wide world.'

'Willingly. But what will Libushe have to say about it? It was quite obvious last time that she's not very keen on me.'

'Women don't have a say in my house. But, just between us, don't do what you did during supper last time in front of her again.'

'You mean when I threw my fork at that rat?'

'No. I mean when you hit it, even in the dark.'

'I thought it would be amusing.'

'It was. But don't do it in front of Libushe. And listen, this . . . what's it called . . . Kiki—'

'Kikimora.'

'Do you need it for anything?'

'What would I want it for? You can have them throw it in the cesspool if there's no reward for it.'

'That's not a bad idea. Hey, Karelka, Borg, Carrypebble! Any of you there?'

A town guard entered with a halberd on his shoulder, the blade catching the doorframe with a crash.

'Carrypebble,' said Caldemeyn. 'Get somebody to help you and take the donkey with that muck wrapped up in the horse-blanket, lead it past the pigsties and chuck the kikimora in the cesspool. Understood?'

'At your command. But . . . Alderman, sir—'

'What?'

'Maybe before we drown that hideous thing—'

'Well?'

'We could show it to Master Irion. It might be useful to him.'

Caldemeyn slapped his forehead with his open palm.

'You're not stupid, Carrypebble. Listen, Geralt, maybe our local wizard will spare you something for that carcass. The fishermen bring him the oddest of fish – octopedes, clabaters or herrongs – many have made some money on them. Come on, let's go to the tower.'

'You've got yourselves a wizard? Is he here for good or only passing?'

'For good. Master Irion. He's been living in Blaviken for a year. A powerful magus, Geralt, you'll see that from his very appearance.'

'I doubt whether a powerful magus will pay for a kikimora,' Geralt grimaced. 'As far as I know it's not needed for any elixirs. Your Irion will only insult me, no doubt. We witchers and wizards don't love each other.'

'I've never heard of Master Irion insulting anyone. I can't swear that he'll pay you but there's no harm in trying. There might be more kikimoras like that on the marshes and what then? Let the wizard look at the monster and cast some sort of spell on the marshlands or something, just in case.'

The witcher thought for a moment.

78

'Very well, Caldemeyn. What the heck, we'll risk a meeting with Master Irion. Shall we go?'

'We're off. Carrypebble, chase the kids away and bring the floppyears. Where's my hat?'

II

The tower, built from smoothly hewn blocks of granite and crowned by tooth-like battlements, was impressive, dominating the broken tiles of homesteads and dipping-roofed thatched cottages.

'He's renovated it, I see,' remarked Geralt. 'With spells, or did he have you working at it?'

'Spells, chiefly.'

'What's he like, this Irion?'

'Decent. He helps people. But he's a recluse, doesn't say much. He rarely leaves the tower.'

On the door, which was adorned with a rosace inlaid with pale wood, hung a huge knocker in the shape of a flat bulging-eyed fish-head holding a brass ring in its toothed jaws. Caldemeyn, obviously well-versed with the workings of its mechanics, approached, cleared his throat and recited:

'Alderman Caldemeyn greets you with a case for Master Irion. With him greets you, Witcher Geralt, with respect to the same case.'

For a long moment nothing happened, then finally the fish-head moved its toothed mandibles and belched a cloud of steam.

'Master Irion is not receiving. Leave, my good people.'

Caldemeyn waddled on the spot and looked at Geralt. The witcher shrugged. Carrypebble picked his nose with serious concentration.

'Master Irion is not receiving,' the knocker repeated metallically. 'Go, my good—'

'I'm not a good person,' Geralt broke in loudly. 'I'm a witcher. That thing on the donkey is a kikimora, and I killed it not far from town. It is the duty of every resident wizard to look after the safety of the neighbourhood. Master Irion does not have to honour me with conversation, does not have to receive me, if that is his will. But let him examine the kikimora and draw his own conclusions. Carrypebble, unstrap the kikimora and throw it down by the door.'

'Geralt,' the alderman said quietly. 'You're going to leave but I'm going to have to—'

'Let's go, Caldemeyn. Carrypebble, take that finger out of your nose and do as I said.'

'One moment,' the knocker said in an entirely different tone. 'Geralt, is that really you?'

The witcher swore quietly.

'I'm losing patience. Yes, it's really me. So what?'

'Come up to the door,' said the knocker, puffing out a small cloud of steam. 'Alone. I'll let you in.'

'What about the kikimora?'

'To hell with it. I want to talk to you, Geralt. Just you. Forgive me, Alderman.'

'What's it to me, Master Irion?' Caldemeyn waved the matter aside. 'Take care, Geralt. We'll see each other later. Carrypebble! Into the cesspool with the monster!'

'As you command.'

The witcher approached the inlaid door, which opened a little bit – just enough for him to squeeze through – and then slammed shut, leaving him in complete darkness.

'Hey!' he shouted, not hiding his anger.

'Just a moment,' answered a strangely familiar voice.

The feeling was so unexpected that the witcher staggered and stretched out his hand, looking for support. He didn't find any.

The orchard was blossoming with white and pink, and smelled of rain. The sky was split by the many-coloured arc of a rainbow, which bound the crowns of the trees to the distant, blue chain of mountains. The house nestled in the orchard, tiny and modest, was drowning in hollyhocks. Geralt looked down and discovered that he was up to his knees in thyme.

'Well, come on, Geralt,' said the voice. 'I'm in front of the house.'

He entered the orchard, walking through the trees. He noticed a movement to his left and looked round. A fair-haired girl, entirely naked, was walking along a row of shrubs carrying a basket full of apples. The witcher solemnly promised himself that nothing would surprise him anymore.

'At last. Greetings, witcher.'

'Stregobor!' Geralt was surprised.

During his life, the witcher had met thieves who looked like town councillors, councillors who looked like beggars, harlots who looked like princesses, princesses who looked like calving cows and kings who looked like thieves. But Stregobor always looked as, according to every rule and notion, a wizard should look. He was tall, thin and stooping, with enormous bushy grey eyebrows and a long, crooked nose. To top it off, he wore a black, trailing robe with improbably wide sleeves, and wielded a long staff capped with a crystal knob. None of the wizards Geralt knew looked like Stregobor. Most surprising of all was that Stregobor was, indeed, a wizard.

They sat in wicker chairs at a white marble-topped table on a porch surrounded by hollyhocks. The naked blonde with the apple basket approached, smiled, turned and, swaying her hips, returned to the orchard.

'Is that an illusion, too?' asked Geralt, watching the sway.

'It is. Like everything here. But it is, my friend, a first-class illusion. The flowers smell, you can eat the apples, the bee can sting you, and she,' the wizard indicated the blonde, 'you can—'

'Maybe later.'

'Quite right. What are you doing here, Geralt? Are you still toiling away, killing the last representatives of dying species for money? How much did you get for the kikimora? Nothing, I guess, or you wouldn't have come here. And to think that there are people who don't believe in destiny. Unless you knew about me. Did you?'

'No, I didn't. It's the last place I could have expected you. If my memory serves me correctly you used to live in a similar tower in Kovir.'

'A great deal has changed since then.'

'Such as your name. Apparently, you're Master Irion now.'

'That's the name of the man who created this tower. He died about two hundred years ago, and I thought it right to honour him in some way since I occupied his abode. I'm living here. Most of the inhabitants live off the sea and, as you know, my speciality, apart from illusions, is weather. Sometimes I'll calm a storm, sometimes conjure one up, sometimes drive schools of whiting and cod closer to the shores with the westerly wind. I can survive. That is,' he added, miserably, 'I could.'

'How come "I could"? Why the change of name?'

'Destiny has many faces. Mine is beautiful on the outside and hideous on the inside. She has stretched her bloody talons towards me—'

'You've not changed a bit, Stregobor.' Geralt grimaced. 'You're talking nonsense while making wise and meaningful faces. Can't you speak normally?'

'I can,' sighed the wizard. 'I can if that makes you happy. I made it all the way here, hiding and running from a monstrous being that wants to murder me. My escape proved in vain – it found me. In all probability, it's going to try to kill me tomorrow, or at the latest, the day after.'

'Aha,' said the witcher, dispassionately. 'Now I understand.'

'My facing death doesn't impress you much, does it?'

'Stregobor,' said Geralt, 'that's the way of the world. One sees all sorts of things when one travels. Two peasants kill each other over a field which, the following day, will be trampled flat by two counts and their retinues trying to kill each other off. Men hang from trees at the roadside, brigands slash merchants' throats. At every step in town you trip over corpses in the gutters. In palaces they stab each other with daggers, and somebody falls under the table at a banquet every minute, blue from poisoning. I'm used to it. So why should a death threat impress me, and one directed at you at that?'

'One directed at me at that,' Stregobor repeated with a sneer. 'And I considered you a friend. Counted on your help.'

'Our last meeting,' said Geralt, 'was in the court of King Idi of Kovir. I'd come to be paid for killing the amphisboena which had been terrorising the neighbourhood. You and your compatriot Zavist vied with each other to call me a charlatan, a thoughtless murdering machine and a scavenger. Consequently not only didn't Idi pay me a penny, he gave me twelve hours to leave Kovir and, since his hourglass was broken, I barely made it. And now you say you're counting on my help. You say a monster's after you. What are you afraid of, Stregobor? If it catches up with you, tell it you like monsters, that you protect them and make sure no witcher scavenger ever troubles their peace. Indeed, if the monster disembowels and devours you, it'll prove terribly ungrateful.'

The wizard turned his head away silently. Geralt laughed. 'Don't get all puffed up like a frog, magician. Tell me what's threatening you. We'll see what can be done.'

'Have you heard of the Curse of the Black Sun?'

'But of course. Except that it was called the Mania of Mad Eltibald after the wizard who started the lark and caused dozens of girls from good, even noble, families to be murdered or imprisoned in towers. They were supposed to have been possessed by demons, cursed, contaminated by the Black Sun, because that's what, in your pompous jargon, you called the most ordinary eclipse in the world.'

'Eltibald wasn't mad at all. He deciphered the writing on Dauk menhirs, on tombstones in the Wozgor necropolises, and examined the legends and traditions of weretots. All of them spoke of the eclipse in no uncertain terms. The Black Sun was to announce the imminent return of Lilit, still honoured in the East under the name of Niya, and the extermination of the human race. Lilit's path was to be prepared by "sixty women wearing gold crowns, who would fill the river valleys with blood".'

'Nonsense,' said the witcher. 'And what's more, it doesn't rhyme. All decent predictions rhyme. Everyone knows what Eltibald and the Council of Wizards had in mind at the time. You took advantage of a madman's ravings to strengthen your own authority. To break up alliances, ruin marriage allegiances, stir up dynasties. In a word: to tangle the strings of crowned puppets even more. And here you are lecturing me about predictions, which any old storyteller at the marketplace would be ashamed of.'

'You can have your reservations about Eltibald's theories, about how the predictions were interpreted. But you can't challenge the fact that there have been horrendous mutations among girls born just after the eclipse.'

'And why not? I've heard quite the opposite.'

'I was present when they did an autopsy on one of them,' said the wizard. 'Geralt, what we found inside the skull and marrow could not be described. Some sort of red sponge. The internal organs were all mixed up, some were missing completely. Everything was covered in moving cilia, bluish-pink shreds. The heart was six-chambered, with two chambers practically atrophied. What do you say to that?'

'I've seen people with eagles' talons instead of hands, people with a wolf's fangs. People with additional joints, additional organs and additional senses. All of which were the effects of your messing about with magic.'

'You've seen all sorts of mutations, you say.' The magician raised his head. 'And how many of them have you slaughtered for money, in keeping with your witcher's calling? Well? Because one can have a wolf's fangs and go no further than baring them at the trollops in taverns, or one can have a wolf's nature, too, and attack children. And that's just how it was with the girls who were born after the eclipse. Their outright insane tendency to cruelty, aggression, sudden bursts of anger and an unbridled temperament, were noted.'

'You can say that about any woman,' sneered Geralt. 'What are you drivelling on about? You're asking me how many mutants I've killed. Why aren't you interested in how many I've extricated from spells, freed from curses? I, a witcher despised by you. And what have you done, you mighty magicians?'

'A higher magic was used. Ours and that of the priests, in various temples. All attempts ended in the girls' deaths.'

'That speaks badly of you, not the girls. And so we've now got the first corpses. I take it the only autopsies were done on them?'

'No. Don't look at me like that, you know very well that there were more corpses, too. It was initially decided to eliminate all of them. We got rid of a few . . . autopsies were done on all of them. One of them was even vivisectioned.'

'And you sons-of-bitches have the nerve to criticise witchers? Oh, Stregobor, the day will come when people will learn, and get the better of you.'

'I don't think a day like that will come soon,' said the wizard caustically. 'Don't forget that we were acting in the people's defence. The mutant girls would have drowned entire countries in blood.'

'So say you magicians, turning your noses up, so high and mighty with your auras of infallibility. While we're on the subject, surely you're not going to tell me that in your hunt for these so-called mutants you haven't once made a mistake?'

'All right,' said Stregobor after a long silence. 'I'll be honest, although for my own sake I shouldn't. We did make a mistake – more than one. Picking them out was extremely difficult. And that's why we stopped . . . getting rid of them, and started isolating them instead.'

'Your famous towers,' snorted the witcher.

'Our towers. But that was another mistake. We underestimated them. Many escaped. Then some mad fashion to free imprisoned beauties took hold of princes, especially the younger ones, who didn't have much to do and still less to lose. Most of them, fortunately, twisted their necks—'

'As far as I know, those imprisoned in the towers died quickly. It's been said you must have helped them somewhat.'

'That's a lie. But it is true that they quickly fell into apathy, refused to eat . . . What is interesting is that shortly before they died they showed signs of the gift of clairvoyance. Further proof of mutation.'

'Your proofs are becoming ever less convincing. Do you have any more?'

'I do. Silvena, the lady of Narok, whom we never managed to get close to because she gained power so quickly. Terrible things are happening in Narok now. Fialka, Evermir's daughter, escaped her tower using a home-made rope and is now terrorising North Velhad. Bernika of Talgar was freed by an idiot prince. Now he's sitting in a dungeon, blinded, and the most common feature of the Talgar landscape is a set of gallows. There are other examples, too.'

'Of course there are,' said the witcher. 'In Yamurlak, for instance, old man Abrad reigns. He's got scrofula, not a single tooth in his head, was probably born some hundred years before this eclipse, and can't fall asleep unless someone's being tortured to death in his presence. He's wiped out all his relatives and emptied half of the country in crazy – how did you put it? – attacks of anger. There are also traces of a rampant temperament. Apparently he was nicknamed Abrad Jack-up-the-Skirt in his youth. Oh, Stregobor, it would be great if the cruelty of rulers could be explained away by mutations or curses.'

'Listen, Geralt—'

'No. You won't win me over with your reasons nor convince me that Eltibad wasn't a murdering madman, so let's get back to the monster threatening you. You'd better understand that, after the introduction you've given me, I don't like the story. But I'll hear you out.'

'Without interrupting with spiteful comments?'

'That I can't promise.'

'Oh well,' Stregobor slipped his hands into the sleeves of his robe, 'then it'll only take longer. Well, the story begins in Creyden, a small principality in the north. The wife of Fredefalk, the Prince of Creyden, was Aridea, a wise, educated woman. She had many exceptional adepts of the magical arts in her family and – through inheritance, no doubt – she came into possession of a rare and powerful artefact. One of Nehalenia's Mirrors. They're chiefly used by prophets and oracles because they predict the future accurately, albeit intricately. Aridea quite often turned to the Mirror—'

'With the usual question, I take it,' interrupted Geralt. '"Who is the fairest of them all?" I know; all Nehalenia's Mirrors are either polite or broken.'

'You're wrong. Aridea was more interested in her country's fate. And the Mirror answered her questions by predicting a horrible death for her and for a great number of others by the hand, or fault, of Fredefalk's daughter from his first marriage. Aridea ensured this news reached the Council, and the Council sent me to Creyden. I don't have to add that Fredefalk's first-born daughter was born shortly after the eclipse. I was quite discreet for a little while. She managed to torture a canary and two puppies during that time, and also gouged out a servant's eye with the handle of a comb. I carried out a few tests using curses, and most of them confirmed that the little one was a mutant. I went to Aridea with the news because Fredefalk's daughter meant the world to him. Aridea, as I said, wasn't stupid—'

'Of course,' Geralt interrupted again, 'and no doubt she wasn't head-over-heels in love with her stepdaughter. She preferred her own children to inherit the throne. I can guess what followed. How come nobody throttled her? And you, too, while they were at it.'

Stregobor sighed, raised his eyes to heaven, where the rainbow was still shimmering colourfully and picturesquely.

'I wanted to isolate her, but Aridea decided otherwise. She sent the little one out into the forest with a hired thug, a trapper. We found him later in the undergrowth . . . without any trousers, so it wasn't hard to recreate the turn of events. She had dug a brooch-pin into his brain, through his ear, no doubt while his attention was on entirely different matters.'

'If you think I feel sorry for him,' muttered Geralt, 'then you're wrong.'

'We organised a manhunt,' continued Stregobor, 'but all traces of the little one had disappeared. I had to leave Creyden in a hurry because Fredefalk was beginning to suspect something.

Then, four years later I received news from Aridea. She'd tracked down the little one, who was living in Mahakam with seven gnomes whom she'd managed to convince it was more profitable to rob merchants on the roads than to pollute their lungs with dust from the mines. She was known as Shrike because she liked to impale the people she caught on a sharp pole while they were still alive. Several times Aridea hired assassins, but none of them returned. Well, then it became hard to find anyone to try – Shrike had already become quite famous. She'd learnt to use a sword so well there was hardly a man who could defy her. I was summoned, and arrived in Creyden secretly, only to learn that someone had poisoned Aridea. It was generally believed that it was the work of Fredefalk, who had found himself a younger, more robust mistress – but I think it was Renfri.'

'Renfri?'

'That's what she was called. I said she'd poisoned Aridea. Shortly afterwards Prince Fredefalk died in a strange hunting accident, and Aridea's eldest son disappeared without a word. That must have been the little one's doing, too. I say "little" but she was seventeen by then. And she was pretty well-developed.

'Meanwhile,' the wizard picked up after a moment's break, 'she and her gnomes had become the terror of the whole of Mahakam. Until, one day, they argued about something, I don't know what – sharing out the loot, or whose turn it was to spend the night with her – anyway, they slaughtered each other with knives. Only Shrike survived. Only her. And I was in the neighbourhood at the time. We met face to face: she recognised me in a flash and knew the part I'd played in Creyden. I tell you, Geralt, I had barely managed to utter a curse – and my hands were shaking like anything – when that wildcat flew at me with a sword. I turned her into a neat slab of mountain crystal, six ells by nine. When she fell into a lethargy I threw the slab into the gnomes' mine and brought the tunnels down on it.'

'Shabby work,' commented Geralt. 'That spell could have been reversed. Couldn't you have burnt her to cinders? You know so many nice spells, after all.'

'No. It's not my speciality. But you're right, I did make a hash of it. Some idiot prince found her, spent a fortune on a counter-curse, reversed the spell and triumphantly took her home to some out-of-the-way kingdom in the east. His father, an old brigand, proved to have more sense. He gave his son a hiding, and questioned Shrike about the treasures which she and the gnomes had seized and which she'd hidden. His mistake was to allow his elder son to assist him when he had her stretched out, naked, on the executioner's bench. Somehow, the following day, that same eldest son – now an orphan bereft of siblings – was ruling the kingdom, and Shrike had taken over the office of first favourite.'

'Meaning she can't be ugly.'

'That's a matter of taste. She wasn't a favourite for long. Up until the first coup d'état at the palace, to give it a grand name – it was more like a barn. It soon became clear that she hadn't forgotten about me. She tried to assassinate me three times in Kovir. I decided not to risk a fourth attempt and to wait her out in Pontar. Again, she found me. This time I escaped to Angren, but she found me there too. I don't know how she does it, I cover my traces well. It must be a feature of her mutation.'

'What stopped you from casting another spell to turn her into crystal? Scruples?'

'No. I don't have any of those. She had become resistant to magic.'

'That's impossible.'

'It's not. It's enough to have the right artefact or aura. Or this could also be associated with her mutation, which is progressing. I escaped from Angren and hid here, in Arcsea, in Blaviken. I've lived in peace for a year, but she's tracked me down again.'

'How do you know? Is she already in town?'

'Yes. I saw her in the crystal ball.' The wizard raised his wand. 'She's not alone. She's leading a gang, which shows that she's brewing something serious. Geralt, I don't have anywhere else to run. I don't know where I could hide. The fact that you've arrived here exactly at this time can't be a coincidence. It's fate.'

The witcher raised his eyebrows. 'What's on your mind?'

'Surely it's obvious. You're going to kill her.'

'I'm not a hired thug, Stregobor.'

'You're not a thug, agreed.'

'I kill monsters for money. Beasts which endanger people. Horrors conjured up by spells and sorceries cast by the likes of you. Not people.'

'She's not human. She's exactly a monster: a mutant, a cursed mutant. You brought a kikimora here. Shrike's worse than a kikimora. A kikimora kills because it's hungry, but Shrike does it for pleasure. Kill her and I'll pay you whatever sum you ask. Within reason, of course.'

'I've already told you. I consider the story about mutations and Lilit's curse to be nonsense. The girl has her reasons for settling her account with you, and I'm not going to get mixed up in it. Turn to the alderman, to the town guards. You're the town wizard, you're protected by municipal law.'

'I spit on the law, the alderman and his help!' exploded Stregobor. 'I don't need defence, I need you to kill her! Nobody's going to get into this tower – I'm completely safe here. But what's that to me? I don't intend to spend the rest of my days here, and Shrike's not going to give up while I'm alive. Am I to sit here, in this tower, and wait for death?'

'They did. Do you know what, magician? You should have left that hunt for the girls to other, more powerful, wizards. You should have foreseen the consequences.'

'Please, Geralt.'

'No, Stregobor.'

The sorcerer was silent. The unreal sun in its unreal sky hadn't moved towards the zenith but the witcher knew it was already dusk in Blaviken. He felt hungry.

'Geralt,' said Stregobor, 'when we were listening to Eltibald, many of us had doubts. But we decided to accept the lesser evil. Now I ask you to make a similar choice.'

'Evil is evil, Stregobor,' said the witcher seriously as he got up. 'Lesser, greater, middling, it's all the same. Proportions are negotiated, boundaries blurred. I'm not a pious hermit, I haven't done only good in my life. But if I'm to choose between one evil and another, then I prefer not to choose at all. Time for me to go. We'll see each other tomorrow.'

'Maybe,' said the wizard. 'If you get here in time.'

III

The Golden Court, the country town's elegant inn, was crowded and noisy. The guests, locals and visitors, were mostly engaged in activities typical for their nation or profession. Serious merchants argued with dwarves over the price of goods and credit interest. Less serious merchants pinched the backsides of the girls carrying beer, cabbage and beans. Local nitwits pretended to be well-informed. Harlots were trying to please those who had money while discouraging those who had none. Carters and fishermen drank as if there were no tomorrow. Some seamen were singing a song which celebrated the ocean waves, the courage of captains and the graces of mermaids, the latter graphically and in considerable detail.

'Exert your memory, friend,' Caldemeyn said to the innkeeper, leaning across the counter in order to be heard over the din. 'Six men and a wench, all dressed in black leather studded with silver in the Novigradian style. I saw them at the turnpike. Are they staying here or at The Tuna Fish?'

The innkeeper wrinkled his bulging forehead and wiped a tankard on his striped apron.

'Here, Alderman,' he finally said. 'They say they've come for the market but they all carry swords, even the woman. Dressed, as you said, in black.'

'Well,' the alderman nodded. 'Where are they now? I don't see them here.'

'In the lesser alcove. They paid in gold.'

'I'll go in alone,' said Geralt. 'There's no point in making this

91

an official affair in front of them all, at least for the time being. I'll bring her here.'

'Maybe that's best. But be careful, I don't want any trouble.'

'I'll be careful.'

The seamen's song, judging by the growing intensity of obscene words, was reaching its grand finale. Geralt drew aside the curtain – stiff and sticky with dirt – which hid the entrance to the alcove.

Six men were seated at the table. Shrike wasn't with them.

'What d'you want?' yelled the man who noticed him first. He was balding and his face was disfigured by a scar which ran across his left eyebrow, the bridge of his nose and his right cheek.

'I want to see Shrike.'

Two identical figures stood up – identical motionless faces and fair, dishevelled, shoulder-length hair, identical tight-fitting black outfits glistening with silver ornaments. And with identical movements the twins took identical swords from the bench.

'Keep calm, Vyr. Sit down, Nimir,' said the man with the scar, leaning his elbows on the table. 'Who d'you say you want to see, brother? Who's Shrike?'

'You know very well who I mean.'

'Who's this then?' asked a half-naked athlete, sweaty, girded crosswise with belts, and wearing spiked pads on his forearms. 'D'you know him, Nohorn?'

'No,' said the man with the scar.

'It's some albino,' giggled a slim, dark-haired man sitting next to Nohorn. Delicate features, enormous black eyes and pointed ears betrayed him to be a half-blood elf. 'Albino, mutant, freak of nature. And this sort of thing is allowed to enter pubs among decent people.'

'I've seen him somewhere before,' said a stocky, weatherbeaten man with a plait, measuring Geralt with an evil look in his narrowed eyes.

'Doesn't matter where you've seen him, Tavik,' said Nohorn. 'Listen here. Civril insulted you terribly a moment ago. Aren't you going to challenge him? It's such a boring evening.'

'No,' said the witcher calmly.

'And me, if I pour this fish soup over your head, are you going to challenge me?' cackled the man sitting naked to the waist.

'Keep calm, Fifteen,' said Nohorn. 'He said no, that means no. For the time being. Well, brother, say what you have to say and clear out. You've got one chance to clear out on your own. You don't take it, the attendants will carry you out.'

'I don't have anything to say to you. I want to see Shrike. Renfri.'

'Do you hear that, boys?' Nohorn looked around at his companions. 'He wants to see Renfri. And may I know why?'

'No.'

Nohorn raised his head and looked at the twins as they took a step forward, the silver clasps on their high boots jangling.

'I know,' the man with the plait said suddenly. 'I know where I've seen him now!'

'What's that you're mumbling, Tavik?'

'In front of the alderman's house. He brought some sort of dragon in to trade, a cross between a spider and a crocodile. People were saying he's a witcher.'

'And what's a witcher?' Fifteen asked. 'Eh? Civril?'

'A hired magician,' said the half-elf. 'A conjurer for a fistful of silver. I told you, a freak of nature. An insult to human and divine laws. They ought to be burned, the likes of him.'

'We don't like magicians,' screeched Tavik, not taking his narrowed eyes off Geralt. 'It seems to me, Civril, that we're going to have more work in this hole than we thought. There's more than one of them here and everyone knows they stick together.'

'Birds of a feather.' The half-breed smiled maliciously. 'To think the likes of you walk the earth. Who spawns you freaks?'

'A bit more tolerance, if you please,' said Geralt, calmly, 'as I see your mother must have wandered off through the forest alone often enough to give you good reason to wonder where you come from yourself.'

'Possibly,' answered the half-elf, the smile not leaving his face. 'But at least I knew my mother. You witchers can't say that much about yourselves.'

93

Geralt grew a little pale and tightened his lips. Nohorn, noticing it, laughed out loud.

'Well, brother, you can't let an insult like that go by. That thing that you have on your back looks like a sword. So? Are you going outside with Civril? The evening's so boring.'

The witcher didn't react.

'Shitty coward,' snorted Tavik.

'What did he say about Civril's mother?' Nohorn continued monotonously, resting his chin on his clasped hands. 'Something extremely nasty, as I understood it. That she was an easy lay, or something. Hey, Fifteen, is it right to listen to some straggler insulting a companion's mother? A mother, you son-of-a-bitch, is sacred!'

Fifteen got up willingly, undid his sword and threw it on the table. He stuck his chest out, adjusted the pads spiked with silver studs on his shoulders, spat and took a step forward.

'If you've got any doubts,' said Nohorn, 'then Fifteen is challenging you to a fist fight. I told you they'd carry you out of here. Make room.'

Fifteen moved closer and raised his fists. Geralt put his hand on the hilt of his sword.

'Careful,' he said. 'One more step and you'll be looking for your hand on the floor.'

Nohorn and Tavik leapt up, grabbing their swords. The silent twins drew theirs with identical movements. Fifteen stepped back. Only Civril didn't move.

'What's going on here, dammit? Can't I leave you alone for a minute?'

Geralt turned round very slowly and looked into eyes the colour of the sea.

She was almost as tall as him. She wore her straw-coloured hair unevenly cut, just below the ears. She stood with one hand on the door, wearing a tight, velvet jacket clasped with a decorated belt. Her skirt was uneven, asymmetrical – reaching down to her calf on the left side and, on the right, revealing a strong thigh above a boot made of elk's leather. On her left side, she carried a sword;

on her right, a dagger with a huge ruby set in its pommel.

'Lost your voices?'

'He's a witcher,' mumbled Nohorn.

'So what?'

'He wanted to talk to you.'

'So what?'

'He's a sorcerer!' Fifteen roared.

'We don't like sorcerers,' snarled Tavik.

'Take it easy, boys,' said the girl. 'He wants to talk to me; that's no crime. You carry on having a good time. And no trouble. Tomorrow's market day. Surely you don't want your pranks to disrupt the market, such an important event in the life of this pleasant town?'

A quiet, nasty giggle reverberated in the silence which fell. Civril, still sprawled out carelessly on the bench, was laughing.

'Come on, Renfri,' chuckled the half-blood. 'Important . . . event!'

'Shut up, Civril. Immediately.'

Civril stopped laughing. Immediately. Geralt wasn't surprised. There was something very strange in Renfri's voice – something associated with the red reflection of fire on blades, the wailing of people being murdered, the whinnying of horses and the smell of blood. Others must also have had similar associations – even Tavik's weather-beaten face grew pale.

'Well, white-hair,' Renfri broke the silence. 'Let's go into the larger room. Let's join the alderman you came with. He wants to talk to me too, no doubt.'

At the sight of them, Caldemeyn, who was waiting at the counter, broke off his quiet conversation with the innkeeper, straightened himself and folded his arms across his chest.

'Listen, young lady,' he said severely, not wasting time with banal niceties, 'I know from this witcher of Rivia here what brings you to Blaviken. Apparently you bear a grudge against our wizard.'

'Maybe. What of it?' asked Renfri quietly, in an equally brusque tone.

'Only that there are tribunals to deal with grudges like that. He who wants to revenge a grudge using steel – here in Arcsea – is considered a common bandit. And also, that either you get out of Blaviken early in the morning with your black companions, or I throw you into prison, pre– How do you say it, Geralt?'

'Preventively.'

'Exactly. Understood, young lady?'

Renfri reached into the purse on her belt and pulled out a parchment which had been folded several times.

'Read this, Alderman. If you're literate. And don't call me "young lady".'

Caldemeyn took the parchment, spent a long time reading it, then, without a word, gave it to Geralt.

'"To my regents, vassals and freemen subjects,"' the witcher read out loud. '"To all and sundry. I proclaim that Renfri, the Princess of Creyden, remains in our service and is well seen by us; whosoever dares maltreet her will incur our wrath. Audoen, King—"' Maltreat is not spelt like that. But the seal appears authentic.'

'Because it is authentic,' said Renfri, snatching the parchment from him. 'It was affixed by Audoen, your merciful lord. That's why I don't advise you to maltreat me. Irrespective of how you spell it, the consequences for you would be lamentable. You are not, honourable Alderman, going to put me in prison. Or call me "young lady". I haven't infringed any law. For the time being.'

'If you infringe by even an inch,' Caldemeyn looked as if he wanted to spit, 'I'll throw you in the dungeon together with this piece of paper. I swear on all the gods, young lady. Come on, Geralt.'

'With you, witcher,' Renfri touched Geralt's shoulder, 'I'd still like a word.'

'Don't be late for supper,' the alderman threw over his shoulder, 'or Libushe will be furious.'

'I won't.'

Geralt leant against the counter. Fiddling with the wolf's head medallion hanging around his neck, he looked into the girl's blue-green eyes.

'I've heard about you,' she said. 'You're Geralt, the white-haired witcher from Rivia. Is Stregobor your friend?'

'No.'

'That makes things easier.'

'Not much. Don't expect me to look on peacefully.'

Renfri's eyes narrowed.

'Stregobor dies tomorrow,' she said quietly, brushing the unevenly cut hair off her forehead. 'It would be the lesser evil if he died alone.'

'If he did, yes. But in fact, before Stregobor dies several other people will die too. I don't see any other possibility.'

'Several, witcher, is putting it mildly.'

'You need more than words to frighten me, Shrike.'

'Don't call me Shrike. I don't like it. The point is, I see other possibilities. It would be worth talking it over . . . but Libushe is waiting. Is she pretty, this Libushe?'

'Is that all you had to say to me?'

'No. But you should go. Libushe's waiting.'

IV

There was someone in his little attic room. Geralt knew it before he even reached the door, sensing it through the barely perceptible vibration of his medallion. He blew out the oil lamp which had lit his path up the stairs, pulled the dagger from his boot, slipped it into the back of his belt and pressed the door handle. The room was dark. But not for a witcher.

He was deliberately slow in crossing the threshold; he closed the door behind him carefully. The next second he dived at the person sitting on his bed, crushed them into the linen, forced his forearm under their chin and reached for his dagger. He didn't pull it out. Something wasn't right.

'Not a bad start,' she said in a muffled voice, lying motionless beneath him. 'I expected something like this, but I didn't think

97

we'd both be in bed so quickly. Take your hand from my throat please.'

'It's you.'

'It's me. Now there are two possibilities. The first: you get off me and we talk. The second: we stay in this position, in which case I'd like to take my boots off at least.'

The witcher released the girl, who sighed, sat up and adjusted her hair and skirt.

'Light the candle,' she said. 'I can't see in the dark, unlike you, and I like to see who I'm talking to.'

She approached the table – tall, slim, agile – and sat down, stretching out her long legs in their high boots. She wasn't carrying any visible weapons.

'Have you got anything to drink here?'

'No.'

'Then it's a good thing I brought something,' she laughed, placing a travelling wine-skin and two leather tumblers on the table.

'It's nearly midnight,' said Geralt, coldly. 'Shall we come to the point?'

'In a minute. Here, have a drink. Here's to you, Geralt.'

'Likewise, Shrike.'

'My name's Renfri, dammit.' She raised her head. 'I will permit you to omit my royal title, but stop calling me Shrike!'

'Be quiet or you'll wake the whole house. Am I finally going to learn why you crept in here through the window?'

'You're slow-witted, witcher. I want to save Blaviken from slaughter. I crawled over the rooftops like a she-cat in March in order to talk to you about it. Appreciate it.'

'I do,' said Geralt. 'Except that I don't know what talk can achieve. The situation's clear. Stregobor is in his tower, and you'd have to lay siege to it in order to get to him. If you do that, your letter of safe-conduct won't help you. Audoen won't defend you if you openly break the law. The alderman, guards, the whole of Blaviken will stand against you.'

'The whole of Blaviken would regret standing up to me.' Renfri smiled, revealing a predator's white teeth. 'Did you take a look at my boys? They know their trade, I assure you. Can you imagine what would happen in a fight between them and those dimwit guards who keep tripping over their own halberds?'

'Do you imagine I would stand by and watch a fight like that? I'm staying at the alderman's, as you can see. If the need arises, I should stand at his side.'

'I have no doubt,' Renfri grew serious, 'that you will. But you'll probably be alone as the rest will cower in the cellars. No warrior in the world could match seven swordsmen. So, white-hair, let's stop threatening each other. As I said: slaughter and bloodshed can be avoided. There are two people who can prevent it.'

'I'm all ears.'

'One,' said Renfri, 'is Stregobor himself. He leaves his tower voluntarily, I take him to a deserted spot, and Blaviken sinks back into blissful apathy and forgets the whole affair.'

'Stregobor may seem crazy, but he's not *that* crazy.'

'Who knows, witcher, who knows. Some arguments can't be denied, like the Tridam ultimatum. I plan to present it to the sorcerer.'

'What is it, this ultimatum?'

'That's my sweet secret.'

'As you wish. But I doubt it'll be effective. Stregobor's teeth chatter when he speaks of you. An ultimatum which would persuade him to voluntarily surrender himself into your beautiful hands would have to be pretty good. So who's the other person? Let me guess.'

'I wonder how sharp you are, white-hair.'

'It's you, Renfri. You'll reveal a truly princely— what am I saying, *royal* magnanimity and renounce your revenge. Have I guessed?'

Renfri threw back her head and laughed, covering her mouth with her hand. Then she grew silent and fixed her shining eyes on the witcher.

'Geralt,' she said, 'I used to be a princess. I had everything I could dream of. Servants at my beck and call, dresses, shoes.

Cambric knickers. Jewels and trinkets, ponies, goldfish in a pond. Dolls, and a doll's house bigger than this room. That was my life until Stregobor and that whore Aridea ordered a huntsman to butcher me in the forest and bring back my heart and liver. Lovely, don't you think?'

'No. I'm pleased you evaded the huntsman, Renfri.'

'Like shit I did. He took pity on me and let me go. After the son-of-a-bitch raped me and robbed me.'

Geralt, fiddling with his medallion, looked her straight in the eyes. She didn't lower hers.

'That was the end of the princess,' she continued. 'The dress grew torn, the cambric grew grubby. And then there was dirt, hunger, stench, stink and abuse. Selling myself to any old bum for a bowl of soup or a roof over my head. Do you know what my hair was like? Silk. And it reached a good foot below my hips. I had it cut right to the scalp with sheep-shears when I caught lice. It's never grown back properly.'

She was silent for a moment, idly brushing the uneven strands of hair from her forehead.

'I stole rather than starve to death. I killed to avoid being killed myself. I was locked in prisons which stank of urine, never knowing if they would hang me in the morning, or just flog me and release me. And through it all my stepmother and your sorcerer were hard on my heels, with their poisons and assassins and spells. And you want me to reveal my magnanimity? To forgive him royally? I'll tear his head off, royally, first.'

'Aridea and Stregobor tried to poison you?'

'With an apple seasoned with nightshade. I was saved by a gnome, and an emetic I thought would turn my insides out. But I survived.'

'Was that one of the seven gnomes?' Renfri, pouring wine, froze holding the wine-skin over the tumbler.

'Ah,' she said. 'You do know a lot about me. Yes? Do you have something against gnomes? Or humanoids? They were better to me than most people, not that it's your business.

'Stregobor and Aridea hunted me like a wild animal as long as they could. Until I became the hunter. Aridea died in her own bed. She was lucky I didn't get to her earlier – I had a special plan for her, and now I've got one for the sorcerer. Do you think he deserves to die?'

'I'm no judge. I'm a witcher.'

'You are. I said that there were two people who could prevent bloodshed in Blaviken. The second is you. The sorcerer will let you into the tower. You could kill him.'

'Renfri,' said Geralt calmly, 'did you fall from the roof onto your head on the way to my room?'

'Are you a witcher or aren't you, dammit? They say you killed a kikimora and brought it here on a donkey to get a price for it. Stregobor is worse than the kikimora. It's just a mindless beast which kills because that's how the gods made it. Stregobor is a brute, a true monster. Bring him to me on a donkey and I won't begrudge you any sum you care to mention.'

'I'm not a hired thug, Shrike.'

'You're not,' she agreed with a smile. She leant back on the stool and crossed her legs on the table without the slightest effort to cover her thighs with her skirt. 'You're a witcher, a defender of people from evil. And evil is the steel and fire which will cause devastation here if we fight each other. Don't you think I'm proposing a lesser evil, a better solution? Even for that son-of-a-bitch Stregobor. You can kill him mercifully, with one thrust. He'll die without knowing it. And I guarantee him quite the reverse.'

Geralt remained silent.

Renfri stretched, raising her arms.

'I understand your hesitation,' she said. 'But I need an answer now.'

'Do you know why Stregobor and the king's wife wanted to kill you?'

Renfri straightened abruptly and took her legs off the table.

'It's obvious,' she snarled. 'I am heir to the throne. Aridea's children were born out of wedlock and don't have any right to—'

'No.'

Renfri lowered her head, but only for a moment. Her eyes flashed. 'Fine. I'm supposed to be cursed. Contaminated in my mother's womb. I'm supposed to be . . .'

'Yes?'

'A monster.'

'And are you?'

For a fleeting moment she looked helpless, shattered. And very sad.

'I don't know, Geralt,' she whispered, and then her features hardened again. 'Because how am I to know, dammit? When I cut my finger, I bleed. I bleed every month, too. I get belly-ache when I overeat, and a hangover when I get drunk. When I'm happy I sing and I swear when I'm sad. When I hate someone I kill them and when— But enough of this! Your answer, witcher.'

'My answer is no.'

'You remember what I said?' she asked after a moment's silence. 'There are offers you can't refuse, the consequences are so terrible, and this is one of them. Think it over.'

'I have thought carefully. And my suggestion was as serious.'

Renfri was silent for some time, fiddling with a string of pearls wound three times around her shapely neck before falling teasingly between her breasts, their curves just visible through the slit of her jacket.

'Geralt,' she said, 'did Stregobor ask you to kill me?'

'Yes. He believed it was the lesser evil.'

'Can I believe you refused him, as you have me?'

'You can.'

'Why?'

'Because I don't believe in a lesser evil.'

Renfri smiled faintly, an ugly grimace in the yellow candlelight.

'You don't believe in it, you say. Well you're right, in a way. Only Evil and Greater Evil exist and beyond them, in the shadows, lurks True Evil. True Evil, Geralt, is something you can barely imagine, even if you believe nothing can still surprise you. And sometimes True Evil seizes you by the throat and demands that you choose between it and another, slightly lesser, Evil.'

102

'What's your goal here, Renfri?

'Nothing. I've had a bit to drink and I'm philosophising, I'm looking for general truths. And I've found one: lesser evils exist, but we can't choose them. Only True Evil can force us to such a choice. Whether we like it or not.'

'Maybe I've not had enough to drink.' The witcher smiled sourly. 'And in the meantime midnight's passed, the way it does. Let's speak plainly. You're not going to kill Stregobor in Blaviken because I'm not going to let you. I'm not going to let it come to a slaughter here. So, for the second time, renounce your revenge. Prove to him, to everyone, that you're not an inhuman and bloodthirsty monster. Prove he has done you great harm through his mistake.'

For a moment Renfri watched the witcher's medallion spinning as he twisted the chain.

'And if I tell you, witcher, that I can neither forgive Stregobor nor renounce my revenge then I admit that he is right, is that it? I'd be proving that I am a monster cursed by the gods? You know, when I was still new to this life a freeman took me in. He took a fancy to me, even though I found him repellent. So every time he wanted to fuck me he had to beat me so hard I could barely move, even the following day. One morning I rose while it was still dark and slashed his throat with a scythe. I wasn't yet as skilled as I am now, and a knife seemed too small. And as I listened to him gurgle and choke, watched him kicking and flailing, I felt the marks left by his feet and fists fade, and I felt, oh, so great, so great that . . . I left him, whistling, sprightly, feeling so joyful, so happy. And it's the same each time. If it wasn't, who'd waste time on revenge?'

'Renfri,' said Geralt. 'Whatever your motives, you're not going to leave here joyful and happy. But you'll leave here alive, early tomorrow morning, as the alderman ordered. You're not going to kill Stregobor in Blaviken.'

Renfri's eyes glistened in the candlelight, reflecting the flame, the pearls glowed in the slit of her jacket, the wolf medallion spinning round on its chain sparkled.

'I pity you,' she said slowly, gazing at the medallion. 'You claim a lesser evil doesn't exist. You're standing on a flagstone running with blood, alone and so very lonely because you can't choose, but you had to. And you'll never know, you'll never be sure, if you were right . . . And your reward will be a stoning, and a bad word. I pity you . . .'

'And you?' asked the witcher quietly, almost in a whisper.

'I can't choose, either.'

'What are you?'

'I am what I am.'

'Where are you?'

'I'm . . . cold . . .'

'Renfri!' Geralt squeezed the medallion tightly in his hand.

She tossed her head as if waking up, and blinked several times, surprised. For a very brief moment she looked frightened.

'You've won,' she said sharply. 'You win, witcher. Tomorrow morning I'll leave Blaviken and never return to this rotten town. Never. Now pass me the wine-skin.'

Her usual derisive smile returned as she put her empty tumbler back on the table. 'Geralt?'

'I'm here.'

'That bloody roof is steep. I'd prefer to leave at dawn than fall and hurt myself in the dark. I'm a princess and my body's delicate. I can feel a pea under a mattress – as long as it's not well-stuffed with straw, obviously. How about it?'

'Renfri,' Geralt smiled despite himself, 'is that really befitting of a princess?'

'What do you know about princesses, dammit? I've lived as one and the joy of it is being able to do what you like. Do I have to tell you straight out what I want?'

Geralt, still smiling, didn't reply.

'I can't believe you don't find me attractive.' Renfri grimaced. 'Are you afraid you'll meet the freeman's sticky fate? Eh, white-hair, I haven't got anything sharp on me. Have a look for yourself.'

She put her legs on his knees. 'Pull my boots off. A high boot is the best place to hide a knife.'

Barefoot, she got up, tore at the buckle of her belt. 'I'm not hiding anything here, either. Or here, as you can see. Put that bloody candle out.'

Outside, in the darkness, a cat yawled.

'Renfri?'

'What?'

'Is this cambric?'

'Of course it is, dammit. Am I a princess or not?'

V

'Daddy,' Marilka nagged monotonously, 'when are we going to the market? To the market, Daddy!'

'Quiet, Marilka,' grunted Caldemeyn, wiping his plate with his bread. 'So what were you saying, Geralt? They're leaving?'

'Yes.'

'I never thought it would end so peacefully. They had me by the throat with that letter from Audoen. I put on a brave face but, to tell you the truth, I couldn't do a thing to them.'

'Even if they openly broke the law? Started a fight?'

'Even if they did. Audoen's a very touchy king. He sends people to the scaffold on a whim. I've got a wife, a daughter, and I'm happy with my office. I don't have to worry where the bacon will come from tomorrow. It's good news that they're leaving. But how, and why, did it happen?'

'Daddy, I want to go to the market!'

'Libushe! Take Marilka away! Geralt, I asked Centurion, the Golden Court's innkeeper, about that Novigradian company. They're quite a gang. Some of them were recognised.'

'Yes?'

'The one with the gash across his face is Nohorn, Abergard's old adjutant from the so-called Free Angren Company – you'll have heard of them. That hulk they call Fifteen was one of theirs too and I don't think his nickname comes from fifteen

105

good deeds. The half-elf is Civril, a brigand and professional murderer. Apparently, he had something to do with the massacre at Tridam.'

'Where?'

'Tridam. Didn't you hear of it? Everyone was talking about it three . . . Yes, three years ago. The Baron of Tridam was holding some brigands in the dungeons. Their comrades – one of whom was that half-blood Civril – seized a river ferry full of pilgrims during the Feast of Nis. They demanded the baron set those others free. The baron refused, so they began murdering pilgrims, one after another. By the time the baron released his prisoners they'd thrown a dozen pilgrims overboard to drift with the current – and following the deaths the baron was in danger of exile, or even of execution. Some blamed him for waiting so long to give in, and others claimed he'd committed a great evil in releasing the men, in setting a pre— precedent or something. The gang should have been shot from the banks, together with the hostages, or attacked on the boats; he shouldn't have given an inch. At the tribunal the baron argued he'd had no choice, he'd chosen the lesser evil to save more than twenty-five people – women and children – on the ferry.'

'The Tridam ultimatum,' whispered the witcher. 'Renfri—'

'What?'

'Caldemeyn, the marketplace.'

'What?'

'She's deceived us. They're not leaving. They'll force Stregobor out of his tower as they forced the Baron of Tridam's hand. Or they'll force me to . . . They're going to start murdering people at the market, it's a real trap!'

'By all the gods— Where are you going? Sit down!'

Marilka, terrified by the shouting, huddled, keening, in the corner of the kitchen.

'I told you!' Libushe shouted, pointing to the witcher. 'I said he only brings trouble!'

'Silence, woman! Geralt? Sit down!'

'We have to stop them. Right now, before people go to the

106

market. And call the guards. As the gang leaves the inn seize them and hold them.'

'Be reasonable. We can't. We can't touch a hair of their heads if they've done nothing wrong. They'll defend themselves and there'll be bloodshed. They're professionals, they'll slaughter my people, and it'll be my head for it if word gets to Audoen. I'll gather the guards, go to the market and keep an eye on them there—'

'That won't achieve anything, Caldemeyn. If the crowd's already in the square you can't prevent panic and slaughter. Renfri has to be stopped right now, while the marketplace is empty.'

'It's illegal. I can't permit it. It's only a rumour the half-elf was at Tridam. You could be wrong, and Audoen would flay me alive.'

'We have to take the lesser evil!'

'Geralt, I forbid it! As Alderman, I forbid it! Leave your sword! Stop!'

Marilka was screaming, her hands pressed over her mouth.

VI

Shading his eyes with his hand, Civril watched the sun emerge from behind the trees. The marketplace was coming to life. Waggons and carts rumbled past and the first vendors were already filling their stalls. A hammer was banging, a cock crowing and seagulls screeched loudly overhead.

'Looks like a lovely day,' Fifteen said pensively.

Civril looked at him askance but didn't say anthing.

'The horses all right, Tavik?' asked Nohorn, pulling on his gloves.

'Saddled and ready. But, there's still not many of them in the marketplace.'

'There'll be more.'

'We should eat.'

'Later.'

'Dead right. You'll have time later. And an appetite.'

'Look,' said Fifteen suddenly.

The witcher was approaching from the main street, walking between stalls, coming straight towards them.

'Renfri was right,' Civril said. 'Give me the crossbow, Nohorn.' He hunched over and, holding the strap down with his foot, pulled the string back. He placed the bolt carefully in the groove as the witcher continued to approach. Civril raised the crossbow.

'Not one step closer, witcher!'

Geralt stopped about forty paces from the group.

'Where's Renfri?'

The half-blood's pretty face contorted. 'At the tower. She's making the sorcerer an offer he can't refuse. But she knew you would come. She left a message for you.'

'Speak.'

'"I am what I am. Choose. Either me, or a lesser." You're supposed to know what it means.'

The witcher nodded, raised his hand above his right shoulder, and drew his sword. The blade traced a glistening arc above his head. Walking slowly, he made his way towards the group.

Civril laughed nastily, ominously.

'Renfri said this would happen, witcher, and left us something special to give you. Right between the eyes.'

The witcher kept walking, and the half-elf raised the crossbow to his cheek. It grew very quiet.

The bowstring hummed, the witcher's sword flashed and the bolt flew upwards with a metallic whine, spinning in the air until it clattered against the roof and rumbled into the gutter.

'He deflected it . . .' groaned Fifteen. 'Deflected it in flight—'

'As one,' ordered Civril. Blades hissed as they were drawn from sheathes, the group pressed shoulder to shoulder, bristling with blades.

The witcher came on faster; his fluid walk became a run – not straight at the group quivering with swords, but circling it in a tightening spiral.

As Geralt circled the group Tavik's nerve failed. He rushed the witcher, the twins following him.

'Don't disperse!' Civril roared, shaking his head and losing sight of the witcher. He swore and jumped aside, seeing the group fall apart, scattering around the market stalls.

Tavik went first. He was chasing the witcher when he saw Geralt running in the opposite direction, towards him. He skidded, trying to stop, but the witcher shot past before he could raise his sword. Tavik felt a hard blow just above his hip, fell to his knees and, when he saw his hip, started screaming.

The twins simultaneously attacked the black, blurred shape rushing towards them, mistimed their attack and collided with each other as Geralt slashed Vyr across the chest and Nimir in the temple, leaving one twin to stagger, head down, into a vegetable stall, and the other to spin in place and fall limply into the gutter.

The marketplace boiled with vendors running away, stalls clattering to the ground and screams rising in the dusty air. Tavik tried to stumble to his trembling legs and fell painfully to the ground.

'From the left, Fifteen!' Nohorn roared, running in a semi-circle to approach the witcher from behind.

Fifteen spun. But not quickly enough. He bore a thrust through the stomach, prepared to strike and was struck again in the neck, just below his ear. He took four unsteady steps and collapsed into a fish cart, which rolled away beneath him. Sliding over the slippery cargo Fifteen fell onto the flagstones, silver with scales.

Civril and Nohorn struck simultaneously from both sides, the elf with a high sweeping cut, Nohorn from a kneeling position, low and flat. The witcher caught both, two metallic clangs merging into one. Civril leapt aside and tripped, catching himself against a stall as Nohorn warded off a blow so powerful it threw him backwards to his knees. Leaping up he parried too slowly, taking a gash in the face parallel to his old scar.

Civril bounced off the stall, jumping over Nohorn as he fell, missed the witcher and jumped away. The thrust was so sharp, so precise, he didn't feel it; his legs only gave way when he tried to attack again. The sword fell from his hand, the tendons severed above the elbow. Civril fell to his knees and shook his head, trying and failing to rise. His head dropped, and among the shattered stalls and market wares, the scattered fish and cabbages, his body stilled in the centre of a growing red puddle.

Renfri entered the marketplace.

She approached slowly with a soft, feline step, avoiding the carts and stalls. The crowd in the streets and by the houses, which had been humming like a hornet's nest, grew silent. Geralt stood motionless, his sword in his lowered hand. Renfri came to within ten paces and stopped, close enough to see that, under her jacket, she wore a short coat of chain-mail, barely covering her hips.

'You've made your choice,' she said slowly. 'Are you sure it's the right one?'

'This won't be another Tridam,' Geralt said with an effort.

'It wouldn't have been. Stregobor laughed in my face. He said I could butcher Blaviken and the neighbouring villages and he wouldn't leave his tower. And he won't let anyone in, not even you. Why are you looking at me like that? Yes, I deceived you. I'll deceive anyone if I have to, why should you be special?'

'Get out of here, Renfri.'

She laughed. 'No, Geralt.' She drew her sword, quickly and nimbly.

'Renfri.'

'No. You made a choice. Now it's my turn.' With one sharp move, she tore the skirt from her hips and spun it in the air, wrapping the material around her forearm. Geralt retreated and raised his hand, arranging his fingers in the Sign.

Renfri laughed hoarsely. 'It doesn't affect me. Only the sword will.'

'Renfri,' he repeated. 'Go. If we cross blades, I— I won't be able—'

'I know,' she said. 'But I, I can't do anything else. I just can't. We are what we are, you and I.'

She moved towards him with a light, swaying step, her sword

110

glinting in her right hand, her skirt dragging along the ground from her left.

She leapt, the skirt fluttered in the air and, veiled in its tracks, the sword flashed in a short, sparing cut. Geralt jumped away; the cloth didn't even brush him, and Renfri's blade slid over his diagonal parry. He attacked instinctively, spinning their blades, trying to knock her weapon aside. It was a mistake. She deflected his blade and slashed, aiming for his face. He barely parried and pirouetted away, dodging her dancing blade and jumping aside again. She fell on him, threw the skirt into his eyes and slashed flatly from short range, spinning. Spinning with her he avoided the blow. She knew the trick and turned with him, their bodies so close he could feel the touch of her breath as she ran the edge across his chest. He felt a twinge of pain, ignored it. He turned again, in the opposite direction, deflected the blade flying towards his temple, made a swift feint and attacked. Renfri sprang away as if to strike from above as Geralt lunged and swiftly slashed her exposed thigh and groin from below with the very tip of his sword.

She didn't cry out. Falling to her side she dropped her sword and clutched her thigh. Blood poured through her fingers in a bright stream over her decorated belt, elk-leather boots, and onto the dirty flagstones. The clamour of the swaying crowd, crammed in the streets, grew as they saw blood.

Geralt put up his sword.

'Don't go . . .' she moaned, curling up in a ball.

He didn't reply.

'I'm . . . cold . . .'

He said nothing. Renfri moaned again, curling up tighter as her blood flowed into the cracks between the stones.

'Geralt . . . Hold me . . .'

The witcher remained silent.

She turned her head, resting her cheek on the flagstones and was still. A fine dagger, hidden beneath her body until now, slipped from her numb fingers.

After a long moment the witcher raised his head, hearing

111

Stregobor's staff tapping against the flagstones. The wizard was approaching quickly, avoiding the corpses.

'What slaughter,' he panted. 'I saw it, Geralt, I saw it all in my crystal ball . . .'

He came closer, bent over. In his trailing black robe, supported by his staff, he looked old.

'It's incredible.' He shook his head. 'Shrike's dead.'

Geralt didn't reply.

'Well, Geralt.' The wizard straightened himself. 'Fetch a cart and we'll take her to the tower for an autopsy.'

He looked at the witcher and, not getting any answer, leant over the body.

Someone the witcher didn't know found the hilt of his sword and drew it. 'Touch a single hair of her head,' said the person the witcher didn't know, 'touch her head and yours will go flying to the flagstones.'

'Have you gone mad? You're wounded, in shock! An autopsy's the only way we can confirm—'

'Don't touch her!'

Stregobor, seeing the raised blade, jumped aside and waved his staff. 'All right!' he shouted. 'As you wish! But you'll never know! You'll never be sure! Never, do you hear, witcher?'

'Be gone.'

'As you wish.' The wizard turned away, his staff hitting the flagstones. 'I'm returning to Kovir. I'm not staying in this hole another day. Come with me rather than rot here. These people don't know anything, they've only seen you killing. And you kill nastily, Geralt. Well, are you coming?'

Geralt didn't reply; he wasn't looking at him. He put his sword away. Stregobor shrugged and walked away, his staff tapping rhythmically against the ground.

A stone came flying from the crowd and clattered against the flagstones. A second followed, whizzing past just above Geralt's shoulder. The witcher, holding himself straight, raised both hands and made a swift gesture with them. The crowd heaved; the stones

112

came flying more thickly but the Sign, protecting him behind an invisible oval shield, pushed them aside.

'Enough!' yelled Caldemeyn. 'Bloody hell, enough of that!'

The crowd roared like a surge of breakers but the stones stopped flying. The witcher stood, motionless.

The alderman approached him.

'Is this,' he said, with a broad gesture indicating the motionless bodies strewn across the square, 'how your lesser evil looks? Is this what you believed necessary?'

'Yes,' replied Geralt slowly, with an effort.

'Is your wound serious?'

'No.'

'In that case, get out of here.'

'Yes,' said the witcher. He stood a moment longer, avoiding the alderman's eyes. Then he turned away slowly, very slowly.

'Geralt.'

The witcher looked round.

'Don't come back,' said Caldemeyn. 'Never come back.'

THE VOICE OF REASON 4

'Let's talk, Iola.

'I need this conversation. They say silence is golden. Maybe it is, although I'm not sure it's worth that much. It has its price certainly; you have to pay for it.

'It's easier for you. Yes it is, don't deny it. You're silent through choice; you've made it a sacrifice to your goddess. I don't believe in Melitele, don't believe in the existence of other gods either, but I respect your choice, your sacrifice. Your belief. Because your faith and sacrifice, the price you're paying for your silence, will make you a better, a greater being. Or, at least, it could. But my faithlessness can do nothing. It's powerless.

'You ask what I believe in, in that case.

'I believe in the sword.

'As you can see, I carry two. Every witcher does. It's said, spitefully, the silver one is for monsters and the iron for humans. But that's wrong. As there are monsters which can be struck down only with a silver blade, so there are those for whom iron is lethal. And Iola, not just any iron, it must come from a meteorite. What is a meteorite, you ask? It's a falling star. You must have seen them – short, luminous streaks in the night. You've probably made a wish on one. Perhaps it was one more reason for you to believe in the gods. For me, a meteorite is nothing more than a bit of metal, primed by the sun and its fall, metal to make swords.

'Yes, of course you can take my sword. Feel how light it— No! Don't touch the edge, you'll cut yourself. It's sharper than a razor. It has to be.

'I train in every spare moment. I don't dare lose my skill. I've come here – this furthest corner of the temple garden – to limber up, to rid my muscles of that hideous, loathsome numbness which has come over me, this coldness flowing through me. And you found me here. Funny, for a few days I was trying to find you. I wanted—

'I need to talk, Iola. Let's sit down for a moment.

'You don't know me at all, do you?

'I'm called Geralt. Geralt of— No. Only Geralt. Geralt of nowhere. I'm a witcher.

'My home is Kaer Morhen, Witcher's Settlement. It's . . . It was a fortress. Not much remains of it.

'Kaer Morhen . . . That's where the likes of me were produced. It's not done anymore, no one lives in Kaer Morhen now. No one but Vesemir. Who's Vesemir? My father. Why are you so surprised? What's so strange about it? Everyone's got a father, and mine is Vesemir. And so what if he's not my real father? I didn't know him, or my mother. I don't even know if they're still alive, and I don't much care.

Yes, Kaer Morhen. I underwent the usual mutation there, through the Trial of Grasses, and then hormones, herbs, viral infections. And then through them all again. And again, to the bitter end. Apparently, I took the changes unusually well; I was only ill briefly. I was considered to be an exceptionally resilient brat . . . and was chosen for more complicated experiments as a result. They were worse. Much worse. But, as you see, I survived. The only one to live out of all those chosen for further trials. My hair's been white ever since. Total loss of pigmentation. A side-effect, as they say. A trifle.

'Then they taught me various things until the day when I left Kaer Morhen and took to the road. I'd earned my medallion, the Sign of the Wolf's School. I had two swords: silver and iron, and my conviction, enthusiasm, incentive and . . . faith. Faith that I was needed in a world full of monsters and beasts, to protect the innocent. As I left Kaer Morhen I dreamed of meeting my first monster. I couldn't wait to stand eye to eye with him. And the moment arrived.

'My first monster, Iola, was bald and had exceptionally rotten teeth. I came across him on the highway where, with some fellow monsters, deserters, he'd stopped a peasant's cart and pulled out a little girl, maybe thirteen years old. His companions held her father while the bald man tore off her dress, yelling it was time for her to meet a real man. I rode up and said the time had come for him, too – I thought I was very witty. The bald monster released the girl and threw himself at me with an axe. He was slow but tough. I hit him twice – not clean cuts, but spectacular, and only then did he fall. His gang ran away when they saw what a witcher's sword could do to a man . . .

'Am I boring you, Iola?

'I need this. I really do need it.

'Where was I? My first noble deed. You see, they'd told me again and again in Kaer Morhen not to get involved in such incidents, not to play at being knight errant or uphold the law. Not to show off, but to work for money. And I joined this fight like an idiot, not fifty miles from the mountains. And do you know why? I wanted the girl, sobbing with gratitude, to kiss her saviour on the hands, and her father to thank me on his knees. In reality her father fled with his attackers, and the girl, drenched in the bald man's blood, threw up, became hysterical and fainted in fear when I approached her. Since then, I've only very rarely interfered in such matters.

'I did my job. I quickly learnt how. I'd ride up to village enclosures or town pickets and wait. If they spat, cursed and threw stones I rode away. If someone came out to give me a commission, I'd carry it out.

'I visited towns and fortresses. I looked for proclamations nailed to posts at the crossroads. I looked for the words "Witcher urgently needed". And then there'd be a sacred site, a dungeon, necropolis or ruins, forest ravine or grotto hidden in the mountains, full of bones and stinking carcasses. Some creature which lived to kill, out of hunger, for pleasure, or invoked by some sick will. A manticore, wyvern, fogler, aeschna, ilyocoris, chimera, leshy, vampire, ghoul, graveir, were-wolf, giant scorpion, striga, black annis, kikimora, vypper . . . so many I've killed. There'd be a

116

dance in the dark and a slash of the sword, and fear and distaste in the eyes of my employer afterwards.

'Mistakes? Of course I've made them. But I keep to my principles. No, not the code. Although I have at times hidden behind a code. People like that. Those who follow a code are often respected and held in high esteem. But no one's ever compiled a witcher's code. I invented mine. Just like that. And keep to it. Always—

'Not always.

'There have been situations where it seemed there wasn't any room for doubt. When I should say to myself "What do I care? It's nothing to do with me, I'm a witcher". When I should listen to the voice of reason. To listen to my instinct, even if it's fear, if not to what my experience dictates.

'I should have listened to the voice of reason that time . . .

'I didn't.

'I thought I was choosing the lesser evil. I chose the lesser evil. Lesser evil! I'm Geralt! Witcher . . . I'm the Butcher of Blaviken—

'Don't touch me! It might . . . You might see . . . and I don't want you to. I don't want to know. I know my fate whirls about me like water in a weir. It's hard on my heels, following my tracks, but I never look back.

'A loop? Yes, that's what Nenneke sensed. What tempted me, I wonder, in Cintra? How could I have taken such a risk so foolishly—?

'No, no, no. I never look back. I'll never return to Cintra. I'll avoid it like the plague. I'll *never* go back there.

'Heh, if my calculations are correct, that child would have been born in May, sometime around the feast of Belleteyn. If that's true it's an interesting coincidence. Because Yennefer was also born on Belleteyn's . . .

'Enough of this, we should go. It's already dusk.

'Thank you for talking to me. Thank you, Iola.

'No, nothing's wrong. I'm fine.

'Quite fine.'

A QUESTION OF PRICE

I

The witcher had a knife at his throat.

He was wallowing in a wooden tub, brimful of soapsuds, his head thrown back against its slippery rim. The bitter taste of soap lingered in his mouth as the knife, blunt as a doorknob, scraped his Adam's apple painfully and moved towards his chin with a grating sound.

The barber, with the expression of an artist who is conscious that he is creating a masterpiece, scraped once more for form's sake, then wiped the witcher's face with a piece of linen soaked in tincture of angelica.

Geralt stood up, allowed a servant to pour a bucket of water over him, shook himself and climbed from the tub, leaving wet footmarks on the brick floor.

'Your towel, sir.' The servant glanced curiously at his medallion.

'Thanks.'

'Clothes,' said Haxo. 'Shirt, underpants, trousers and tunic. And boots.'

'You've thought of everything. But can't I go in my own shoes?'

'No. Beer?'

'With pleasure.'

He dressed slowly. The touch of someone else's coarse, unpleasant clothes against his swollen skin spoilt his relaxed mood.

'Castellan?'

'Yes, Geralt?'

'You don't know what this is all about, do you? Why they need me here?'

'It's not my business,' said Haxo, squinting at the servants. 'My job is to get you dressed—'

'Dressed up, you mean.'

'—get you dressed and take you to the banquet, to the queen. Put the tunic on, sir. And hide the medallion beneath it.'

'My dagger was here.'

'It isn't anymore. It's in a safe place, like your swords and your possessions. Nobody carries arms where you're going.'

The witcher shrugged, pulling on the tight purple tunic.

'And what's this?' he asked indicating the embroidery on the front of his outfit.

'Oh yes,' said Haxo. 'I almost forgot. During the banquet you will be the Honourable Ravix of Fourhorn. As guest of honour you will sit at the queen's right hand, such is her wish, and that, on the tunic, is your coat of arms. A bear passant sable, damsel vested azure riding him, her hair loose and arms raised. You should remember it – one of the guests might have a thing about heraldry. It often happens.'

'Of course I'll remember it,' said Geralt seriously. 'And Fourhorn, where's that?'

'Far enough. Ready? Can we go?'

'We can. Just tell me, Haxo, what's this banquet in aid of?'

'Princess Pavetta is turning fifteen and, as is the custom, contenders for her hand have turned up in their dozens. Queen Calanthe wants her to marry someone from Skellige; an alliance with the islanders would mean a lot to us.'

'Why them?'

'Those they're allied with aren't attacked as often as others.'

'A good reason.'

'And not the sole one. In Cintra women can't rule. King Roegner died some time ago and the queen doesn't want another husband: our Lady Calanthe is wise and just, but a king is a king. Whoever marries the princess will sit on the throne, and we want a tough, decent fellow. They have to be found on the islands. They're a hard nation. Let's go.'

Geralt stopped halfway down the gallery surrounding the small inner courtyard and looked around.

'Castellan,' he said under his breath, 'we're alone. Quickly, tell me why the queen needs a witcher. You of all people must know something.'

'For the same reasons as everyone else,' Haxo grunted. 'Cintra is just like any other country. We've got werewolves and basilisks and a manticore could be found, too, if you looked hard enough. So a witcher might also come in useful.'

'Don't twist my words, Castellan. I'm asking why the queen needs a witcher in disguise as a bear passont, with hair loose at that, at the banquet.'

Haxo also looked around, and even leant over the gallery balustrade.

'Something bad's happening, Geralt,' he muttered. 'In the castle. Something's frightening people.'

'What?'

'What usually frightens people? A monster. They say it's small, hunchbacked, bristling like a Urcheon. It creeps around the castle at night, rattles chains. Moans and groans in the chambers.'

'Have you seen it?'

'No,' Haxo spat, 'and I don't want to.'

'You're talking nonsense, Castellan,' grimaced the witcher. 'It doesn't make sense. We're going to an engagement feast. What am I supposed to do there? Wait for a hunchback to jump out and groan? Without a weapon? Dressed up like a jester? Haxo?'

'Think what you like,' grumbled the castellan. 'They told me not to tell you anything, but you asked. So I told you. And you tell me I'm talking nonsense. How charming.'

'I'm sorry, I didn't mean to offend you, Castellan. I was simply surprised . . .'

'Stop being surprised.' Haxo turned away, still sulking. 'Your job isn't to be surprised. And I strongly advise you, witcher, that if the queen orders you to strip naked, paint your arse blue and hang yourself upside down in the entrance hall like a chandelier, you do it without surprise or hesitation. Otherwise you might meet with a fair amount of unpleasantness. Have you got that?'

'I've got it. Let's go, Haxo. Whatever happens, that bath's given me an appetite.'

II

Apart from the curt, ceremonious greetings with which she welcomed him as 'Lord of Fourhorn', Queen Calanthe didn't exchange a single word with the witcher. The banquet was about to begin and the guests, loudly announced by the herald, were gathering.

The table was huge, rectangular, and could seat more than forty men. Calanthe sat at the head of the table on a throne with a high backrest. Geralt sat on her right and, on her left, a grey-haired bard called Drogodar, with a lute. Two more chairs at the head of the table, on the queen's left, remained empty.

To Geralt's right, along the table, sat Haxo and a voivode whose name he'd forgotten. Beyond them were guests from the Duchy of Attre – the sullen and silent knight Rainfarn and his charge, the chubby twelve-year-old Prince Windhalm, one of the pretenders to the princess's hand. Further down were the colourful and motley knights from Cintra, and local vassals.

'Baron Eylembert of Tigg!' announced the herald.

'Coodcoodak!' murmured Calanthe, nudging Drogodar. 'This will be fun.'

A thin and whiskered, richly attired knight bowed low, but his lively, happy eyes and cheerful smirk belied his subservience.

'Greetings, Coodcoodak,' said the queen ceremoniously. Obviously the baron was better known by his nickname than by his family name. 'We are happy to see you.'

'And I am happy to be invited,' declared Coodcoodak, and sighed. 'Oh well, I'll cast an eye on the princess, if you permit, my queen. It's hard to live alone, ma'am.'

'Aye, Coodcoodak,' Calanthe smiled faintly, wrapping a lock of hair around her finger. 'But you're already married, as we well know.'

'Aaahh.' The baron was miffed. 'You know yourself, ma'am, how weak and delicate my wife is, and smallpox is rife in the neighbourhood. I bet my belt and sword against a pair of old slippers that in a year I'll already be out of mourning.'

'Poor man, Coodcoodak. But lucky, too,' Calanthe's smile grew wider. 'Lucky your wife isn't stronger. I hear that last harvest, when she caught you in the haystack with a strumpet, she chased you for almost a mile with a pitchfork but couldn't catch you. You have to feed her better, cuddle her more and take care that her back doesn't get cold during the night. Then, in a year, you'll see how much better she is.'

Coodcoodak pretended to grow doleful. 'I take your point. But can I stay for the feast?'

'We'd be delighted, Baron.'

'The legation from Skellige!' shouted the herald, becoming increasingly hoarse.

The islanders – four of them, in shiny leather doublets trimmed with seal fur and belted with chequered woollen sashes – strode in with a sprightly, hollow step. They were led by a sinewy warrior with a dark face and aquiline nose and, at his side, a broad-shouldered youth with a mop of red hair. They all bowed before the queen.

'It is a great honour,' said Calanthe, a little flushed, 'to welcome such an excellent knight as Eist Tuirseach of Skellige to my castle again. If it weren't for your well-known disdain for marriage, I'd be delighted to think you're here to court my Pavetta. Has loneliness got the better of you after all, sir?'

'Often enough, beautiful Calanthe,' replied the dark-faced islander, raising his glistening eyes to the queen. 'But my life is too dangerous for me to contemplate a lasting union. If it weren't for that . . . Pavetta is still a young girl, an unopened bud, but I can see . . .'

'See what?'

'The apple does not fall far from the tree,' smiled Eist Tuirseach,

122

flashing his white teeth. 'Suffice it to look at you, my queen, to know how beautiful the princess will be when she reaches the age at which a woman can please a warrior. In the meantime, it is young men who ought to court her. Such as our King Bran's nephew here, Crach an Craite, who travelled here for exactly that purpose.'

Crach, bowing his red head, knelt on one knee before the queen.

'Who else have you brought, Eist?'

A thickset, robust man with a bushy beard, and a strapping fellow with bagpipes on his back, knelt by Crach an Craite.

'This is the gallant druid Mousesack, who, like me, is a good friend and advisor to King Bran. And this is Draig Bon-Dhu, our famous skald. And thirty seamen from Skellige are waiting in the courtyard, burning with hope to catch a glimpse of the beautiful Calanthe of Cintra.'

'Sit down, noble guests. Tuirseach, sir, sit here.'

Eist took the vacant seat at the narrower end of the table, only separated from the queen by Drogodar and an empty chair. The remaining islanders sat together on the left, between Marshal Vissegerd and the three sons of Lord Strept, Tinglant, Fodcat and Wieldhill.

'That's more or less everyone.' The queen leant over to the marshal. 'Let's begin, Vissegerd.'

The marshal clapped his hands. The servants, carrying platters and jugs, moved towards the table in a long line, greeted by a joyful murmur from the guests.

Calanthe barely ate, reluctantly picking at the morsels served her with a silver fork. Drogodar, having bolted his food, kept strumming his lute. The rest of the guests, on the other hand, laid waste to the roast piglets, birds, fish and molluscs on offer – with the red-haired Crach an Craite in the lead. Rainfarn of Attre reprimanded the young Prince Windhalm severely, even slapping his hand when he reached for a jug of cider. Coodcoodak stopped picking bones for a moment and entertained his neighbours by imitating the whistle of a mud turtle. The atmosphere grew merrier by the minute. The first toasts were being raised, and already becoming less and less coherent.

Calanthe adjusted the narrow golden circlet on her curled ash-grey hair and turned to Geralt, who was busy cracking open a huge red lobster.

'It's loud enough that we can exchange a few words discreetly. Let us start with courtesies: I'm pleased to meet you.'

'The pleasure's mutual, your Majesty.'

'After the courtesies come hard facts. I've got a job for you.'

'So I gathered. I'm rarely invited to feasts for the pleasure of my company.'

'You're probably not very interesting company, then. What else have you gathered?'

'I'll tell you when you've outlined my task, your Majesty.'

'Geralt,' said Calanthe, her fingers tapping an emerald necklace, the smallest stone of which was the size of a bumble-bee, 'what sort of task do you expect, as a witcher? What? Digging a well? Repairing a hole in the roof? Weaving a tapestry of all the positions King Vridank and the beautiful Cerro tried on their wedding night? Surely you know what your profession's about?'

'Yes, I do. I'll tell you what I've gathered, your Majesty.'

'I'm curious.'

'I gathered that. And that, like many others, you've mistaken my trade for an altogether different profession.'

'Oh?' Calanthe, casually leaning towards the lute-strumming Drogodar, gave the impression of being pensive and absent. 'Who, Geralt, makes up this ignorant horde with whom you equate me? And for what profession do those fools mistake your trade?'

'Your Majesty,' said Geralt calmly, 'while I was riding to Cintra, I met villagers, merchants, peddlers, dwarves, tinkers and woodcutters. They told me about a black annis who has its hide-out somewhere in these woods, a little house on a chicken-claw tripod. They mentioned a chimera nestling in the mountains. Aeschnes and centipedeanomorphs. Apparently a manticore could also be found if you look hard enough. So many tasks a witcher could perform without having to dress up in someone else's feathers and coat of arms.'

'You didn't answer my question.'

'Your Majesty, I don't doubt that a marriage alliance with Skellige is necessary for Cintra. It's possible, too, that the schemers who want to prevent it deserve a lesson – using means which don't involve you. It's convenient if this lesson were to be given by an unknown lord from Fourhorn, who would then disappear from the scene. And now I'll answer your question. You mistake my trade for that of a hired killer. Those others, of whom there are so many, are rulers. It's not the first time I've been called to a court where the problems demand the quick solutions of a sword. But I've never killed people for money, regardless of whether it's for a good or bad cause. And I never will.'

The atmosphere at the table was growing more and more lively as the beer diminished. The red-haired Crach an Craite found appreciative listeners to his tale of the battle at Thwyth. Having sketched a map on the table with the help of meat bones dipped in sauce, he marked out the strategic plan, shouting loudly. Coodcoodak, proving how apt his nickname was, suddenly cackled like a very real sitting hen, creating general mirth among the guests, and consternation among the servants who were convinced that a bird, mocking their vigilance, had somehow managed to make its way from the courtyard into the hall.

'Thus fate has punished me with too shrewd a witcher,' Calanthe smiled, but her eyes were narrowed and angry. 'A witcher who, without a shadow of respect or, at the very least, of common courtesy, exposes my intrigues and infamous plans. But hasn't fascination with my beauty and charming personality clouded your judgement? Don't ever do that again, Geralt. Don't speak to those in power like that. Few of them would forget your words, and you know kings – they have all sorts of things at their disposal: daggers, poisons, dungeons, red-hot pokers. There are hundreds, thousands, of ways kings can avenge their wounded pride. And you wouldn't believe how easy it is, Geralt, to wound some rulers' pride. Rarely will any of them take words such as "No", "I won't",

125

and "Never" calmly. But that's nothing. Interrupt one of them or make inappropriate comments, and you'll condemn yourself to the wheel.'

The queen clasped her narrow white hands together and lightly rested her chin on them. Geralt didn't interrupt, nor did he comment.

'Kings,' continued Calanthe, 'divide people into two categories – those they order around, and those they buy – because they adhere to the old and banal truth that everyone can be bought. Everyone. It's only a question of price. Don't you agree? Ah, I don't need to ask. You're a witcher, after all, you do your job and take the money. As far as you're concerned the idea of being bought has lost its scornful undertone. The question of your price, too, is clear, related as it is to the difficulty of the task and how well you execute it. And your fame, Geralt. Old men at fairs and markets sing of the exploits of the white-haired witcher from Rivia. If even half of it is true then I wager your services are not cheap. So it would be a waste of money to engage you in such simple, trite matters as palace intrigue or murder. Those can be dealt with by other, cheaper hands.'

'BRAAAK! Ghaaa-braaak!' roared Coodcoodak suddenly, to loud applause. Geralt didn't know which animal he was imitating, but he didn't want to meet anything like it. He turned his head and caught the queen's venomously green glance. Drogodar, his lowered head and face concealed by his curtain of grey hair, quietly strummed his lute.

'Ah, Geralt,' said Calanthe, with a gesture forbidding a servant from refilling her goblet. 'I speak and you remain silent. We're at a feast. We all want to enjoy ourselves. Amuse me. I'm starting to miss your pertinent remarks and perceptive comments. I'd also be pleased to hear a compliment or two, homage or assurance of your obedience. In whichever order you choose.'

'Oh well, your Majesty,' said the witcher, 'I'm not a very interesting dinner companion. I'm amazed to be singled out for the honour of occupying this place. Indeed, someone far more appropriate should have been seated here. Anyone you wished. It would have sufficed for you to give them the order, or to buy them. It's only a question of price.'

'Go on, go on,' Calanthe tilted her head back and closed her eyes, the semblance of a pleasant smile on her lips.

'So I'm honoured and proud to be sitting by Queen Calanthe of Cintra, whose beauty is surpassed only by her wisdom. I also regard it as a great honour that the queen has heard of me and that, on the basis of what she has heard, does not wish to use me for trivial matters. Last winter Prince Hrobarik, not being so gracious, tried to hire me to find a beauty who, sick of his vulgar advances, had fled the ball, losing a slipper. It was difficult to convince him that he needed a huntsman, and not a witcher.'

The queen was listening with an enigmatic smile.

'Other rulers, too, unequal to you in wisdom, didn't refrain from proposing trivial tasks. It was usually a question of the murder of a stepson, stepfather, stepmother, uncle, aunt – it's hard to mention them all. They were all of the opinion that it was simply a question of price.'

The queen's smile could have meant anything.

'And so I repeat,' Geralt bowed his head a little, 'that I can't contain my pride to be sitting next to you, ma'am. And pride means a very great deal to us witchers. You wouldn't believe how much. A lord once offended a witcher's pride by proposing a job that wasn't in keeping with either honour or the witcher's code. What's more, he didn't accept a polite refusal and wished to prevent the witcher from leaving his castle. Afterwards everyone agreed this wasn't one of his best ideas.'

'Geralt,' said Calanthe, after a moment's silence, 'you were wrong. You're a very interesting dinner companion.'

Coodcoodak, shaking beer froth from his whiskers and the front of his jacket, craned his neck and gave the penetrating howl of a she-wolf in heat. The dogs in the courtyard, and the entire neighbourhood, echoed the howl.

One of the brothers from Strept dipped his finger in his beer and touched up the thick line around the formation drawn by Crach an Craite.

'Error and incompetence!' he shouted. 'They shouldn't have done that! Here, towards the wing, that's where they should have directed the cavalry, struck the flanks!'

'Ha!' roared Crach an Craite, whacking the table with a bone and splattering his neighbours' faces and tunics with sauce. 'And so weaken the centre? A key position? Ludicrous!'

'Only someone who's blind or sick in the head would miss the opportunity to manoeuvre in a situation like that!'

'That's it! Quite right!' shouted Windhalm of Attre.

'Who's asking you, you little snot?'

'Snot yourself!'

'Shut your gob or I'll wallop you—'

'Sit on your arse and keep quiet, Crach,' called Eist Tuirseach, interrupting his conversation with Vissegerd. 'Enough of these arguments. Drogodar, sir! Don't waste your talent! Indeed, your beautiful though quiet tunes should be listened to with greater concentration and gravity. Draig Bon-Dhu, stop scoffing and guzzling! You're not going to impress anyone here like that. Pump up your bagpipes and delight our ears with decent martial music. With your permission, noble Calanthe!'

'Oh mother of mine,' whispered the queen to Geralt, raising her eyes to the vault for a moment in silent resignation. But she nodded her permission, smiling openly and kindly.

'Draig Bon-Dhu,' said Eist, 'play us the song of the battle of Hochebuz. It won't leave us in any doubt as to the tactical manoeuvres of commanders – or as to who acquired immortal fame there! To the health of the heroic Calanthe of Cintra!'

'The health! And glory!' The guests roared, emptying their goblets and clay cups.

Draig Bon-Dhu's bagpipes gave out an ominous drone and burst into a terrible, drawn-out, modulated wail. The guests took up the song, beating out a rhythm on the table with whatever came to hand. Coodcoodak was staring avidly at the goat-leather sack, captivated by the idea of adopting its dreadful tones in his own repertoire.

'Hochebuz,' said Calante, looking at Geralt, 'my first battle.

Although I fear rousing the indignation and contempt of such a proud witcher, I confess that we were fighting for money. Our enemy was burning villages which paid us levies and we, greedy for our tributes, challenged them on the field. A trivial reason, a trivial battle, a trivial three thousand corpses pecked to pieces by the crows. And look – instead of being ashamed I'm proud as a peacock that songs are sung about me. Even when sung to such awful music.'

Again she summoned her parody of a smile full of happiness and kindness, and answered the toast raised to her by lifting her own, empty, goblet. Geralt remained silent.

'Let's go on.' Calanthe accepted a pheasant leg offered to her by Drogodar and picked at it gracefully. 'As I said, you've aroused my interest. I've been told that witchers are an interesting caste, but I didn't really believe it. Now I do. When hit you give a note which shows you're fashioned of pure steel, unlike these men moulded from bird shit. Which doesn't, in any way, change the fact that you're here to execute a task. And you'll do it without being so clever.'

Geralt didn't smile disrespectfully or nastily, although he very much wanted to. He held his silence.

'I thought,' murmured the queen, appearing to give her full attention to the pheasant's thigh, 'that you'd say something. Or smile. No? All the better. Can I consider our negotiations concluded?'

'Unclear tasks,' said the witcher dryly, 'can't be clearly executed.'

'What's unclear? You did, after all, guess correctly. I have plans regarding a marriage alliance with Skellige. These plans are threatened, and I need you to eliminate the treat. But here your shrewdness ends. The supposition that I mistake your trade for that of a hired thug has piqued me greatly. Accept, Geralt, that I belong to that select group of rulers who know exactly what witchers do, and how they ought to be employed. On the other hand, if someone kills as efficiently as you do, even though not for money, he shouldn't be surprised if people credit him with being a professional in that field. Your fame runs ahead of you,

Geralt, it's louder than Draig Bon-Dhu's accursed bagpipes, and there are equally few pleasant notes in it.'

The bagpipe player, although he couldn't hear the queen's words, finished his concert. The guests rewarded him with an uproarious ovation and dedicated themselves with renewed zeal to the remains of the banquet, recalling battles and making rude jokes about womenfolk. Coodcoodak was making a series of loud noises, but there was no way to tell if these were yet another animal imitation, or an attempt to relieve his overloaded stomach.

Eist Tuirseach leant far across the table. 'Your Majesty,' he said, 'there are good reasons, I am sure, for your dedication to the lord from Fourhorn, but it's high time we saw Princess Pavetta. What are we waiting for? Surely not for Crach an Craite to get drunk? And even that moment is almost here.'

'You're right as usual, Eist,' Calanthe smiled warmly. Geralt was amazed by her arsenal of smiles. 'Indeed, I do have important matters to discuss with the Honourable Ravix. I'll dedicate some time to you too, but you know my principle: duty then pleasure. Haxo!'

She raised her hand and beckoned the castellan. Haxo rose without a word, bowed, and quickly ran upstairs, disappearing into the dark gallery. The queen turned to the witcher.

'You heard? We've been debating for too long. If Pavetta has stopped preening in front of the looking-glass she'll be here presently. So prick up your ears because I won't repeat this. I want to achieve the ends which, to a certain degree, you have guessed. There can be no other solution. As for you, you have a choice. You can be forced to act by my command – I don't wish to dwell on the consequences of disobedience, although obedience will be generously rewarded – or you can render me a paid service. Note that I didn't say "I can buy you", because I've decided not to offend your witcher's pride. There's a huge difference, isn't there?'

'The magnitude of this difference has somehow escaped my notice.'

'Then pay greater attention. The difference, my dear witcher, is that one who is bought is paid according to the buyer's whim, whereas one who renders a service sets his own price. Is that clear?'

'To a certain extent. Let's say, then, that I choose to serve. Surely I should know what that entails?'

'No. Only a command has to be specific and explicit. A paid service is different. I'm interested in the results, nothing more. How you achieve it is your business.'

Geralt, raising his head, met Mousesack's penetrating black gaze. The druid of Skellige, without taking his eyes from the witcher, was crumbling bread in his hands and dropping it as if lost in thought. Geralt looked down. There on the oak table, crumbs, grains of buckwheat and fragments of lobster shell were moving like ants. They were forming runes which joined up – for a moment – into a word. A question.

Mousesack waited without taking his eyes off him. Geralt, almost imperceptibly, nodded. The druid lowered his eyelids and, with a stony face, swiped the crumbs off the table.

'Honourable gentlemen!' called the herald. 'Pavetta of Cintra!'

The guests grew silent, turning to the stairs.

Preceded by the castellan and a fair-haired page in a scarlet doublet, the princess descended slowly, her head lowered. The colour of her hair was identical to her mother's – ash-grey but she wore it braided into two thick plaits which reached below her waist. Pavetta was adorned only with a tiara ornamented with a delicately worked jewel and a belt of tiny golden links which girded her long silvery-blue dress at the hips.

Escorted by the page, herald, castellan and Vissegerd, the princess occupied the empty chair between Drogodar and Eist Tuirseach. The knightly islander immediately filled her goblet and entertained her with conversation. Geralt didn't notice her answer with more than a word. Her eyes were permanently lowered, hidden behind her long lashes even during the noisy toasts raised to her around the table. There was no doubt her beauty had impressed the guests – Crach an Craite stopped shouting and stared at Pavetta in silence, even forgetting his tankard of beer.

Windhalm of Attre was also devouring the princess with his eyes, flushing shades of red as though only a few grains in the hourglass separated them from their wedding night. Coodcoodak and the brothers from Strept were studying the girl's petite face, too, with suspicious concentration.

'Aha,' said Calanthe quietly, clearly pleased. 'And what do you say, Geralt? The girl has taken after her mother. It's even a shame to waste her on that red-haired lout, Crach. The only hope is that the pup might grow into someone with Eist Tuirseach's class. It's the same blood, after all. Are you listening, Geralt? Cintra has to form an alliance with Skellige because the interest of the state demands it. My daughter has to marry the right person. Those are the results you must ensure me.'

'I have to ensure that? Isn't your will alone sufficient for it to happen?'

'Events might take such a turn that it won't be sufficient.'

'What can be stronger than your will?'

'Destiny.'

'Aha. So I, a poor witcher, am to face down a destiny which is stronger than the royal will. A witcher fighting destiny! What irony!'

'Yes, Geralt? What irony?'

'Never mind. Your Majesty, it seems the service you demand borders on the impossible.'

'If it bordered on the possible,' Calanthe drawled, 'I would manage it myself. I wouldn't need the famous Geralt of Rivia. Stop being so clever. Everything can be dealt with – it's only a question of price. Bloody hell, there must be a figure on your witchers' pricelist for work that borders on the impossible. I can guess one, and it isn't low. You ensure me my outcome and I will give you what you ask.'

'What did you say?'

'I'll give you whatever you ask for. And I don't like being told to repeat myself. I wonder, witcher, do you always try to dissuade your employers as strongly as you are me? Time is slipping away. Answer, yes or no?'

'Yes.'

'That's better. That's better, Geralt. Your answers are much closer to the ideal. They're becoming more like those I expect when I ask a question. So. Discreetly stretch your left hand out and feel behind my throne.'

Geralt slipped his hand under the yellow-blue drapery. Almost immediately he felt a sword secured to the leather-upholstered backrest. A sword well-known to him.

'Your Majesty,' he said quietly, 'not to repeat what I said earlier about killing people, you do realise that a sword alone will not defeat destiny?'

'I do,' Calanthe turned her head away. 'A witcher is also necessary. As you see, I took care of that.'

'Your Maje—'

'Not another word, Geralt. We've been conspiring for too long. They're looking at us, and Eist is getting angry. Talk to the castellan. Have something to eat. Drink, but not too much. I want you to have a steady hand.'

He obeyed. The queen joined a conversation between Eist, Vissegerd and Mousesack, with Pavetta's silent and dreamy participation. Drogodar had put away his lute and was making up for his lost eating time. Haxo wasn't talkative. The voivode with the hard-to-remember name, who must have heard something about the affairs and problems of Fourhorn, politely asked whether the mares were foaling well. Geralt answered yes, much better than the stallions. He wasn't sure if the joke had been well taken, but the voivode didn't ask any more questions.

Mousesack's eyes constantly sought the witcher's, but the crumbs on the table didn't move again.

Crach an Craite was becoming more and more friendly with the two brothers from Strept. The third, the youngest brother, was paralytic, having tried to match the drinking speed imposed by Draig Bon-Dhu. The skald had emerged from it unscathed.

The younger and less important lords gathered at the end of the table, tipsy, started singing a well-known song – out of tune –

133

about a little goat with horns and a vengeful old woman with no sense of humour.

A curly-haired servant and a captain of the guards wearing the gold and blue of Cintra ran up to Vissegerd. The marshal, frowning, listened to their report, rose, and leaned down from behind the throne to murmur something to the queen. Calanthe glanced at Geralt and answered with a single word. Vissegerd leant over even further and whispered something more; the queen looked at him sharply and, without a word, slapped her armrest with an open palm. The marshal bowed and passed the command to the captain of the guards. Geralt didn't hear it but he did notice that Mousesack wriggled uneasily and glanced at Pavetta – the princess was sitting motionless, her head lowered.

Heavy footsteps, each accompanied by the clang of metal striking the floor, could be heard over the hum at the table. Everyone raised their heads and turned.

The approaching figure was clad in armour of iron sheets and leather treated with wax. His convex, angular, black and blue breast-plate overlapped a segmented apron and short thigh pads. The armour-plated brassards bristled with sharp, steel spikes and the visor, with its densely grated screen extending out in the shape of a dog's muzzle, was covered with spikes like a conker casing.

Clattering and grinding, the strange guest approached the table and stood motionless in front of the throne.

'Noble queen, honourable gentlemen,' said the newcomer, bowing stiffly. 'Please forgive me for disrupting your ceremonious feast. I am Urcheon of Erlenwald.'

'Greetings, Urcheon of Erlenwald,' said Calanthe slowly. 'Please take your place at the table. In Cintra we welcome every guest.'

'Thank you, your Majesty,' Urcheon of Erlenwald bowed once again and touched his chest with a fist clad in an iron gauntlet. 'But I haven't come to Cintra as a guest but on a matter of great importance and urgency. If your Majesty permits I will present my case immediately, without wasting your time.'

'Urcheon of Erlenwald,' said the queen sharply, 'a praiseworthy concern about our time does not justify lack of respect. And such is your speaking to us from behind an iron trellis. Remove your helmet, and we'll endure the time wasted while you do.'

'My face, your Majesty, must remain hidden for the time being. With your permission.'

An angry ripple, punctuated here and there with the odd curse, ran through the gathered crowd. Mousesack, lowering his head, moved his lips silently. The witcher felt the spell electrify the air for a second, felt it stir his medallion. Calanthe was looking at Urcheon, narrowing her eyes and drumming her fingers on her armrest.

'Granted,' she said finally. 'I choose to believe your motive is sufficiently important. So – what brings you here, Urcheon-without-a-face?'

'Thank you,' said the newcomer. 'But I'm unable to suffer the accusation of lacking respect, so I explain that it is a matter of a knight's vows. I am not allowed to reveal my face before midnight strikes.'

Calanthe, raising her hand perfunctorily, accepted his explanation. Urcheon advanced, his spiked armour clanging.

'Fifteen years ago,' he announced loudly, 'your husband King Roegner lost his way while hunting in Erlenwald. Wandering around the pathless tracts, he fell from his horse into a ravine and sprained his leg. He lay at the bottom of the gully and called for help but the only answer he got was the hiss of vipers and the howling of approaching werewolves. He would have died without the help he received.'

'I know what happened,' the queen affirmed. 'If you know it, too, then I guess you are the one who helped him.'

'Yes. It is only because of me he returned to you in one piece, and well.'

'I am grateful to you then, Urcheon of Erlenwald. That gratitude is none the lesser for the fact that Roegner, gentleman of my heart and bed, has left this world. Tell me, if the implication that your aid was not disinterested does not offend another of your knightly vows, how I can express my gratitude.'

'You well know my aid was not disinterested. You know, too,

that I have come to collect the promised reward for saving the king's life.'

'Oh yes?' Calanthe smiled but green sparks lit up her eyes. 'So you found a man at the bottom of a ravine, defenceless, wounded, at the mercy of vipers and monsters. And only when he promised you a reward did you help? And if he didn't want to or couldn't promise you something, you'd have left him there, and, to this day, I wouldn't know where his bones lay? How noble. No doubt your actions were guided by a particularly chivalrous vow at the time.'

The murmur around the hall grew louder.

'And today you come for your reward, Urcheon?' continued the queen, smiling even more ominously. 'After fifteen years? No doubt you are counting the interest accrued over this period? This isn't the dwarves' bank, Urcheon. You say Roegner promised you a reward? Ah, well, it will be difficult to get him to pay you. It would be simpler to send you to him, into the other world, to reach an agreement over who owes what. I loved my husband too dearly, Urcheon, to forget that I could have lost him then, fifteen years ago, if he hadn't chosen to bargain with you. The thought of it arouses rather-ill feeling towards you. Masked newcomer, do you know that here in Cintra, in my castle and in my power, you are just as helpless and close to death as Roegner was then, at the bottom of the ravine? What will you propose, what price, what reward will you offer, if I promise you will leave here alive?'

The medallion on Geralt's neck twitched. The witcher caught Mousesack's clearly uneasy gaze. He shook his head a little and raised his eyebrows questioningly. The druid also shook his head and, with a barely perceptible move of his curly beard, indicated Urcheon. Geralt wasn't sure.

'Your words, your Majesty,' called Urcheon, 'are calculated to frighten me, to kindle the anger of the honourable gentlemen gathered here, and the contempt of your pretty daughter, Pavetta. But above all, your words are untrue. And you know it!'

'You accuse me of lying like a dog.' An ugly grimace crept across Calanthe's lips.

'You know very well, your Majesty,' the newcomer continued adamantly, 'what happened then in Erlenwald. You know Roegner, once saved, vowed of his own will to give me whatever I asked for. I call upon every one to witness my words! When the king, rescued from his misadventure, reached his retinue, he asked me what I demanded and I answered. I asked him to promise me whatever he had left at home without knowing or expecting it. The king swore it would be so, and on his return to the castle he found you, Calanthe, in labour. Yes, your Majesty, I waited for fifteen years and the interest on my reward has grown. Today I look at the beautiful Pavetta and see that the wait has been worth it! Gentlemen and knights! Some of you have come to Cintra to ask for the princess's hand. You have come in vain. From the day of her birth, by the power of the royal oath, the beautiful Pavetta has belonged to me!'

An uproar burst forth among the guests. Some shouted, someone swore, someone else thumped his fist on the table and knocked the dishes over. Wieldhill of Strept pulled a knife out of the roast lamb and waved it about. Crach an Craite, bent over, was clearly trying to break a plank from the table trestle.

'That's unheard of!' yelled Vissegerd. 'What proof do you have? Proof?'

'The queen's face,' exclaimed Urcheon, extending his hand, 'is the best proof!'

Pavetta sat motionless, not raising her head. The air was growing thick with something very strange. The witcher's medallion was tearing at its chain under the tunic. He saw the queen summon a page and whisper a short command. Geralt couldn't hear it, but he was puzzled by the surprise on the boy's face and the fact that the command had to be repeated. The page ran towards the exit.

The uproar at the table continued as Eist Tuirseach turned to the queen.

'Calanthe,' he said calmly, 'is what he says true?'

'And if it is,' the queen muttered through her teeth, biting her lips and picking at the green sash on her shoulder, 'so what?'

'If what he says is true,' Eist frowned, 'then the promise will have to be kept.'

'Is that so?'

'Or am I to understand,' the islander asked grimly, 'that you treat all promises this lightly, including those which have etched themselves so deeply in my memory?'

Geralt, who had never expected to see Calanthe blush deeply, with tears in her eyes and trembling lips, was surprised.

'Eist,' whispered the queen, 'this is different—'

'Is it, really?'

'Oh, you son-of-a-bitch!' Crach an Craite yelled unexpectedly, jumping up. 'The last fool who said I'd acted in vain was pinched apart by crabs at the bottom of Allenker bay! I didn't sail here from Skellig to return empty-handed! A suitor has turned up, some son of a trollop! Someone bring me a sword and give that idiot some iron! We'll soon see who—'

'Maybe you could just shut up, Crach?' Eist snapped scathingly, resting both fists on the table. 'Draig Bon-Dhu! I render you responsible for his future behaviour!'

'And are you going to silence me, too, Tuirseach?' shouted Rainfarn of Attre, standing up. 'Who is going to stop me from washing the insult thrown at my prince away with blood? And his son, Windhalm, the only man worthy of Pavetta's hand and bed! Bring the swords! I'll show that Urcheon, or whatever he's called, how we of Attre take revenge for such abuse! I wonder whether anybody or anything can hold me back?'

'Yes. Regard for good manners,' said Eist Tuirseach calmly. 'It is not proper to start a fight here or challenge anyone without permission from the lady of the house. What is this? Is the throne room of Cintra an inn where you can punch each other's heads and stab each other with knives as the fancy takes you?'

Everybody started to shout again, to curse and swear and wave their arms about. But the uproar suddenly stopped, as if cut by a knife, at the short, furious roar of an enraged bison.

'Yes,' said Coodcoodak, clearing his throat and rising from his chair. 'Eist has it wrong. This doesn't even look like an inn anymore. It's more like a zoo, so a bison should be at home here. Honourable Calanthe, allow me to offer my opinion.'

'A great many people, I see,' said Calanthe in a drawling voice, 'have an opinion on this problem and are offering it even without my permission. Strange that you aren't interested in mine? And in my opinion, this bloody castle will sooner collapse on my head than I give my Pavetta to this crank. I haven't the least intention—'

'Roegner's oath—' Urcheon began, but the queen silenced him, banging her golden goblet on the table.

'Roegner's oath means about as much to me as last year's snows! And as for you, Urcheon, I haven't decided whether to allow Crach or Rainfarn to meet you outside, or to simply hang you. You're greatly influencing my decision with your interruption!'

Geralt, still disturbed by the way his medallion was quivering, looked around the hall. Suddenly he saw Pavetta's eyes, emerald green like her mother's. The princess was no longer hiding them beneath her long lashes – she swept them from Mousesack to the witcher, ignoring the others. Mousesack, bent over, was wriggling and muttering something.

Coodcoodak, still standing, cleared his throat meaningfully.

'Speak,' the queen nodded. 'But be brief.'

'As you command, your Majesty. Noble Calanthe and you, knights! Indeed, Urcheon of Erlenwald made a strange request of King Roegner, a strange reward to demand when the king offered him his wish. But let us not pretend we've never heard of such requests, of the Law of Surprise, as old as humanity itself. Of the price a man who saves another can demand, of the granting of a seemingly impossible wish. "You will give me the first thing that comes to greet you." It might be a dog, you'll say, a halberdier at the gate, even a mother-in-law impatient to holler at her son-in-law when he returns home. Or: "You'll give me what you find at home yet don't expect." After a long journey, honourable gentlemen, and an unexpected return, this could be a lover in the wife's bed. But sometimes it's a child. A child marked out by destiny.'

139

'Briefly, Coodcoodak,' Calanthe frowned.

'As you command. Sirs! Have you not heard of children marked out by destiny? Was not the legendary hero, Zatret Voruta, given to the dwarves as a child because he was the first person his father met on his return? And Mad Deï, who demanded a traveller give him what he left at home without knowing it? That surprise was the famous Supree, who later liberated Mad Deï from the curse which weighed him down. Remember Zivelena, who became the Queen of Metinna with the help of the gnome Rumplestelt, and in return promised him her first-born? Zivelena didn't keep her promise when Rumplestelt came for his reward and, by using spells, she forced him to run away. Not long after that, both she and the child died of the plague. You do not dice with Destiny with impunity!'

'Don't threaten me, Coodcoodak,' Calanthe grimaced. 'Midnight is close, the time for ghosts. Can you remember any more legends from your undoubtedly difficult childhood? If not, then sit down.'

'I ask your Grace,' the baron turned up his long whiskers, 'to allow me to remain standing. I'd like to remind everybody of another legend. It's an old, forgotten legend – we've all probably heard it in our difficult childhoods. In this legend, the kings kept their promises. And we, poor vassals, are only bound to kings by the royal word: treaties, alliances, our privileges and fiefs all rely on it. And now? Are we to doubt all this? Doubt the inviolability of the king's word? Wait until it is worth as much as yesteryear's snow? If this is how things are to be then a difficult old age awaits us after our difficult childhoods!'

'Whose side are you on, Coodcoodak?' hollered Rainfarn of Attre.

'Silence! Let him speak!'

'This cackler, full of hot air, insults her Majesty!'

'The Baron of Tigg is right!'

'Silence,' Calanthe said suddenly, getting up. 'Let him finish.'

'I thank you graciously,' bowed Coodcoodak. 'But I have just finished.'

Silence fell, strange after the commotion his words had caused.

Calanthe was still standing. Geralt didn't think anyone else had noticed her hand shake as she wiped her brow.

'My lords,' she said finally, 'you deserve an explanation. Yes, this . . . Urcheon . . . speaks the truth. Roegner did swear to give him that which he did not expect. It looks as if our lamented king was an oaf as far as a woman's affairs are concerned, and couldn't be trusted to count to nine. He confessed the truth on his death-bed, because he knew what I'd do to him if he'd admitted it earlier. He knew what a mother, whose child is disposed of so recklessly, is capable of.'

The knights and magnates remained silent. Urcheon stood motionless, like a spiked, iron statue.

'And Coodcoodak,' continued Calanthe, 'well, Coodcoodak has reminded me that I am not a mother but a queen. Very well then. As queen, I shall convene a council tomorrow. Cintra is not a tyranny. The council will decide whether a dead king's oath is to decide the fate of the successor to the throne. It will decide whether Pavetta and the throne of Cintra are to be given to a stranger, or to act according to the kingdom's interest.' Calanthe was silent for a moment, looking askance at Geralt. 'And as for the noble knights who have come to Cintra in the hope of the princess's hand . . . It only remains for me to express my deep regret at the cruel disrespect and dishonour they have experienced here, at the ridicule poured on them. I am not to blame.'

Amidst the hum of voices which rumbled through the guests, the witcher managed to pick out Eist Tuirseach's whisper.

'On all the gods of the sea,' sighed the islander. 'This isn't befitting. This is open incitement to bloodshed. Calanthe, you're simply setting them against each other—'

'Be quiet, Eist,' hissed the queen furiously, 'because I'll get angry.'

Mousesack's black eyes flashed as – with a glance – the druid indicated Rainfarn of Attre who, with a gloomy, grimacing face, was preparing to stand. Geralt reacted immediately, standing up first and banging the chair noisily.

'Maybe it will prove unnecessary to convene the council,' he said in ringing tones.

Everyone grew silent, watching him with astonishment. Geralt felt Pavetta's emerald eyes on him, he felt Urcheon's gaze fall on him from behind the lattice of his black visor, and he felt the Force surging like a flood-wave and solidifying in the air. He saw how, under the influence of this Force, the smoke from the torches and oil lamps was taking on fantastic forms. He knew that Mousesack saw it too. He also knew that nobody else saw it.

'I said,' he repeated calmly, 'that convening the council may not prove necessary. You understand what I have in mind, Urcheon of Erlenwald?'

The spiked knight took two grating steps forward.

'I do,' he said, his words hollow beneath his helmet. 'It would take a fool not to understand. I heard what the merciful and noble lady Calanthe said a moment ago. She has found an excellent way of getting rid of me. I accept your challenge, knight unknown to me!'

'I don't recall challenging you,' said Geralt. 'I don't intend to duel you, Urcheon of Erlenwald.'

'Geralt!' called Calanthe, twisting her lips and forgetting to call the witcher Ravix, 'don't overdo it! Don't put my patience to the test!'

'Or mine,' added Rainfarn ominously. Crach an Craite growled, and Eist Tuirseach meaningfully showed him a clenched fist. Crach growled even louder.

'Everyone heard,' spoke Geralt, 'Baron Tigg tell us about the famous heroes taken from their parents on the strength of the same oath that Urcheon received from King Roegner. But why should anyone want such an oath? You know the answer, Urcheon of Erlenwald. It creates a powerful, indissoluble tie of destiny between the person demanding the oath and its object, the child-surprise. Such a child, marked by blind fate, can be destined for extraordinary things. It can play an incredibly important role in the life of the person to whom fate has tied it. That is why, Urcheon, you demanded the prize you claim today. You don't want the throne of Cintra. You want the princess.'

'It is exactly as you say, knight unknown to me,' Urcheon laughed out loud. 'That is exactly what I claim! Give me the one who is my destiny!'

'That,' said Geralt, 'will have to be proved.'

'You dare doubt it? After the queen confirmed the truth of my words? After what you've just said?'

'Yes. Because you didn't tell us everything. Roegner knew the power of the Law of Surprise and the gravity of the oath he took. And he took it because he knew law and custom have a power which protects such oaths, ensuring they are only fulfilled when the force of destiny confirms them. I declare, Urcheon, that you have no right to the princess as yet. You will win her only when—'

'When what?'

'When the princess herself agrees to leave with you. This is what the Law of Surprise states. It is the child's, not the parent's, consent which confirms the oath, which proves that the child was born under the shadow of destiny. That's why you returned after fifteen years, Urcheon, and that's the condition King Roegner stipulated in his oath.'

'Who are you?'

'I am Geralt of Rivia.'

'Who are you, Geralt of Rivia, to claim to be an oracle in matters of laws and customs?'

'He knows this law better than anyone else,' Mousesack said in a hoarse voice, 'because it applied to him once. He was taken from his home because he was what his father hadn't expected to find on his return. Because he was destined for other things. And by the power of destiny he became what he is.'

'And what is he?'

'A witcher.'

In the silence that reigned the guardhouse bell struck, announcing midnight in a dull tone. Everyone shuddered and raised their heads. Mousesack watched Geralt with surprise. But it was Urcheon who flinched most noticeably and moved uneasily. His

143

hands, clad in their armour gauntlets, fell to his sides lifelessly, and the spiked helmet swayed unsteadily.

The strange, unknown Force suddenly grew thicker, filling the hall like a grey mist.

'It's true,' said Calanthe. 'Geralt, present here, is a witcher. His trade is worthy of respect and esteem. He has sacrificed himself to protect us from monsters and nightmares born in the night, those sent by powers ominous and harmful to man. He kills the horrors and monsters that await us in the forests and ravines. And those which have the audacity to enter our dwellings.' Urcheon was silent. 'And so,' continued the queen, raising her ringed hand, 'let the law be fulfilled, let the oath which you, Urcheon of Erlenwald, insist should be satisfied, be satisfied. Midnight has struck. Your vow no longer binds you. Lift your visor. Before my daughter expresses her will, before she decides her destiny, let her see your face. We all wish to see your face.'

Urcheon of Erlenwald slowly raised his armoured hand, pulled at the helmet's fastenings, grabbed it by the iron horn and threw it against the floor with a crash. Someone shouted, someone swore, someone sucked in their breath with a whistle. On the queen's face appeared a wicked, very wicked, smile. A cruel smile of triumph.

Above the wide, semi-circular breastplate two bulbous, black, button eyes looked out. Eyes set to either side of a blunt, elongated muzzle covered in reddish bristles and full of sharp white fangs. Urcheon's head and neck bristled with a brush of short, grey, twitching prickles.

'This is how I look,' spoke the creature, 'which you well knew, Calanthe. Roegner, in telling you of his oath, wouldn't have omitted describing me. Urcheon of Erlenwald to whom – despite my appearance – Roegner swore his oath. You prepared well for my arrival, queen. Your own vassals have pointed out your haughty and contemptuous refusal to keep Roegner's word. When your attempt to set the other suitors on me didn't succeed, you still had a killer witcher in reserve, ready at your right-hand. And finally, common, low deceit. You wanted to humiliate me, Calanthe. Know that it is yourself you have humiliated.'

'Enough,' Calanthe stood up and rested her clenched fist on her hip. 'Let's put an end to this. Pavetta! You see who, or rather what, is standing in front of you, claiming you for himself. In accordance with the Law of Surprise and eternal custom, the decision is yours. Answer. One word from you is enough. Yes, and you become the property, the conquest, of this monster. No, and you will never have to see him again.'

The Force pulsating in the hall was squeezing Geralt's temples like an iron vice, buzzing in his ears, making the hair on his neck stand on end. The witcher looked at Mousesack's whitening knuckles, clenched at the edge of the table. At the trickle of sweat running down the queen's cheek. At the breadcrumbs on the table, moving like insects, forming runes, dispersing and again gathering into one word: CAREFUL!

'Pavetta!' Calanthe repeated. 'Answer. Do you choose to leave with this creature?'

Pavetta raised her head. 'Yes.'

The Force filling the hall echoed her, rumbling hollowly in the arches of the vault. No one, absolutely no one, made the slightest sound.

Calanthe very slowly, collapsed into her throne. Her face was completely expressionless.

'Everyone heard,' Urcheon's calm voice resounded in the silence. 'You, too, Calanthe. As did you, witcher, cunning, hired thug. My rights have been established. Truth and destiny have triumphed over lies and deviousness. What do you have left, noble queen, disguised witcher? Cold steel?' No one answered. 'I'd like to leave with Pavetta immediately,' continued Urcheon, his bristles stirring as he snapped his jaw shut, 'but I won't deny myself one small pleasure. It is you, Calanthe, who will lead your daughter here to me and place her white hand in mine.'

Calanthe slowly turned her head in the witcher's direction. Her eyes expressed a command. Geralt didn't move, sensing that the Force condensing in the air was concentrated on him. Only on

145

him. Now he understood. The queen's eyes narrowed, her lips quivered . . .

'What?! What's this?' yelled Crach an Craite, jumping up. 'Her white hand? In his? The princess with this bristly stinker? With this . . . pig's snout?'

'And I wanted to fight him like a knight!' Rainfarn chimed in. 'This horror, this beast! Loose the dogs on him! The dogs!'

'Guards!' cried Calanthe.

Everything happened at once. Crach an Craite seized a knife from the table and knocked his chair over with a crash. Obeying Eist's command Draig Bon-Dhu, without a thought, whacked the back of his head with his bagpipes, as hard as he could. Crach dropped onto the table between a sturgeon in grey sauce and the few remaining arched ribs of a roast boar. Rainfarn leapt towards Urcheon, flashing a dagger drawn from his sleeve. Coodcoodak, springing up, kicked a stool under his feet which Rainfarn jumped agilely, but a moment's delay was enough – Urcheon deceived him with a short feint and forced him to his knees with a mighty blow from his armoured fist. Coodcoodak fell to snatch the dagger from Rainfarn but was stopped by Prince Windhalm, who clung to his thigh like a bloodhound.

Guards, armed with guisarmes and lances, ran in from the entrance. Calanthe, upright and threatening, with an authoritative, abrupt gesture indicated Urcheon to them. Pavetta started to shout, Eist Tuirseach to curse. Everyone jumped up, not quite knowing what to do.

'Kill him!' shouted the queen.

Urcheon, huffing angrily and baring his fangs, turned to face the attacking guards. He was unarmed but clad in spiked steel, from which the points of the guisarmes bounced with a clang. But the blows knocked him back, straight onto Rainfarn, who was just getting up and immobilised him by grabbing his legs. Urcheon let out a roar and, with his iron elbow-guards, deflected the blades aimed at his head. Rainfarn jabbed him with his dagger but the blade slid off the breast-plate. The guards, crossing their spear-shafts, pinned him to the sculpted chimney. Rainfarn, who was hanging onto his belt, found a chink in the armour and dug the dagger into it. Urcheon curled up.

'Dunyyyyyyy!' Pavetta shrilled as she jumped onto the chair.

The witcher, sword in hand, sprang onto the table and ran towards the fighting men, knocking plates, dishes and goblets all over the place. He knew there wasn't much time. Pavetta's cries were sounding more and more unnatural. Rainfarn was raising his dagger to stab again.

Geralt cut, springing from the table into a crouch. Rainfarn wailed and staggered to the wall. The witcher spun and, with the centre of his blade, slashed a guard who was trying to dig the sharp tongue of his lance between Urcheon's apron and breast-plate. The guard tumbled to the ground, losing his helmet. More guards came running in from the entrance.

'This is not befitting!' roared Eist Tuirseach, grabbing a chair. He shattered the unwieldly piece of furniture against the floor with great force and, with what remained in his hand, threw himself at those advancing on Urcheon.

Urcheon, caught by two guisarme hooks at the same time, collapsed with a clang, cried out and huffed as he was dragged along the floor. A third guard raised his lance to stab down and Geralt cut him in the temple with the point of his sword. Those dragging Urcheon stepped back quickly, throwing down their guisarmes, while those approaching from the entrance backed away from the remnants of chair brandished by Eist like the magic sword Balmur in the hand of the legendary Zatreta Voruta.

Pavetta's cries reached a peak and suddenly broke off. Geralt, sensing what was about to happen, fell to the floor watching for a greenish flash. He felt an excruciating pain in his ears, heard a terrible crash and a horrifying wail ripped from numerous throats. And then the princess's even, monotonous and vibrating cry.

The table, scattering dishes and food all around, was rising and spinning; heavy chairs were flying around the hall and shattering against the walls; tapestries and hangings were flapping, raising clouds of dust. Cries and the dry crack of guisarme shafts snapping like sticks came from the entrance.

The throne, with Calanthe sitting on it, sprang up and flew across the hall like an arrow, smashing into the wall with a crash and falling apart. The queen slid to the floor like a ragged puppet. Eist Tuirseach, barely on his feet, threw himself towards her, took her in his arms and sheltered her from the hail pelting against the walls and floor with his body.

Geralt, grasping the medallion in his hand, slithered as quickly as he could towards Mousesack, miraculously still on his knees, who was lifting a short hawthorn wand with a rat's skull affixed to the tip. On the wall behind the druid a tapestry depicting the siege and fire of Fortress Ortagar was burning with very real flames.

Pavetta wailed. Turning round and round, she lashed everything and everybody with her cries as if with a whip. Anyone who tried to stand tumbled to the ground or was flattened against the wall. An enormous silver sauce-boat in the shape of a many-oared vessel with an upturned bow came whistling through the air in front of Geralt's eyes and knocked down the voivode with the hard-to-remember name just as he was trying to dodge it. Plaster rained down silently as the table rotated beneath the ceiling, with Crach an Craite flattened on it and throwing down vile curses.

Geralt crawled to Mousesack and they hid behind the heap formed by Fodcat of Strept, a barrel of beer, Drogodar, a chair and Drogodar's lute.

'It's pure, primordial Force!' the druid yelled over the racket and clatter. 'She's got no control over it!'

'I know!' Geralt yelled back. A roast pheasant with a few striped feathers still stuck in its rump, fell from nowhere and thumped him in the back.

'She has to be restrained! The walls are starting to crack!'

'I can see!'

'Ready?'

'Yes!'

'One! Two! Now!'

They both hit her simultaneously, Geralt with the Sign of Aard and Mousesack with a terrible, three-staged curse powerful enough to make the floor melt. The chair on which the princess was standing disintegrated into splinters. Pavetta barely noticed – she hung in the air within a transparent green sphere. Without ceasing to shout, she turned her head towards them and her petite face shrunk into a sinister grimace.

'By all the demons—!' roared Mousesack.

'Careful!' shouted the witcher, curling up. 'Block her, Mousesack! Block her or it's the end of us!'

The table thudded heavily to the ground, shattering its trestle and everything beneath it. Crach an Craite, who was lying on the table, was thrown into the air. A heavy rain of plates and remnants of food fell; crystal carafes exploded as they hit the ground. The cornice broke away from the wall, rumbling like thunder, making the floors of the castle quake.

'Everything's letting go!' Mousesack shouted, aiming his wand at the princess. 'The whole Force is going to fall on us!'

Geralt, with a blow of his sword, deflected a huge double-pronged fork which was flying straight at the druid.

'Block it, Mousesack!'

Emerald eyes sent two flashes of green lightning at them. They coiled into blinding, whirling funnels from the centres of which the Force – like a battering ram which exploded the skull, put out the eyes and paralysed the breath – descended on them. Together with the Force, glass, majolica, platters, candlesticks, bones, nibbled loaves of bread, planks, slats and smouldering firewood from the hearth poured over them. Crying wildly like a great capercaillie, Castellan Haxo flew over their heads. The enormous head of a boiled carp splattered against Geralt's chest, on the bear passant sable and damsel of Fourhorn.

Through Mousesack's wall-shattering curses, through his own shouting and the wailing of the wounded, the din, clatter and racket, through Pavetta's wailing, the witcher suddenly heard the most terrible sound.

Coodcoodak, on his knees, was strangling Draig Bon-Dhu's bagpipes with his hands, while, with his head thrown back, he shouted over the monstrous sounds emerging from the bag, wailed and roared, cackled and croaked, bawled and squawked in a cacophony of sounds made by all known, unknown, domestic, wild and mythical animals.

Pavetta fell silent, horrified, and looked at the baron with her mouth agape. The Force eased off abruptly.

'Now!' yelled Mousesack, waving his wand. 'Now, witcher!'

They hit her. The greenish sphere surrounding the princess burst under their blow like a soap bubble and the vacuum instantly sucked in the Force raging through the room. Pavetta flopped heavily to the ground and started to weep.

After the pandemonium a moment's silence rang in their ears; then, with difficulty, laboriously, voices started to break through the rubble and destruction, through the broken furniture and the inert bodies.

'*Cuach op arse, ghoul y badraigh mal an cuach,*' spat Crach an Craite, spraying blood from his bitten lip.

'Control yourself, Crach,' said Mousesack with effort, shaking buckwheat from his front. 'There are women present.'

'Calanthe. My beloved. My Calanthe!' Eist Tuirseach said in the pauses between kisses.

The queen opened her eyes but didn't try to free herself from his embrace.

'Eist. People are watching,' she said.

'Let them watch.'

'Would somebody care to explain what that was?' asked Marshal Vissegerd, crawling from beneath a fallen tapestry.

'No,' said the witcher.

'A doctor!' Windhalm of Attre, leaning over Rainfarn, shouted shrilly.

'Water!' Wieldhill, one of the brothers from Strept, called, stifling the smouldering tapestry with his jacket. 'Water, quickly!'

'And beer!' Coodcoodak croaked.

A few knights, still able to stand, were trying to lift Pavetta, but she pushed their hands aside, got up on her own and, unsteadily, walked towards the hearth. There, with his back resting against the wall, sat Urcheon, awkwardly trying to remove his blood-smeared armour.

'The youth of today,' snorted Mousesack, looking in their direction. 'They start early! They've only got one thing on their minds.'

'What's that?'

'Didn't you know, witcher, that a virgin, that is one who's untouched, wouldn't be able to use the Force?'

'To hell with her virginity,' muttered Geralt. 'Where did she get such a gift anyway? Neither Calanthe nor Roegner—'

'She inherited it, missing a generation, and no mistake,' said the druid. 'Her grandmother, Adalia, could raise a drawbridge with a twitch of her eyebrows. Hey, Geralt, look at that! She still hasn't had enough!'

Calanthe, supported by Eist Tuirseach's arm, indicated the wounded Urcheon to the guards. Geralt and Mousesack approached quickly but unnecessarily. The guards recoiled from the semi-reclining figure and, whispering and muttering, backed away.

Urcheon's monstrous snout softened, blurred and was beginning to lose its contours. The spikes and bristles rippled and became black, shiny, wavy hair and a beard which bordered a pale, angular, masculine face, dominated by a prominent nose.

'What . . .' stammered Eist Tuirseach. 'Who's that? Urcheon?'

'Duny,' said Pavetta softly.

Calanthe turned away with pursed lips.

'Cursed?' murmured Eist. 'But how—'

'Midnight has struck,' said the witcher. 'Just this minute. The bell we heard before was early. The bell-ringer's mistake. Am I right, Calanthe?'

'Right, right,' groaned the man called Duny, answering instead of the queen, who had no intention of replying anyway. 'But maybe instead of standing there talking, someone could help me with this armour and call a doctor. That madman Rainfarn stabbed me under the ribs.'

'What do we need a doctor for?' said Mousesack, taking out his wand.

151

'Enough.' Calanthe straightened and raised her head proudly. 'Enough of this. When all this is over, I want to see you in my chamber. All of you, as you stand. Eist, Pavetta, Mousesack, Geralt and you . . . Duny. Mousesack?'

'Yes, your Majesty.'

'That wand of yours . . . I've bruised my backbone. And thereabouts.'

'At your command, your Majesty.'

III

'. . . a curse,' continued Duny, rubbing his temple. 'Since birth. I never found a reason for it, or who did it to me. From midnight to dawn, an ordinary man, from dawn . . . you saw what. Akerspaark, my father, wanted to hide it. People are superstitious in Maecht; spells and curses in the royal family could prove fatal for the dynasty. One of my father's knights took me away from court and brought me up. The two of us wandered around the world – the knight errant and his squire, and later, when he died, I journeyed alone. I can't remember who told me that a child-surprise could free me from the curse. Not long after that I met Roegner. The rest you know.'

'The rest we know, or can guess,' nodded Calanthe. 'Especially that you didn't wait the fifteen years agreed upon with Roegner but turned my daughter's head before that. Pavetta! Since when?'

The princess lowered her head and raised a finger.

'There. You little sorceress. Right under my nose! Let me just find out who let him into the castle at night! Let me at the ladies-in-waiting you went gathering primroses with. Primroses, dammit! Well, what am I to do with you now?'

'Calanthe—' began Eist.

'Hold on, Tuirseach. I haven't finished yet. Duny, the matter's become very complicated. You've been with Pavetta for a year now, and what? And nothing. So you negotiated the oath from the wrong father. Destiny has made a fool of you. What irony, as Geralt of Rivia, present here, is wont to say.'

'To hell with destiny, oaths and irony,' grimaced Duny. 'I love Pavetta and she loves me, that's all that counts. You can't stand in the way of our happiness.'

'I can, Duny, I can, and how.' Calanthe smiled one of her unfailing smiles. 'You're lucky I don't want to. I have a certain debt towards you, Duny. I'd made up my mind . . . I ought to ask your forgiveness, but I hate doing that. So I'm giving you Pavetta and we'll be quits. Pavetta? You haven't changed your mind, have you?'

The princess shook her head eagerly.

'Thank you, your Majesty. Thank you,' smiled Duny. 'You're a wise and generous queen.'

'Of course I am. And beautiful.'

'And beautiful.'

'You can both stay in Cintra if you wish. The people here are less superstitious than the inhabitants of Maecht and adjust to things quicker. Besides, even as Urcheon you were quite pleasant. But you can't count on having the throne just yet. I intend to reign a little longer beside the new king of Cintra. The noble Eist Tuirseach of Skellige has made me a very interesting proposition.'

'Calanthe—'

'Yes, Eist, I accept. I've never before listened to a confession of love while lying on the floor amidst fragments of my own throne but . . . How did you put it, Duny? This is all that counts and I don't advise anyone to stand in the way of my happiness. And you, what are you staring at? I'm not as old as you think.'

'Today's youth,' muttered Mousesack. 'The apple doesn't fall far—'

'What are you muttering, sorcerer?'

'Nothing, ma'am.'

'Good. While we're at it, I've got a proposition for you, Mouse-sack. Pavetta's going to need a teacher. She ought to learn how to use her gift. I like this castle, and I'd prefer it to remain standing.

It might fall apart at my talented daughter's next attack of hysteria. How about it, Druid?'

'I'm honoured.'

'I think,' the queen turned her head towards the window. 'It's dawn. Time to—'

She suddenly turned to where Pavetta and Duny were whispering to each other, holding hands, their foreheads all but touching.

'Duny!'

'Yes, your Majesty?'

'Do you hear? It's dawn! It's already light. And you . . .'

Geralt glanced at Mousesack and both started laughing.

'And why are you so happy, sorcerers? Can't you see—?'

'We can, we can,' Geralt assured her.

'We were waiting until you saw for yourself,' snorted Mousesack. 'I was wondering when you'd catch on.'

'To what?'

'That you've lifted the curse. It's you who's lifted it,' said the witcher. 'The moment you said "I'm giving you Pavetta" destiny was fulfilled.'

'Exactly,' confirmed the druid.

'Oh gods,' said Duny slowly. 'So, finally. Damn, I thought I'd be happier, that some sort of trumpets would play or . . . Force of habit. Your Majesty! Thank you. Pavetta, do you hear?'

'Mhm,' said the princess without raising her eyes.

'And so,' sighed Calanthe, looking at Geralt with tired eyes, 'all's well that ends well. Don't you agree, witcher? The curse has been lifted, two weddings are on their way, it'll take about a month to repair the throne-room, there are four dead, countless wounded and Rainfarn of Attre is half-dead. Let's celebrate. Do you know, witcher, that there was a moment when I wanted to have you—'

'I know.'

'But now I have to do you justice. I demanded a result and got one. Cintra is allied to Skellige. My daughter's marrying the right man. For a moment I thought all this would have been fulfilled according to destiny anyway, even if I hadn't had you brought in for the feast and sat you next to me. But I was wrong. Rainfarn's dagger could have changed destiny. And Rainfarn was stopped by a sword held by a witcher. You've done an honest job, Geralt. Now it's a question of price. Tell me what you want.'

'Hold on,' said Duny, fingering his bandaged side. 'A question of price, you say. It is I who am in debt, it's up to me—'

'Don't interrupt.' Calanthe narrowed her eyes. 'Your mother-in-law hates being interrupted. Remember that. And you should know that you're not in any debt. It so happens that you were the subject of my agreement with Geralt. I said we're quits and I don't see the sense of my having to endlessly apologise to you for it. But the agreement still binds me. Well, Geralt. Your price.'

'Very well,' said the witcher. 'I ask for your green sash, Calanthe. May it always remind me of the colour of the eyes of the most beautiful queen I have ever known.'

Calanthe laughed, and unfastened her emerald necklace.

'This trinket,' she said, 'has stones of the right hue. Keep it, and the memory.'

'May I speak?' asked Duny modestly.

'But of course, Son-in-law, please do, please do.'

'I still say I am in your debt, witcher. It is my life that Rainfarn's dagger endangered. I would have been beaten to death by the guards without you. If there's talk of a price then I should be the one to pay. I assure you I can afford it. What do you ask, Geralt?'

'Duny,' said Geralt slowly, 'a witcher who is asked such a question has to ask to have it repeated.'

'I repeat, therefore. Because, you see, I am in your debt for still another reason. When I found out who you were, there in the hall, I hated you and thought very badly of you. I took you for a blind, bloodthirsty tool, for someone who kills coldly and without question, who wipes his blade clean of blood and counts the cash. But I've become convinced that the witcher's profession is worthy of respect. You protect us not only from the evil lurking in the darkness, but also from that which lies within ourselves. It's a shame there are so few of you.'

Calanthe smiled.

For the first time that night Geralt was inclined to believe it was genuine.

'My son-in-law has spoken well. I have to add two words to what he said. Precisely two. Forgive, Geralt.'

'And I,' said Duny, 'ask again. What do you ask for?'

'Duny,' said Geralt seriously, 'Calanthe, Pavetta. And you, righteous knight Tuirseach, future king of Cintra. In order to become a witcher, you have to be born in the shadow of destiny, and very few are born like that. That's why there are so few of us. We're growing old, dying, without anyone to pass our knowledge, our gifts, on to. We lack successors. And this world is full of Evil which waits for the day none of us are left.'

'Geralt,' whispered Calanthe.

'Yes, you're not wrong, queen. Duny! You will give me that which you already have but do not know. I'll return to Cintra in six years to see if destiny has been kind to me.'

'Pavetta,' Duny opened his eyes wide. 'Surely you're not—'

'Pavetta!' exclaimed Calanthe. 'Are you . . . are you—?'

The princess lowered her eyes and blushed. Then replied.

THE VOICE OF REASON 5

'Geralt! Hey! Are you there?'

He raised his head from the coarse, yellowed pages of *The History of the World* by Roderick de Novembre, an interesting if controversial work which he had been studying since the previous day.

'Yes, I am. What's happened, Nenneke? Do you need me?'

'You've got a guest.'

'Again? Who's it this time? Duke Hereward himself?'

'No. It's Dandilion this time, your fellow. That idler, parasite and good-for-nothing, that priest of art, the bright-shining star of the ballad and love poem. As usual he's radiant with fame, puffed up like a pig's bladder and stinking of beer. Do you want to see him?'

'Of course. He's my friend, after all.'

Nenneke, peeved, shrugged her shoulders. 'I can't understand that friendship. He's your absolute opposite.'

'Opposites attract.'

'Obviously. There, he's coming,' she indicated with her head. 'Your famous poet.'

'He really is a famous poet, Nenneke. Surely you're not going to claim you've never heard his ballads.'

'I've heard them.' The priestess winced. 'Yes, indeed. Well, I don't know much about it, but maybe the ability to jump from touching lyricism to obscenities so easily is a talent. Never mind. Forgive me, but I won't keep you company. I'm not in the mood for either his poetry or his vulgar jokes.'

A peal of laughter and the strumming of a lute resounded in the corridor and there, on the threshold of the library, stood Dandilion in a lilac jerkin with lace cuffs, his hat askew. The troubadour bowed exaggeratedly at the sight of Nenneke, the heron feather pinned to his hat sweeping the floor.

'My deepest respects, venerable mother,' he whined stupidly. 'Praise be the Great Melitele and her priestesses, the springs of virtue and wisdom—'

'Stop talking bullshit,' snorted Nenneke. 'And don't call me mother. The very idea that you could be my son fills me with horror.'

She turned on her heel and left, her trailing robe rustling. Dandilion, aping her, sketched a parody bow.

'She hasn't changed a bit,' he said cheerfully. 'She still can't take a joke. She's furious because I chatted a bit to the gate-keeper when I got here, a pretty blonde with long lashes and a virgin's plait reaching down to her cute little bottom, which it would be a sin not to pinch. So I did and Nenneke, who had just arrived . . . Ah, what the deuce. Greetings, Geralt.'

'Greetings, Dandilion. How did you know I was here?'

The poet straightened himself and yanked his trousers up. 'I was in Wyzim,' he said. 'I heard about the striga, and that you were wounded. I guessed where you would come to recuperate. I see you're well now, are you?'

'You see correctly, but try explaining that to Nenneke. Sit, let's talk.'

Dandilion sat and peeped into the book lying on the lectern. 'History?' he smiled. 'Roderick de Novembre? I've read him, I have. History was second on my list of favourite subjects when I was studying at the Academy in Oxenfurt.'

'What was first?'

'Geography,' said the poet seriously. 'The atlas was bigger and it was easier to hide a demijohn of vodka behind it.'

Geralt laughed dryly, got up, removed Lunin and Tyrss's *The Arcane Mysteries of Magic and Alchemy* from the shelf and pulled a round-bellied vessel wrapped in straw from behind the bulky volume and into the light of day.

'Oho.' The bard visibly cheered up. 'Wisdom and inspiration, I see, are still to be found in libraries. Oooh! I like this! Plum,

158

isn't it? Yes, this is true alchemy. This is a philosopher's stone well worth studying. Your health, brother. Ooooh, it's strong as the plague!'

'What brings you here?' Geralt took the demijohn over from the poet, took a sip and started to cough, fingering his bandaged neck. 'Where are you going?'

'Nowhere. That is, I could go where you're going. I could keep you company. Do you intend staying here long?'

'Not long. The local duke let it be known I'm not welcome.'

'Hereward?' Dandilion knew all the kings, princes, lords and feudal lords from Jaruga to the Dragon Mountains. 'Don't you give a damn. He won't dare fall foul of Nenneke, or Melitele. The people would set fire to his castle.'

'I don't want any trouble. And I've been sitting here for too long anyway. I'm going south, Dandilion. Far south. I won't find any work here. Civilisation. What the hell do they need a witcher here for? When I ask after employment, they look at me as if I'm a freak.'

'What are you talking about? What civilisation? I crossed Buina a week ago and heard all sorts of stories as I rode through the country. Apparently there are water sprites here, myriapodans, chimerea, flying drakes, every possible filth. You should be up to your ears in work.'

'Stories, well, I've heard them too. Half of them are either made up or exaggerated. No, Dandilion. The world is changing. Something's coming to an end.'

The poet took a long pull at the demijohn, narrowed his eyes and sighed heavily. 'Are you crying over your sad fate as a witcher again? And philosophising on top of that? I perceive the disastrous effects of inappropriate literature, because the fact that the world is changing occurred even to that old fart Roderick de Novembre. The changeability of the world is, as it happens, the only thesis in this treatise you can agree with. But it's not so innovative you have to ply me with it and put on the face of a great thinker – which doesn't suit you in the least.'

Instead of answering Geralt took a sip from the demijohn.

159

'Yes, yes,' sighed Dandilion anew. 'The world is changing, the sun sets, and the vodka is coming to an end. What else, in your opinion, is coming to an end? You mentioned something about endings, philosopher.'

'I'll give you a couple of examples,' said Geralt after a moment's silence, 'all from two months this side of the Buina. One day I ride up and what do I see? A bridge. And under that bridge sits a troll and demands every passerby pays him. Those who refuse have a leg injured, sometimes both. So I go to the alderman: "How much will you give me for that troll?" He's amazed. "What are you talking about?" he asks, "Who will repair the bridge if the troll's not there? He repairs it regularly with the sweat of his brow, solid work, first rate. It's cheaper to pay his toll." So I ride on, and what do I see? A forktail. Not very big, about four yards nose-tip to tail-tip. It's flying, carrying a sheep in its talons. I go to the village. "How much?" I ask, "will you pay me for the forktail?" The peasants fall on their knees. "No!" they shout, "it's our baron's youngest daughter's favourite dragon. If a scale falls from its back, the baron will burn our hamlet, and skin us." I ride on, and I'm getting hungrier and hungrier. I ask around for work. Certainly it's there, but what work? To catch a rusalka for one man, a nymph for another, a dryad for a third . . . They've gone completely mad – the villages are teeming with girls but they want humanoids. Another asks me to kill a mecopteran and bring him a bone from its hand because, crushed and poured into a soup, it cures impotence—'

'That's rubbish,' interrupted Dandilion. 'I've tried it. It doesn't strengthen anything and it makes the soup taste of old socks. But if people believe it and are inclined to pay—'

'I'm not going to kill mecopterans. Nor any other harmless creatures.'

'Then you'll go hungry. Unless you change your line of work.'

'To what?'

'Whatever. Become a priest. You wouldn't be bad at it with all your scruples, your morality, your knowledge of people and of everything. The fact that you don't believe in any gods shouldn't be a problem – I don't know many priests who do. Become a priest and stop feeling sorry for yourself.'

'I'm not feeling sorry for myself. I'm stating the facts.'

Dandilion crossed his legs and examined his worn sole with interest. 'You remind me, Geralt, of an old fisherman who, towards the end of his life, discovers that fish stink and the breeze from the sea makes your bones ache. Be consistent. Talking and regretting won't get you anywhere. If I were to find that the demand for poetry had come to an end, I'd hang up my lute and become a gardener. I'd grow roses.'

'Nonsense. You're not capable of giving it up.'

'Well,' agreed the poet, still staring at his sole, 'maybe not. But our professions differ somewhat. The demand for poetry and the sound of lute strings will never decline. It's worse with your trade. You witchers, after all, deprive yourselves of work, slowly but surely. The better and the more conscientiously you work, the less work there is for you. After all, your goal is a world without monsters, a world which is peaceful and safe. A world where witchers are unnecessary. A paradox, isn't it?'

'True.'

'In the past, when unicorns still existed, there was quite a large group of girls who took care of their virtue in order to be able to hunt them. Do you remember? And the ratcatchers with pipes? Everybody was fighting over their services. But they were finished off by alchemists and their effective poisons and then domesticated ferrets and weasels. The little animals were cheaper, nicer and didn't guzzle so much beer. Notice the analogy?'

'I do.'

'So use other people's experiences. The unicorn virgins, when they lost their jobs, immediately popped their cherry. Some, eager to make up for the years of sacrifice, became famous far and wide for their technique and zeal. The ratcatchers . . . Well, you'd better not copy them, because they, to a man, took to drink and went to the dogs. Well, now it looks as if the time's come for witchers. You're reading Roderick de Novembre? As far as I remember, there are mentions of witchers there, of the first ones who started work some three hundred years ago. In the days when the peasants used to go to reap the harvest in armed bands, when villages were surrounded by a triple stockade, when merchant caravans looked like the march of regular troops, and loaded catapults stood on the ramparts of the few towns night and day. Because it was us, human beings, who were the intruders here. This land was ruled by dragons, manticores, griffins and amphisboenas, vampires and werewolves, striga, kikimoras, chimerae and flying drakes. And this land had to be taken from them bit by bit, every valley, every mountain pass, every forest and every meadow. And we didn't manage that without the invaluable help of witchers. But those times have gone, Geralt, irrevocably gone. The baron won't allow a forktail to be killed because it's the last draconid for a thousand miles and no longer gives rise to fear but rather to compassion and nostalgia for times passed. The troll under the bridge gets on with people. He's not a monster used to frighten children. He's a relic and a local attraction – and a useful one at that. And chimerae, manticores and amphisboenas? They dwell in virgin forests and inaccessible mountains—'

'So I was right. Something is coming to an end. Whether you like it or not, something's coming to an end.'

'I don't like you mouthing banal platitudes. I don't like your expression when you do it. What's happening to you? I don't recognise you, Geralt. Ah, plague on it, let's go south as soon as possible, to those wild countries. As soon as you've cut down a couple of monsters, your blues will disappear. And there's supposed to be a fair number of monsters down there. They say that when an old woman's tired of life, she goes alone and weaponless into the woods to collect brushwood. The consequences are guaranteed. You should go and settle there for good.'

'Maybe I should. But I won't.'

'Why? It's easier for a witcher to make money there.'

'Easier to make money,' Geralt took a sip from the demijohn. 'But harder to spend it. And on top of that, they eat pearl barley and millet, the beer tastes like piss, the girls don't wash and the mosquitoes bite.'

Dandilion chuckled loudly and rested his head against the bookshelf, on the leather-bound volumes.

'Millet and mosquitoes! That reminds me of our first expedition together to the edge of the world,' he said. 'Do you remember? We met at the fête in Gulet and you persuaded me—'

'You persuaded me! You had to flee from Gulet as fast as your horse could carry you because the girl you'd knocked up under the musicians' podium had four sturdy brothers. They were looking for you all over town, threatening to geld you and cover you in pitch and sawdust. That's why you hung on to me then.'

'And you almost jumped out of your pants with joy to have a companion. Until then you only had your horse for company. But you're right, it was as you say. I did have to disappear for a while, and the Valley of Flowers seemed just right for my purpose. It was, after all, supposed to be the edge of the inhabited world, the last outpost of civilisation, the furthest point on the border of two worlds . . . Remember?'

'I remember.'

THE EDGE OF THE WORLD

I

Dandilion came down the steps of the inn carefully, carrying two tankards dripping with froth. Cursing under his breath he squeezed through a group of curious children and crossed the yard at a diagonal, avoiding the cowpats.

A number of villagers had already gathered round the table in the courtyard where the witcher was talking to the alderman. The poet set the tankards down and found a seat. He realised straight away that the conversation hadn't advanced a jot during his short absence.

'I'm a witcher, sir,' Geralt repeated for the umpteenth time, wiping beer froth from his lips. 'I don't sell anything. I don't go around enlisting men for the army and I don't know how to treat glanders. I'm a witcher.'

'It's a profession,' explained Dandilion yet again. 'A witcher, do you understand? He kills strigas and spectres. He exterminates all sorts of vermin. Professionally, for money. Do you get it, alderman?'

'Aha!' The alderman's brow, deeply furrowed in thought, grew smoother. 'A witcher! You should have said so right away!'

'Exactly,' agreed Geralt. 'So now I'll ask you: is there any work to be found around here for me?'

'Aaaa.' The alderman quite visibly started to think again. 'Work? Maybe those . . . Well . . . werethings? You're asking are there any werethings hereabouts?'

The witcher smiled and nodded, rubbing an itching eyelid with his knuckles.

'That there are,' the alderman concluded after a fair while.

'Only look ye yonder, see ye those mountains? There's elves live there, that there is their kingdom. Their palaces, hear ye, are all of pure gold. Oh aye, sir! Elves, I tell ye. 'Tis awful. He who yonder goes, never returns.'

'I thought so,' said Geralt coldly. 'Which is precisely why I don't intend going there.'

Dandilion chuckled impudently.

The alderman pondered a long while, just as Geralt had expected.

'Aha,' he said at last. 'Well, aye. But there be other werethings here too. From the land of elves they come, to be sure. Oh, sir, there be many, many. 'Tis hard to count them all. But the worst, that be the Bane, am I right, my good men?'

The 'good men' came to life and besieged the table from all sides.

'Bane!' said one. 'Aye, aye, 'tis true what the alderman says. A pale virgin, she walks the cottages at daybreak, and the children, they die!'

'And imps,' added another, a soldier from the watchtower. 'They tangle up the horses' manes in the stables!'

'And bats! There be bats here!'

'And myriapodans! You come up all in spots because of them!'

The next few minutes passed in a recital of the monsters which plagued the local peasants with their dishonourable doings, or their simple existence. Geralt and Dandilion learnt of misguids and mamunes, which prevent an honest peasant from finding his way home in a drunken stupour, of the flying drake which drinks milk from cows, of the head on spider's legs which runs around in the forest, of hobolds which wear red hats and about a dangerous pike which tears linen from women's hands as they wash it – and just you wait and it'll be at the women themselves. They weren't spared hearing that old Nan the Hag flies on a broom at night and performs abortions in the day, that the miller tampers with the flour by mixing it with powdered acorns and that a certain Duda believed the royal steward to be a thief and scoundrel.

Geralt listened to all this calmly, nodding with feigned interest,

165

and asked a few questions about the roads and layout of the land, after which he rose and nodded to Dandilion.

'Well, take care, my good people,' he said. 'I'll be back soon, then we'll see what can be done.'

They rode away in silence alongside the cottages and fences, accompanied by yapping dogs and screaming children.

'Geralt,' said Dandilion, standing in the stirrups to pick a fine apple from a branch which stretched over the orchard fence, 'all the way you've been complaining about it being harder and harder to find work. Yet from what I just heard, it looks as if you could work here without break until winter. You'd make a penny or two, and I'd have some beautiful subjects for my ballads. So explain why we're riding on.'

'I wouldn't make a penny, Dandilion.'

'Why?'

'Because there wasn't a word of truth in what they said.'

'I beg your pardon?'

'None of the creatures they mentioned exist.'

'You're joking!' Dandilion spat out a pip and threw the apple core at a patched mongrel. 'No, it's impossible. I was watching them carefully, and I know people. They weren't lying.'

'No,' the witcher agreed. 'They weren't lying. They firmly believed it all. Which doesn't change the facts.'

The poet was silent for a while.

'None of those monsters . . . None? It can't be. Something of what they listed must be here. At least one! Admit it.'

'All right. I admit it. One does exist for sure.'

'Ha! What?'

'A bat.'

They rode out beyond the last fences, on to a highway between beds yellow with oilseed and cornfields rolling in the wind. Loaded carts travelled past them in the opposite direction. The bard pulled his leg over the saddle-bow, rested his lute on his knee and strummed nostalgic tunes, waving from time to time at the giggling, scantily clad girls wandering along the sides of the road carrying rakes on their robust shoulders.

'Geralt,' he said suddenly, 'but monsters do exist. Maybe not as many as before, maybe they don't lurk behind every tree in the forest, but they are there. They exist. So how do you account for people inventing ones, then? What's more, believing in what they invent? Eh, famous witcher? Haven't you wondered why?'

'I have, famous poet. And I know why.'

'I'm curious.'

'People,' Geralt turned his head, 'like to invent monsters and monstrosities. Then they seem less monstrous themselves. When they get blind-drunk, cheat, steal, beat their wives, starve an old woman, when they kill a trapped fox with an axe or riddle the last existing unicorn with arrows, they like to think that the Bane entering cottages at daybreak is more monstrous than they are. They feel better then. They find it easier to live.'

'I'll remember that,' said Dandilion, after a moment's silence. 'I'll find some rhymes and compose a ballad about it.'

'Do. But don't expect a great applause.'

They rode slowly but lost the last cottages of the hamlet from sight. Soon they had climbed the row of forested hills.

'Ha.' Dandilion halted his horse and looked around. 'Look, Geralt. Isn't it beautiful here? Idyllic, damn it. A feast for the eyes!'

The land sloped gently down to a mosaic of flat, even fields picked out in variously coloured crops. In the middle, round and regular like a leaf of clover, sparkled the deep waters of three lakes surrounded by dark strips of alder thickets. The horizon was traced by a misty blue line of mountains rising above the black, shapeless stretch of forest.

'We're riding on, Dandilion.'

The road led straight towards the lakes alongside dykes and ponds hidden by alder trees and filled with quacking mallards, garganeys, herons and grebes. The richness of bird life was surprising alongside the signs of human activity – the dykes were well maintained and covered with fascines, while the sluice gates had been reinforced with stones and beams. The outlet boxes, which were not in the least rotten, trickled merrily with water.

Canoes and jetties were visible in the reeds by the lakes and bars of set nets and fish-pots were poking out of the deep waters.

Dandilion suddenly looked around.

'Someone's following us,' he said, excited. 'In a cart!'

'Incredible,' scoffed the witcher without looking around. 'In a cart? And I thought that the locals rode on bats.'

'Do you know what?' growled the troubadour. 'The closer we get to the edge of the world, the sharper your wit. I dread to think what it will come to!'

They weren't riding fast and the empty cart, drawn by two piebald horses, quickly caught up with them.

'Wooooooaaaaahhhh!' The driver brought the horses to a halt just behind them. He was wearing a sheepskin over his bare skin and his hair reached down to his brows. 'The gods be praised, noble sirs!'

'We, too,' replied Dandilion, familiar with the custom, 'praise them.'

'If we want to,' murmured the witcher.

'I call myself Nettly,' announced the carter. 'I was watching ye speak to the alderman at Upper Posada. I know ye tae be a witcher.'

Geralt let go of the reins and let his mare snort at the roadside nettles.

'I did hear,' Nettly continued, 'the alderman prattle ye stories. I marked your expression and 'twas nae strange to me. In a long time now I've nae heard such balderdash and lies.'

Dandilion laughed.

Geralt was looking at the peasant attentively, silently.

Nettly cleared his throat. 'Care ye nae to be hired for real, proper work, sir?' he asked. 'There'd be something I have for ye.'

'And what is that?'

Nettly didn't lower his eyes. 'It be nae good to speak of business on the road. Let us drive on to my home, to Lower Posada. There we'll speak. Anyways, 'tis that way ye be heading.'

'Why are you so sure?'

'As 'cos ye have nae other way here, and yer horses' noses be turned in that direction, not their butts.'

168

Dandilion laughed again. 'What do you say to that, Geralt?'

'Nothing,' said the witcher. 'It's no good to talk on the road. On our way then, honourable Nettly.'

'Tie ye the horses to the frame, and sit yerselves down in the cart,' the peasant proposed. 'It be more comfortable for ye. Why rack yer arses on the saddle?'

'Too true.'

They climbed onto the cart. The witcher stretched out comfortably on the straw. Dandilion, evidently afraid of getting his elegant green jerkin dirty, sat on the plank. Nettly clucked his tongue at the horses and the vehicle clattered along the beam-reinforced dyke.

They crossed a bridge over a canal overgrown with water-lilies and duckweed, and passed a strip of cut meadows. Cultivated fields stretched as far as the eye could see.

'It's hard to believe that this should be the edge of the world, the edge of civilisation,' said Dandilion. 'Just look, Geralt. Rye like gold, and a mounted peasant could hide in that corn. Or that oilseed, look, how enormous.'

'You know about agriculture?'

'We poets have to know about everything,' said Dandilion haughtily. 'Otherwise we'd compromise our work. One has to learn, my dear fellow, learn. The fate of the world depends on agriculture, so it's good to know about it. Agriculture feeds, clothes, protects from the cold, provides entertainment and supports art.'

'You've exaggerated a bit with the entertainment and art.'

'And booze, what's that made of?'

'I get it.'

'Not very much, you don't. Learn. Look at those purple flowers. They're lupins.'

'They's be vetch, to be true,' interrupted Nettly. 'Have ye nae seen lupins, or what? But ye have hit exact with one thing, sir. Everything seeds mightily here, and grows as to make the heart sing. That be why 'tis called the Valley of Flowers. That be why our forefathers settled here, first ridding the land of the elves.'

'The Valley of Flowers, that's Dol Blathanna,' Dandilion nudged

169

the witcher, who was stretched out on the straw, with his elbow. 'You paying attention? The elves have gone but their name remains. Lack of imagination. And how do you get on with the elves here, dear host? You've got them in the mountains across the path, after all.'

'We nae mix with each other. Each to his own.'

'The best solution,' said the poet. 'Isn't that right, Geralt?'

The witcher didn't reply.

II

'Thank you for the spread.' Geralt licked the bone spoon clean and dropped it into the empty bowl. 'A hundred thanks, dear host. And now, if you permit, we'll get down to business.'

'Well, that we can,' agreed Nettly. 'What say ye, Dhun?'

Dhun, the elder of Lower Posada, a huge man with a gloomy expression, nodded to the girls who swiftly removed the dishes from the table and left the room, to the obvious regret of Dandilion who had been grinning at them ever since the feast began, and making them giggle at his gross jokes.

'I'm listening,' said Geralt, looking at the window from where the rapping of an axe and the sound of a saw drifted. Some sort of woodwork was going on in the yard and the sharp, resinous smell was penetrating the room. 'Tell me how I can be of use to you.'

Nettly glanced at Dhun.

The elder of the village nodded and cleared his throat. 'Well, it be like this,' he said. 'There be this field hereabouts—'

Geralt kicked Dandilion – who was preparing to make a spiteful comment – under the table.

'—a field,' continued Dhun. 'Be I right, Nettly? A long time, that field there, it lay fallow, but we set it to the plough and now, 'tis on it we sow hemp, hops and flax. It be a grand piece of field, I tell ye. Stretches right up to the forest—'

'And what?' The poet couldn't help himself. 'What's on that field there?'

'Well,' Dhun raised his head and scratched himself behind the ear. 'Well, there be a deovel prowls there.'

'What?' snorted Dandilion. 'A what?'

'I tell ye: a deovel.'

'What deovel?'

'What can he be? A deovel and that be it.'

'Devils don't exist!'

'Don't interrupt, Dandilion,' said Geralt in a calm voice. 'And go on, honourable Dhun.'

'I tell ye: it's a deovel.'

'I heard you.' Geralt could be incredibly patient when he chose. 'Tell me, what does he look like, where did he come from, how does he bother you? One thing at a time, if you please.'

'Well,' Dhun raised his gnarled hand and started to count with great difficulty, folding his fingers over, one at a time, 'one thing at a time. Forsooth, ye be a wise man. Well, it be like this. He looks, sir, like a deovel, for all the world like a deovel. Where did he come from? Well, nowhere. Crash, bang, wallop and there we have him: a deovel. And bother us, forsooth he doesnae bother us overly. There be times he even helps.'

'Helps?' cackled Dandilion, trying to remove a fly from his beer. 'A devil?'

'Don't interrupt, Dandilion. Carry on, Dhun, sir. How does he help you, this, as you say—'

'Deovel,' repeated the freeman with emphasis. 'Well, this be how he helps: he fertilises the land, he turns the soil, he gets rid of the moles, scares birds away, watches over the turnips and beetroots. Oh, and he eats the caterpillars he does, they as do hatch in the cabbages. But the cabbages, he eats them too, forsooth. Nothing but guzzle, be what he does. Just like a deovel.'

Dandilion cackled again, then flicked a beer-drenched fly at a cat sleeping by the hearth. The cat opened one eye and glanced at the bard reproachfully.

'Nevertheless,' the witcher said calmly, 'you're ready to pay me

171

to get rid of him, am I right? In other words, you don't want him in the vicinity?'

'And who,' Dhun looked at him gloomily, 'would care to have a deovel on his birthright soil? This be our land since forever, bestowed upon us by the king and it has nought to do with the deovel. We spit on his help. We've got hands ourselves, have we not? And he, sir, is nay a deovel but a malicious beast and has got so much, forgive the word, shite in his head as be hard to bear. There be no knowing what will come into his head. Once he fouled the well, then chased a lass, frightening and threatening to fuck her. He steals, sir, our belongings and victuals. He destroys and breaks things, makes a nuisance of himself, churns the dykes, digs ditches like some muskrat or beaver – the water from one pond trickled out completely and the carp in it died. He smoked a pipe in the haystack he did, the son-of-a-whore, and all the hay it went up in smoke—'

'I see,' interrupted Geralt. 'So he does bother you.'

'Nay,' Dhun shook his head. 'He doesnae bother us. He be simply up to mischief, that's what he be.'

Dandilion turned to the window, muffling his laughter.

The witcher kept silent.

'Oh, what be there to talk about,' said Nettly who had been silent until then. 'Ye be a witcher, nae? So do ye something about this deovel. It be work ye be looking for in Upper Posada, I heard so myself. So ye have work. We'll pay ye what needs be. But take note: we don't want ye killing the deovel. No way.'

The witcher raised his head and smiled nastily. 'Interesting,' he said. 'Unusual, I'd say.'

'What?' frowned Dhun.

'An unusual condition. Why all this mercy?'

'He should nae be killed,' Dhun frowned even more, 'because in this Valley—'

'He should nae and that be it,' interrupted Nettly. 'Only catch him, sir, or drive him off yon o'er the seventh mountain. And ye will nae be hard done by when ye be paid.'

The witcher stayed silent, still smiling.

'Seal it, will ye, the deal?' asked Dhun.

'First, I'd like a look at him, this devil of yours.'

The freemen glanced at each other.

'It be yer right,' said Nettly, then stood up. 'And yer will. The deovel he do prowl the whole neighbourhood at night but at day he dwells somewhere in the hemp. Or among the old willows on the marshland. Ye can take a look at him there. We won't hasten ye. Ye be wanting rest, then rest as long as ye will. Ye will nae go wanting in comfort and food as befits the custom of hospitality. Take care.'

'Geralt.' Dandilion jolted up from his stool and looked out into the yard at the freemen walking away from the cottage. 'I can't understand anything anymore. A day hasn't gone by since our chat about imagined monsters and you suddenly get yourself hired hunting devils. And everybody – except ignorant freemen obviously – knows that devils are an invention, they're mythical creatures. What's this unexpected zeal of yours supposed to mean? Knowing you a little as I do, I take it you haven't abased yourself so as to get us bed, board and lodging, have you?'

'Indeed,' grimaced Geralt. 'It does look as if you know me a little, singer.'

'In that case, I don't understand.'

'What is there to understand?'

'There's no such things as devils!' yelled the poet, shaking the cat from sleep once and for all. 'No such thing! To the devil with it, devils don't exist!'

'True,' Geralt smiled. 'But Dandilion, I could never resist the temptation of having a look at something that doesn't exist.'

III

'One thing is certain,' muttered the witcher, sweeping his eyes over the tangled jungle of hemp spreading before them. 'this devil is not stupid.'

'How did you deduce that?' Dandilion was curious. 'From the fact that he's sitting in an impenetrable thicket? Any old hare has enough brains for that.'

'It's a question of the special qualities of hemp. A field of this size emits a strong aura against magic. Most spells will be useless here. And there, look, do you see those poles? Those are hops – their pollen has the same effect. It's not mere chance. The rascal senses the aura and knows he's safe here.'

Dandilion coughed and adjusted his breeches. 'I'm curious.' He scratched his forehead beneath his hat, 'How are you going to go about it, Geralt? I've never seen you work. I take it you know a thing or two about catching devils – I'm trying to recall some ballads. There was one about a devil and a woman. Rude, but amusing. The woman, you see—'

'Spare me, Dandilion.'

'As you wish. I only wanted to be helpful, that's all. And you shouldn't scorn ancient songs. There's wisdom in them, accumulated over generations. There's a ballad about a farmhand called Slow, who—'

'Stop wittering. We have to earn our board and lodging.'

'What do you want to do?'

'Rummage around a bit in the hemp.'

'That's original,' snorted the troubadour. 'Though not too refined.'

'And you, how would you go about it?'

'Intelligently,' Dandilion sniffed. 'Craftily. With a hounding, for example. I'd chase the devil out of the thicket, chase him on horseback, in the open field, and lasso him. What do you think of that?'

'Interesting. Who knows, maybe it could be done, if you took part – because at least two of us are needed for an enterprise like that. But we're not going hunting yet. I want to find out what this thing is, this devil. That's why I'm going to rummage about in the hemp.'

'Hey!' The bard had only just noticed. 'You haven't brought your sword!'

'What for? I know some ballads about devils, too. Neither the woman nor Slow the farmhand used a sword.'

'Hmm . . .' Dandilion looked around. 'Do we have to squeeze through the very middle of this thicket?'

'You don't have to. You can go back to the village and wait for me.'

'Oh, no,' protested the poet. 'And miss a chance like this? I want to see a devil too, see if he's as terrible as they claim. I was asking if we have to force our way through the hemp when there's a path.'

'Quite right,' Geralt shaded his eyes with his hand. 'There is a path. So let's use it.'

'And what if it's the devil's path?'

'All the better. We won't have to walk too far.'

'Do you know, Geralt,' babbled the bard, following the witcher along the narrow, uneven path among the hemp. 'I always thought the devil was just a metaphor invented for cursing: "go to the devil", "to the devil with it", "may the devil". Lowlanders say: "The devils are bringing us guests", while dwarves have "Duvvel hoael" when they get something wrong, and call poor-blooded livestock devvelsheyss. And in the Old Language, there's a saying, "A d'yaebl aep arse", which means—'

'I know what it means. You're babbling, Dandilion.'

Dandilion stopped talking, took off the hat decorated with a heron's feather, fanned himself with it and wiped his sweaty brow. The humid, stifling heat, intensified by the smell of grass and weeds in blossom, dominated the thicket. The path curved a little and, just beyond the bend, ended in a small clearing which had been stamped in the weeds.

'Look, Dandilion.'

In the very centre of the clearing lay a large, flat stone, and on it stood several clay bowls. An almost burnt-out tallow candle was set among the bowls. Geralt saw some grains of corn and broad beans among the unrecognisable pips and seeds stuck in the flakes of melted fat.

'As I suspected,' he muttered. 'They're bringing him offerings.'

'That's just it,' said the poet, indicating the candle. 'And they burn a tallow candle for the devil. But they're feeding him seeds, I see, as if he were a finch. Plague, what a bloody pigsty. Everything here is all sticky with honey and birch tar. What—'

The bard's next words were drowned by a loud, sinister bleating. Something rustled and stamped in the hemp, then the strangest creature Geralt had ever seen emerged from the thicket.

The creature was about half a rod tall with bulging eyes and a goat's horns and beard. The mouth, a soft, busy slit, also brought a chewing goat to mind. Its nether regions were covered with long, thick, dark-red hair right down to the cleft hooves. The devil had a long tail ending in a brush-like tassel which wagged energetically.

'Uk! Uk!' barked the monster, stamping his hooves. 'What do you want here? Leave! Leave or I'll ram you down. Uk! Uk!'

'Has anyone ever kicked your arse, little goat?' Dandilion couldn't stop himself.

'Uk! Uk! Beeeeee!' bleated the goathorn in agreement, or denial, or simply bleating for the sake of it.

'Shut up, Dandilion,' growled the witcher. 'Not a word.'

'Blebleblebeeeee!' The creature gurgled furiously, his lips parting wide to expose yellow horse-like teeth. 'Uk! Uk! Bleubeeee-ubleuuuuubleeeeeeee!'

'Most certainly,' nodded Dandilion, 'you can take the barrel-organ and bell when you go home—'

'Stop it, damn you,' hissed Geralt. 'Keep your stupid jokes to yourself—'

'Jokes!' roared the goathorn loudly and leapt up. 'Jokes? New jokers have come, have they? They've brought iron balls, have they? I'll give you iron balls, you scoundrels, you. Uk! Uk! Uk! You want to joke, do you? Here are some jokes for you! Here are your balls!'

The creature sprang up and gave a sudden swipe with his hand. Dandilion howled and sat down hard on the path, clasping his forehead. The creature bleated and aimed again. Something whizzed past Geralt's ear.

'Here are your balls!' Brrreee!'

176

An iron ball, an inch in diameter, thwacked the witcher in the shoulder and the next hit Dandilion in the knee. The poet cursed foully and scrambled away, Geralt running after him as balls whizzed above his head.

'Uk! Uk! ' screamed the goathorn, leaping up and down. 'I'll give you balls! You shitty jokers!'

Another ball whizzed through the air. Dandilion cursed even more foully as he grabbed the back of his head. Geralt threw himself to one side, among the hemp, but didn't avoid the ball that hit him in the shoulder. The goathorn's aim was true and he appeared to have an endless supply of balls. The witcher, stumbling through the thicket, heard yet another triumphant bleat from the victorious goathorn, followed by the whistle of a flying ball, a curse and the patter of Dandilion's feet scurrying away along the path.

And then silence fell.

IV

'Well, well, Geralt.' Dandilion held a horseshoe he'd cooled in a bucket to his forehead. 'That's not what I expected. A horned freak with a goatee like a shaggy billy-goat, and he chased you away like some upstart. And I got it in the head. Look at that bump!'

'That's the sixth time you've shown it to me. And it's no more interesting now than it was the first time.'

'How charming. And I thought I'd be safe with you!'

'I didn't ask you to traipse after me in the hemp, and I did ask you to keep that foul tongue of yours quiet. You didn't listen, so now you can suffer. In silence, please, because they're just coming.'

Nettly and Dhun walked into the dayroom. Behind them hobbled a grey-haired old woman, twisted as a pretzel, led by a fair-haired and painfully thin teenage girl.

'Honourable Dhun, honourable Nettly,' the witcher began

without introduction. 'I asked you, before I left, whether you yourselves had already tried to do something with that devil of yours. You told me you hadn't done anything. I've grounds to think otherwise. I await your explanation.'

The villagers murmured amongst themselves, after which Dhun coughed into his fist and took a step forward. 'Ye be right, sir. Asking forgiveness. We lied – it be guilt devours us. We wanted to outwit the deovel ourselves, for him to go away—'

'By what means?'

'Here in this Valley,' said Dhun slowly, 'there be monsters in the past. Flying dragons, earth myriapodans, were-brawls, ghosts, gigantous spiders and various vipers. And all the times we be searching in our great booke for a way to deal with all that vermin.'

'What great book?'

'Show the booke, old woman. Booke, I say. The great booke! I'll be on the boil in a minute! Deaf as a doorknob, she be! Lille, tell the old woman to show the booke!'

The girl tore the huge book from the talonned fingers of the old woman and handed it to the witcher.

'In this here great booke,' continued Dhun, 'which be in our family clan for time immemorial, be ways to deal with every monster, spell and wonder in the world that has been, is, or will be.'

Geralt turned the heavy, thick, greasy, dust-encrusted volume in his hands. The girl was still standing in front of him, wringing her apron in her hands. She was older than he had initially thought – her delicate figure had deceived him, so different from the robust build of the other girls in the village.

He lay the book down on the table and turned its heavy wooden cover. 'Take a look at this, Dandilion.'

'The first Runes,' the bard worked out, peering over his shoulder, the horseshoe still pressed to his forehead. 'The writing used before the modern alphabet. Still based on elfin runes and dwarves' ideograms. A funny sentence construction, but that's how they spoke then. Interesting etchings and illuminations. It's not often you get to see something like this, Geralt, and if you do, it's in

178

libraries belonging to temples and not villages at the edge of the world. By all the gods, where did you get that from, dear peasants? Surely you're not going to try to convince me that you can read this? Woman? Can you read the First Runes? Can you read any runes?'

'Whaaaat?'

The fair-haired girl moved closer to the woman and whispered something into her ear.

'Read?' the crony revealed her toothless gums in a smile. 'Me? No, sweetheart. 'Tis a skill I've ne'er mastered.'

'Explain to me,' said Geralt coldly, turning to Dhun and Nettly, 'how do you use the book if you can't read runes?'

'Always the oldest woman knows what stands written in the booke,' said Dhun gloomily. 'And what she knows, she teaches some young one, when 'tis time for her to turn to earth. Heed ye, yerselves, how 'tis time for our old woman. So our old woman has taken Lille in and she be teaching her. But for now, 'tis the old woman knows best.'

'The old witch and the young witch,' muttered Dandilion.

'The old woman knows the whole book by heart?' Geralt asked with disbelief. 'Is that right, Grandma?'

'Nae the whole, oh nae,' answered the woman, again through Lille, 'only what stands written by the picture.'

'Ah,' Geralt opened the book at random. The picture on the torn page depicted a dappled pig with horns in the shape of a lyre. 'Well then – what's written here?'

The old woman smacked her lips, took a careful look at the etching, then shut her eyes.

'The horned aurochs or Taurus,' she recited, 'erroneously called bison by ignoramuses. It hath horns and useth them to ram—'

'Enough. Very good, indeed.' the witcher turned several sticky pages. 'And here?'

'Cloud sprites and wind sprites be varied. Some rain pour, some wind roar, and others hurl their thunder. Harvests to protect from them, takest thou a knife of iron, new, of a mouse's droppings a half ounce, of a grey heron's fat—'

'Good, well done. Hmm . . . And here? What's this?'

The etching showed a dishevelled monstrosity with enormous eyes and even larger teeth, riding a horse. In its right hand, the monstrous being wielded a substantial sword, in its left, a bag of money.

'A witchman,' mumbled the woman. 'Called by some a witcher. To summon him is most dangerous, albeit one must; for when against the monster and the vermin there be no aid, the witchman can contrive. But careful one must be—'

'Enough,' muttered Geralt. 'Enough, Grandma. Thank you.'

'No, no,' protested Dandilion with a malicious smile. 'How does it go on? What a greatly interesting book! Go on, Granny, go on.'

'Eeee . . . But careful one must be to touch not the witchman, for thus the mange can one acquire. And lasses do from him hide away, for lustful the witchman is above all measure—'

'Quite correct, spot on,' laughed the poet, and Lille, so it seemed to Geralt, smiled almost imperceptibly.

'—though the witchman greatly covetous and greedy for gold be,' mumbled the old woman, half-closing her eyes, 'giveth ye not such a one more than: for a drowner, one silver penny or three halves; for a werecat, silver pennies two; for a plumard, silver pennies—'

'Those were the days,' muttered the witcher. 'Thank you, Grandma. And now show us where it speaks of the devil and what the book says about devils. This time 'tis grateful I'd be to heareth more, for to learn the ways and meanes ye did use to deal with him most curious am I.'

'Careful, Geralt,' chuckled Dandilion. 'You're starting to fall into their jargon. It's an infectious mannerism.'

The woman, controlling her shaking hands with difficulty, turned several pages. The witcher and the poet leaned over the table. The etching did, in effect, show the ball-thrower: horned, hairy, tailed and smiling maliciously.

'The deovel,' recited the woman. 'Also called "willower" or "sylvan". For livestock and domestic fowl, a tiresome and great

180

pest is he. Be it your will to chase him from your hamlet, takest thou—'

'Well, well,' murmured Dandilion.

' takest thou of nuts, one fistful,' continued the woman, running her finger along the parchment. 'Next, takest thou of iron balls a second fistful. Of honey an utricle, of birch tar a second. Of grey soap a firkin; of soft cheese another. There where the deovel dwelleth, goest thou when 'tis night. Commenceth then to eat the nuts. Anon, the deovel who hath great greed, will hasten and ask if they are tasty indeed. Givest to him then the balls of iron—'

'Damn you,' murmured Dandilion. 'Pox take—'

'Quiet,' said Geralt. 'Well, Grandma. Go on.'

'. . . having broken his teeth he will be attentive as thou eatest the honey. Of said honey will he himself desire. Givest him of birch tar, then yourself eateth soft cheese. Soon, hearest thou, will the deovel grumbleth and tumbleth, but makest of it as naught. Yet if the deovel desireth soft cheese, givest him soap. For soap the deovel withstandeth not—'

'You got to the soap?' interrupted Geralt with a stony expression turning towards Dhun and Nettly.

'In no way,' groaned Nettly. 'If only we had got to the balls. But he gave us what for when he bit a ball—'

'And who told you to give him so many?' Dandilion was enraged. 'It stands written in the book, one fistful to take. Yet ye gaveth of balls a sackful! Ye furnished him with ammunition for two years, the fools ye be!'

'Careful,' smiled the witcher. 'You're starting to fall into their jargon. It's infectious.'

'Thank you.'

Geralt suddenly raised his head and looked into the eyes of the girl standing by the woman. Lille didn't lower her eyes. They were pale and wildly blue. 'Why are you bringing the devil offerings in the form of grain?' he asked sharply. 'After all, it's obvious that he's a typical herbivore.'

Lille didn't answer.

'I asked you a question, girl. Don't be frightened, you won't get the mange by talking to me.'

'Don't ask her anything, sir,' said Nettly, with obvious unease in his voice. 'Lille . . . She . . . She be strange. She won't answer you, don't force her.'

Geralt kept looking into Lille's eyes, and Lille still met his gaze. He felt a shiver run down his back and creep along his shoulders.

'Why didn't you attack the devil with stancheons and pitchforks,' he raised his voice. 'Why didn't you set a trap for him? If you'd wanted to, his goat's head would already be spiked on a pole to frighten crows away. You warned me not to kill him. Why? You forbade it, didn't you, Lille?'

Dhun got up from the bench. His head almost touched the beams.

'Leave, lass,' he growled. 'Take the old woman and leave.'

'Who is she, honourable Dhun?' the witcher demanded as the door closed behind Lille and the woman. 'Who is that girl? Why does she enjoy more respect from you than that bloody book?'

'It be nae yer business.' Dhun looked at him, and there was no friendliness in his eyes. 'Persecute wise women in your own town, burn stakes in yer own land. There has been none of it here, nor will there be.'

'You didn't understand me,' said the witcher coldly.

'Because I did nae try,' growled Dhun.

'I noticed,' Geralt said through his teeth, making no effort to be cordial. 'But be so gracious as to understand something, honourable Dhun. We have no agreement. I haven't committed myself to you in any way. You have no reason to believe that you've bought yourself a witcher who, for a silver penny or three halves, will do what you can't do yourselves. Or don't want to do. Or aren't allowed to. No, honourable Dhun. You have not bought yourself a witcher yet, and I don't think you'll succeed in doing so. Not with your reluctance to understand.'

Dhun remained silent, measuring Geralt with a gloomy stare.

Nettly cleared his throat and wriggled on the bench, shuffling his rag sandals on the dirt floor, then suddenly straightened up.

'Witcher, sir,' he said. 'Do nae be enraged. We will tell ye, what and how. Dhun?'

The elder of the village nodded and sat down.

'As we be riding here,' began Nettly, 'ye did notice how everything here grows, the great harvests we have? There be nae many places ye see all grow like this, if there be any such. Seedlings and seeds be so important to us that 'tis with them we pay our levies and we sell them and use them to barter—'

'What's that got to do with the devil?'

'The deovel was wont to make a nuisance of himself and play silly tricks, and then he be starting to steal a great deal of grain. At the beginning, we be bringing him a little to the stone in the hemp, thinking his fill he'd eat and leave us in peace. Naught of it. With a vengeance he went on stealing. And when we started to hide our supplies in shops and sheds, well locked and bolted, 'tis furious he grew, sir, he roared, bleated. "Uk! Uk!" he called, and when he goes "Uk! Uk!" ye'd do best to run for yer life. He threatened to—'

'—screw,' Dandilion threw in with a ribald smile.

'That too,' agreed Nettly. 'Oh, and he mentioned a fire. Talk long as we may, he could nae steal so 'tis levies he demanded. He ordered grain and other goods be brought him by the sackful. Riled we were then and intending to beat his tailed arse. But—'

The freeman cleared his throat and lowered his head.

'Ye need nae beat about the bush,' said Dhun suddenly. 'We judged the witcher wrong. Tell him everything, Nettly.'

'The old woman forbade us to beat the devil,' said Nettly quickly, 'but we know 'tis Lille, because the woman . . . The woman only says what Lille tell her to. And we . . . Ye know yerself, sir. We listen.'

'I've noticed.' Geralt twisted his lips in a smile. 'The woman can only waggle her chin and mumble a text which she doesn't understand herself. And you stare at the girl, with gaping mouths, as if she were the statue of a goddess. You avoid her eyes but try to guess her wishes. And her wishes are your command. Who is this Lille of yours?'

'But ye have guessed that, sir. A prophetess. A Wise One. But say naught of this to anyone. We ask ye. If word were to get to the steward, or, gods forbid, to the viceroy—'

'Don't worry,' said Geralt seriously. 'I know what that means and I won't betray you.'

The strange women and girls, called prophetesses or Wise Ones, who could be found in villages, didn't enjoy the favour of those noblemen who collected levies and profited from farming. Farmers always consulted prophetesses on everything and believed them, blindly and boundlessly. Decisions based on their advice were often completely contrary to the politics of lords and overlords. Geralt had heard of incomprehensible decrees – the slaughter of entire pedigree herds, the cessation of sowing or harvesting, and even the migration of entire villages. Local lords therefore opposed the superstition, often brutally, and freemen very quickly learnt to hide the Wise Ones. But they didn't stop listening to their advice. Because experience proved the Wise Ones were always right in the long run.

'Lille did not permit us to kill the deovel,' continued Nettly. 'She told us to do what the booke says. As ye well know, it did nae work out. There has already been trouble with the steward. If we give less grain in levy than be normal, 'tis bawl he will, shout and fulminate. Thus we have nay even squeaked to him of the deovel, the reason being the steward be ruthless and knows cruelly little about jokes. And then ye happened along. We asked Lille if we could . . . hire ye—'

'And?'

'She said, through the woman, that she need first of all to look at ye.'

'And she did.'

'That she did. And accepted ye she has, that we know. We can tell what Lille accepts and what she doesnae.'

'She never said a word to me.'

'She ne'er has spoken word to anyone – save the old woman. But if she had not accepted ye, she would nay have entered the room for all in the world—'

184

'Hm . . .' Geralt reflected. 'That's interesting. A prophetess who, instead of prophesying, doesn't say a word. How did she come to be among you?'

'We nae know, witcher, sir,' muttered Dhun. 'But as for the old woman, so the older folk remember, it be like this. The old woman afore her took a close-tongued girl under her wing too, one as which came from no one knows. And that girl she be our old woman. My grandfather would say the old woman be reborn that way. Like the moon she be reborn in the sky and ever new she be. Do nae laugh—'

'I'm not laughing.' Geralt shook his head. 'I've seen too much to laugh at things like that. Nor do I intend to poke my nose into your affairs, honourable Dhun. My questions aim to establish the bond between Lille and the devil. You've probably realised yourselves that one exists. So if you're anxious to be on good terms with your prophetess, then I can give you only one way to deal with the devil: you must get to like him.'

'Know ye, sir,' said Nettly, 'it be nae only a matter of the deovel. Lille does nae let us harm anything. Any creature.'

'Of course,' Dandilion butted in, 'country prophetesses grow from the same tree as druids. And a druid will go so far as to wish the gadfly sucking his blood to enjoy its meal.'

'Ye hits it on the head,' Nettly faintly smiled. 'Ye hits the nail right on the head. 'Twas the same with us and the wild boars that dug up our vegetable beds. Look out the window: beds as pretty as a picture. We have found a way, Lille doesnae even know. What the eyes do nay see, the heart will nae miss. Understand?'

'I understand,' muttered Geralt. 'And how. But we can't move forward. Lille or no Lille, your devil is a sylvan. An exceptionally rare but intelligent creature. I won't kill him, my code doesn't allow it.'

'If he be intelligent,' said Dhun, 'go speak reason to him.'

'Just so,' Nettly joined in. 'If the deovel has brains that will mean he steals grain according to reason. So ye, witcher, find out what he wants. He does nae eat that grain, after all – not so much, at least. So what does he want grain for? To spite us? What does he want? Find out and chase him off in some witcher way. Will ye do that?'

'I'll try,' decided Geralt. 'But . . .'

'But what?'

'Your book, my friends, is out of date. Do you see what I'm getting at?'

'Well, forsooth,' grunted Dhun, 'not really.'

'I'll explain. Honourable Dhun, honourable Nettly, if you're counting on my help costing you a silver penny or three halves, then you are bloody well mistaken.'

V

'Hey!'

A rustle, an angry *Uk! Uk!* and the snapping of stakes, reached them from the thicket.

'Hey!' repeated the witcher, prudently remaining hidden. 'Show yourself, willower.'

'Willower yourself.'

'So what is it? Devil?'

'Devil yourself.' The sylvan poked his head out from the hemp, baring his teeth. 'What do you want?'

'To talk.'

'Are you making fun of me or what? Do you think I don't know who you are? The peasants hired you to throw me out of here, eh?'

'That's right,' admitted Geralt indifferently. 'And that's precisely what I wanted to chat to you about. What if we were to come to an understanding?'

'That's where it hurts,' bleated the sylvan. 'You'd like to get off lightly, wouldn't you? Without making an effort, eh? Pull the other one! Life, my good man, means competition. The best man wins. If you want to win with me, prove you're the best. Instead of coming to an understanding, we'll have competitions. The

186

winner dictates the conditions. I propose a race from here to the old willow on the dyke.'

'I don't know where the dyke is, or the old willow.'

'I wouldn't suggest the race if you knew. I like competitions but I don't like losing.'

'I've noticed. No, we won't race each other. It's very hot today.'

'Pity. So maybe we'll pit ourselves against each other in a different way?' The sylvan bared his yellow teeth and picked up a large stone from the ground. 'Do you know the game "Who shouts loudest?" I shout first. Close your eyes.'

'I have a different proposition.'

'I'm all ears.'

'You leave here without any competitions, races or shouting. Of your own accord, without being forced.'

'You can shove such a proposition a *d'yeabl aep arse*.' The devil demonstrated his knowledge of the Old Language. 'I won't leave here. I like it here.'

'But you've made too much of a nuisance of yourself here. Your pranks have gone too far.'

'*Duvvelsheyss* to you with my pranks.' The sylvan, as it turned out, also knew the dwarves' tongue. 'And your proposition is also worth as much as a duvvelsheyss. I'm not going anywhere unless you beat me at some game. Shall I give you a chance? We'll play at riddles if you don't like physical games. I'll give you a riddle in a minute and if you guess it, you win and I leave. If you don't, I stay and you leave. Rack your brains because the riddle isn't easy.'

Before Geralt could protest the sylvan bleated, stamped his hooves, whipped the ground with his tail and recited:

> *Little pink leaves, pods small and full,*
> *It grows in soft clay, not far from the stream,*
> *On a long stalk, its flower is moist,*
> *But to a cat, please show it not,*
> *'Cos if you do, he'll eat the lot.*

187

Well, what is it? Guess.'

'I haven't the faintest idea,' the witcher said, not even trying to think it over. 'Sweet pea, perhaps?'

'Wrong. You lose.'

'And what is the correct answer? What has . . . hmm . . . moist pods?'

'Cabbage.'

'Listen,' growled Geralt. 'You're starting to get on my nerves.'

'I warned you,' chuckled the sylvan, 'that the riddle wasn't easy. Tough. I won, I stay. And you leave. I wish you, sir, a cold farewell.'

'Just a moment.' The witcher surreptitiously slipped a hand into his pocket. 'And my riddle? I have the right to a revenge match, haven't I?'

'No!' protested the devil. 'I might not guess it, after all. Do you take me for a fool?'

'No,' Geralt shook his head. 'I take you for a spiteful, arrogant dope. We're going to play quite a new game shortly, one which you don't know.'

'Ha! After all! What game?'

'The game is called,' said the witcher slowly, 'don't do unto, others what you would not have them do to you". You don't have to close your eyes.'

Geralt stooped in a lightning throw; the one-inch iron ball whizzed sharply through the air and thwacked the sylvan straight between the horns. The creature collapsed onto his back as if hit by a thunderbolt. Geralt dived between the poles and grabbed him by one shaggy leg. The sylvan bleated and kicked. The witcher sheltered his head with his arm, but to little effect. The sylvan, despite his mean posture, kicked with the strength of an enraged mule. The witcher tried and failed to catch a kicking hoof. The sylvan flapped, thrashed his hands on the ground and kicked him again in the forehead. The witcher cursed, feeling the sylvan's leg slip from his fingers. Both, having parted, rolled in opposite directions, kicked the poles with a crash and tangled themselves up in the creeping hemp.

The sylvan was the first to jump up, and, lowering his horned head, charged. But Geralt was already on his feet and effortlessly dodged the attack, grabbed the creature by a horn, tugged hard, threw him to the ground and crushed him with his knees. The sylvan bleated and spat straight into the witcher's eyes like a camel suffering from excess saliva. The witcher instinctively stepped back without releasing the devil's horns. The sylvan, trying to toss his head, kicked with both hooves at once and – strangely – hit the mark with both. Geralt swore nastily, but didn't release his grip. He pulled the sylvan up, pinned him to the creaking poles and kicked him in a shaggy knee with all his might, then he leant over and spat right into his ear. The sylvan howled and snapped his blunt teeth.

'Don't do unto others . . .' panted the witcher, '. . . what you would not have them do to you. Shall we play on?' The sylvan gurgled, howled and spat fiercely, but Geralt held him firmly by the horns and pressed his head down hard, making the spittle hit the sylvan's own hooves, which tore at the ground, sending up clouds of dust and weeds.

The next few minutes passed in an intense skirmish and exchange of insults and kicks. If Geralt was pleased about anything, it was only that nobody could see him – for it was a truly ridiculous sight.

The force of the next kick tore the combatants apart and threw them in opposite directions, into the hemp thicket. The sylvan got up before the witcher and rushed to escape, limping heavily. Geralt, panting and wiping his brow, rushed in pursuit. They forced their way through the hemp and ran into the hops. The witcher heard the pounding of a galloping horse, the sound he'd been waiting for.

'Here, Dandilion! Here!' he yelled. 'In the hops!'

He saw the mount breast right in front of him and was knocked over. He bounced off the horse as though it were a rock and tumbled onto his back. The world darkened. He managed to roll to the side, behind the hop poles, to avoid the hooves. He sprung up nimbly but another rider rode into him, knocking him down again. Then suddenly, someone threw themselves at him and pinned him to the ground.

Then there was a flash, and a piercing pain in the back of his head.

And darkness.

VI

There was sand on his lips. When he tried to spit it out he realised he was lying face-down on the ground. And he was tied up. He raised his head a little and heard voices.

He was lying on the forest floor, by a pine tree. Some twenty paces away stood unsaddled horses. They were obscured behind the feathery fronds of ferns, but one of those horses was, without a doubt, Dandilion's chestnut.

'Three sacks of corn,' he heard. 'Good, Torque. Very good. You've done well.'

'That's not all,' said the bleating voice, which could only be the sylvan devil. 'Look at this, Galarr. It looks like beans but it's completely white. And the size of it! And this, this is called oilseed. They make oil from it.'

Geralt squeezed his eyes shut, then opened them again. No, it wasn't a dream. The devil and Galarr, whoever he was, were using the Old Language, the language of elves. But the words corn, beans, and oilseed were in the common tongue.

'And this? What's this?' asked Galarr.

'Flaxseed. Flax, you know? You make shirts from flax. It's much cheaper than silk, and more hardwearing. It's quite a complicated process as far as I know but I'll find out the ins and outs.'

'As long as it takes root, this flax of yours; as long as it doesn't go to waste like the turnip,' grumbled Galarr, in the same strange Volapuk. 'Try to get some new turnip seedlings, Torque.'

'Have no fear,' bleated the sylvan. 'There's no problem with that here. Everything grows like hell. I'll get you some, don't worry.'

'And one more thing,' said Galarr. 'Finally find out what that three-field system of theirs is all about.'

The witcher carefully raised his head and tried to turn round.

'Geralt . . .' he heard a whisper. 'Are you awake?'

'Dandilion . . .' he whispered back. 'Where are we . . .? What's happening?'

Dandilion only grunted quietly. Geralt had had enough. He cursed, tensed himself and turned on to his side.

In the middle of the glade stood the sylvan devil with – as he now knew – the sweet name of Torque. He was busy loading sacks, bags and packs on to the horses. He was being helped by a slim, tall man who could only be Galarr. The latter, hearing the witcher move, turned around. His hair was black with a distinct hint of dark blue. He had sharp features, big, bright eyes and pointed ears.

Galarr was an elf. An elf from the mountains. A pure-blooded Aen Seidhe, a representative of the Old People.

Galarr wasn't alone. Six more sat at the edge of the glade. One was busy emptying Dandilion's packs, another strummed the troubadour's lute. The remainder, gathered around an untied sack, were greedily devouring turnips and raw carrots.

'Vanadain, Toruviel,' said Galarr, indicating the prisoners with a nod of his head. 'Vedrai! Enn'le!'

Torque jumped up and bleated. 'No, Galarr! No! Filavandrel has forbidden it! Have you forgotten?'

'No, I haven't forgotten.' Galarr threw two tied sacks across the horse's back. 'But we have to check if they haven't loosened the knots.'

'What do you want from us?' the troubadour moaned as one of the elves knocked him to the ground with his knee and checked the knots. 'Why are you holding us prisoners? What do you want? I'm Dandilion, a poe—'

Geralt heard the sound of a blow. He turned round, twisted his head.

The elf standing over Dandilion had black eyes and raven hair, which fell luxuriantly over her shoulders, except for two thin plaits braided at her temples. She was wearing a short leather camisole over a loose shirt of green satin, and tight woollen leggings tucked into riding boots. Her hips were wrapped around with a coloured shawl which reached halfway down her thighs.

'*Que glosse?*' she asked, looking at the witcher and playing with the hilt of the long dagger in her belt. '*Que l'en pavienn, ell'ea?*'

'*Nell'ea,*' he contested. '*T'en pavienn, Aen Seidhe.*'

'Did you hear?' The elf turned to her companion, the tall Seidhe who, not bothering to check Geralt's knots, was strumming away at Dandilion's lute with an expression of indifference on his long face. 'Did you hear, Vanadain? The ape-man can talk! He can even be impertinent!'

Seidhe shrugged, making the feathers decorating his jacket rustle. 'All the more reason to gag him, Toruviel.'

The elf leant over Geralt. She had long lashes, an unnaturally pale complexion and parched, cracked lips. She wore a necklace of carved golden birch pieces on a thong, wrapped around her neck several times.

'Well, say something else, ape-man,' she hissed. 'We'll see what your throat, so used to barking, is capable of.'

'What's this? Do you need an excuse to hit a bound man?' The witcher turned over on his back with an effort and spat out the sand. 'Hit me without any excuses. I've seen how you like it. Let off some steam.'

The elf straightened. 'I've already let off some steam on you, while your hands were free,' she said. 'I rode you down and swiped you on the head. And I'll also finish you off when the time comes.'

He didn't answer.

'I'd much rather stab you from close-up, looking you in the eyes,' continued the elf. 'But you stink most hideously, human, so I'll shoot you.'

'As you wish.' The witcher shrugged, as far as the knots let him. 'Do as you like, noble Aen Seidhe. You shouldn't miss a tied-up, motionless target.'

192

The elf stood over him, legs spread, and leant down, flashing her teeth.

'No, I shouldn't,' she hissed. 'I hit whatever I want. But you can be sure you won't die from the first arrow. Or the second. I'll try to make sure you can feel yourself dying.'

'Don't come so close,' he grimaced, pretending to be repulsed. 'You stink most hideously, Aen Seidhe.'

The elf jumped back, rocked on her narrow hips and forcefully kicked him in the thigh. Geralt drew his legs in and curled up, knowing where she was aiming next. He succeeded, and got her boot in the hip, so hard his teeth rattled.

The tall elf standing next to her echoed each kick with a sharp chord on the lute.

'Leave him, Toruviel!' bleated the sylvan. 'Have you gone mad? Galarr, tell her to stop!'

'*Thaesse!*' shrieked Toruviel, and kicked the witcher again. The tall Seidhe tore so violently at the strings that one snapped with a protracted whine.

'Enough of that! Enough, for gods' sake!' Dandilion yelled fretfully, wriggling and tumbling in the ropes. 'Why are you bullying him, you stupid whore? Leave us alone! And you leave my lute alone, all right?'

Toruviel turned to him with an angry grimace on her cracked lips. 'Musician!' she growled. 'A human, yet a musician! A lutenist!'

Without a word, she pulled the instrument from the tall elf's hand, forcefully smashed the lute against the pine and threw the remains, tangled in the strings, on Dandilion's chest.

'Play on a cow's horn, you savage, not a lute.'

The poet turned as white as death, his lips quivered. Geralt, feeling cold fury rising up somewhere within him, drew Toruviel's eyes with his own.

'What are you staring at?' hissed the elf, leaning over. 'Filthy ape-man! Do you want me to gouge out those insect eyes of yours?'

Her necklace hung down just above him. The witcher tensed,

193

lunged, and caught the necklace in his teeth, tugging powerfully, curling his legs in and turning on his side.

Toruviel lost her balance and fell on top of him.

Geralt wriggled in the ropes like a fish, crushed the elf beneath him, tossed his head back with such force that the vertebrae in his neck cracked and, with all his might, butted her in the face with his forehead. Toruviel howled and struggled.

They pulled him off her brutally and, tugging at his clothes and hair, lifted him. One of them struck him; he felt rings cut the skin over his cheekbone and the forest danced and swam in front of his eyes. He saw Toruviel lurch to her knees, blood pouring from her nose and mouth. The elf wrenched the dagger from its sheath but gave a sob, hunched over, grasped her face and dropped her head between her knees.

The tall elf in the jacket adorned with colourful feathers took the dagger from her hand and approached the witcher. He smiled as he raised the blade. Geralt saw him through a red haze; blood from his forehead, which he'd cut against Toruviel's teeth, poured into his eye-sockets.

'No!' bleated Torque, running up to the elf and hanging on to his arm. 'Don't kill him! No!'

'Voe'rle, Vanadain,' a sonorous voice suddenly commanded. 'Quess aen? Caelm, evellienn! Galarr!'

Geralt turned his head as far as the fist clutching his hair permitted.

The horse which had just reached the glade was as white as snow, its mane long, soft and silky as a woman's hair. The hair of the rider sitting in the sumptuous saddle was identical in colour, pulled back at the forehead by a bandana studded with sapphires.

Torque, bleating now and then, ran up to the horse, caught hold of the stirrup and showered the white-haired elf with a torrent of words. The Seidhe interrupted him with an authoritative gesture and jumped down from his saddle. He approached Toruviel, who was being supported by two elves, and carefully removed the bloodied handkerchief from her face. Toruviel gave a heartrending groan. The Seidhe shook his head and approached the witcher.

His burning black eyes, shining like stars in his pale face, had dark rings beneath them, as if he had not slept for several nights in a row.

'You stink even when bound,' he said quietly in unaccented common tongue. 'Like a basilisk. I'll draw my conclusions from that.'

'Toruviel started it,' bleated the devil. 'She kicked him when he was tied up, as if she'd lost her mind—'

With a gesture the elf ordered him to be quiet. At his command the other Seidhe dragged the witcher and Dandilion under the pine tree and fastened them to the trunk with belts. Then they all knelt by the prostrate Toruviel, sheltering her. After a moment Geralt heard her yell and fight in their arms.

'I didn't want this,' said the sylvan, still standing next to them. 'I didn't, human. I didn't know they'd arrive just when we— When they stunned you and tied your companion up, I asked them to leave you there, in the hops. But—'

'They couldn't leave any witnesses,' muttered the witcher.

'Surely they won't kill us, will they?' groaned Dandilion. 'Surely they won't . . .'

Torque said nothing, wiggling his soft nose.

'Bloody hell.' The poet groaned. 'They're going to kill us? What's all this about, Geralt? What did we witness?'

'Our sylvan friend is on a special mission in the Valley of Flowers. Am I right, Torque? At the elves' request he's stealing seeds, seedlings, knowledge about farming . . . What else, devil?'

'Whatever I can,' bleated Torque. 'Everything they need. And show me something they don't need. They're starving in the mountains, especially in winter. And they know nothing about farming. And before they've learned to domesticate game or poultry, and to cultivate what they can in their plots of land . . . They haven't got the time, human.'

'I don't care a shit about their time. What have I done to them?' groaned Dandilion. 'What wrong have I done them?'

'Think carefully,' said the white-haired elf, approaching without a sound, 'and maybe you can answer the question yourself.'

'He's simply taking revenge for all the wrong that man has done the elves.' The witcher smiled wryly. 'It's all the same to him who he takes his revenge on. Don't be deluded by his noble bearing and elaborate speech, Dandilion. He's no different than the black-eyes who knocked us down. He has to unload his powerless hatred on somebody.'

The elf picked up Dandilion's shattered lute. For a moment, he looked at the ruined instrument in silence, and finally threw it into the bushes.

'If I wanted to give vent to hatred or a desire for revenge,' he said, playing with a pair of soft white leather gloves, 'I'd storm the valley at night, burn down the village and kill the villagers. Childishly simple. They don't even put out a guard. They don't see or hear us when they come to the forest. Can there be anything simpler, anything easier, than a swift, silent arrow from behind a tree? But we're not hunting you. It is you, man with strange eyes, who is hunting our friend, the sylvan Torque.'

'Eeeeee, that's exaggerating,' bleated the devil. 'What hunt? We were having a bit of fun—'

'It is you humans who hate anything that differs from you, be it only by the shape of its ears,' the elf went on calmly, paying no attention to the sylvan. 'That's why you took our land from us, drove us from our homes, forced us into the savage mountains. You took our Dol Blathanna, the Valley of Flowers. I am Fila-vandrel aen Fidhail of Silver Towers, of the Feleaorn family from White Ships. Now, exiled and hounded to the edge of the world, I am Filavandrel of the Edge of the World.'

'The world is huge,' muttered the witcher. 'We can find room. There's enough space.'

'The world is huge,' repeated the elf. 'That's true, human. But you have changed this world. At first, you used force to change it. You treated it as you treat anything that falls into your hands. Now it looks as if the world has started to fit in with you. It's given way to you. It's given in.'

Geralt didn't reply.

'Torque spoke the truth,' continued Filavandrel. 'Yes, we are starving. Yes, we are threatened with annihilation. The sun shines differently, the air is different, water is not as it used to be. The things we used to eat, made use of, are dying, diminishing, deteriorating. We never cultivated the land. Unlike you humans we never tore at it with hoes and ploughs. To you, the earth pays a bloody tribute. It bestowed gifts on us. You tear the earth's treasures from it by force. For us, the earth gave birth and blossomed because it loved us. Well, no love lasts forever. But we still want to survive.'

'Instead of stealing grain, you can buy it. As much as you need. You still have a great many things that humans consider valuable. You can trade.'

Filavandrel smiled contemptuously. 'With you? Never.'

Geralt frowned, breaking up the dried blood on his cheek. 'The devil with you then, and your arrogance and contempt. By refusing to cohabit you're condemning yourselves to annihilation. To cohabit, to come to an understanding, that's your only chance.'

Filavandrel leaned forwards, his eyes blazing.

'Cohabit on your terms?' he asked in a changed, yet still calm, voice. 'Acknowledging your sovereignty? Losing our identity? Cohabit as what? Slaves? Pariahs? Cohabit with you from beyond the walls you've built to fence yourselves away in towns? Cohabit with your women and hang for it? Or look on at what half-blood children must live with? Why are you avoiding my eyes, strange human? How do you find cohabiting with neighbours from whom, after all, you do differ somewhat?'

'I manage.' The witcher looked him straight in the eyes. 'I manage because I have to. Because I've no other way out. Because I've overcome the vanity and pride of being different. I've understood that they are a pitiful defence against being different. Because I've understood that the sun shines differently when something changes, but I'm not the axis of those changes. The sun shines differently, but it will continue to shine, and jumping at it with a hoe isn't going to do anything. We've got to accept facts, elf. That's what we've got to learn.'

'That's what you want, isn't it?' With his wrist Filavandrel wiped away the sweat above his white brows. 'Is that what you want to impose on others? The conviction that your time has come, your human era and age, and that what you're doing to other races is as natural as the rising and the setting of the sun? That everybody has to come to terms with it, to accept it? And you accuse me of vanity? And what are the views you're proclaiming? Why don't you humans finally realise that your domination of the world is as natural and repellant as lice multiplying in a sheepskin coat? You could propose we cohabit with lice and get the same reaction – and I'd listen to the lice as attentively if they, in return for our acknowledgment of their supremacy, were to agree to allow common use of the coat.'

'So don't waste time discussing it with such an unpleasant insect, elf,' said the witcher, barely able to control his voice. 'I'm surprised you want to arouse a feeling of guilt and repentance in such a louse as me. You're pitiful, Filavandrel. You're embittered, hungry for revenge and conscious of your own powerlessness. Go on, thrust the sword into me. Revenge yourself on the whole human race. You'll see what relief that'll bring you. First kick me in the balls or the teeth, like Toruviel.'

Filavandrel turned his head.

'Toruviel is sick,' he said.

'I know that disease and its symptoms.' Geralt spat over his shoulder. 'The treatment I gave her ought to help.'

'This conversation is senseless,' Filavandrel stepped away. 'I'm sorry we've got to kill you. Revenge has nothing to do with it, it's purely practical. Torque has to carry on with his task and no one can suspect who he's doing it for. We can't afford to go to war with you, and we won't be taken in by trade and exchange. We're not so naïve that we don't know your merchants are just outposts of your way of life. We know what follows them. And what sort of cohabitation they bring.'

'Elf,' Dandilion, who had remained silent until now, said quietly, 'I've got friends. People who'll pay ransom for us. In the form of provisions, if you like, or any form. Think about it. After all, those stolen seeds aren't going to save you—'

'Nothing will save them anymore,' Geralt interrupted him. 'Don't grovel, Dandilion, don't beg him. It's pointless and pitiful.'

'For someone who has lived such a short time,' Filavandrel forced a smile, 'you show an astounding disdain for death, human.'

'Your mother gives birth to you only once and only once do you die,' the witcher said calmly. 'An appropriate philosophy for a louse, don't you agree? And your longevity? I pity you, Filavandrel.'

The elf raised his eyebrows.

'Why?'

'You're pathetic, with your little stolen sacks of seeds on pack horses, with your handful of grain, that tiny crumb thanks to which you plan to survive. And with that mission of yours which is supposed to turn your thoughts from imminent annihilation. Because you know this is the end. Nothing will sprout or yield crops on the plateaux, nothing will save you now. But you live long, and you will live very long in arrogant isolation, fewer and fewer of you, growing weaker and weaker, more and more bitter. And you know what'll happen then, Filavandrel. You know that desperate young men with the eyes of hundred-year-old men and withered, barren and sick girls like Toruviel will lead those who can still hold a sword and bow in their hands, down into the valleys. You'll come down into the blossoming valleys to meet death, wanting to die honourably, in battle, and not in sick beds of misery, where anaemia, tuberculosis and scurvy will send you. Then, long-living Aen Seidhe, you'll remember me. You'll remember that I pitied you. And you'll understand that I was right.'

'Time will tell who was right,' said the elf quietly. 'And herein lies the advantage of longevity. I've got a chance of finding out, if only because of that stolen handful of grain. You won't have a chance like that. You'll die shortly.'

'Spare him, at least,' Geralt indicated Dandilion with his head. 'No, not out of lofty mercy. Out of common sense. Nobody's going to ask after me, but they are going to take revenge for him.'

'You judge my common sense poorly,' the elf said after some

hesitation. 'If he survives thanks to you he'll undoubtedly feel obliged to avenge you.'

'You can be sure of that!' Dandilion burst out, pale as death. 'You can be sure, you son-of-a-bitch. Kill me too, because I promise otherwise I'll set the world against you. You'll see what lice from a fur coat can do! We'll finish you off even if we have to level those mountains of yours to the ground! You can be sure of that!'

'How stupid you are, Dandilion,' sighed the witcher.

'Your mother gives birth to you only once and only once do you die,' said the poet haughtily, the effect somewhat spoilt by his teeth rattling like castanets.

'That settles it.' Filavandrel took his gloves from his belt and pulled them on. 'It's time to end this.'

At his command the elves positioned themselves opposite Geralt and Dandilion with bows. They did it quickly; they'd obviously been waiting for this a long time. One of them, the witcher noticed, was still chewing a turnip. Toruviel, her mouth and nose bandaged with cloth and birch bark, stood next to the archers. Without a bow.

'Shall I bind your eyes?' asked Filavandrel.

'Go away.' The witcher turned his head. 'Go—'

'*A d'yeable aep arse*,' Dandilion finished for him, his teeth chattering.

'Oh, no!' the sylvan suddenly bleated, running up and sheltering the condemned men with his body. 'Have you lost your mind? Filavandrel! This is not what we agreed! Not this! You were supposed to take them up to the mountains, hold them somewhere in some cave, until we'd finished—'

'Torque,' said the elf, 'I can't. I can't risk it. Did you see what he did to Toruviel while tied up? I can't risk it.'

'I don't care what you can or can't! What do you imagine? You think I'll let you murder them? Here, on my land? Right next to my hamlet? You accursed idiots! Get out of here with your bows or I'll ram you down. Uk! Uk!'

'Torque.' Filavandrel rested his hands on his belt. 'This is necessary.'

'Duvvelsheyss, not necessary!'

'Move aside, Torque.'

The sylvan shook his ears, bleated even louder, stared and bent his elbow in an abusive gesture popular among dwarves.

'You're not going to murder anybody here! Get on your horses and out into the mountains, beyond the passes! Otherwise you'll have to kill me too!'

'Be reasonable,' said the white-haired elf slowly. 'If we let them live, people are going to learn what you're doing. They'll catch you and torture you. You know what they're like, after all.'

'I do,' bleated the sylvan still sheltering Geralt and Dandilion. 'It turns out I know them better than I know you! And, verily, I don't know who to side with. I regret allying myself with you, Filavandrel!'

'You wanted to,' said the elf coldly, giving a signal to the archers. 'You wanted to, Torque. L'sparellean! Evellienn!'

The elves drew arrows from their quivers. 'Go away, Torque,' said Geralt, gritting his teeth. 'It's senseless. Get aside.' The sylvan, without budging from the spot, showed him the dwarves' gesture.

'I can hear . . . music . . .' Dandilion suddenly sobbed.

'It happens,' said the witcher, looking at the arrowheads. 'Don't worry. There's no shame in fear.'

Filavandrel's face changed, screwed up in a strange grimace. The white-haired Seidhe suddenly turned round and gave a shout to the archers. They lowered their weapons.

Lille entered the glade.

She was no longer a skinny peasant girl in a sackcloth dress. Through the grasses covering the glade walked – no, not walked – floated a queen, radiant, golden-haired, fiery-eyed, ravishing. The Queen of the Fields, decorated with garlands of flowers, ears of corn, bunches of herbs. At her left-hand side a young stag pattered on stiff legs, at her right rustled an enormous hedgehog.

'Dana Meadbh,' said Filavandrel with veneration. And then bowed and knelt.

The remaining elves also knelt; slowly, reluctantly, they fell to their knees one after the other and bowed their heads low in veneration. Toruviel was the last to kneel.

'*Hael*, Dana Meadbh,' repeated Filavandrel.

Lille didn't answer. She stopped several paces short of the elf and swept her blue eyes over Dandilion and Geralt. Torque, while bowing, started cutting through the knots. None of the Seidhe moved.

Lille stood in front of Filavandrel. She didn't say anything, didn't make the slightest sound, but the witcher saw the changes on the elf's face, sensed the aura surrounding them and was in no doubt they were communicating. The devil suddenly pulled at his sleeve.

'Your friend,' he bleated quietly, 'has decided to faint. Right on time. What shall we do?'

'Slap him across the face a couple of times.'

'With pleasure.'

Filavandrel got up from his knees. At his command the elves fell to saddling the horses as quick as lightening.

'Come with us, Dana Meadbh,' said the white-haired elf. 'We need you. Don't abandon us, Eternal One. Don't deprive us of your love. We'll die without it.'

Lille slowly shook her head and indicated east, the direction of the mountains. The elf bowed, crumpling the ornate reins of his white-maned mount in his hands.

Dandilion walked up, pale and dumbfounded, supported by the sylvan. Lille looked at him and smiled. She looked into the witcher's eyes. She looked long. She didn't say a word. Words weren't necessary.

Most of the elves were already in their saddles when Filavandrel and Toruviel approached. Geralt looked into the elf's black eyes, visible above the bandages.

'Toruviel . . .' he said. And didn't finish.

The elf nodded. From her saddle-bow, she took a lute, a

marvellous instrument of light, tastefully inlaid wood with a slender, engraved neck. Without a word, she handed the lute to Dandilion. The poet accepted the instrument and smiled. Also without a word, but his eyes said a great deal.

'Farewell, strange human,' Filavandrel said quietly to Geralt. 'You're right. Words aren't necessary. They won't change anything.'

Geralt remained silent.

'After some consideration,' added the Seidhe, 'I've come to the conclusion that you were right. When you pitied us. So goodbye. Goodbye until we meet again, on the day when we descend into the valleys to die honourably. We'll look out for you then, Toruviel and I. Don't let us down.'

For a long time, they looked at each other in silence. And then the witcher answered briefly and simply:

'I'll try.'

VII

'By the gods, Geralt.' Dandilion stopped playing, hugged the lute and touched it with his cheek. 'This wood sings on its own! These strings are alive! What wonderful tonality! Bloody hell, a couple of kicks and a bit of fear is a pretty low price to pay for such a superb lute. I'd have let myself be kicked from dawn to dusk if I'd known what I was going to get. Geralt? Are you listening to me at all?'

'It's difficult not to hear you two.' Geralt raised his head from the book and glanced at the sylvan, who was still stubbornly squeaking on a peculiar set of pipes made from reeds of various lengths. 'I hear you, the whole neighbourhood hears you.'

'Duvvelsheyss, not neighbourhood,' Torque put his pipes aside. 'A desert, that's what it is. A wilderness. A shit-hole. Eh, I miss my hemp!'

'He misses his hemp,' laughed Dandilion, carefully turning the

203

delicately engraved lute pegs. 'You should have sat in the thicket quiet as a dormouse instead of scaring girls, destroying dykes and sullying the well. I think you're going to be more careful now and give up your tricks, eh, Torque?'

'I like tricks,' declared the sylvan, baring his teeth. 'And I can't imagine life without them. But have it your way, I promise to be more careful on new territory. I'll be more restrained.'

The night was cloudy and windy. The gale beat down the reeds and rustled in the branches of the bushes surrounding their camp. Dandilion threw some dry twigs into the fire. Torque wriggled around on his makeshift bed, swiping mosquitoes away with his tail. A fish leapt in the lake with a splash.

'I'll describe our whole expedition to the edge of the world in a ballad,' declared Dandilion. 'And I'll describe you in it, too, Torque.'

'Don't think you'll get away with it,' growled the sylvan. 'I'll write a ballad too then and describe you, but in such a way as you won't be able to show your face in decent company for twelve years. So watch out! Geralt?'

'What?'

'Have you read anything interesting in that book which you so disgracefully wheedled out of those freemen?'

'I have.'

'So read it to us, before the fire burns out.'

'Yes, yes,' Dandilion strummed the melodious strings of Toruviel's lute, 'read us something, Geralt.'

The witcher leant on his elbow, edging the volume closer to the fire.

'"Glimpsed she may be,"' he began, '"during the time of sumor, from the days of Mai and Juyn to the days of October, but most oft this haps on the Feste of the Scythe, which ancients would call Lammas. She revealeth herself as the Fairhaired Ladie, in flowers all, and all that liveth followeth her path and clingeth to her, as one, plant or beast. Hence her name is Lyfia. Ancients call her Danamebi and venerate her greatly. Even the Bearded, albeit in

204

mountains not on fields they dwell, respect and call her Blo-emenmagde."'

'Danamebi,' muttered Dandilion. 'Dana Meadbh, the Lady of the Fields.'

'"Whence Lyfia treads the earth blossometh and bringeth forth, and abundantly doth each creature breed, such is her might. All nations to her offer sacrifice of harvest in vain hope their field not another's will by Lyfia visited be. Because it is also said that there cometh a day at end when Lyfia will come to settle among that tribe which above all others will rise, but these be mere womenfolk tales. Because, forsooth, the wise do say that Lyfia loveth but one land and that which groweth on it and liveth alike, with no difference, be it the smallest of common apple trees or the most wretched of insects, and all nations are no more to her than that thinnest of trees because, forsooth, they too will be gone and new, different tribes will follow. But Lyfia eternal is, was and ever shall be until the end of time."'

'Until the end of time!' sang the troubadour and strummed his lute. Torque joined in with a high trill on his reed pipes. 'Hail, Lady of the Fields! For the harvest, for the flowers in Dol Blathanna, but also for the hide of the undersigned, which you saved from being riddled with arrows. Do you know what? – I'm going to tell you something.' He stopped playing, hugged the lute like a child and grew sad. 'I don't think I'll mention the elves and the difficulties they've got to struggle with, in the ballad. There'd be no shortage of scum wanting to go into the mountains . . . Why hasten the—' The troubadour grew silent.

'Go on, finish,' said Torque bitterly. 'You wanted to say: hasten what can't be avoided. The inevitable.'

'Let's not talk about it,' interrupted Geralt. 'Why talk about it? Words aren't necessary. Follow Lille's example.'

'She spoke to the elf telepathically,' muttered the bard. 'I sensed it. I'm right, aren't I, Geralt? After all, you can sense communication like that. Did you understand what . . . What she was getting across to the elf?'

'Some of it.'

'What was she talking about?'

'Hope. That things renew themselves, and won't stop doing so.'

'Is that all?'

'That was enough.'

'Hm . . . Geralt? Lille lives in the village, among people. Do you think that—'

'—that she'll stay with them? Here, in Dol Blathanna? Maybe. If . . .'

'If what?'

'If people prove worthy of it. If the edge of the world remains the edge of the world. If we respect the boundaries. But enough of this talk, boys. Time to sleep.'

'True. It's nearly midnight, the fire's burning out. I'll sit up for a little while yet. I've always found it easiest to invent rhymes beside a dying fire. And I need a title for my ballad. A nice title.'

'Maybe *The Edge of the World*?'

'Banal,' snorted the poet. 'Even if it really is the edge, it's got to be described differently. Metaphorically. I take it you know what a metaphor is, Geralt? Hmm . . . Let me think . . . "Where . . ." Bloody hell. "Where—"'

'Goodnight,' said the devil.

THE VOICE OF REASON 6

The witcher unlaced his shirt and peeled the wet linen from his neck. It was very warm in the cave, hot, even, the air hung heavy and moist, the humidity condensing in droplets on the moss-covered boulders and basalt blocks of the walls.

Plants were everywhere. They grew out of beds hewn into the bedrock and filled with peat, in enormous chests, troughs and flowerpots. They climbed up rocks, up wooden trellises and stakes. Geralt examined them with interest, recognising some rare specimens – those which made up the ingredients of a witcher's medicines and elixirs, magical philtres and a sorcerer's decoctions, and others, even rarer, whose qualities he could only guess at. Some he didn't know at all, or hadn't even heard of. He saw stretches of star-leafed melilote, compact balls of puffheads pouring out of huge flowerpots, shoots of arenaria strewn with berries as red as blood. He recognised the meaty, thickly-veined leaves of fastaim, the crimson-golden ovals of measure-me-nots and the dark arrows of sawcuts. He noticed pinnated pondblood moss huddled against stone blocks, the glistening tubers of raven's eye and the tiger-striped petals of the mousetail orchid.

In the shady part of the grotto bulged caps of the sewant mushroom, grey as stones in a field. Not far from them grew reachcluster, an antidote to every known toxin and venom. The modest yellow-grey brushes peering from chests deeply sunken into the ground revealed scarix, a root with powerful and universal medicinal qualities.

The centre of the cave was taken up by aqueous plants. Geralt saw vats full of hornwort and turtle duckweed, and tanks covered in a compact skin of liverwort, fodder for the parasitic giant oyster. Glass reservoirs full of gnarled rhizomes of the hallucinogenic bitip, slender, dark-green cryptocorines and clusters of nematodes. Muddy, silted troughs were breeding grounds for innumerable phycomycetes, algae, moulds and swamp lichen.

Nenneke, rolling up the sleeves of her priestess's robe, took a pair of scissors and a little bone rake from her basket and got to work. Geralt sat on a bench between shafts of light falling through huge crystal blocks in the cave's vault.

The priestess muttered and hummed under her breath, deftly plunging her hands into the thicket of leaves and shoots, snipping with her scissors and filling the basket with bunches of weeds. She adjusted the stakes and frames supporting the plants and, now and again, turned the soil with her small rake. Sometimes, muttering angrily, she pulled out dried or rotted stalks, threw them into the humus containers as food for mushrooms and other squamous and snake-like twisted plants which the witcher didn't recognise. He wasn't even sure they were plants at all – it seemed to him the glistening rhizomes moved a little, stretching their hair-like off-shoots towards the priestess's hands.

It was warm. Very warm.

'Geralt?'

'Yes?' He fought off an overwhelming sleepiness. Nenneke, playing with her scissors, was looking at him from behind the huge pinnated leaves of sand-spurry flybush.

'Don't leave yet. Stay. A few more days.'

'No, Nenneke. It's time for me to be on my way.'

'Why the hurry? You don't have to worry about Hereward. And let that vagabond Dandilion go and break his neck on his own. Stay, Geralt.'

'No, Nenneke.'

The priestess snipped with scissors. 'Are you in such haste to leave the temple because you're afraid that she'll find you here?'

'Yes,' he admitted reluctantly. 'You've guessed.'

'It wasn't exactly difficult,' she muttered. 'But don't worry. Yennefer's already been here. Two months ago. She won't be back in a hurry, because we quarrelled. No, not because of you. She didn't ask about you.'

'She didn't ask?'

'That's where it hurts,' the priestess laughed. 'You're egocentric, like all men. There's nothing worse than a lack of interest, is there? Than indifference? No, but don't lose heart. I know Yennefer only too well. She didn't ask anything, but she did look around attentively, looking for signs of you. And she's mighty furious at you, that I did feel.'

'What did you quarrel about?'

'Nothing that would interest you.'

'I know anyway.'

'I don't think so,' said Nenneke calmly, adjusting the stakes. 'You know her very superficially. As, incidentally, she knows you. It's quite typical of the relationship which binds you, or did bind you. Both parties aren't capable of anything other than a strongly emotional evaluation of the consequences, while ignoring the causes.'

'She came looking for a cure,' he remarked coldly. 'That's what you quarrelled about, admit it.'

'I won't admit anything.'

The witcher got up and stood in full light under one of the crystal sheets in the grotto's vault.

'Come here a minute, Nenneke. Take a look at this.' He unknotted a secret pocket in his belt, dug out a tiny bundle, a miniature purse made of goat-leather, and poured the contents into his palm.

'Two diamonds, a ruby, three pretty nephrites, and an interesting agate.' Nenneke was knowledgeable about everything. 'How much did they cost you?'

'Two and a half thousand Temeria orens. Payment for the Wyzim striga.'

'For a torn neck,' grimaced the priestess. 'Oh, well, it's a question of price. But you did well to turn cash into these trinkets. The oren is weak and the cost of stones in Wyzim isn't high; it's too near to the dwarves' mines in Mahakam. If you sell those in Novigrad, you'll get at least five hundred Novigrad crowns, and

209

the crown, at present, stands at six and a half orens and is going up.'

'I'd like you to take them.'

'For safe-keeping?'

'No. Keep the nephrites for the temple as, shall we say, my offering to the goddess Melitele. And the remaining stones . . . are for her. For Yennefer. Give them to her when she comes to visit you again, which will no doubt be soon.'

Nenneke looked him straight in the eyes.

'I wouldn't do this if I were you. You'll make her even more furious, if that's possible, believe me. Leave everything as it is, because you're no longer in a position to mend anything or make anything better. Running away from her, you behaved . . . well, let's say, in a manner not particularly worthy of a mature man. By trying to wipe away your guilt with precious stones, you'll behave like a very, very over-mature man. I really don't know what sort of man I can stand less.'

'She was too possessive,' he muttered, turning away his face. 'I couldn't stand it. She treated me like—'

'Stop it,' she said sharply. 'Don't cry on my shoulder. I'm not your mother, and I won't be your confidante either. I don't give a shit how she treated you and I care even less how you treated her. And I don't intend to be a go-between or give these stupid jewels to her. If you want to be a fool, do it without using me as an intermediary.'

'You misunderstand. I'm not thinking of appeasing or bribing her. But I do owe her something, and the treatment she wants to undergo is apparently very costly. I want to help her, that's all.'

'You're more of an idiot than I thought.' Nenneke picked up the basket from the ground. 'A costly treatment? Help? Geralt, these jewels of yours are, to her, knick-knacks not worth spitting on. Do you know how much Yennefer can earn for getting rid of an unwanted pregnancy for a great lady?'

'I do happen to know. And that she earns even more for curing infertility. It's a shame she can't help herself in that respect. That's why she's seeking help from others – like you.'

'No one can help her, it's impossible. She's a sorceress. Like most female magicians, her ovaries are atrophied and it's irreversible. She'll never be able to have children.'

'Not all sorceresses are handicapped in this respect. I know something about that, and you do, too.'

Nenneke closed her eyes. 'Yes, I do.'

'Something can't be a rule if there are exceptions to it. And please don't give me any banal untruths about exceptions proving the rule. Tell me something about exceptions as such.'

'Only one thing,' she said coldly, 'can be said about exceptions. They exist. Nothing more. But Yennefer . . . Well, unfortunately, she isn't an exception. At least not as regards the handicap we're talking about. In other respects it's hard to find a greater exception than her.'

'Sorcerers,' Geralt wasn't put off by Nenneke's coldness, or her allusion, 'have raised the dead. I know of proven cases. And it seems to me that raising the dead is harder than reversing the atrophy of any organs.'

'You're mistaken. Because I don't know of one single, proven, fully successful case of reversing atrophy or regenerating endocrine glands. Geralt, that's enough. This is beginning to sound like a consultation. You don't know anything about these things. I do. And if I tell you that Yennefer has paid for certain gifts by losing others, then that's how it is.'

'If it's so clear then I don't understand why she keeps on trying to—'

'You understand very little,' interrupted the priestess. 'Bloody little. Stop worrying about Yennefer's complaints and think about your own. Your body was also subjected to changes which are irreversible. She surprises you, but what about you? It ought to be clear to you too, that you're never going to be human, but you still keep trying to be one. Making human mistakes. Mistakes a witcher shouldn't be making.'

He leant against the wall of the cave and wiped the sweat from his brow.

'You're not answering,' stated Nenneke, smiling faintly. 'I'm not surprised. It's not easy to speak with the voice of reason. You're sick, Geralt. You're not fully fit. You react to elixirs badly. You've got a rapid pulse rate, the dilation of your eyes is slow, your reactions are delayed. You can't get the simplest Signs right. And you want to hit the trail? You have to be treated. You need therapy. And before that, a trance.'

'Is that why you sent Iola to me? As part of the therapy? To make the trance easier?'

'You're a fool!'

'But not to such an extent.'

Nenneke turned away and slipped her hands among the meaty stalks of creepers which the witcher didn't recognise.

'Well, have it your way,' she said easily. 'Yes, I sent her to you. As part of the therapy. And let me tell you, it worked. Your reactions were much better the following day. You were calmer. And Iola needed some therapy, too. Don't be angry.'

'I'm not angry because of the therapy, or because of Iola.'

'But at the voice of reason you're hearing?'

He didn't answer.

'A trance is necessary,' repeated Nenneke, glancing around at her cave garden. 'Iola's ready. She's made both physical and psychic contact with you. If you want to leave, let's do it tonight.'

'No. I don't want to. Look, Nenneke, Iola might start to prophesy during the trance. To predict, read the future.'

'That's just it.'

'Exactly. And I don't want to know the future. How could I do what I'm doing if I knew it? Besides, I know it anyway.'

'Are you sure?' He didn't answer. 'Oh, well, all right,' she sighed. 'Let's go. Oh, and Geralt? I don't mean to pry but tell me . . . How did you meet? You and Yennefer? How did it all start?'

The witcher smiled. 'It started with me and Dandilion not having anything for breakfast and deciding to catch some fish.'

'Am I to understand that instead of fish you caught Yennefer?'

'I'll tell you what happened. But maybe after supper. I'm hungry.'

'Let's go then. I've got everything I need.'

The witcher made a move towards the exit and once more looked around the cave hothouse.

'Nenneke?'

'Aha?'

'Half of the plants you've got here don't grow anywhere else anymore. Am I right?'

'Yes. More than half.'

'How come?'

'If I said it was through the goddess Melitele's grace, I daresay that wouldn't be enough for you, would it?'

'I daresay it wouldn't.'

'That's what I thought.' Nenneke smiled. 'You see, Geralt, this bright sun of ours is still shining, but not quite the way it used to. Read the great books if you like. But if you don't want to waste time on it maybe you'll be happy with the explanation that the crystal roof acts like a filter. It eliminates the lethal rays which are increasingly found in sunlight. That's why plants which you can't see growing wild anywhere in the world grow here.'

'I understand,' nodded the witcher. 'And us, Nenneke? What about us? The sun shines on us, too. Shouldn't we shelter under a roof like that?'

'In principle, yes,' sighed the priestess. 'But . . .'

'But what?'

'It's too late.'

THE LAST WISH

I

The catfish stuck its barbelled head above the surface, tugged with force, splashed, stirred the water and flashed its white belly.

'Careful, Dandilion!' shouted the witcher, digging his heels into the wet sand. 'Hold him, damn it!'

'I am holding him . . .' groaned the poet. 'Heavens, what a monster! It's a leviathan, not a fish! There'll be some good eating on that, dear gods!'

'Loosen it. Loosen it or the line will snap!'

The catfish clung to the bed and threw itself against the current towards the bend in the river. The line hissed as Dandilion's and Geralt's gloves smouldered.

'Pull, Geralt, pull! Don't loosen it or it'll get tangled up in the roots!'

'The line will snap!'

'No, it won't. Pull!'

They hunched up and pulled. The line cut the water with a hiss, vibrated and scattered droplets which glistened like mercury in the rising sun. The catfish suddenly surfaced, set the water seething just below the surface, and the tension of the line eased. They quickly started to gather up the slack.

'We'll smoke it,' panted Dandilion. 'We'll take it to the village and get it smoked. And we'll use the head for soup!'

'Careful!'

Feeling the shallows under its belly, the catfish threw half of its twelve-foot-long body out of the water, tossed its head, whacked its flat tail and took a sharp dive into the depths. Their gloves smouldered anew.

'Pull, pull! To the bank, the son-of-a-bitch!'

'The line is creaking! Loosen it, Dandilion!'

'It'll hold, don't worry! We'll cook the head . . . for soup . . .'

The catfish, dragged near to the bank again, surged and strained furiously against them as if to let them know he wasn't that easy to get into the pot. The spray flew six feet into the air.

'We'll sell the skin . . .' Dandilion, red with effort, pulled the line with both hands. 'And the barbels . . . We'll use the barbels to make—'

Nobody ever found out what the poet was going to make from the catfish's barbels. The line snapped with a crack and both fishermen, losing their balance, fell onto the wet sand.

'Bloody hell!' Dandilion yelled so loud that the echo resounded though the osiers. 'So much grub escaped! I hope you die, you son-of-a-catfish.'

'I told you,' Geralt shook his wet trousers. 'I told you not to use force when you pull. You screwed up, my friend. You make as good a fisherman as a goat's arse makes a trumpet.'

'That's not true.' The troubadour was outraged. 'It's my doing that the monster took the bait in the first place.'

'Oh really? You didn't lift a finger to help me set the line. You played the lute and hollered so the whole neighbourhood could hear you, nothing more.'

'You're wrong,' Dandilion bared his teeth. 'When you fell asleep, you see, I took the grubs off the hook and attached a dead crow, which I'd found in the bushes. I wanted to see your face in the morning when you pulled the crow out. And the catfish took the crow. Your grubs would have caught shit-all.'

'They would have, they would have.' The witcher spat into the water, winding the line on to a little wooden rake. 'But it snapped because you tugged like an idiot. Wind up the rest of the lines instead of gabbling. The sun's already up, it's time to go. I'm going to pack up.'

'Geralt!'

'What?'

'There's something on the other line, too . . . No, dammit, it only got caught. Hell, it's holding like a stone, I can't do it! Ah, that's it . . . Ha, ha, look what I'm bringing in. It must be the wreck of a barge from King Dezmod's time! What great stuff! Look, Geralt!'

Dandilion was clearly exaggerating; the clump of rotted ropes, net and algae pulled out of the water was impressive but it was far from being the size of a barge dating from the days of the legendary king. The bard scattered the jumble over the bank and began to dig around in it with the tip of his shoe. The algae was alive with leeches, scuds and little crabs.

'Ha! Look what I've found!'

Geralt approached, curious. The find was a chipped stoneware jar, something like a two-handled amphora, tangled up in netting, black with rotten algae, colonies of caddis-larvae and snails, dripping with stinking slime.

'Ha!' Dandilion exclaimed again, proudly. 'Do you know what this is?'

'It's an old pot.'

'You're wrong,' declared the troubadour, scraping away shells and hardened, shiny clay. 'This is a charmed jar. There's a djinn inside who'll fulfil my three wishes.'

The witcher snorted.

'You can laugh,' Dandilion finished his scraping, bent over and rinsed the amphora. 'But there's a seal on the spigot and a wizard's mark on the seal.'

'What mark? Let's see.'

'Oh, sure.' The poet hid the jar behind his back. 'And what more do you want? I'm the one who found it and I need all the wishes.'

'Don't touch that seal! Leave it alone!'

'Let go, I tell you! It's mine!'

'Dandilion, be careful!'

'Sure!'

'Don't touch it! Oh, bloody hell!'

The jar fell to the sand during their scuffle, and luminous red smoke burst forth.

The witcher jumped back and rushed towards the camp for his sword. Dandilion, folding his arms across his chest, didn't move.

The smoke pulsated and collected in an irregular sphere level with Dandilion's eyes. The sphere formed a six-foot-wide distorted head with no nose, enormous eyes and a sort of beak.

'Djinn!' said Dandilion, stamping his foot. 'I freed thee and as of this day, I am thy lord. My wishes—'

The head snapped its beak, which wasn't really a beak but something in the shape of drooping, deformed and ever-changing lips.

'Run!' yelled the witcher. 'Run, Dandilion!'

'My wishes,' continued the poet, 'are as follows. Firstly, may Valdo Marx, the troubadour of Cidaris, die of apoplexy as soon as possible. Secondly, there's a count's daughter in Caelf called Virginia who refuses all advances. May she succumb to mine. Thirdly—'

No one ever found out Dandilion's third wish.

Two monstrous paws emerged from the horrible head and grabbed the bard by the throat. Dandilion screeched.

Geralt reached the head in three leaps, swiped his silver sword and slashed it through the middle. The air howled, the head exhaled smoke and rapidly doubled in diameter. The monstrous jaw, now also much larger, flew open, snapped and whistled; the paws pulled the struggling Dandilion around and crushed him to the ground.

The witcher crossed his fingers in the Sign of Aard and threw as much energy as he could muster at the head. The energy materialised in a blinding beam, sliced through the glow surrounding the head and hit its mark. The boom was so loud that it stabbed Geralt's ears, and the air sucked in by the implosion made the willows rustle. The roar of the monster was deafening as it grew even larger, but it released the poet, soared up, circled and, waving its paws, flew away over the water.

The witcher rushed to pull Dandilion – who was lying motionless – away. At that moment, his fingers touched a round object buried in the sand.

It was a brass seal decorated with the sign of a broken cross and a nine-pointed star.

The head, suspended above the river, had become the size of a haystack, while the open, roaring jaws looked like the gates of an average-sized barn. Stretching out its paws, the monster attacked.

Geralt, not having the least idea of what to do, squeezed the seal in his fist and, extending his hand towards the assailant, screamed out the words of an exorcism a priestess had once taught him. He had never used those words until now because, in principle, he didn't believe in superstitions.

The effect surpassed his expectations.

The seal hissed and grew hot, burning his hand. The gigantic head froze in the air, suspended, motionless above the river. It hung like that for a moment then, at last, it began to howl, roar, and dispersed into a pulsating bundle of smoke, into a huge, whirling cloud. The cloud whined shrilly and whisked upstream with incredible speed, leaving a trail of churned-up water on the surface. In a matter of seconds, it had disappeared into the distance; only a dwindling howl lingered across the water.

The witcher rushed to the poet, cowering on the sand.

'Dandilion? Are you dead? Dandilion, damn it! What's the matter with you?'

The poet jerked his head, shook his hands and opened his mouth to scream. Geralt grimaced and narrowed his eyes – Dandilion had a trained – loud – tenor voice and, when frightened, could reach extraordinary registers. But what emerged from the bard's throat was a barely audible, hoarse croak.

'Dandilion! What's the matter with you? Answer me!'

'Hhhh . . . eeee . . . kheeeee . . . theeee whhhhorrrrrrre . . .'

'Are you in pain? What's the matter? Dandilion!'

'Hhhh . . . Whhhooo . . .'

'Don't say anything. If everything's all right, nod.'

Dandilion grimaced and, with great difficulty, nodded and then immediately turned on his side, curled up and – choking and coughing – vomited blood.

Geralt cursed.

'By all the gods!' The guard stepped back and lowered the lantern. 'What's the matter with him?'

'Let us through, my good man,' said the witcher quietly, supporting Dandilion, who was huddled up in the saddle. 'We're in great haste, as you see.'

'I do.' The guard swallowed, looking at the poet's pale face and chin covered in black, dried blood. 'Wounded? It looks terrible, sir.'

'I'm in haste,' repeated Geralt. 'We've been travelling since dawn. Let us through, please.'

'We can't,' said the other guard. 'You're only allowed through between sunrise and sunset. None may pass at night. That's the order. There's no way through for anyone unless they've got a letter of safe-conduct from the king or the mayor. Or they're nobility with a coat of arms.'

Dandilion croaked, huddled up even more, resting his forehead on the horse's mane, shuddered, shook and retched dryly. Another stream of blood trickled down the branched, dried pattern on his mount's neck.

'My good men,' Geralt said as calmly as he could, 'you can see for yourselves how badly he fares. I have to find someone who can treat him. Let us through. Please.'

'Don't ask.' The guard leant on his halberd. 'Orders are orders. I'll go to the pillory if I let you through. They'll chase me from service, and then how will I feed my children? No, sir, I can't. Take your friend down from the horse and put him in the room in the barbican. We'll dress him and he'll last out until dawn, if that's his fate. It's not long now.'

'A dressing's not enough.' The witcher ground his teeth. 'We need a healer, a priest, a gifted doctor—'

'You wouldn't be waking up anyone like that at night anyway,' said the second guard. 'The most we can do is see that you don't have to camp out under the gate until dawn. It's warm in there and there's somewhere to put your friend; he'll fare better there than in the saddle. Come on, let us help you lower him from the horse.'

It was warm, stuffy and cosy in the room within the barbican. A fire crackled merrily in the hearth, and behind it a cricket chirped fiercely.

Three men sat at the heavy square table laid with jugs and plates.

'Forgive us for disturbing you, squires . . .' said the guard, holding Dandilion up. 'I trust you won't mind . . . This one here is a knight, hmm . . . And the other one is wounded, so I thought—'

'You thought well,' one of the men turned his slender, sharp, expressive face towards them and got up. 'Here, lay him down on the pallet.'

The man was an elf, like the other one sitting at the table. Both, judging by their clothes, which were a typical mixture of human and elven fashion, were elves who had settled and integrated. The third man, who looked the eldest, was human, a knight, judging by the way he was dressed and by his salt-and-pepper hair, cut to fit beneath a helmet.

'I'm Chireadan,' the taller of the elves, with an expressive face, introduced himself. As was usual with representatives of the Old People, it was difficult to guess his age; he could have been twenty or one hundred and twenty. 'This is my cousin Errdil. And this nobleman is the knight Vratimir.'

'A nobleman,' muttered Geralt, but a closer look at the coat of arms embroidered on his tunic shattered his hopes: a shield divided per cross and bearing golden lilies was cut diagonally by a silver bar. Vratimir was not only illegitimate but came from a mixed, human-nonhuman union. As a result, although he was entitled to use a coat of arms, he couldn't consider himself a true nobleman, and the privilege of crossing the city gate after dusk most certainly wasn't extended to him.

'Unfortunately,' – the witcher's scrutiny did not escape the elf's attention – 'we, too, have to remain here until dawn. The law knows no exceptions, at least not for the likes of us. We invite you to join our company, sir knight.'

'Geralt, of Rivia,' the witcher introduced himself. 'A witcher, not a knight.'

'What's the matter with him?' Chireadan indicated Dandilion, whom the guards had laid on a pallet in the meantime. 'It looks like poisoning. If it is poisoning, then I can help. I've got some good medicine with me.'

Geralt sat down, then quickly gave a guarded account of events at the river. The elves looked at each other, and the knight spat through his teeth and frowned.

'Extraordinary,' Chireadan remarked. 'What could it have been?'

'A djinn in a bottle,' muttered Vratimir. 'Like a fairy tale—'

'Not quite.' Geralt indicated Dandilion, curled up on the pallet. 'I don't know of any fairy tale that ends like this.'

'That poor fellow's injuries,' said Chireadan, 'are evidently of a magical nature. I fear that my medicine will not be of much use. But I can at least lessen his suffering. Have you already given him a remedy, Geralt?'

'A painkilling elixir.'

'Come and help me. You can hold his head up.'

Dandilion greedily drank the medicine, diluted with wine, choked on his last sip, wheezed and covered the leather pillow with spittle.

'I know him,' Errdil said. 'He's Dandilion, the troubadour and poet. I saw him singing at the court of King Ethain in Cidaris once.'

'A troubadour,' repeated Chireadan, looking at Geralt. 'That's bad. Very bad. The muscles of his neck and throat are attacked. Changes in his vocal cords are starting to take place. The spell's action has to be halted as soon as possible otherwise . . . This might be irreversible.'

'That means . . . Does that mean he won't be able to talk?'

'Talk, yes. Maybe. Not sing.'

Geralt sat down at the table without saying a word and rested his forehead on his clenched fists.

'A wizard,' said Vratimir. 'A magical remedy or a curative spell is needed. You have to take him to some other town, witcher.'

'What?' Geralt raised his head. 'And here, in Rinde? Isn't there a wizard here?'

'Magicians are hard to come by in the whole of Redania,' said the knight. 'Isn't that true? Ever since King Heribert placed an exorbitant tax on spells, magicians have boycotted the capital and those towns which are rigorous in executing the king's edicts. And the councillors of Rinde are famous for their zeal in this respect. Chireadan, Errdil, am I right?'

'You are,' confirmed Errdil. 'But . . . Chireadan, may I?'

'You have to,' said Chireadan, looking at the witcher. 'There's no point in making a secret of it; everyone knows anyway. There's a sorceress staying in the town right now, Geralt.'

'Incognito, no doubt?'

'Not very,' smiled the elf. 'The sorceress in question is something of an individualist. She's ignoring both the boycott imposed on Rinde by the Council of Wizards, and the disposition of the local councillors, and is doing rather splendidly out of it: the boycott means there's tremendous demand for magical services here and, of course, the sorceress isn't paying any levies.'

'And the town council puts up with it?'

'The sorceress is staying with a merchant, a trade broker from Novigrad, who is also the honorary ambassador. Nobody can touch her there. She has asylum.'

'It's more like house arrest than asylum,' corrected Errdil. 'She's just about imprisoned there. But she has no shortage of clients. Rich clients. She ostentatiously makes light of the councillors, holds balls and extravagant parties—'

'While the councillors are furious, turn whoever they can against her and tarnish her reputation as best they can,' Chireadan cut in. 'They spread foul rumours about her and hope, no doubt, that the Novigrad hierarchy will forbid the merchant to grant her asylum.'

'I don't like meddling in things like that,' muttered Geralt, 'but I've got no choice. What's the merchant-ambassador's name?'

'Beau Berrant.'

The witcher thought that Chireadan grimaced as he pronounced the name.

'Oh well, it really is your only hope. Or rather, the only hope for that poor fellow moaning on the bed. But whether the sorceress will want to help you . . . I don't know.'

'Be careful when you go there,' said Errdil. 'The mayor's spies are watching the house. You know what to do if they stop you. Money opens all doors.'

'I'll go as soon as they open the gates. What's the sorceress called?'

Geralt thought he detected a slight flush on Chireadan's expressive face. But it could have been the glow from the fire in the hearth.

'Yennefer of Vergerberg.'

III

'My lord's asleep,' repeated the doorman, looking down at Geralt. He was taller by a head and nearly twice as broad in the shoulders. 'Are you deaf, you vagabond? The lord's asleep, I said.'

'Then let him sleep,' agreed the witcher. 'I've not got business with your lord but with the lady who is staying here.'

'Business, you say.' The doorman, as it turned out, was surprisingly witty for someone of such stature and appearance. 'Then go, you loiterer, to the whorehouse to satisfy your need. Scram.'

Geralt unfastened the purse on his belt and, holding it by the straps, weighed it in his palm.

'You won't bribe me,' the Cerberus said proudly.

'I don't intend to.'

The porter was too huge to have the reflexes which would let him dodge or shield himself from a quick blow given by an ordinary man. He didn't even have time to blink before the witcher's blow landed. The heavy purse struck him in the temple with a metallic crash. He collapsed against the door, grabbing the frame with both hands. Geralt tore him away from it with a kick in the knee, shoved him with his shoulder and fetched him another blow with the purse. The doorman's eyes grew hazy and diverged in a comical squint, and his legs folded under him like two pen-knives. The witcher, seeing the strapping fellow moving, although almost unconscious, walloped him with force for the third time, right on the crown of his head.

'Money,' he muttered, 'opens all doors.'

It was dark in the vestibule. A loud snoring came from the door on the left. The witcher peeped in carefully. A fat woman, her nightdress hitched up above her hips, was asleep on a tumbled pallet, snoring and snorting through her nose. It wasn't the most beautiful sight. Geralt dragged the porter into the little room and closed the door.

On the right was another door, half-opened, and behind it stone steps led down. The witcher was about to pass them when an indistinct curse, a clatter and the dry crash of a vessel cracking reached him from below.

The room was a big kitchen, full of utensils, smelling of herbs and resinous wood. On the stone floor, among fragments of a clay jug, knelt a completely naked man with his head hanging low.

'Apple juice, bloody hell,' he mumbled, shaking his head like a sheep which had rammed a wall by a mistake. 'Apple . . . juice. Where . . . Where're the servants?'

'I beg your pardon?' the witcher asked politely.

The man raised his head and swallowed. His eyes were vague and very bloodshot.

'She wants juice from apples,' he stated, then got up with evident difficulty, sat down on a chest covered with a sheepskin coat, and leant against the stove. 'I have to . . . take it upstairs because—'

'Do I have the pleasure of speaking to the merchant Beau Berrant?'

'Quieter,' the man grimaced painfully. 'Don't yell. Listen, in that barrel there . . . Juice. Apple. Pour it into something . . . and help me get upstairs, all right?'

Geralt shrugged, then nodded sympathetically. He generally avoided overdoing the alcohol but the state in which the merchant found himself was not entirely unknown to him. He found a jug and a tin mug among the crockery and drew some juice from the barrel. He heard snoring and turned. Beau Berrant was fast asleep, his head hanging on his chest.

For a moment, the witcher considered pouring juice over him to wake him up, but he changed his mind. He left the kitchen, carrying the jug. The corridor ended in a heavy inlaid door. He entered carefully, opening it just enough to slip inside. It was dark, so he dilated his pupils. And wrinkled his nose.

A heavy smell of sour wine, candles and overripe fruit hung in the air. And something else, that brought to mind a mixture of the scents of lilac and gooseberries.

He looked around. The table in the middle of the chamber bore a battlefield of jugs, carafes, goblets, silver plates, dishes and ivory-handled cutlery. A creased tablecloth, which had been pushed aside, was soaked in wine, covered in purple stains and stiff with wax which had trickled down the candlesticks. Orange peel glowed like flowers among plum and peach stones, pear cores and grape stalks. A goblet had fallen over and smashed. The other was in one piece, half full, with a turkey bone sticking out of it. Next to the goblet stood a black, high-heeled slipper. It was made of basilisk skin. There wasn't a more expensive raw material which could be used in the making of shoes.

The other slipper lay under a chair on top of a carelessly discarded black dress with white frills and an embroidered flowery pattern.

For a moment Geralt stood undecided, struggling with embarrassment and the desire to turn on his heel and leave. But that would have meant his tussle with the Cerberus below had been unnecessary. And the witcher didn't like doing anything unnecessarily. He noticed winding stairs in the corner of the chamber.

On the steps he found four withered white roses and a napkin stained with wine and crimson lipstick. The scent of lilac and gooseberries grew stronger. The stairs led to a bedroom, the floor of which was covered in an enormous, shaggy animal skin. A white shirt with lace cuffs, and umpteen white roses, lay on the skin. And a black stocking.

The other stocking hung from one of the four engraved posts which supported the domed canopy over the bed. The engravings on the posts depicted nymphs and fauns in various positions. Some of the positions were interesting. Others funny. Many repeated themselves.

Geralt cleared his throat loudly, looking at the abundant black locks visible from under the eiderdown. The eiderdown moved and moaned. Geralt cleared his throat even louder.

'Beau?' the abundance of black locks asked indistinctly. 'Have you brought the juice?'

'Yes.'

A pale triangular face, violet eyes and narrow, slightly contorted lips appeared beneath the black tresses.

'Ooooh . . .' The lips became even more contorted. 'Ooooh . . . I'm dying of thirst . . .'

'Here you are.'

The woman sat up, scrambling out of the bedclothes. She had pretty shoulders, a shapely neck and, around it, a black velvet choker with a star-shaped jewel sparkling with diamonds. Apart from the choker she had nothing on.

'Thank you.' She took the mug from his hand, drank greedily, then raised her arms and touched her temples. The eiderdown slipped down even further. Geralt averted his eyes – politely, but unwillingly.

'Who are you?' asked the black-haired woman, narrowing her eyes and covering herself with the eiderdown. 'What are you doing here? And where, dammit, is Berrant?'

'Which question shall I answer first?'

He immediately regretted his sarcasm. The woman raised her hand and a golden streak shot out from her fingers. Geralt reacted instinctively, crossing both hands in the Sign of Heliotrope, and caught the spell just in front of his face, but the discharge was so strong that it threw him back against the wall. He sank to the floor.

226

'No need!' he shouted, seeing the woman raise her hand again. 'Lady Yennefer! I come in peace, with no evil intentions!'

A stamping came from the stairs and servants loomed in the bedroom doorway.

'Lady Yennefer!'

'Leave,' the sorceress ordered calmly. 'I don't need you. You're paid to keep an eye on the house. But since this individual has, nevertheless, managed to get in, I'll take care of him myself. Pass that on to Berrant. And prepare a bath for me.'

The witcher got up with difficulty. Yennefer observed him in silence, narrowing her eyes.

'You parried my spell,' she finally said. 'You're not a sorcerer, that's obvious. But you reacted exceptionally fast. Tell me who you are, stranger who has come in peace. And I advise you to speak quickly.'

'I'm Geralt of Rivia. A witcher.'

Yennefer leant out of the bed, grasping a faun – engraved on the pole – by a piece of anatomy well adapted to being grasped. Without taking her eyes off Geralt, she picked a coat with a fur collar up off the floor and wrapped herself up in it tightly before getting up. She poured herself another mug of juice without hurrying, drank it in one go, coughed and came closer. Geralt discreetly rubbed his lower back which, a moment ago, had collided painfully with the wall.

'Geralt of Rivia,' repeated the sorceress, looking at him from behind black lashes. 'How did you get in here? And for what reason? You didn't hurt Berrant, I hope?'

'No. I didn't. Lady Yennefer, I need your help.'

'A witcher,' she muttered, coming up even closer and wrapping the coat around her more tightly. 'Not only is it the first one I've seen up close but it's none other than the famous White Wolf. I've heard about you.'

'I can imagine.'

'I don't know what you can imagine.' She yawned, then came even closer. 'May I?' She touched his cheek and looked him in the eyes. He clenched his jaw. 'Do your pupils automatically adapt to

227

light or can you narrow and dilate them according to your will?'

'Yennefer,' he said calmly, 'I rode nonstop all day from Rinde. I waited all night for the gates to open. I gave your doorman, who didn't want to let me in, a blow to the head. I disturbed your sleep and peace, discourteously and importunately. All because my friend needs help which only you can give him. Give it to him, please, and then, if you like, we can talk about mutations and aberrations.'

She took a step back and contorted her lips unpleasantly. 'What sort of help do you mean?'

'The regeneration of organs injured through magic. The throat, larynx and vocal cords. An injury caused by a scarlet mist. Or something very much like it.'

'Very much like it,' she repeated. 'To put it in a nutshell, it wasn't a scarlet mist which has injured your friend. So what was it? Speak out. Being torn from my sleep at dawn, I have neither the strength nor the desire to probe your brain.'

'Hmm . . . It's best I start from the beginning.'

'Oh, no,' she interrupted him. 'If it's all that complicated then wait. An aftertaste in my mouth, dishevelled hair, sticky eyes and other morning inconveniences strongly affect my perceptive faculties. Go downstairs to the bath-chamber in the cellar. I'll be there in a minute and then you'll tell me everything.'

'Yennefer, I don't want to be persistent but time is pressing. My friend—'

'Geralt,' she interrupted sharply, 'I climbed out of bed for you and I didn't intend to do that before the chime of midday. I'm prepared to do without breakfast. Do you know why? Because you brought me the apple juice. You were in a hurry, your head was troubled with your friend's suffering, you forced your way in here, and yet you thought of a thirsty woman. You won me over, so my help is not out of the question. But I won't do anything without hot water and soap. Go. Please.'

'Very well.'

'Geralt.'

'Yes,' he stopped on the threshold.

228

'Make use of the opportunity to have a bath yourself. I can not only guess the age and breed of your horse, but also its colour, by the smell.'

IV

She entered the bath-chamber just as Geralt, sitting naked on a tiny stool, was pouring water over himself from a bucket. He cleared his throat and modestly turned his back to her.

'Don't be embarrassed,' she said, throwing an armful of clothing on the hook. 'I don't faint at the sight of a naked man. Triss Merigold, a friend, says if you've seen one, you've seen them all.'

He got up, wrapping a towel round his hips.

'Beautiful scar,' she smiled, looking at his chest. 'What was it? Did you fall under the blade in a saw-mill?'

He didn't answer. The sorceress continued to observe him, tilting her head coquettishly.

'The first witcher I can look at from close up, and completely naked at that. Aha!' She leant over, listening. 'I can hear your heart beat. It's very slow. Can you control how much adrenalin you secrete? Oh, forgive me my professional curiosity. Apparently, you're touchy about the qualities of your own body. You're wont to describe these qualities using words which I greatly dislike, lapsing into pompous sarcasm with it, something I dislike even more.'

He didn't answer.

'Well, enough of that. My bath is getting cold.' Yennefer moved as if she wanted to discard her coat, then hesitated. 'I'll take my bath while you talk, to save time. But I don't want to embarrass you and, besides, we hardly know each other. So then, taking decency into account—'

'I'll turn round,' he proposed hesitantly.

'No. I have to see the eyes of the person I'm talking to. I've got a better idea.'

He heard an incantation being recited, felt his medallion quiver and saw the black coat softly slip to the floor. Then he heard the water splashing.

'Now I can't see your eyes, Yennefer,' he said. 'And that's a pity.'

The invisible sorceress snorted and splashed in the tub. 'Go on.'

Geralt finished struggling with his trousers, pulling them on under his towel, and sat on the bench. Buckling up his boots, he related the adventure by the river, cutting out most of the skirmish with the catfish. Yennefer didn't seem the type to be interested in fishing.

When he got to the part where the cloud-creature escaped from the jar, the huge soapy sponge froze.

'Well, well,' he heard, 'that's interesting. A djinn in a bottle.'

'No djinn,' he contested. 'It was some variant of scarlet mist. Some new, unknown type—'

'The new and unknown type deserves to be called something,' said the invisible Yennefer. 'The name djinn is no worse than any other. Continue, please.'

He obeyed. The soap in the tub foamed relentlessly as he continued his tale, and the water overflowed. Something caught his eye. Looking more carefully he discerned outlines and shapes revealed by the soap covering the invisible Yennefer. They fascinated him to the extent that he was struck dumb.

'Go on!' a voice coming from nothingness, from above the outlines which so absorbed him, urged. 'What happened next?'

'That's all,' he said. 'I chased him away, that djinn, as you call him—'

'How?' The ladle rose and poured water. The soap vanished, as did the shapes.

Geralt sighed. 'With an incantation,' he said. 'An exorcism.'

'Which one?' The ladle poured water once more. The witcher started to observe the ladle's action more diligently because the water, albeit briefly, also revealed this and that. He repeated the incantation, substituting the vowel 'e' with an intake of breath, according to the safety rule. He thought he'd impress the sorceress by knowing the rule so he was surprised when he heard laughter coming from the tub.

'What's so funny?'

'That exorcism of yours . . .' The towel flew off its peg and suddenly began to wipe the rest of the outlines. 'Triss is going to kill herself laughing when I tell her. Who taught you that, witcher? That incantation?'

'A priestess from Huldra's sanctuary. It's a secret language of the temple—'

'Secret to some.' The towel slapped against the brim of the tub, water sprayed on to the floor and wet footprints marked the sorceress's steps. 'That wasn't an incantation, Geralt. Nor would I advise you to repeat those words in other temples.'

'What was it, if not an incantation?' he asked, watching two black stockings outline shapely legs, one after the other.

'A witty saying.' Frilly knickers clung to nothing in an unusually interesting manner. 'If rather indecent.'

A white shirt with an enormous flower-shaped ruffle fluttered upwards and outlined Yennefer's body. She didn't, the witcher noticed, bother with the whalebone nonsense usually worn by women. She didn't have to.

'What saying?' he asked.

'Never mind.'

The cork sprang from a rectangular crystal bottle standing on the stool. The bath-chamber started to smell of lilac and goose-berries. The cork traced several circles and jumped back into place. The sorceress fastened the cuffs of her shirt, pulled on a dress and materialised.

'Fasten me up.' She turned her back to him while combing her hair with a tortoiseshell comb. He noticed that the comb had a long, sharp prong which could, if need be, easily take the place of a dagger.

He took a deliberately long time fastening her dress, one hook at a time, enjoying the scent of her hair, which fell halfway down her back in a black cascade.

'Going back to the bottle creature,' said Yennefer, putting diamond earrings in her ears, 'it's obvious that it wasn't your funny incantation that drove him away. The hypothesis that he discharged his fury on your friend and left seems closer to the truth.'

'Probably,' Geralt agreed, gloomily. 'I don't think he flew off to Cidaris to do away with Valdo Marx.'

'Who's Valdo Marx?'

'A troubadour who considers my companion, also a poet and musician, a talentless wastrel who panders to the taste of the masses.'

The sorceress turned round with a strange glimmer in her eyes. 'Could it be that your friend managed to express a wish?'

'Two. Both stupid. Why do you ask? This fulfilling of wishes by genies is nonsense, after all, djinns, spirits of the lamp—'

'Clearly nonsense,' repeated Yennefer with a smile. 'Of course. It's an invention, a fairy tale devoid of any sense, like all the legends in which good spirits and fortune tellers fulfil wishes. Stories like that are made up by poor simpletons, who can't even dream of fulfilling their wishes and desires themselves. I'm pleased you're not one of them, Geralt of Rivia. It makes you closer in spirit to me. If I want something, I don't dream of it – I act. And I always get what I want.'

'I don't doubt it. Are you ready?'

'I am.' The sorceress finished fastening the straps of her slippers and stood up. Even in high heels, she wasn't impressively tall. She shook her hair which, he found, had retained its picturesque, dishevelled and curling disarray despite the furious combing.

'I've got a question, Geralt. The seal which closed the bottle . . . Has your friend still got it?'

The witcher reflected. He had the seal, not Dandilion. But experience had taught him that sorcerers shouldn't be told too much.

'Hmm . . . I think so.' He deceived her as to the reason for his delay in replying. 'Yes, he probably does. Why? Is the seal important?'

'That's a strange question,' she said sharply, 'for a witcher and a specialist in supernatural monstrosities. Someone who ought to know that such a seal is important enough not to touch. And not to let their friend touch.'

He clenched his jaw. The blow was well aimed.

'Oh, well.' Yennefer changed her tone to a much gentler one. 'No one's infallible and no witcher's infallible, as we see. Everyone can make a mistake. Well, we can get it on our way. Where's your comrade?'

'Here, in Rinde. At Errdil's. The elf's.'

She looked at him carefully.

'At Errdil's?' she repeated, contorting her lips in a smile. 'I know where that is. And I gather his cousin Chireadan is there too?'

'That's right. But what—?'

'Nothing,' she interrupted, raised her arms and closed her eyes.

The medallion around the witcher's neck pulsed, tugged at the chain.

On the damp bath-chamber wall shone the luminous outline of a door which framed a swirling phosphorescent milky nothingness. The witcher cursed. He didn't like magical portals, or travelling by them.

'Do we have to . . .' He cleared his throat. 'It's not far—'

'I can't walk the streets of this town,' she cut him short. 'They're not too crazy about me here. They might insult me and throw stones – or do something worse. Several people are effectively ruining my reputation here, thinking they can get away with it. Don't worry, my portals are safe.'

Geralt had once watched as only half a traveller using a safe portal flew through. The other half was never found. He knew of several cases where people had entered a portal and never been seen again.

The sorceress adjusted her hair again and pinned a pearl-embossed purse to her belt. The purse looked too small to hold anything other than a handful of coppers and a lipstick, but Geralt knew it was no ordinary purse.

'Hold me. Tighter. I'm not made of china. On our way!'

The medallion vibrated, something flashed and Geralt suddenly found himself in black nothingness, in penetrating cold. He couldn't see, hear or feel anything. Cold was all that his senses could register.

He wanted to curse, but didn't have time.

V

'It's an hour since she went in,' Chireadan turned over the hourglass standing on the table. 'I'm starting to get worried. Was Dandilion's throat really so bad? Don't you think we ought to go and have a look?'

'She made it quite clear that she didn't want us to.' Geralt finished his mug of herb tea, grimacing dreadfully. He valued and liked the settled elves for their intelligence, calm reserve and sense of humour, but he couldn't understand or share their taste in food or drink. 'I don't intend to disturb her, Chireadan. Magic requires time. It can take all day and night, as long as Dandilion gets better.'

'Oh well, you're right.'

A sound of hammering came from the room next door. Errdil, as it turned out, lived in a deserted inn which he had bought intending to renovate and then open with his wife, a quiet, taciturn elf. Vratimir, who had taken to their company after a night spent with the elves in the guardroom, volunteered to help with the repairs. He got down to renovating the wood panelling, working alongside the married couple, as soon as the confusion created by the witcher and Yennefer leaping through the wall in the flash of a portal had subsided.

'I didn't think you'd find it so easy, if I'm to be honest,' Chireadan went on. 'Yennefer isn't the most spontaneous of people when it comes to help. Others' troubles don't particularly bother her, and don't disturb her sleep. In a word, I've never heard of her helping anyone if there wasn't something in it for her. I wonder what's in it for her to help you and Dandilion.'

'Aren't you exaggerating?' The witcher smiled. 'I didn't have such a bad impression of her. She likes to demonstrate her superiority, it's true, but compared with other wizards, with that whole arrogant bunch, she's walking charm and kindliness personified.'

Chireadan also smiled. 'It's almost as though you thought a scorpion were prettier than a spider,' he said, 'because it's got such a lovely tail. Be careful, Geralt. You're not the first to have judged her like that without knowing she's turned her charm and beauty into weapons. Weapons she uses skilfully and without scruple. Which, of course, doesn't change the fact that she's a fascinating and good-looking woman. You wouldn't disagree, would you?'

Geralt glanced keenly at the elf. For a second time, he thought he saw traces of a blush on his face. It surprised him no less than Chireadan's words. Pure-blooded elves were not wont to admire human women, even the very beautiful ones, and Yennefer, although attractive in her own way, couldn't pass as a great beauty.

Each to their own taste but, in actual fact, not many would describe sorceresses as good-looking. Indeed, all of them came from social circles where the only fate for daughters would be marriage. Who would have thought of condemning their daughter to years of tedious studies and the tortures of somatic mutations if she could be given away in marriage and advantageously allied? Who wished to have a sorceress in their family? Despite the respect enjoyed by magicians, a sorceress's family did not benefit from her in the least because by the time the girl had completed her education, nothing tied her to her family anymore – only brotherhood counted, to the exclusion of all else. So only daughters with no chance of finding a husband become sorceresses.

Unlike priestesses and druidesses, who only unwillingly took ugly or crippled girls, sorcerers took anyone who showed evidence of a predisposition. If the child passed the first years of training, magic entered into the equation – straightening and evening out legs, repairing bones which had badly knitted, patching hare-lips,

235

removing scars, birthmarks and pox scars. The young sorceress would become attractive because the prestige of her profession demanded it. The result was pseudo-pretty women with the angry and cold eyes of ugly girls. Girls who couldn't forget their ugliness had been covered by the mask of magic only for the prestige of their profession.

No, Geralt couldn't understand Chireadan. His eyes, the eyes of a witcher, registered too many details.

'No, Chireadan,' he answered. 'I wouldn't disagree. Thank you for the warning. But this only concerns Dandilion. He suffered at my side, in my presence. I didn't manage to save him and I couldn't help him. I'd sit on a scorpion with my bare backside if I knew it would help him.'

'That's precisely what you've got to beware of most.' The elf smiled enigmatically. 'Because Yennefer knows it and she likes to make the most of such knowledge. Don't trust her, Geralt. She's dangerous.'

He didn't answer.

Upstairs, the door squeaked. Yennefer stood at the stairs, leaning on the gallery balustrade.

'Witcher, could you come here?'

'Of course.'

The sorceress leant her back against the door of one of the few rooms with furniture, where they had put the suffering troubadour.

The witcher approached, watchful and silent. He saw her left shoulder, slightly higher than her right. Her nose, slightly too long. Her lips, a touch too narrow. Her chin, receding a little too much. Her brows a little too irregular. Her eyes . . .

He saw too many details. Quite unnecessarily.

'How's Dandilion?'

'Do you doubt my capabilities?'

He continued watching. She had the figure of a twenty-year-old, although he preferred not to guess at her real age. She moved with natural, unaffected grace. No, there was no way of guessing what she had been like before, what had been improved. He stopped thinking about it; there wasn't any sense.

236

'Your talented friend will be well,' she said. 'He'll recover his vocal talents.'

'You have my gratitude, Yennefer.'

She smiled. 'You'll have an opportunity to prove it.'

'Can I look in on him?'

She remained silent for a moment, watching him with a strange smile and drumming her fingers on the door-frame. 'Of course. Go in.'

The medallion on the witcher's neck started to quiver, sharply and rhythmically.

A glass sphere the size of a small watermelon, aflame with a milky light, lay in the centre of the floor. The sphere marked the heart of a precisely traced nine-pointed star whose arms reached the corners and walls of the small chamber. A red pentagram was inscribed within the star. The tips of the pentagram were marked by black candles standing in weirdly shaped holders. Black candles had also been lit at the head of the bed where Dandilion, covered with sheepskins, rested. The poet was breathing peacefully; he didn't wheeze or rasp anymore and the rictus of pain had disappeared from his face, to be replaced by an idiotic smile of happiness.

'He's asleep,' said Yennefer. 'And dreaming.'

Geralt examined the patterns traced on the floor. The magic hidden within them was palpable, but he knew it was a dormant magic. It brought to mind the purr of a sleeping lion, without suggesting how the roar might sound.

'What is this, Yennefer?'

'A trap.'

'For what?'

'For you, for the time being.' The sorceress turned the key in the lock, then turned it over in her hand. The key disappeared.

'And thus I'm trapped,' he said coldly. 'What now? Are you going to assault my virtue?'

'Don't flatter yourself.' Yennefer sat on the edge of the bed. Dandilion, still smiling like a moron, groaned quietly. It was, without a doubt, a groan of bliss.

'What's this all about, Yennefer? If it's a game, I don't know the rules.'

'I told you,' she began, 'that I always get what I want. As it happens, I desire something that Dandilion has. I'll get it from him and we can part ways. Don't worry, he won't come to any harm—'

'The things you've set on the floor,' he interrupted, 'are used to summon demons. Someone always comes to harm where demons are summoned. I won't allow it.'

'—not a hair of his head will be harmed,' continued the sorceress, without paying any attention to his words. 'His voice will be even more beautiful and he'll be very pleased, even happy. We'll all be happy. And we'll part with no ill-feelings or resentment.'

'Oh, Virginia,' moaned Dandilion without opening his eyes. 'Your breasts are so beautiful, more delicate than a swan's down . . . Virginia . . .'

'Has he lost his mind? Is he raving?'

'He's dreaming,' smiled Yennefer. 'His dream wish is being satisfied in his sleep. I probed his mind to the very depths. There wasn't much there. A few obscenities, several dreams and masses of poetry. But be that as it may. The seal which plugged the bottle with the djinn, Geralt, I know he doesn't have it. You do. Please give it to me.'

'What do you need the seal for?'

'How should I answer your question?' The sorceress smiled coquettishly. 'Let's try this: it's none of your damned business, witcher. Does that satisfy you?'

'No.' His smile was equally nasty. 'It doesn't. But don't reproach yourself for it, Yennefer. I'm not easily satisfied. Only those who are above average have managed so far.'

'Pity. So you'll remain unsatisfied. It's your loss. The seal, please. Don't pull that face, it doesn't suit either your good looks or your complexion. In case you hadn't noticed, let me tell you that you are now beginning to repay the gratitude you owe me. The seal is the first instalment for the price to be paid for the singer's voice.'

238

'I see you've divided the price into several instalments,' he said coldly. 'Fine. I might have expected that. But let it be a fair trade, Yennefer. I bought your help. And I'll pay.'

She contorted her lips in a smile, but her violet eyes remained wide open and cold.

'You shouldn't have any doubts as to that, witcher.'

'Me,' he repeated. 'Not Dandilion. I'm taking him to a safe place. When I've done that I'll come back and pay your second instalment, and all the others. Because as to the first . . .'

He reached into a secret pocket of his belt and pulled out the brass seal with the sign of a star and broken cross.

'Here, take it. Not as an instalment. Accept it from a witcher as proof of his gratitude for having treated him more kindly, albeit in a calculated manner, than the majority of your brethren would have done. Accept it as evidence of goodwill, which ought to convince you that, having seen to my friend's safety, I'll return to repay you. I didn't see the scorpion amidst the flowers, Yennefer. I'm prepared to pay for my inattention.'

'A pretty speech.' The sorceress folded her arms. 'Touching and pompous. Pity it's in vain. I need Dandilion, so he's staying here.'

'He's already been close to the creature you intend to draw here.' Geralt indicated the patterns on the floor. 'When you've finished your handiwork and brought the djinn here Dandilion is most certainly going to suffer despite all your promises, maybe even more than before. Because it's the creature from the bottle that you want, isn't it? Do you intend to master it, force it to serve you? You don't have to answer, I know it's none of my damned business. Do what you want, draw ten demons in if you like. But without Dandilion. If you put him at risk, this will no longer be an honest trade, Yennefer, and you don't have the right to demand payment for that. I won't allow—' He broke off.

'I wondered when you'd feel it,' giggled the sorceress.

Geralt tensed his muscles and, clenching his jaw until it hurt, strained his entire will. It didn't help. He was paralysed, like a stone statue, like a post which had been dug into the ground. He couldn't even wiggle a toe.

'I knew you could deflect a spell thrown straight at you,' said Yennefer. 'I also knew that before you tried anything you'd try to impress me with your eloquence. You were talking while the spell hanging over you was working and slowly breaking you. Now you can only talk. But you don't have to impress me anymore. I know you're eloquent. Any further efforts in that direction will only spoil the effect.'

'Chireadan—' he said with an effort, still fighting the magical paralysis. 'Chireadan will realise that you're up to something. He'll soon work it out, suspect something any minute now, because he doesn't trust you, Yennefer. He hasn't trusted you from the start—'

The sorceress swept her hand in a broad gesture. The walls of the chamber became blurred and took on a uniform dull grey appearance and colour. The door disappeared, the windows disappeared, even the dusty curtains and pictures on the wall, splattered with flies, vanished.

'What if Chireadan does figure it out?' She grimaced maliciously. 'Is he going to run for help? Nobody will get through my barrier. But Chireadan's not going to run anywhere. He won't do anything against me. Anything. He's under my spell. No, it's not a question of black sorcery. I didn't do anything in that way. It's a simple question of body chemistry. He's fallen in love with me, the blockhead. Didn't you know? Can you imagine, he even intended to challenge Beau to a duel. A jealous elf. That rarely happens. Geralt, it's not for nothing that I chose this house.'

'Beau Berrant, Chireadan, Errdil, Dandilion. You really are heading for your goal as straight as you can. But me, Yennefer, you're not going to use me.'

'Oh I am, I am.' The sorceress got up from the bed and approached him, carefully avoiding the signs and symbols marked out on the floor. 'After all, I did say that you owe me something for curing the poet. It's a matter of a trifle, a small favour. After what I've done, what I intend to do here in a moment, I'm leaving Rinde and I've still got unpaid accounts in this town. I've promised several people here something, and I always keep my promises. Since I won't have time to do so myself, you'll keep those promises for me.'

He wrestled with all his might. In vain.

'Don't struggle, my little witcher.' She smiled spitefully. 'It's pointless. You've got a strong will and quite a bit of resistance to magic but you can't contend with me and my spell. And don't act out a farce for me, don't try to charm me with your hard and insolent masculinity. You are the only one to think you're insolent and hard. You'd do anything for me in order to save your friend, even without spells at that. You'd pay any price. You'd lick my boots. And maybe something else, too, if I unexpectedly wished to amuse myself.'

He remained silent. Yennefer was standing in front of him, smiling and fiddling with the obsidian star sparkling with diamonds pinned to her velvet ribbon.

'I already knew what you were like,' she continued, 'after exchanging a few words with you in Beau's bedroom. And I knew what form of payment I'd demand from you. My accounts in Rinde could be settled by anyone, including Chireadan. But you're the one who's going to do it because you have to pay me. For your insolence, for the cold way you look at me, for the eyes which fish for every detail, for your stony face and sarcastic tone of voice. For thinking that you could stand face to face with Yennefer of Vergerberg and believe her to be full of self-admiration and arrogance, a calculating witch, while staring at her soapy tits. Pay up, Geralt of Rivia!'

She grabbed his hair with both hands and kissed him violently on the lips, sinking her teeth into them like a vampire. The medallion on his neck quivered and it felt to Geralt as if the chain was shrinking and strangling him. Something blazed in his head while a terrible humming filled his ears. He stopped seeing the sorceress's violet eyes and fell into darkness.

He was kneeling. Yennefer was talking to him in a gentle, soft voice.

'You remember?'

241

'Yes, my lady.' It was his own voice.

'So go and carry out my instructions.'

'At your command, my lady.'

'You may kiss my hand.'

'Thank you, my lady.'

He felt himself approach her on his knees. Ten thousand bees buzzed in his head. Her hand smelt of lilac and gooseberries. Lilac and gooseberries . . . Lilac and gooseberries . . . A flash. Darkness.

A balustrade, stairs. Chireadan's face.

'Geralt! What's the matter with you? Geralt, where are you going?'

'I have to . . .' His own voice. 'I have to go—'

'Oh, gods! Look at his eyes!'

Vratimir's face, contorted with horror. Errdil's face. And Chireadan's voice.

'No! Errdil! Don't touch him! Don't try to stop him! Out of his way – get out of his way!'

The scent of lilac and gooseberries. Lilac and gooseberries . . .

A door. The explosion of sunlight. It's hot. Humid. The scent of lilac and gooseberries. There's going to be a storm, he thought.

And that was his last thought.

VI

Darkness. The scent . . .

Scent? No, smell. Stench of urine, rotten straw and wet rags. The stink of a smouldering torch stuck into an iron grip set in a wall of uneven stone blocks. A shadow thrown by the light of the torch, a shadow on the dirt floor—

The shadow of a grille.

The witcher cursed.

'At last.' He felt someone lift him up, rest his back against the damp wall. 'I was beginning to worry, you didn't regain consciousness for so long.'

'Chireadan? Where – dammit, my head's splitting – where are we?'

'Where do you think?'

Geralt wiped his face and looked around. Three rogues were sitting by the opposite wall. He couldn't see them clearly; they were sitting as far from the torch light as possible, in near complete darkness. Something which looked like a heap of rags crouched under the grille which separated them from the lit corridor. It was, in fact, a thin old man with a nose like a stork's beak. The length of his matted stringy hair and the state of his clothes showed that he hadn't arrived yesterday.

'They've thrown us in the dungeon,' he said gloomily.

'I'm glad you've regained your ability to draw logical conclusions,' said the elf.

'Bloody hell . . . And Dandilion? How long have we been here? How much time has gone by since—?'

'I don't know. I was unconscious, just like you, when I was thrown in here.' Chireadan raked up the straw to sit more comfortably. 'Is it important?'

'And how, dammit! Yennefer— And Dandilion— Dandilion's there, with her, and she's planning— Hey, you! How long have we been in here?'

The other prisoners whispered among themselves. None replied.

'Have you gone deaf?' Geralt spat, still unable to get rid of the metallic taste in his mouth. 'I'm asking you, what time of day is it? Or night? Surely you know what time they feed you?'

They muttered again, cleared their throats. 'Sirs,' said one of them at last. 'Leave us in peace and don't talk to us. We be decent thieves, not some politicals. We didn't try to attack the authorities. We was only stealing.'

'That be it,' said another. 'You've your corner, we've ours. And let each look after his own.'

Chireadan snorted. The witcher spat.

'That's the way it goes,' mumbled the hairy old man with a long nose. 'Everyone in the clink guards his own corner and holds with his own.'

'And you, old man,' asked the elf sneeringly, 'are you with them or with us? Which camp do you count yourself in?'

'None,' he answered proudly, 'because I'm innocent.'

Geralt spat again. 'Chireadan?' he asked, rubbing his temple. 'This attempt on the authorities . . . Is it true?'

'Absolutely. You don't remember?'

'I walked out into the street . . . People were looking at me . . . Then . . . Then there was a shop—'

'A pawnbroker's.' The elf lowered his voice. 'You went into the pawnbroker's. As soon as you walked in, you punched the owner in the teeth. Hard. Very hard.'

The witcher ground his teeth and cursed.

'The pawnbroker fell,' Chireadan continued quietly. 'And you kicked him several times in delicate places. The assistant ran to help his master and you threw him out of the window, into the street.'

'I fear,' muttered Geralt, 'that wasn't the end of it.'

'Your fears are well founded. You left the pawnbroker's and marched down the centre of the street, jostling passersby and shouting some nonsense about a lady's honour. There was quite a crowd following you, Errdil, Vratimir and I among them. Then you stopped in front of Laurelnose the apothecary's house, went in, and were back in the street a moment later, dragging Laurelnose by the leg. And you made something of a speech to the crowd.'

'What sort of a speech?'

'To put it simply, you stated that a self-respecting man shouldn't ever call a professional harlot a whore because it's base and repugnant, while using the word whore to describe a woman one has never knocked off or paid any money for doing so, is childish and punishable. The punishment, you announced, would be dealt there and then, and it would be fitting for a spoilt child. You thrust the apothecary's head between his knees, pulled down his pants and thrashed his arse with a belt.'

'Go on, Chireadan. Go on. Don't spare me.'

'You beat Laurelnose on the backside and the apothecary howled and sobbed, called to gods and men alike for help, begged for mercy – he even promised to be better in the future, but you clearly didn't believe him. Then several armed bandits, who in Rinde go by the name of guards, came running up.'

'And,' Geralt nodded, 'that's when I made a hit at the authorities?'

'Not at all. You made a hit at them much earlier. Both the pawnbroker and Laurelnose are on the town council. Both had called for Yennefer to be thrown out of town. Not only did they vote for it at the council but they badmouthed her in taverns and spread vulgar gossip.'

'I guessed that. Carry on. You stopped when the guards appeared. They threw me in here?'

'They wanted to. Oh, Geralt, what a sight it was. What you did to them, it's hard to describe. They had swords, whips, clubs, hatchets, and you only had an ash cane with a pommel, which you'd snatched from some dandy. And when they were all lying on the ground, you walked on. Most of us knew where you were going.'

'I'd be happy to know too.'

'You were going to the temple. Because the priest Krepp, who's also a member of the council, dedicated a lot of time to Yennefer in his sermons. You promised him a lesson in respect for the fair sex. When you spoke of him you omitted his title and threw in other descriptions, to the delight of the children trailing after you.'

'Aha,' muttered Geralt. 'So blasphemy came into it, too. What else? Desecration of the temple?'

'No. You didn't manage to get in there. An entire unit of municipal guards, armed – it seemed to me – with absolutely everything they could lay their hands on in the armoury apart from a catapult, was waiting in front of the temple. It looked as if they were going to slaughter you, but you didn't reach them. You suddenly grasped your head with both hands and fainted.'

'You don't have to finish. So, Chireadan, how were you imprisoned?'

'Several guards ran to attack you when you fell. I got into a dispute with them. I got a blow over the head with a mace and came to here, in this hole. No doubt they'll accuse me of taking part in an anti-human conspiracy.'

'Since we're talking about accusations,' the witcher ground his teeth again, 'what's in store for us, do you think?'

'If Neville, the mayor, gets back from the capital on time,' muttered Chireadan, 'who knows . . . he's a friend. But if he doesn't, then sentence will be passed by the councillors, including Laurelnose and the pawnbroker, of course. And that means—'

The elf made a brief gesture across his neck. Despite the darkness the gesture left little doubt as to Chireadan's meaning. The witcher didn't reply. The thieves mumbled to each other and the tiny old man, locked up for his innocence, seemed to be asleep.

'Great,' said Geralt finally, and cursed vilely. 'Not only will I hang, but I'll do so with the knowledge that I'm the cause of your death, Chireadan. And Dandilion's, too, no doubt. No, don't interrupt. I know it's Yennefer's prank, but I'm the guilty one. It's my foolishness. She deceived me, took the piss out of me, as the dwarves say.'

'Hmm . . .' muttered the elf. 'Nothing to add, nothing to take away. I warned you against her. Dammit, I warned you, and I turned out to be just as big an – pardon the word – idiot. You're worried that I'm here because of you, but it's quite the opposite. You're locked up because of me. I could have stopped you in the street, overpowered you, not allowed— But I didn't. Because I was afraid that when the spell she'd cast on you had dispelled, you'd go back and . . . harm her. Forgive me.'

'I forgive you, because you've no idea how strong that spell was. My dear elf, I can break an ordinary spell within a few minutes and I don't faint while doing it. You wouldn't have managed to break Yennefer's spell and you would have had difficulty overpowering me. Remember the guards.'

'I wasn't thinking about you. I repeat: I was thinking about her.'

'Chireadan?'

'Yes?'

'Do you . . . Do you—'

'I don't like grand words,' interrupted the elf, smiling sadly. 'I'm greatly, shall we say, fascinated by her. No doubt you're surprised that anyone could be fascinated by her?'

Geralt closed his eyes to recall an image which, without using grand words, fascinated him inexplicably.

'No, Chireadan,' he said. 'I'm not surprised.'

Heavy steps sounded in the corridor, and a clang of metal. The dungeon was filled with the shadows of four guards. A key grated. The innocent old man leapt away from the bars like a lynx and hid among the criminals.

'So soon?' The elf, surprised, half-whispered. 'I thought it would take longer to build the scaffold . . .'

One of the guards, a tall, strapping fellow, bald as a knee, his mug covered with bristles like a boar, pointed at the witcher.

'That one,' he said briefly.

Two others grabbed Geralt, hauled him up and pressed him against the wall. The thieves squeezed into their corner; the long-nosed grandad buried himself in the straw. Chireadan wanted to jump up, but he fell to the dirt floor, retreating from the short sword pointed at his chest.

The bald guard stood in front of the witcher, pulled his sleeves up and rubbed his fist.

'Councillor Laurelnose,' he said, 'told me to ask if you're enjoying our little dungeon. Perhaps there's something you need? Perhaps the chill is getting to you? Eh?'

Geralt did not answer. Nor could he kick the bald man, as the guards who restrained him were standing on his feet in their heavy boots.

The bald man took a short swing and punched the witcher in the stomach. It didn't help to tense his muscles in defence. Geralt, catching his breath with an effort, looked at the buckle of his own belt for a while, then the guards hauled him up again.

'Is there nothing you need?' the guard continued, stinking of onions and rotting teeth. 'The councillor will be pleased that you have no complaints.'

Another blow, in the same place. The witcher choked and would have puked, but he had nothing to throw up.

The bald guard turned sideways. He was changing hands.

Wham! Geralt looked at the buckle of his belt again. Although it seemed strange, there was no hole above it through which the wall could be seen.

'Well?' The guard backed away a little, no doubt planning to take a wider swing. 'Don't you have any wishes? Mr Laurelnose asked whether you have any. But why aren't you saying anything? Tongue-tied? I'll get it straight for you!'

Wham!

Geralt didn't faint this time either. And he had to faint because he cared for his internal organs. In order to faint, he had to force the guard to—

The guard spat, bared his teeth and rubbed his fist again.

'Well? No wishes at all?'

'Just one . . .' moaned the witcher, raising his head with difficulty. 'That you burst, you son-of-a-whore.'

The bald guard ground his teeth, stepped back and took a swing – this time, according to Geralt's plan, aiming for his head. But the blow never came. The guard suddenly gobbled like a turkey, grew red, grabbed his stomach with both hands, howled, roared with pain . . .

And burst.

VII

'And what am I to do with you?'

A blindingly bright ribbon of lightning cut the darkened sky outside the window, followed by a sharp, drawn-out crash of thunder. The downpour was getting harder as the storm cloud passed over Rinde.

Geralt and Chireadan, seated on a bench under a huge tapestry depicting the Prophet Lebiodus pasturing his sheep, remained

248

silent, modestly hanging their heads. Mayor Neville was pacing the chamber, snorting and panting with anger.

'You bloody, shitty sorcerers!' he yelled suddenly, standing still. 'Are you persecuting my town, or what? Aren't there any other towns in the world?'

The elf and witcher remained silent.

'To do something like—' the mayor choked. 'To turn the warder . . . Like a tomato! To pulp! To red pulp! It's inhuman!'

'Inhuman and godless,' repeated the priest, also present. 'So inhuman that even a fool could guess who's behind it. Yes, mayor. We both know Chireadan and the man here, who calls himself a witcher, wouldn't have enough Force to do this. It is all the work of Yennefer, that witch cursed by the gods!' There was a clap of thunder outside, as if confirming the priest's words. 'It's her and no one else,' continued Krepp. 'There's no question about it. Who, if not Yennefer, would want revenge upon Laurelnose?'

'Hehehe,' chuckled the mayor suddenly. 'That's the thing I'm least angry about. Laurelnose has been scheming against me; he's been after my office. And now the people aren't going to respect him. When they remember how he got it in the arse—'

'That's all it needs, Mr Neville, you to applaud the crime,' Krepp frowned. 'Let me remind you that had I not thrown an exorcism at the witcher, he would have raised his hand to strike me and the temple's majesty—'

'And that's because you spoke vilely about her in your sermons, Krepp. Even Berrant complained about you. But what's true is true. Do you hear that, you scoundrels?' The mayor turned to Geralt and Chireadan again. 'Nothing justifies what you've done! I don't intend to tolerate such things here! That's enough, now get on with it, tell me everything, tell me what you have for your defence, because if you don't, I swear by all the relics that I'll lead you such a dance as you won't forget to your dying day! Tell me everything, right now, as you would in a confessional!'

Chireadan sighed deeply and looked meaningfully and pleadingly at the witcher.

Geralt also sighed, then cleared his throat. And he recounted everything. Well, almost everything.

'So that's it,' said the priest after a moment's silence. 'A fine kettle of fish. A genie released from captivity. And an enchantress who has her sights on the genie. Not a bad arrangement. This could end badly, very badly.'

'What's a genie?' asked Neville. 'And what does this Yennefer want?'

'Enchanters,' explained Krepp, 'draw their power from the forces of nature, or to put it more accurately, from the so-called Four Elements or Principles, commonly called the natural forces. Air, Water, Fire and Earth. Each of these elements has its own Dimension which is called a Plane in the jargon used by enchanters. There's a Water Plane, Fire Plane and so on. These Dimensions, which are beyond our reach, are inhabited by what are called genies—'

'That's what they're called in legends,' interrupted the witcher. 'Because as far as I know—'

'Don't interrupt,' Krepp cut him short. 'The fact that you don't know much was evident in your tale, witcher. So be quiet and listen to what those wiser than you have to say. Going back to the genies, there are four sorts, just as there are four Planes. Djinns are air creatures; marides are associated with the principle of water; afreet are Fire genies and d'ao, the genies of Earth—'

'You've run away with yourself, Krepp,' Neville butted in. 'This isn't a temple school, don't lecture us. Briefly, what does Yennefer want with this genie?'

'A genie like this, mayor, is a living reservoir of magical energy. A sorcerer who has a genie at their beck and call can direct that energy in the form of spells. They don't have to draw the Force from Nature, the genie does it for them. The power of such an enchanter is enormous, close to omnipotence—'

'Somehow I've never heard of a wizard who can do everything,' contradicted Neville. 'On the contrary, the power of most of them is clearly exaggerated. They can't do this, they can't—'

'The enchanter Stammelford,' interrupted the priest, once more taking on the tone and poise of an academic lecturer, 'once moved a mountain because it obstructed the view from his tower. Nobody has managed to do the like, before or since. Because Stammelford, so they say, had the services of a d'ao, an Earth genie. There are records of deeds accomplished by other magicians on a similar scale. Enormous waves and catastrophic rains are certainly the work of marides. Fiery columns, fires and explosions the work of afreets—'

'Whirlwinds, hurricanes, flights above the earth,' muttered Geralt, 'Geoffrey Monck.'

'Exactly. I see you do know something after all.' Krepp glanced at him more kindly. 'Word has it old Monck had a way of forcing a djinn to serve him. There were rumours that he had more than one. He was said to keep them in bottles and make use of them when need arose. Three wishes from each genie, then it's free and escapes into its own dimension.'

'The one at the river didn't fulfil anything,' said Geralt emphatically. 'He immediately threw himself at Dandilion's throat.'

'Genies,' Krepp turned up his nose, 'are spiteful and deceitful beings. They don't like being packed into bottles and ordered to move mountains. They do everything they possibly can to make it impossible for you to express your wishes and then they fulfil them in a way which is hard to control and foresee, sometimes literally, so you have to be careful what you say. To subjugate a genie you need a will of iron, nerves of steel, a strong Force and considerable abilities. From what you say, it looks like your abilities, witcher, were too modest.'

'Too modest to subjugate the cad,' agreed Geralt. 'But I did chase him away; he bolted so fast the air howled. And that's also something. Yennefer, it's true, ridiculed my exorcism—'

'What was the exorcism? Repeat it.'

Geralt repeated it, word for word.

'What?!' The priest first turned pale, then red and finally blue. 'How dare you! Are you making fun of me?'

'Forgive me,' stuttered Geralt. 'To be honest, I don't know . . . what the words mean.'

'So don't repeat what you don't know! I've no idea where you could have heard such filth!'

'Enough of that.' The mayor waved it all aside. 'We're wasting time. Right. We now know what the sorceress wants the genie for. But you said, Krepp, that it's bad. What's bad? Let her catch him and go to hell, what do I care? I think—'

No one ever found out what Neville was thinking, even if it wasn't a boast. A luminous rectangle appeared on the wall next to the tapestry of Prophet Lebiodus, something flashed and Dandilion landed in the middle of the town hall.

'Innocent!' yelled the poet in a clear, melodious tenor, sitting on the floor and looking around, his eyes vague. 'Innocent! The witcher is innocent! I wish you to believe it!'

'Dandilion!' Geralt shouted, holding Krepp back, who was clearly getting ready to perform an exorcism or a curse. 'Where have you . . . here . . . Dandilion!'

'Geralt!' The bard jumped up.

'Dandilion!'

'Who's this?' Neville growled. 'Dammit, if you don't put an end to your spells, there's no guarantee what I'll do. I've said that spells are forbidden in Rinde! First you have to put in a written application, then pay a tax and stamp duty . . . Eh? Isn't it that singer, the witch's hostage?'

'Dandilion,' repeated Geralt, holding the poet by the shoulders. 'How did you get here?'

'I don't know,' admitted the bard with a foolish, worried expression. 'To be honest, I'm rather unaware of what happened to me. I don't remember much and may the plague take me if I know what of that is real and what's a nightmare. But I do remember quite a pretty, black-haired female with fiery eyes—'

'What are you telling me about black-haired women for?' Neville interrupted angrily. 'Get to the point, squire, to the point. You yelled that the witcher is innocent. How am I to understand that? That Laurelnose thrashed his own arse with his hands? Because if the witcher's innocent, it couldn't have been otherwise. Unless it was a mass hallucination.'

'I don't know anything about any arses or hallucinations,' said Dandilion proudly. 'Or anything about laurel noses. I repeat, that the last thing I remember was an elegant woman dressed in tastefully co-ordinated black and white. She threw me into a shiny hole, a magic portal for sure. But first she gave me a clear and precise errand. As soon as I'd arrived I was immediately to say, I quote: "My wish is for you to believe the witcher is not guilty for what occurred. That, and no other, is my wish." Word for word. Indeed, I tried to ask what all this was, what it was all about, and why. The black-haired woman didn't let me get a word in edgeways. She scolded me most inelegantly, grasped me by the neck and threw me into the portal. That's all. And now . . .' Dandilion pulled himself up, brushed his doublet, adjusted his collar and fancy − if dirty − ruffles. '. . . perhaps, gentlemen, you'd like to tell me the name of the best tavern in town and where it can be found.'

'There are no bad taverns in my town,' said Neville slowly. 'But before you see them for yourself, you'll inspect the best dungeon in this town very thoroughly. You and your companions. Let me remind you that you're still not free, you scoundrels! Look at them! One tells incredible stories while the other leaps out of the wall and shouts about innocence, I wish, he yells, you to believe me. He has the audacity to wish—'

'My gods!' the priest suddenly grasped his bald crown. 'Now I understand! The wish! The last wish!'

'What's happened to you, Krepp?' the mayor frowned. 'Are you ill?'

'The last wish!' repeated the priest. 'She made the bard express the last, the third wish. And Yennefer set a magical trap and, no doubt, captured the genie before he managed to escape into his own dimension! Mr Neville, we must—'

It thundered outside. So strongly that the walls shook.

'Dammit,' muttered the mayor, going up to the window. 'That was close. As long as it doesn't hit a house. All I need now is a fire— Oh gods! Just look! Just look at this! Krepp! What is it?'

All of them, to a man, rushed to the window.

'Mother of mine!' yelled Dandilion, grabbing his throat. 'It's him! It's that son-of-a-bitch who strangled me!'

'The djinn!' shouted Krepp. 'The Air genie!'

'Above Errdil's tavern!' shouted Chireadan, 'above his roof!'

'She's caught him!' The priest leant out so far he almost fell. 'Can you see the magical light? The sorceress has caught the genie!'

Geralt watched in silence.

Once, years ago, when a little snot-faced brat following his studies in Kaer Morhen, the Witchers' Settlement, he and a friend, Eskel, had captured a huge forest bumble-bee and tied it to a jug with a thread. They were in fits of laughter watching the antics of the tied bumble-bee, until Vesemir, their tutor, caught them at it and tanned their hides with a leather strap.

The djinn, circling above the roof of Errdil's tavern, behaved exactly like that bumble-bee. He flew up and fell, he sprang up and dived, he buzzed furiously in a circle. Because the djinn, exactly like the bumble-bee in Kaer Morhen, was tied down. Twisted threads of blindingly bright light of various colours were tightly wrapped around him and ended at the roof. But the djinn had more options than the bumble-bee, which couldn't knock down surrounding roofs, rip thatches to shreds, destroy chimneys, and shatter towers and garrets. The djinn could. And did.

'It's destroying the town,' wailed Neville. 'That monster's destroying my town!'

'Hehehe,' laughed the priest. 'She's found her match, it seems! It's an exceptionally strong djinn! I really don't know who's caught whom, the witch him or he the witch! Ha, it'll end with the djinn grinding her to dust. Very good! Justice will be done!'

'I shit on justice!' yelled the mayor, not caring if there were any voters under the window. 'Look what's happening there, Krepp! Panic, ruin! You didn't tell me that, you bald idiot! You played the wise guy, gabbled on, but not a word about what's most important! Why didn't you tell me that that demon . . . Witcher! Do something! Do you hear, innocent sorcerer? Do something about that demon! I forgive you all your offences, but—'

'There's nothing can be done here, Mr Neville,' snorted Krepp. 'You didn't listen to what I was saying, that's all. You never listen to me. This, I repeat, is an exceptionally strong djinn. If it wasn't for that, the sorceress would have hold of him already. Her spell is soon going to weaken, and then the djinn is going to crush her and escape. And we'll have some peace.'

'And in the meantime, the town will go to ruins?'

'We've got to wait,' repeated the priest, 'but not idly. Give out the orders, mayor. Tell the people to evacuate the surrounding houses and get ready to extinguish fires. What's happening there now is nothing compared to the hell that's going to break loose when the genie has finished with the witch.'

Geralt raised his head, caught Chireadan's eye and looked away.

'Mr Krepp,' he suddenly decided, 'I need your help. It's about the portal through which Dandilion appeared here. The portal still links the town hall to—'

'There's not even a trace of the portal anymore,' the priest said coldly, pointing to the wall. 'Can't you see?'

'A portal leaves a trace, even when invisible. A spell can stabilise such a trace. I'll follow it.'

'You must be mad. Even if a passage like that doesn't tear you to pieces, what do you expect to gain by it? Do you want to find yourself in the middle of a cyclone?'

'I asked if you can cast a spell which could stabilise the trace.'

'Spell?' the priest proudly raised his head. 'I'm not a godless sorcerer! I don't cast spells! My power comes from faith and prayer!'

'Can you or can't you?'

'I can.'

'Then get on with it, because time's pressing on.'

'Geralt,' said Dandilion, 'you've gone stark raving mad! Keep away from that bloody strangler!'

'Silence, please,' said Krepp, 'and gravity. I'm praying.'

'To hell with your prayers!' Neville hollered. 'I'm off to gather the people. We've got to do something and not stand here gabbling! Gods, what a day! What a bloody day!'

The witcher felt Chireadan touch his shoulder. He turned. The elf looked him in the eyes, then lowered his own.

'You're going there because you have to, aren't you?'

Geralt hesitated. He thought he smelled the scent of lilac and gooseberries.

'I think so,' he said reluctantly. 'I do have to. I'm sorry, Chireadan—'

'Don't apologise. I know what you feel.'

'I doubt it. Because I don't know myself.'

The elf smiled. The smile had little to do with joy. 'That's just it, Geralt. Precisely it.'

Krepp pulled himself upright and took a deep breath. 'Ready,' he said, pointing with pride at the barely visible outline on the wall. 'But the portal is unsteady and won't stay there for long. And there's no way to be sure it won't break. Before you step through, sir, examine your conscience. I can give you a blessing, but in order to forgive you your sins—'

'—there's no time,' Geralt finished the sentence for him. 'I know, Mr Krepp. There's never enough time for it. Leave the chamber, all of you. If the portal explodes it'll burst your eardrums.'

'I'll stay,' said Krepp, when the door had closed behind Dandilion and the elf. He waved his hands in the air, creating a pulsating aura around himself. 'I'll spread some protection, just in case. And if the portal does burst . . . I'll try and pull you out, witcher. What are eardrums to me? They grow back.'

Geralt looked at him more kindly.

The priest smiled. 'You're a brave man,' he said. 'You want to save her, don't you? But bravery isn't going to be of much use to you. Djinns are vengeful beings. The sorceress is lost. And if you go there, you'll be lost, too. Examine your conscience.'

'I have.' Geralt stood in front of the faintly glowing portal. 'Mr Krepp, sir?'

'Yes.'

'That exorcism which made you so angry . . . What do the words mean?'

'Indeed, what a moment for quips and jokes—'

'Please, Mr Krepp, sir.'

'Oh, well,' said the priest, hiding behind the mayor's heavy oak table. 'It's your last wish, so I'll tell you. It means . . . Hmm . . . Hmm . . . essentially . . . *get out of here and go fuck yourself!*'

Geralt entered the nothingness, where cold stifled the laughter which was shaking him.

VIII

The portal, roaring and whirling like a hurricane, spat him out with a force that bruised his lungs. The witcher collapsed on the floor, panting and catching his breath with difficulty.

The floor shook. At first he thought he was trembling after his journey through the splitting hell of the portal, but he rapidly realised his mistake. The whole house was vibrating, trembling and creaking.

He looked around. He was not in the small room where he had last seen Yennefer and Dandilion but in the large communal hall of Errdil's renovated tavern.

He saw her. She was kneeling between tables, bent over the magical sphere. The sphere was aflame with a strong, milky light, so bright, enough to shine red through her fingers. The light from the sphere illuminated a scene, flickering and swaying, but clear. Geralt saw the small room with a star and pentagram traced on the floor, blazing with white heat. He saw many-coloured, creaking, fiery lines shooting from the pentagram and disappearing up over the roof towards the furious roar of the captured djinn.

Yennefer saw him, jumped up and raised her hand.

'No!' he shouted, 'don't do this! I want to help you!'

'Help?' She snorted. 'You?'

'Me.'

'In spite of what I did to you?'

'In spite of it.'

'Interesting. But not important. I don't need your help. Get out of here.'

'No.'

'Get out of here!' she yelled, grimacing ominously. 'It's getting dangerous! The whole thing's getting out of control, do you understand? I can't master him. I don't get it, but the scoundrel isn't weakening at all! I caught him once he'd fulfilled the troubadour's third wish and I should have him in the sphere by now. But he's not getting any weaker! Dammit, it looks as if he's getting stronger! But I'm still going to get the better of him, I'll break—'

'You won't break him, Yennefer. He'll kill you.'

'It's not so easy to kill me—'

She broke off. The whole roof of the tavern suddenly flared up. The vision projected by the sphere dissolved in the brightness. A huge fiery rectangle appeared on the ceiling. The sorceress cursed as she lifted her hands, and sparks gushed from her fingers.

'Run, Geralt!'

'What's happening, Yennefer?'

'He's located me . . .' She groaned, flushing red with effort. 'He wants to get at me. He's creating his own portal to get in. He can't break loose but he'll get in by the portal. I can't— I can't stop him!'

'Yennefer—'

'Don't distract me! I've got to concentrate . . . Geralt, you've got to get out of here. I'll open my portal, a way for you to escape. Be careful, it'll be a random portal, I haven't got time or strength for any other . . . I don't know where you'll end up . . . but you'll be safe . . . Get ready—'

A huge portal on the ceiling suddenly flared blindingly, expanded and grew deformed. Out of the nothingness appeared the shapeless mouth already known to the witcher, snapping its drooping lips and howling loudly enough to pierce his ears. Yennefer jumped, waved her arms and shouted an incantation. A net of light shot from her palm and fell on the djinn. It gave a roar and sprouted long paws which shot towards the sorceress's throat like attacking cobras. Yennefer didn't back away.

Geralt threw himself towards her, pushed her aside and sheltered her. The djinn, tangled in the magical light, sprang from the portal like a cork from a bottle and threw himself at them, opening his jaws. The witcher clenched his teeth and hit him with the Sign without any apparent effect. But the genie didn't attack. He hung in the air just below the ceiling, swelled to an impressive size, goggled at Geralt with his pale eyes and roared. There was something in that roar, something like a command, an order. He didn't understand what it was.

'This way!' shouted Yennefer, indicating the portal which she had conjured up on the wall by the stairs. In comparison to the one created by the genie, the sorceress's portal looked feeble, extremely inferior. 'This way, Geralt! Run for it!'

'Only with you!'

Yennefer, sweeping the air with her hands, was shouting incantations and the many-coloured fetters showered sparks and creaked. The djinn whirled like the bumble-bee, pulling the bonds tight, then loosening them. Slowly but surely he was drawing closer to the sorceress. Yennefer did not back away.

The witcher leapt to her, deftly tripped her up, grabbed her by the waist with one hand and dug the other into her hair at the nape. Yennefer cursed nastily and thumped him in the neck with her elbow. He didn't let go of her. The penetrating smell of ozone, created by the curses, didn't kill the smell of lilac and gooseberries. Geralt stilled the sorceress's kicking legs and jumped, raising her straight up to the opalescently flickering nothingness of the lesser portal.

The portal which led into the unknown.

They flew out in a tight embrace, fell onto a marble floor and slid across it, knocking over an enormous candlestick and a table from which crystal goblets, platters of fruit and a huge bowl of crushed ice, seaweed and oysters showered down with a crash. Screams and squeals came from around the room.

They were lying in the very centre of a ballroom, bright with candelabra. Richly-clad gentlemen and ladies, sparkling with jewels, had stopped dancing and were watching them in stunned silence. The musicians in the gallery finished their piece in a cacophony which grated on the ears.

'You moron!' Yennefer yelled, trying to scratch out his eyes. 'You bloody idiot! You stopped me! I nearly had him!'

'You had shit-all!' he shouted back, furious. 'I saved your life, you stupid witch!'

She hissed like a furious cat, her palms showered sparks.

Geralt, turning his face away, caught her by both wrists and they rolled among the oysters, seaweed and crushed ice.

'Do you have an invitation?' A portly man with the golden chain of a chamberlain on his chest was looking at them with a haughty expression.

'Screw yourself!' screamed Yennefer, still trying to scratch Geralt's eyes out.

'It's a scandal,' the chamberlain said emphatically. 'Verily, you're exaggerating with this teleportation. I'm going to complain to the Council of Wizards. I'll demand—'

No one ever heard what the chamberlain would demand. Yennefer wrenched herself free, slapped the witcher in the ear with her open palm, kicked him forcefully in the shin and jumped into the fading portal in the wall.

Geralt threw himself after her, catching her hair and belt with a practised move.

Yennefer, also having gained practise, landed him a blow with her elbow.

The sudden move split her dress at the armpit, revealing a shapely breast. An oyster flew from her torn dress.

They both fell into the nothingness of the portal. Geralt could still hear the chamberlain's voice.

'Music! Play on! Nothing has happened. Please take no notice of that pitiful incident!'

The witcher was convinced that with every successive journey through the portal, the risk of misfortune was multiplying and he wasn't mistaken. They hit the target, Errdil's tavern, but they materialised just under the ceiling. They fell, shattering the stair balustrade and, with a deafening crash, landed on the table. The table had the right not to withstand the blow, and it didn't.

Yennefer found herself under the table. He was sure she had lost consciousness. He was mistaken.

She punched him in the eye and fired a volley of insults straight at him which would do credit to a dwarven undertaker – and they were renowned for their foul language. The curses were accompanied by furious, chaotic blows dealt blindly, randomly.

Geralt grabbed her by the hands and, to avoid being hit by her forehead, thrust his face into the sorceress's cleavage which smelled of lilac, gooseberries and oysters.

'Let me go!' she screamed, kicking like a pony. 'You idiot! Let go! The fetters are going to break any moment now. I've got to strengthen them or the djinn will escape!'

He didn't answer, although he wanted to. He grasped her even more tightly, trying to pin her down to the floor. Yennefer swore horribly, struggled, and with all her strength, kicked him in the crotch with her knee. Before he could catch his breath she broke free and screamed an incantation. He felt a terrible force drag him from the ground and hurl him across the hall until, with a violence that near-stunned him, he slammed against a carved two-doored chest of drawers and shattered it completely.

IX

'What's happening there?!' Dandilion, clinging to the wall, strained his neck, trying to see through the downpour. 'Tell me what's happening there, dammit!'

'They're fighting!' yelled an urchin, springing away from the tavern window as if he'd burnt himself. His tattered friends also escaped, slapping the mud with their bare heels. 'The sorcerer and the witch are fighting!'

'Fighting?' Neville was surprised. 'They're fighting, and that shitty demon is ruining my town! Look, he's knocked another chimney down. And damaged the brick-kiln! Hey, you get over there, quick! Gods, we're lucky it's raining or there'd be a fire like nobody's business!'

'This won't last much longer,' Krepp said gloomily. 'The magical light is weakening, the bonds will break at any moment. Mr Neville! Order the people to move back! All hell's going to break loose over there at any minute! There'll be only splinters left of that house! Mr Errdil, what are you laughing at? It's your house. What makes you so amused?'

'I had that wreck insured for a massive sum!'

'Does the policy cover magical and supernatural events?'

'Of course.'

'That's wise, Mr Elf. Very wise. Congratulations. Hey, you people, get to some shelter! Don't get any closer, if you value your lives!'

A deafening crash came from within Errdil's house, and lightning flashed. The small crowd retreated, hiding behind the pillars.

'Why did Geralt go there?' groaned Dandilion. 'What the hell for? Why did he insist on saving that witch? Why, dammit? Chireadan, do you understand?'

The elf smiled sadly. 'Yes, I do, Dandilion,' he said. 'I do.'

X

Geralt leapt away from another blazing orange shaft which shot from the sorceress's fingers. She was clearly tired, the shafts were weak and slow, and he avoided them with no great difficulty.

'Yennefer!' he shouted. 'Calm down! Will you listen!? You won't be able—'

He didn't finish. Thin red bolts of lightning spurted from the sorceress's hands, reaching him in many places and wrapping him up thoroughly. His clothes hissed and started to smoulder.

'I won't be able to?' she said through her teeth, standing over

262

him. 'You'll soon see what I'm capable of. It will suffice for you to lie there for a while and not get in my way.'

'Get this off me!' he roared, struggling in the blazing spider's web. 'I'm burning, dammit!'

'Lie there and don't move,' she advised, panting heavily. 'It only burns when you move . . . I can't spare you any more time, witcher. We had a romp, but enough's enough. I've got to take care of the djinn; he's ready to run away—'

'Run away?' Geralt screamed. 'It's you who should run away! That djinn . . . Yennefer, listen to me carefully. I've got to tell you the truth.'

XI

The djinn gave a tug at the fetters, traced a circle, tightened the lines holding it, and swept the little tower off Beau Berrant's house.

'What a roar he's got!' Dandilion frowned, instinctively clasping his throat. 'What a terrible roar! It looks as if he's bloody furious!'

'That's because he is,' said Krepp. Chireadan glanced at him.

'What?'

'He's furious,' repeated Krepp. 'And I'm not surprised. I'd be furious too if I had to fulfil, to the letter, the first wish accidentally expressed by the witcher—'

'How's that?' shouted Dandilion. 'Geralt? Wish?'

'He's the one who held the seal which imprisoned the djinn. The djinn's fulfilling his wishes. That's why the witch can't master it. But the witcher mustn't tell her, even if he's caught on to it by now. He shouldn't tell her.'

'Dammit,' muttered Chireadan. 'I'm beginning to understand. The warder in the dungeon burst . . .'

'That was the witcher's second wish. He's still got one left. The last one. But, gods help us, he shouldn't reveal that to Yennefer!'

She stood motionless, leaning over him, paying no attention to the djinn struggling at its bonds above the tavern roof. The building shook, lime and splinters poured from the ceiling, furniture crept along the floor, shuddering spasmodically.

'So that's how it is,' she hissed. 'Congratulations. You deceived me. Not Dandilion, but you. That's why the djinn's fighting so hard! But I haven't lost yet, Geralt. You underestimate me, and you underestimate my power. I've still got the djinn and you in my hand. You've still got one last wish, haven't you? So make it. You'll free the djinn and then I'll bottle it.'

'You haven't got enough strength left, Yennefer.'

'You underestimate my strength. The wish, Geralt!'

'No, Yennefer. I can't . . . The djinn might fulfil it, but it won't spare you. It'll kill you when it's free. It'll take its revenge on you . . . You won't manage to catch it and you won't manage to defend yourself against it. You're weakened, you can barely stand. You'll die, Yennefer.'

'That's my risk!' she shouted, enraged. 'What's it to you what happens to me? Think rather what the djinn can give you! You've still got one wish! You can ask what you like! Make use of it! Use it, witcher! You can have anything! Anything!'

'Are they both going to die?' wailed Dandilion. 'How come? Krepp, why? After all, the witcher— Why, by all perfidious and unexpected plagues, isn't he escaping? Why? What's keeping him? Why doesn't he leave that bloody witch to her fate and run away? It's senseless!'

'Absolutely senseless,' repeated Chireadan bitterly. 'Absolutely.'

'It's suicide. And plain idiocy!'

'It's his job, after all,' interrupted Neville. 'The witcher's saving my town. May the gods be my witness – if he defeats the witch and chases the demon away, I'll reward him handsomely . . .'.

Dandilion snatched the hat decorated with a heron's feather from his head, spat into it, threw it in the mud and trampled on it, spitting out words in various languages as he did.

'But he's . . .' he groaned suddenly, 'still got one wish in reserve! He could save both her and himself! Mr Krepp!'

'It's not that simple,' the priest pondered. 'But if . . . If he expressed the right wish . . . If he somehow tied his fate to the fate . . . No, I don't think it would occur to him. And it's probably better that it doesn't.'

XIV

'The wish, Geralt! Hurry up! What do you desire? Immortality? Riches? Fame? Power? Might? Privileges? Hurry, we haven't any time!' He was silent. 'Humanity,' she said suddenly, smiling nastily. 'I've guessed, haven't I? That's what you want, that's what you dream of! Of release, of the freedom to be who you want, not who you have to be. The djinn will fulfil that wish, Geralt. Just say it.'

He stayed silent.

She stood over him in the flickering radiance of the wizard's sphere, in the glow of magic, amidst the flashes of rays restraining the djinn, streaming hair and eyes blazing violet, erect, slender, dark, terrible . . .

And beautiful.

All of a sudden she leant over and looked him in the eyes. He caught the scent of lilac and gooseberries.

'You're not saying anything,' she hissed. 'So what is it you desire, witcher? What is your most hidden dream? Is it that you don't know or you can't decide? Look for it within yourself, look deeply and carefully because, I swear by the Force, you won't get another chance like this!'

But he suddenly knew the truth. He knew it. He knew what she used to be. What she remembered, what she couldn't forget, what she lived with. Who she really was before she had become a sorceress.

Her cold, penetrating, angry and wise eyes were those of a hunchback.

He was horrified. No, not of the truth. He was horrified that she would read his thoughts, find out what he had guessed. That she would never forgive him for it. He deadened that thought within himself, killed it, threw it from his memory forever, without trace, feeling, as he did so, enormous relief. Feeling that—

The ceiling cracked open. The djinn, entangled in the net of the now fading rays, tumbled right on top of them, roaring, and in that roar were triumph and murder lust. Yennefer leapt to meet him. Light beamed from her hands. Very feeble light.

The djinn opened his mouth and stretched his paws towards her.

The witcher suddenly understood what it was he wanted.

And he made his wish.

XV

The house exploded. Bricks, beams and planks flew up in a cloud of smoke and sparks. The djinn spurted from the dust-storm, huge as a barn. Roaring and choking with triumphant laughter the Air genie, free now, not tied to anyone's will, traced three circles above the town, tore the spire from the town hall, soared into the sky and vanished.

'It's escaped! It's escaped!' called Krepp. 'The witcher's had his way! The genie has flown away! It won't be a threat to anyone anymore!'

'Ah,' said Errdil with genuine rapture, 'what a wonderful ruin!'

'Dammit, dammit!' hollered Dandilion, huddled behind the

wall. 'It's shattered the entire house! Nobody could survive that! Nobody, I tell you!'

'The witcher, Geralt of Rivia, has sacrificed himself for the town,' mayor Neville said ceremoniously. 'We won't forget him. We'll revere him. We'll think of a statue . . .'

Dandilion shook a piece of wicker matting bound with clay from his shoulder, brushed his jerkin free of lumps of rain-dampened plaster, looked at the mayor and, in a few well-chosen words, expressed his opinion about sacrifice, reverence, memory and all the statues in the world.

XVI

Geralt looked around. Water was slowly dripping from the hole in the ceiling. There were heaps of rubble and stacks of timber all around. By a strange coincidence, the place where they lay was completely clear. Not one plank or one brick had fallen on them. It was as if they were being protected by an invisible shield.

Yennefer, slightly flushed, knelt by him, resting her hands on her knees.

'Witcher.' She cleared her throat. 'Are you dead?'

'No.' Geralt wiped the dust from his face and hissed.

Slowly, Yennefer touched his wrist and delicately ran her fingers along his palm. 'I burnt you—'

'It's nothing. A few blisters—'

'I'm sorry. You know, the djinn's escaped. For good.'

'Do you regret it?'

'Not much.'

'Good. Help me up, please.'

'Wait,' she whispered. 'That wish of yours . . . I heard what you wished for. I was astounded, simply astounded. I'd have expected anything but to . . . What made you do it, Geralt? Why . . . Why me?'

'Don't you know?'

She leant over him, touched him. He felt her hair, smelling of lilac and gooseberries, brush his face and he suddenly knew that he'd never forget that scent, that soft touch, knew that he'd never be able to compare it to any other scent or touch. Yennefer kissed him and he understood that he'd never desire any lips other than hers, so soft and moist, sweet with lipstick. He knew that, from that moment, only she would exist, her neck, shoulders and breasts freed from her black dress, her delicate, cool skin, which couldn't be compared to any other he had ever touched. He gazed into her violet eyes, the most beautiful eyes in the world, eyes which he feared would become . . .

Everything. He knew.

'Your wish,' she whispered, her lips very near his ear. 'I don't know whether such a wish can ever be fulfilled. I don't know whether there's such a Force in Nature that could fulfil such a wish. But if there is, then you've condemned yourself. Condemned yourself to me.'

He interrupted her with a kiss, an embrace, a touch, caresses and then with everything, his whole being, his every thought, his only thought, everything, everything, everything. They broke the silence with sighs and the rustle of clothing strewn on the floor. They broke the silence very gently, lazily, and they were considerate and very thorough. They were caring and tender and, although neither quite knew what caring and tenderness were, they succeeded because they very much wanted to. And they were in no hurry whatsoever. The whole world had ceased to exist for a brief moment, but to them, it seemed like a whole eternity.

And then the world started to exist again; but it existed very differently.

'Geralt?'

'Mmm?'

'What now?'

'I don't know.'

'Nor do I. Because, you see, I . . . I don't know whether it was worth condemning yourself to me. I don't know how— Wait, what are you doing . . .? I wanted to tell you—'

268

'Yennefer . . . Yen.'

'Yen,' she repeated, giving in to him completely. 'Nobody's ever called me that. Say it again.'

'Yen.'

'Geralt.'

XVII

It had stopped raining. A rainbow appeared over Rinde and cut the sky with a broken, coloured arc. It looked as if it grew straight from the tavern's ruined roof.

'By all the gods,' muttered Dandilion, 'what silence . . . They're dead, I tell you. Either they've killed each other or my djinn's finished them off.'

'We should go and see,' said Vratimir, wiping his brow with his crumpled hat. 'They might be wounded. Should I call a doctor?'

'An undertaker, more like it,' said Krepp. 'I know that witch, and that witcher's got the devil in his eyes too. There's no two ways about it, we've got to start digging two pits in the cemetery. I'd advise sticking an aspen stake into that Yennefer before burying her.'

'What silence,' repeated Dandilion. 'Beams were flying all over the place a moment ago and now it's as quiet as a grave.'

They approached the tavern ruins very cautiously and slowly.

'Let the carpenter get the coffins ready,' said Krepp. 'Tell the carpenter—'

'Quiet,' interrupted Errdil. 'I heard something. What was it, Chireadan?'

The elf brushed the hair off his pointed ear and tilted his head.

'I'm not sure . . . Let's get closer.'

'Yennefer's alive,' said Dandilion suddenly, straining his musical ear. 'I heard her moan. There, she moaned again!'

'Uhuh,' confirmed Errdil. 'I heard it, too. She moaned. She

must really be suffering. Chireadan, where are you going? Careful!'

The elf backed away from the shattered window through which he had carefully peeped.

'Let's get out of here,' he said quietly. 'Let's not disturb them.'

'They're both alive? Chireadan? What are they doing?'

'Let's get out of here,' repeated the elf. 'Let's leave them alone for a bit. Let them stay there, Yennefer, Geralt and his last wish. Let's wait in a tavern; they'll join us before long. Both of them.'

'What are they doing?' Dandilion was curious. 'Tell me, dammit!'

The elf smiled. Very, very sadly. 'I don't like grand words,' he said. 'And it's impossible to give it a name without using grand words.'

THE VOICE OF REASON 7

Falwick, in full armour, without a helmet and with the crimson coat of the Order flung over his shoulder, stood in the glade. Next to him, with his arms across his chest, was a stocky, bearded dwarf in an overcoat lined with fox-fur over a chain-mail shirt of iron rings. Tailles, wearing no armour but a short, quilted doublet, paced slowly, brandishing his unsheathed sword from time to time.

The witcher looked about, restraining his horse. All around glinted the cuirasses and flat helmets of soldiers armed with lances.

'Bloody hell,' muttered Geralt. 'I might have expected this.'

Dandilion turned his horse and quietly cursed at the sight of the lances cutting off their retreat.

'What's this about, Geralt?'

'Nothing. Keep your mouth shut and don't butt in. I'll try to lie my way out of it somehow.'

'What's it about, I ask you? More trouble?'

'Shut up.'

'It was a stupid idea after all, to ride into town,' groaned the troubadour, glancing towards the nearby towers of the temple visible above the forest. 'We should have stayed at Nenneke's and not stirred beyond the walls—'

'Shut up. It'll all become clear, you'll see.'

'Doesn't look like it.'

Dandilion was right. It didn't. Tailles, brandishing his naked sword, continued pacing without looking in their direction. The soldiers, leaning on their spears, were watching gloomily and indifferently, with the expression of professionals for whom killing does not provoke much interest.

They dismounted. Falwick and the dwarf slowly approached.

'You've insulted Tailles, a man of good birth, witcher,' said the count without preamble or the customary courtesies. 'And Tailles, as you no doubt remember, threw down the gauntlet. It was not fit to press you within the grounds of the temple, so we waited until you emerged from behind the priestess's skirt. Tailles is waiting. You must fight.'

'Must?'

'Must.'

'But do you not think, Falwick,' Geralt smiled disapprovingly, 'that Tailles, a man of good birth, does me too much honour? I never attained the honour of being knighted, and it's best not to mention the circumstances of my birth. I fear I'm not sufficiently worthy of . . . How does one say it, Dandilion?'

'Unfit to give satisfaction and joust in the lists,' recited the poet, pouting. 'The code of chivalry proclaims—'

'The Chapter of the Order is governed by its own code,' interrupted Falwick. 'If it were you who challenged a Knight of the Order, he could either refuse or grant you satisfaction, according to his will. But this is the reverse: it is the knight who challenges you and by this he raises you to his own level – but, of course, only for the time it takes to avenge the insult. You can't refuse. The refusal of accepting the dignity would render you unworthy.'

'How logical,' said Dandilion with an ape-like expression. 'I see you've studied the philosophers, sir Knight.'

'Don't butt in.' Geralt raised his head and looked into Falwick's eyes. 'Go on, sir. I'd like to know where this is leading. What would happen if I turned out to be . . . unworthy?'

'What would happen?' Falwick gave a malicious smile. 'I'd order you hung from a branch, you rat-catcher.'

'Hold on,' the dwarf said hoarsely. 'Take it easy, sir. And no invective, all right?'

'Don't you teach me manners, Cranmer,' hissed the knight. 'And remember, the prince has given you orders which you're to execute to the letter.'

'It's you who shouldn't be teaching me, Count.' The dwarf rested his hand on the double-headed axe thrust into his belt. 'I know how to carry out orders, and I can do without your advice.

272

Allow me, Geralt sir. I'm Dennis Cranmer, captain of Prince Hereward's guards.'

The witcher bowed stiffly, looking into the dwarf's eyes, light grey and steel-like beneath the bushy flaxen eyebrows.

'Stand your ground with Tailles, sir,' Dennis Cranmer continued calmly. 'It'll be better that way. It's not a fight to the death, only until one of you is rendered helpless. So fight in the field and let him render you helpless.'

'I beg your pardon?'

'Sir Tailles is the prince's favourite,' said Falwick, smiling spitefully. 'If you touch him with your sabre during the fight, you mutant, you will be punished. Captain Cranmer will arrest you and take you to face his Highness. To be punished. Those are his orders.'

The dwarf didn't even glance at the knight; his cold, steel eyes did not leave Geralt.

The witcher smiled faintly but quite nastily. 'If I understand correctly,' he said, 'I'm to fight the duel because, if I refuse, I'll be hanged. If I fight I'm to allow my opponent to injure me because if I wound him I'll be put to the rack. What charming alternatives. Maybe I should save you the bother? I'll thump my head against the pine tree and render myself helpless. Will that grant you satisfaction?'

'Don't sneer,' hissed Falwick. 'Don't make your situation any worse. You've insulted the Order, you vagabond, and you have to be punished for it, do you understand? And young Tailles needs the fame of defeating a witcher, so the Chapter wants to give it to him. Otherwise you'd be hanging already. You allow yourself to be defeated and you save your miserable life. We don't care about your corpse, we want Tailles to nick your skin. And your mutant skin heals quickly. So, go ahead. Decide. You've got no choice.'

'That's what you think, is it, sir?' Geralt smiled even more nastily and looked around at the soldiers appraisingly. 'But I think I do.'

'Yes, that's true,' admitted Dennis Cranmer. 'You do. But then there'll be bloodshed, great bloodshed. Like at Blaviken. Is that what you want? Do you want to burden your conscience with blood and death? Because the alternative you're thinking of, Geralt, is blood and death.'

'Your argument is charming, Captain, fascinating even,' mocked Dandilion. 'You're trying to bait a man ambushed in the forest with humanitarianism, calling on his nobler feelings. You're asking him, as I understand, to deign not to spill the blood of the brigands who attacked him. He's to take pity on the thugs because the thugs are poor, have got wives, children and, who knows, maybe even mothers. But don't you think, Captain Cranmer, that your worrying is premature? Because I look at your lancers and see that their knees are shaking at the very thought of fighting with Geralt of Rivia, the witcher who dealt with a striga alone, with his bare hands. There won't be any bloodshed here; nobody will be harmed here – aside from those who might break their legs running away.'

'I,' said the dwarf calmly and pugnaciously, 'have nothing to reproach my knees with. I've never run away from anyone and I'm not about to change my ways. I'm not married, don't know anything about any children and I'd prefer not to bring my mother, a woman with whom I'm not very well acquainted, into this. But I will carry out the orders I've been given. To the letter, as always. Without calling on any feelings, I ask Geralt of Rivia to make a decision. I will accept whatever he decides and will behave accordingly.'

They looked each other in the eyes, the dwarf and the witcher.

'Very well,' Geralt said finally. 'Let's deal with it. It's a pity to waste the day.'

'You agree then.' Falwick raised his head and his eyes glistened. 'You'll fight a duel with the high-born Tailles of Dorndal?'

'Yes.'

'Good. Prepare yourself.'

'I'm ready.' Geralt pulled on his gauntlets. 'Let's not waste time. There'll be hell if Nenneke finds out about this. So let's sort it out quickly. Dandilion, keep calm. It's got nothing to do with you. Am I right, Cranmer, sir?'

'Absolutely,' the dwarf stated firmly and looked at Falwick. 'Absolutely, sir. Whatever happens, it only concerns you.'

The witcher took the sword from his back.

'No,' said Falwick, drawing his. 'You're not going to fight with that razor of yours. Take my sword.'

Geralt shrugged. He took the count's blade and swiped it to try it out.

'Heavy,' he said coldly. 'We could just as easily use spades.'

'Tailles has the same. Equal chances.'

'You're very funny, Falwick.'

The soldiers surrounded the glade, forming a loose circle. Tailles and the witcher stood facing each other.

'Tailles? What do you say to an apology?'

The young knight screwed up his lips, folded his left arm behind his back and froze in a fencing position.

'No?' Geralt smiled. 'You don't want to listen to the voice of reason? Pity.'

Tailles squatted down, leapt and attacked without warning. The witcher didn't even make an effort to parry and avoided the flat point with a swift half-turn. The knight swiped broadly. The blade cut through the air once more. Geralt dodged beneath it in an agile pirouette, jumped softly aside and, with a short, light feint, threw Tailles off his rhythm. Tailles cursed, cut broadly from the right, lost his balance for a moment and tried to regain it while, instinctively, clumsily, holding his sword high to defend himself. The witcher struck with the speed and force of a lightning bolt, extending his arm to its full length and slashing straight ahead. The heavy sword thundered against Tailles' blade, deflecting it so hard it hit the knight in the face. Tailles howled, fell to his knees and touched the grass with his forehead.

Falwick ran up to him.

Geralt dug his sword into the ground and turned around.

'Hey, guards!' yelled Falwick, getting up. 'Take him!'

'Stand still! To your places!' growled Dennis Cranmer, touching his axe. The soldiers froze.

'No, Count,' the dwarf said slowly. 'I always execute orders to the letter. The witcher did not touch Tailles. The kid hit himself with his own iron. His hard luck.'

'His face is destroyed! He's disfigured for life!'

'Skin heals.' Dennis Cranmer fixed his steel eyes on the witcher and bared his teeth. 'And the scar? For a knight, a scar is a commendable reminder, a reason for fame and glory, which the Chapter so desired for him. A knight without a scar is a prick, not a knight. Ask him, Count, and you'll see that he's pleased.'

Tailles was writhing on the ground, spitting blood, whimpering and wailing; he didn't look pleased in the least.

'Cranmer!' roared Falwick, tearing his sword from the ground, 'you'll be sorry for this, I swear!'

The dwarf turned around, slowly pulled the axe from his belt, coughed and spat into his palm. 'Oh, Count, sir,' he rasped. 'Don't perjure yourself. I can't stand perjurers and Prince Hereward has given me the right to punish them. I'll turn a deaf ear to your stupid words. But don't repeat them, if you please.'

'Witcher,' Falwick, puffing with rage, turned to Geralt. 'Get yourself out of Ellander. Immediately. Without a moment's delay!'

'I rarely agree with him,' muttered Dennis, approaching the witcher and returning his sword, 'but in this case he's right. I'd ride out pretty quick.'

'We'll do as you advise.' Geralt slung the belt across his back. 'But before that I have words for the count. Falwick!'

The Knight of the White Rose blinked nervously and wiped his palms on his coat.

'Let's just go back to your Chapter's code for a minute,' continued the witcher, trying not to smile. 'One thing really interests me. If I, let us say, felt disgusted and insulted by your attitude in this whole affair, if I challenged you to the sword right now, what would you do? Would you consider me sufficiently worthy to cross blades with? Or would you refuse, even though you knew that by doing so I would take you to be unworthy even to be spat on, punched in the face and kicked in the arse under

276

the eyes of the foot soldiers? Count Falwick, be so gracious as to satisfy my curiosity.'

Falwick grew pale, took a step back, looked around. The soldiers avoided his eyes. Dennis Cranmer grimaced, stuck his tongue out and sent a jet of saliva a fair distance.

'Even though you're not saying anything,' continued Geralt, 'I can hear the voice of reason in your silence, Falwick, sir. You've satisfied my curiosity, now I'll satisfy yours. If the Order bothers Mother Nenneke or the priestesses in any way, or unduly intrudes upon Captain Cranmer, then may you know, Count, that I'll find you and, not caring about any code, will bleed you like a pig.'

The knight grew even paler.

'Don't forget my promise, Count. Come on, Dandilion. It's time for us to leave. Take care, Dennis.'

'Good luck, Geralt.' The dwarf gave a broad smile. 'Take care. I'm very pleased to have met you, and hope we'll meet again.'

'The feeling's mutual, Dennis.'

They rode away with ostensible slowness, not looking back. They began to canter only once they were hidden by the forest.

'Geralt,' the poet said suddenly, 'surely we won't head straight south? We'll have to make a detour to avoid Ellander and Hereward's lands, won't we? Or do you intend to continue with this show?'

'No, Dandilion, I don't. We'll go through the forests and then join the Traders' Trail. Remember, not a word in Nenneke's presence about this quarrel. Not a word.'

'We are riding out without any delay, I hope?'

'Immediately.'

II

Geralt leant over, checked the repaired hoop of his stirrup and fitted the stirrup leather, still stiff, smelling of new skins and hard to buckle. He adjusted the saddle-girth, the travel bags, the horse-blanket rolled up behind the saddle and the silver sword strapped to it. Nenneke was motionless next to him, her arms folded.

Dandilion approached, leading his bay gelding.

'Thank you for the hospitality, Venerable One,' he said seriously. 'And don't be angry with me anymore. I know that, deep down, you like me.'

'Indeed,' agreed Nenneke without smiling. 'I do, you dolt, although I don't know why myself. Take care.'

'So long, Nenneke.'

'So long, Geralt. Look after yourself.'

The witcher's smile was surly.

'I prefer to look after others. It turns out better in the long run.'

From the temple, from between columns entwined with ivy, Iola emerged in the company of two younger pupils. She was carrying the witcher's small chest. She avoided his eyes awkwardly and her troubled smile combined with the blush on her freckled, chubby face made a charming picture. The pupils accompanying her didn't hide their meaningful glances and barely stopped themselves from giggling.

'For Great Melitele's sake,' sighed Nenneke, 'an entire parting procession. Take the chest, Geralt. I've replenished your elixirs. You've got everything that was in short supply. And that medicine, you know the one. Take it regularly for two weeks. Don't forget. It's important.'

'I won't. Thanks, Iola.'

The girl lowered her head and handed him the chest. She so wanted to say something. She had no idea what ought to be said, what words ought to be used. She didn't know what she'd say, even if she could. She didn't know. And yet she so much wanted to.

Their hands touched.

Blood. Blood. Blood. Bones like broken white sticks. Tendons like whitish cords exploding from beneath cracking skin cut by enormous paws bristling with thorns, and sharp teeth. The hideous sound of torn flesh, and shouting – shameless and horrifying in its shamelessness. The shamelessness of the end. Of death. Blood and shouting. Shouting. Blood. Shouting—

'Iola!'

Nenneke, with extraordinary speed considering her girth, rushed to the girl lying on the ground, shaken by convulsions, and held her down by her shoulders and hair. One of the pupils stood as if paralysed, the other, more clear-headed, knelt on Iola's legs. Iola arched her back, opened her mouth in a soundless, mute cry.

'Iola!' Nenneke shouted. 'Iola! Speak! Speak, child! Speak!'

The girl stiffened even more, clenched her jaws, and a thin trickle of blood ran down her cheek. Nenneke, growing red with the effort, shouted something which the witcher didn't understand, but his medallion tugged at his neck so hard that he was forced to bend under the pressure of its invisible weight.

Iola stilled.

Dandilion, pale as a sheet, sighed deeply. Nenneke raised herself to her knees and stood with an effort.

'Take her away,' she said to the pupils. There were more of them now; they'd gathered, grave and silent.

'Take her,' repeated the priestess, 'carefully. And don't leave her alone. I'll be there in a minute.'

She turned to Geralt. The witcher was standing motionless, fiddling with the reins in his sweaty hands.

'Geralt . . . Iola—'

'Don't say anything, Nenneke.'

'I saw it, too . . . for a moment. Geralt, don't go.'

'I've got to.'

'Did you see . . . did you see that?'

'Yes. And not for the first time.'

'And?'

'There's no point in looking over your shoulder.'

'Don't go, please.'

'I've got to. See to Iola. So long, Nenneke.'

The priestess slowly shook her head, sniffed and, in an abrupt move, wiped a tear away with her wrist.

'Farewell,' she whispered, not looking him in the eye.

ABOUT GOLLANCZ

Gollancz is the oldest SF publishing imprint in the world. Since being founded in 1927 Gollancz has continued to publish a focused selection of bestselling and award-winning authors. The front-list includes **Ben Aaronovitch**, **Joe Abercrombie**, **Charlaine Harris**, **Joanne Harris**, **Joe Hill**, **Alastair Reynolds**, **Patrick Rothfuss**, **Nalini Singh** and **Brandon Sanderson**.

As one of the largest Science Fiction and Fantasy imprints in the UK it is no surprise we have one of the most extensive backlists in the world. Find high-quality SF on Gateway written by such authors as **Philip K. Dick**, **Ursula Le Guin**, **Connie Willis**, **Sir Arthur C. Clarke**, **Pat Cadigan**, **Michael Moorcock** and **George R.R. Martin**.

We also have a strand of publishing in translation, which includes French, Polish and Russian authors. Gollancz is home to more award-winning authors than any other imprint, with names including **Aliette de Bodard**, **M. John Harrison**, **Paul McAuley**, **Sarah Pinborough**, **Pierre Pevel**, **Justina Robson** and many more.

The SF Gateway
More than 3,000 classic, rare and previously out-of-print SF novels at your fingertips.
www.sfgateway.com

The Gollancz Blog
Bringing you news from our worlds to yours. Stories, interviews, articles and exclusive extracts just for you!
www.gollancz.co.uk

GOLLANCZ
LONDON

START A BRAND NEW ADVENTURE

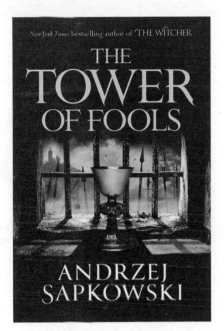

THE
TOWER
OF FOOLS

ANDRZEJ SAPKOWSKI

Chapter One

In which the reader makes the acquaintance of Reinmar of Bielawa, called Reynevan, and of his better features, including his knowledge of the *ars amandi*, the arcana of horse-riding, and the Old Testament, though not necessarily in that order.

Through the small chamber's window, against a background of the recently stormy sky, could be seen three towers. The first belonged to the town hall. Further off, the slender spire of the Church of Saint John the Evangelist, its shiny red tiles glistening in the sun. And beyond that, the round tower of the ducal castle. Swifts winged around the church spire, frightened by the recent tolling of the bells, the ozone-rich air still shuddering from the sound.

The bells had also quite recently tolled in the towers of the Churches of the Blessed Virgin Mary and Corpus Christi. Those towers, however, weren't visible from the window of the chamber in the garret of a wooden building affixed like a swallow's nest to the complex of the Augustinian hospice and priory.

It was time for Sext. The monks began the *Deus in adjutorium* while Reinmar of Bielawa – known to his friends as 'Reynevan' – kissed the sweat-covered collarbone of Adèle of Stercza, freed himself from her embrace and lay down beside her, panting, on bedclothes hot from lovemaking.

Outside, Priory Street echoed with shouts, the rattle of wagons, the dull thud of empty barrels and the melodious clanking of tin and copper pots. It was Wednesday, market day, which always attracted large numbers of merchants and customers.

Memento, salutis Auctor
quod nostri quondam corporis,
ex illibata Virgine
nascendo, formam sumpseris.
Maria mater gratiae,
mater misericordiae,
tu nos ab hoste protege,
et hora mortis suscipe . . .

They're already singing the hymn, thought Reynevan, lazily embracing Adèle, a native of distant Burgundy and the wife of the knight Gelfrad of Stercza. *The hymn has begun. It beggars belief how swiftly moments of happiness pass. One wishes they would last for ever, but they fade like a fleeting dream.*

'Reynevan . . . *Mon amour* . . . My divine boy . . .' Adèle interrupted his dreamy reverie. She, too, was aware of the passing of time, but evidently had no intention of wasting it on philosophical deliberations.

Adèle was utterly, completely, totally naked.

Every country has its customs, thought Reynevan. *How fascinating it is to learn about the world and its peoples. Silesian and German women, for example, when they get down to it, never allow their shifts to be lifted higher than their navels. Polish and Czech women gladly lift theirs themselves, above their breasts, but not for all the world would they remove them completely. But Burgundians, oh, they cast off everything at once, their hot blood apparently unable to bear any cloth on their skin during the throes of passion. Ah, what a joy it is to learn about the world. The countryside of Burgundy must be beautiful. Lofty mountains . . . Steep hillsides . . . Vales . . .*

'Ah, aaah, *mon amour*,' moaned Adèle of Stercza, thrusting her entire Burgundian landscape against Reynevan's hand.

Reynevan, incidentally, was twenty-three and quite lacking in worldly experience. He had known very few Czech women, even fewer Silesians and Germans, one Polish woman, one Gypsy, and had once been spurned by a Hungarian woman. Far from impressive, his erotic experiences were actually quite meagre in terms of both quantity and quality, but they still made him swell with pride and conceit. Reynevan – like every testosterone-fuelled young man – regarded himself as a great seducer and erotic connoisseur to whom the female race was an open book. The truth was that his eleven trysts with Adèle of Stercza had taught Reynevan more about the *ars amandi* than his three-year studies in Prague. Reynevan hadn't understood, however, that Adèle was teaching him, certain that all that counted was his inborn talent.

Ad te levavi oculos meos
qui habitas in caelis.
Ecce sicut oculi servorum
In manibus dominorum suorum.
Sicut oculi ancillae in manibus dominae suae
ita oculi nostri ad Dominum Deum nostrum,
Donec misereatur nostri.
Miserere nostri Domine...

Adèle seized Reynevan by the back of the neck and pulled him onto her. Reynevan, understanding what was required of him, made love to her powerfully and passionately, whispering assurances of devotion into her ear. He was happy. Very happy.

Reynevan owed the happiness intoxicating him to the Lord's saints – indirectly, of course – as follows:

Feeling remorse for some sins or other – known only to himself and his confessor – the Silesian knight Gelfrad of Stercza had set off on a penitential pilgrimage to the grave of Saint James. But on the way, he decided that Compostela was definitely too far, and that a pilgrimage to Saint-Gilles would absolutely suffice. But Gelfrad wasn't fated to reach Saint-Gilles, either. He only made it to Dijon, where by chance he met a sixteen-year-old Burgundian, the gorgeous Adèle of Beauvoisin. Adèle, who utterly enthralled Gelfrad with her beauty, was an orphan, and her two hell-raising and good-for-nothing brothers gave their sister to be married to the Silesian knight without a second thought. Although, in the brothers' opinion, Silesia lay somewhere between the Tigris and the Euphrates, Stercza was the ideal brother-in-law in their eyes because he didn't argue too much over the dowry. Thus, the Burgundian came to Heinrichsdorf, a village near Ziębice held in endowment by Gelfrad. While in Ziębice, Adèle caught Reinmar of Bielawa's eye. And vice versa.

'Aaaah!' screamed Adèle of Stercza, wrapping her legs around Reynevan's back. 'Aaaaa-aaah!'

Never would those moans have occurred, and nothing more than surreptitious glances and furtive gestures have passed between them, if not for a third saint: George, to be precise. For on Saint George's Day, Gelfrad of Stercza had sworn an oath and joined one of the many anti-Hussite crusades organised by the Brandenburg Prince-Elector and the Meissen margraves. The crusaders didn't achieve any great victories – they entered Bohemia and left very soon after, not even risking a skirmish with the Hussites. But although there was no fighting, there were casualties, one of which turned out to be Gelfrad, who fractured his leg very badly falling from his horse and was still recuperating somewhere in Pleissnerland. Adèle, a grass widow, staying in the meanwhile with her husband's family in Bierutów, was able to freely tryst with Reynevan in a chamber in the complex of the Augustinian priory in Oleśnica, not far from the hospice where Reynevan had his workshop.

The monks in the Church of Corpus Christi began to sing the second of three psalms making up the Sext. *We'll have to hurry*, thought Reynevan. *During the* capitulum, *at the latest the* Kyrie, *and not a moment after, Adèle must vanish from the hospice. She cannot be seen here.*

> *Benedictus Dominus*
> *qui non dedit nos*
> *in captionem dentibus eorum.*
> *Anima nostra sicut passer erepta est*
> *de laqueo venantium ...*

Reynevan kissed Adèle's hip, and then, inspired by the monks' singing, took a deep breath and plunged himself into her orchard of pomegranates. Adèle tensed, straightened her arms and dug her fingers in his hair, augmenting his biblical initiatives with gentle movements of her hips.

'Oh, oooooh ... *Mon amour* ... *Mon magicien* ... My divine boy ... My sorcerer ...'

Qui confidunt in Domino, sicut mons Sion
non commovebitur in aeternum,
qui habitat in Hierusalem ...

The third already, thought Reynevan. *How fleeting are these moments of happiness ...*

'*Revertere*,' he muttered, kneeling. 'Turn around, turn around, Shulamith.'

Adèle turned, knelt and leaned forward, seizing the linden-wood planks of the bedhead tightly and presenting Reynevan with her entire ravishingly gorgeous posterior. *Aphrodite Kallipygos*, he thought, moving closer. The ancient association and erotic sight made him approach like the aforementioned Saint George, charging with his lance thrust out towards the dragon of Silene. Kneeling behind Adèle like King Solomon behind the throne of wood of the cedar of Lebanon, he seized her vineyards of Engedi in both hands.

'May I compare you, my love,' he whispered, bent over a neck as shapely as the Tower of David, 'may I compare you to a mare among Pharaoh's chariots.'

And he did. Adèle screamed through clenched teeth. Reynevan slowly slid his hands down her sides, slippery with sweat, and the Burgundian threw back her head like a mare about to clear a jump.

Gloria Patri, et Filio et Spiritui sancto.
Sicut erat in principio, et nunc, et semper
et in saecula saeculorum, Amen.
Alleluia!

As the monks concluded the Gloria, Reynevan, kissing the back of Adèle of Stercza's neck, placed his hand beneath her orchard of pomegranates, engrossed, mad, like a young hart skipping upon the mountains to his beloved ...

A mailed fist struck the door, which thudded open with such force that the lock was torn off the frame and shot through the window like a meteor. Adèle screamed shrilly as the Stercza brothers burst into the chamber.

Reynevan tumbled out of bed, positioning it between himself and the intruders, grabbed his clothes and began to hurriedly put them on. He largely succeeded, but only because the brothers Stercza had directed their frontal attack at their sister-in-law.

'You vile harlot!' bellowed Morold of Stercza, dragging a naked Adèle from the bedclothes.

'Wanton whore!' chimed in Wittich, his older brother, while Wolfher – next oldest after Adèle's husband Gelfrad – did not even open his mouth, for pale fury had deprived him of speech. He struck Adèle hard in the face. The Burgundian screamed. Wolfher struck her again, this time backhanded.

'Don't you dare hit her, Stercza!' yelled Reynevan, but his voice broke and trembled with fear and a paralysing feeling of impotence, caused by his trousers being round his knees. 'Don't you dare!'

His cry achieved its effect, although not the way he had intended. Wolfher and Wittich, momentarily forgetting their adulterous sister-in-law, pounced on Reynevan, raining down a hail of punches and kicks on the boy. He cowered under the blows, but rather than defend or protect himself, he stubbornly pulled on his trousers as though they were some kind of magical armour. Out of the corner of one eye, he saw Wittich drawing a knife. Adèle screamed.

'Don't,' Wolfher snapped at his brother. 'Not here!'

Reynevan managed to get onto his knees. Wittich, face white with fury, jumped at him and punched him, throwing him to the floor again. Adèle let out a piercing scream which broke off as Morold struck her in the face and pulled her hair.

'Don't you dare ...' Reynevan groaned '... hit her, you scoundrels!'

'Bastard!' yelled Wittich. 'Just you wait!'

Wittich leaped forward, punched and kicked once and twice. Wolfher stopped him at the third.

'Not here,' Wolfher repeated calmly, but it was a baleful calm. 'Into the courtyard with him. We'll take him to Bierutów. That slut, too.'

'I'm innocent!' wailed Adèle of Stercza. 'He bewitched me! Enchanted me! He's a sorcerer! *Sorcier! Diab—*'

Morold silenced her with another punch. 'Hold your tongue, trollop,' he growled. 'You'll get the chance to scream. Just wait a while.'

'Don't you *dare* hit her!' yelled Reynevan.

'We'll give you a chance to scream, too, little rooster,' Wolfher added, still menacingly calm. 'Come on, out with him.'

The Stercza brothers threw Reynevan down the garret's steep stairs and the boy tumbled onto the landing, splintering part of the wooden balustrade. Before he could get up, they seized him again and threw him out into the courtyard, onto sand strewn with steaming piles of horse shit.

'Well, well, well,' said Nicolaus of Stercza, the youngest of the brothers, barely a stripling, who was holding the horses. 'Look who's stopped by. Could it be Reinmar of Bielawa?'

'The scholarly braggart Bielawa,' snorted Jentsch of Knobelsdorf, known as Eagle Owl, a comrade and relative of the Sterczas. 'The arrogant know-all Bielawa!'

'Shitty poet,' added Dieter Haxt, another friend of the family. 'Bloody Abélard!'

'And to prove to him we're well read, too,' said Wolfher as he descended the stairs, 'we'll do to him what they did to Abélard when he was caught with Héloïse. Well, Bielawa? How do you fancy being a capon?'

'Go fuck yourself, Stercza.'

'What? What?' Although it seemed impossible, Wolfher Stercza had turned even paler. 'The rooster still has the audacity to open his beak? To crow? The bullwhip, Jentsch!'

'Don't you dare beat him!' Adèle called impotently as she was led down the stairs, now clothed, albeit incompletely. 'Don't you dare! Or I'll tell everyone what you are like! That you courted me yourself, pawed me and tried to debauch me behind your brother's back! That you swore vengeance on me if I spurned you! Which is why you are so . . . so . . .'

She couldn't find the German word and the entire tirade fell apart. Wolfher just laughed.

'Verily!' he mocked. 'People will listen to the Frenchwoman, the lewd strumpet. The bullwhip, Eagle Owl!'

The courtyard was suddenly awash with black Augustinian habits.

'What is happening here?' shouted the venerable Prior Erasmus Steinkeller, a bony and sallow old man. 'Christians, what are you doing?'

'Begone!' bellowed Wolfher, cracking the bullwhip. 'Begone, shaven-heads, hurry off to your prayer books! Don't interfere in knightly affairs, or woe betide you, blackbacks!'

'Good Lord.' The prior put his liver-spotted hands together. 'Forgive them, for they know not what they do. *In nomine Patris, et Filii—*'

'Morold, Wittich!' roared Wolfher. 'Bring the harlot here! Jentsch, Dieter, bind her paramour!'

'Or perhaps,' snarled Stefan Rotkirch, another friend of the family who had been silent until then, 'we'll drag him behind a horse a little?'

'We could. But first, we'll give him a flogging!'

Wolfher aimed a blow with the horsewhip at the still-prone Reynevan but did not connect, as his wrist was seized by Brother Innocent, nicknamed by his fellow friars 'Brother Insolent', whose impressive height and build were apparent despite his humble monkish stoop. His vicelike grip held Wolfher's arm motionless.

Stercza swore coarsely, jerked himself away and gave the monk a hard shove. But he might as well have shoved the tower in Oleśnica Castle for all the effect it had. Brother Innocent didn't budge an inch. He shoved Wolfher back, propelling him halfway across the courtyard and dumping him in a pile of muck.

For a moment, there was silence. And then they all rushed the huge monk. Eagle Owl, the first to attack, was punched in the teeth and tumbled across the sand. Morold of Stercza took a thump to the ear and staggered off to one side, staring vacantly. The others swarmed over the Augustinian like ants, raining blows on the monk's huge form. Brother Insolent retaliated just as savagely and in a distinctly unchristian way, quite at odds with Saint Augustine's rule of humility.

The sight enraged the old prior. He flushed like a beetroot, roared like a lion and rushed into the fray, striking left and right with heavy blows of his rosewood crucifix.

'*Pax!*' he bellowed as he struck. '*Pax! Vobiscum!* Love thy neighbour! *Proximum tuum! Sicut te ipsum!* Whoresons!'

Dieter Haxt punched him hard. The old man was flung over backwards and his sandals flew up, describing pretty trajectories in the air. The Augustinians cried out and several of them charged into battle, unable to restrain themselves. The courtyard was seething in earnest.

Wolfher of Stercza, who had been shoved out of the confusion, drew a short sword and brandished it – bloodshed looked inevitable. But Reynevan, who had finally managed to stand up, whacked him in the back of the head with the handle of the bullwhip he had picked up. Stercza held his head and turned around, only for Reynevan to lash him across the face. As Wolfher fell to the ground, Reynevan rushed towards the horses.

'Adèle! Here! To me!'

Adèle didn't even budge, and the indifference painted on her face was alarming. Reynevan leaped into the saddle. The horse neighed and fidgeted.

'Adèèèèle!'

Morold, Wittich, Haxt and Eagle Owl were now running towards him. Reynevan reined the horse around, whistled piercingly and spurred it hard, making for the gate.

'After him!' yelled Wolfher. 'To your horses and get after him!'

Reynevan's first thought was to head towards Saint Mary's Gate and out of the town into the woods, but the stretch of Cattle Street leading to the gate was totally crammed with wagons. Furthermore, the horse, urged on and frightened by the cries of an unfamiliar rider, was showing great individual initiative, so before he knew it,

Reynevan was hurtling along at a gallop towards the town square, splashing mud and scattering passers-by. He didn't have to look back to know the others were hot on his heels given the thudding of hooves, the neighing of horses, the angry roaring of the Sterczas and the furious yelling of people being jostled.

He jabbed the horse to a full gallop with his heels, hitting and knocking over a baker carrying a basket. A shower of loaves and pastries flew into the mud, soon to be trodden beneath the hooves of the Sterczas' horses. Reynevan didn't even look back, more concerned with what was ahead of him than behind. A cart piled high with faggots of brushwood loomed up before his eyes. The cart was blocking almost the entire street, the rest of which was occupied by a group of half-clothed urchins, kneeling down and busily digging something extremely engrossing out of the muck.

'We have you, Bielawa!' thundered Wolfher from behind, also seeing the obstruction.

Reynevan's horse was racing so swiftly there was no chance of stopping it. He pressed himself against its mane and closed his eyes. As a result, he didn't see the half-naked children scatter with the speed and grace of rats. He didn't look back, so nor did he see a peasant in a sheepskin jerkin turn around, somewhat stupefied, as he hauled a cart into the road. Nor did he see the Sterczas riding broadside into the cart. Nor Jentsch of Knobelsdorf soaring from the saddle and sweeping half of the faggots from the cart with his body.

Reynevan galloped down Saint John's Street, between the town hall and the burgermeister's house, hurtling at full speed into Oleśnica's huge and crowded town square. Pandemonium erupted. Aiming for the southern frontage and the squat, square tower of the Oława Gate visible above it, Reynevan galloped through the crowds, leaving havoc behind him. Townsfolk yelled and pigs squealed, as overturned stalls and benches showered a hail of household goods and foodstuffs of every kind in all directions. Clouds of feathers flew everywhere as the Sterczas – hot on Reynevan's heels – added to the destruction.

Reynevan's horse, frightened by a goose flying past its nose, recoiled and hurtled into a fish stall, shattering crates and bursting open barrels. The enraged fishmonger made a great swipe with a keep net, missing Reynevan but striking the horse's rump. The horse whinnied and slewed sideways, upending a stall selling thread and ribbons, and only a miracle prevented Reynevan from falling. Out of the corner of one eye, he saw the stallholder running after him brandishing a huge cleaver (serving God only knew what purpose in the haberdashery trade). Spitting out some goose feathers stuck to his lips, he brought the horse under control and galloped through the shambles, knowing that the Oława Gate was very close.

'I'll tear your balls off, Bielawa!' Wolfher of Stercza roared from behind. 'I'll tear them off and stuff them down your throat!'

'Kiss my arse!'

Only four men were chasing him now – Rotkirch had been pulled from his horse and was being roughed up by some infuriated market traders.

Reynevan darted like an arrow down an avenue of animal carcasses suspended by their legs. Most of the butchers leaped back in alarm, but one carrying a large haunch of beef on one shoulder tumbled under the hooves of Wittich's horse, which took fright, reared up and was ploughed into by Wolfher's horse. Wittich flew from the saddle straight onto the meat stall, nose-first into livers, lights and kidneys, and was then landed on by Wolfher. His foot was caught in the stirrup and before he could free himself, he had smashed a large number of stalls and covered himself in mud and blood.

At the last moment, Reynevan quickly lowered his head over the horse's neck to duck under a wooden sign with a piglet's head painted on it. Dieter Haxt, who was bearing down on him, wasn't quick enough and the cheerfully grinning piglet slammed into his forehead. Dieter flew from the saddle and crashed into a pile of refuse, frightening some cats. Reynevan turned around. Now only Nicolaus of Stercza was keeping up with him.

Reynevan shot out of the chaos at a full gallop and into a small square where some tanners were working. As a frame hung with wet hides loomed up before him, he urged his horse to jump. It did. And Reynevan didn't fall off. Another miracle.

Nicolaus wasn't as lucky. His horse skidded to a halt in front of the frame and collided with it, slipping on the mud and scraps of meat and fat. The youngest Stercza shot over his horse's head, with very unfortunate results. He flew belly-first right onto a scythe used for scraping leather which the tanners had left propped up against the frame.

At first, Nicolaus had no idea what had happened. He got up from the ground, caught hold of his horse, and only when it snorted and stepped back did his knees sag and buckle beneath him. Still not really knowing what was happening, the youngest Stercza slid across the mud after the panicked horse, which was still moving back and snorting. Finally, as he released the reins and tried to get to his feet again, he realised something was wrong and looked down at his midriff.

And screamed.

He dropped to his knees in the middle of a rapidly spreading pool of blood.

Dieter Haxt rode up, reined in his horse and dismounted. A moment later, Wolfher and Wittich followed suit.

Nicolaus sat down heavily. Looked at his belly again. Screamed and then burst into tears. His eyes began to glaze over as the blood gushing from him mingled with the blood of the oxen and hogs butchered that morning.

'Nicolaaaaus!' yelled Wolfher.

Nicolaus of Stercza coughed and choked. And died.

'You are dead, Reinmar of Bielawa!' Wolfher of Stercza, pale with fury, bellowed towards the gate. 'I'll catch you, kill you, destroy you. Exterminate you and your entire viperous family. Your entire viperous family, do you hear?'

Reynevan didn't. Amid the thud of horseshoes on the bridge planks, he was leaving Oleśnica and dashing south, straight for the Wrocław highway.